"GRIPPING"

Sea...

"RIVETING"

Booklist

"SCARY"

Toronto Globe and Mail

"STYLISH"

Providence Journal

"INTENSE"

Ft. Lauderdale Sun-Sentinel

Praise for J.A. JANCE and
KISS OF THE BEES

"Reminiscent of Tony Hillerman's mysteries, *Kiss of the Bees'* strongest point is deftly defined characters. . . . The storyline works."

San Francisco Examiner

"Searing. . . . intense. . . . a penetrating story. . . . The author uncovers the individual nuances of each of her Anglo and Native American characters and makes it easy to care about them."

Ft. Lauderdale Sun-Sentinel

"A many-layered suspense novel. . . . Jance has a sure hand. . . .She creates a coherent and engrossing novel that uses the dreamlike Papago creation myth to artfully combine magic and reality."

Publishers Weekly

"A riveting tale of psychological suspense."

Booklist

"A surreal and enlightening journey through the table mountains, canyons, and deserts of the Southwest . . . a talented mystery writer with the prowess to make a game of pin the tail on the donkey appear menacing . . . simply wonderful. . . . Her loyal readers, of which she has many, will not be disappointed with *Kiss of the Bees*."

Providence Journal

J. A. JANCE

KISS OF THE BEES

AVON BOOKS
An Imprint of HarperCollins*Publishers*

AVON BOOKS
An Imprint of HarperCollins *Publishers*
10 East 53rd Street
New York, New York 10022-5299

First Avon Books paperback printing: January 2001
First Avon Books hardcover printing: January 2000

10 9 8 7 6 5 4 3 2 1

For Rita Pablo,
Pauline Hendricks,
and Melissa Juan

Prologue

June 1976

There were three of them—a *viejo*—an older man—and two younger ones—trudging up the sandy arroyo, each lugging two gallon-sized plastic containers of water. Mitch Johnson watched them through the gunsight on his rifle, wondering should he or shouldn't he? In the end, he did. He shot them for the same reason Edmund Hillary climbed Mount Everest—because they were there.

The older one was still alive and moaning when Johnson stopped his Jeep on the rim of the wash to check his handiwork. It offended him that one shot had been so far off, hitting the man in the lower spine rather than where he'd meant to. The Marines had taught him better than that. He had the expert rifle badge to prove it, along with a Purple Heart and a bum leg as well.

He slid down the crumbling bank of Brawley Wash. The sand was ankle-deep and powdery underfoot, so there was no question of leaving a trail of identifiable footprints. Besides, as soon as the rains came, the bodies would be washed far downstream, into the Santa Rita, eventually, and from there into the Gila. When the bodies showed up, weeks or months from now, Johnson figured no one would be smart enough to trace three dead wetbacks back to the son-in-law of a well-to-do cotton farmer with a prosperous place off Sandario Road.

The three men lay facedown in the sand. The one who was still alive lay with his fist clasped shut around the handle of the water bottle. In the hot mid-June sun, water meant life. Approaching them, Johnson held his rifle at the ready, just in case. He walked up and kicked the bottle, shattering its brittle white plastic. The water sank instantly into the sand, like bathwater disappearing down a drain. Then slowly, systematically, he kicked each of the other five bottles in turn, sending their contents, too, spilling deep into the parched earth of the wash bed.

Only when the water was gone did he return to the injured man. The guy was quiet now, no doubt playing dead and hoping there wouldn't be another shot. And there wouldn't be. Why bother? The man was already dead; he just didn't know it. Why waste another bullet?

"Welcome to the United States of America, greaser," Mitch Johnson said aloud in English. "Have a nice day."

With that he turned and walked away—limped away—leaving the hot afternoon sun to finish his deadly work. What he didn't see as he scrambled back up the side of the wash to his waiting Jeep was that he was not alone. There was one other person there in the wash with him—another wetback—armed with his own two gallons of water and with his own unquenchable belief that somehow life north of the international border would be better than it was back home in Mexico.

For several minutes after the Jeep drove off in a plume of dust the fourth man didn't move, didn't venture out of his hiding place. Juan Ruiz Romero had been resting through the hottest part of the day in the sparse shade of a mesquite tree when the other three men passed by. Because groups are always easier to spot and apprehend than a single man traveling alone, Juan had stayed where he was, hidden and safe under his sheltering mesquite, as the trio walked unwittingly to the slaughter. Lying there quietly, Juan alone had heard and seen the Jeep come wheeling up the dirt road on the far side of the wash.

Somehow, a strangled sob escaped his lips. Sure the gunman must have heard it and would turn on him next. Juan shrank back into the mesquite. He stayed there for some time, holding his breath and expecting another gunshot at any moment, one that would spill his own life's blood deep into the thirsty, waiting sand.

With his heart beating a terrified tattoo in his chest, Juan watched the killer go up to each of the fallen men in turn, looking down at them, as if examining whether they lived or not. Juan saw the ferocity of the kicks that shattered the life-giving water jugs. He witnessed the killer limp back up the bank, climb into his waiting Jeep, and drive away.

For several long minutes after the Jeep had disappeared from view, a shaken Juan stayed where he was. At last, though, he ventured out, moving forward as tentatively as a spooked deer. By the time he reached the three motionless bodies, Juan was convinced that all three men were dead. How could they be anything else?

He was standing less than two feet away when one of them stirred and moaned. Juan started at the sound, leaping backward as if dodging away from the warning rattle of an unseen snake.

It took a moment for Juan to collect himself. Two of the men were dead then, he ascertained finally, when he could think clearly once again. One was still alive. One of the three still had a chance to live, and Juan Ruiz Romero was it.

He straightened up and peered out over the rim of the wash. Far to the north, a dust plume from the fast moving but invisible Jeep still ballooned upward. To the south, although Juan had done his best to avoid them, were other people, including numerous officers from the Border Patrol. A few miles that way as well lay a fairly busy blacktop road that ran east and west. Juan had waited until after dark the night before and had used the protection of a culvert to duck under the highway. And far off to the east was an airfield of some kind. Airplanes had been coming and going from there all morning long.

In those few moments, Juan was torn by indecision. The easiest thing for him—the cowardly thing—would have been to leave the dead and wounded where they were and walk away. All he had to do was turn his back on them and mind his own business. The old man would no doubt die anyway, no matter what someone did for him. He was old. Clearly his life would soon be over one way or the other. Juan's was just beginning. He had a job waiting for him in Casa Grande—a job arranged by his mother's second cousin—if only he could get there before the foreman gave it away to someone else.

But standing there, Juan had a flash of insight. He realized that what had happened to these three men was perhaps the very thing that had happened to Juan's own father. Some fifteen years earlier, Ignacio Romero had left home for the last time. He had planned to walk across the border fence west of Nogales just as he had done countless times before. Other years when Ignacio had gone north to look for work, he had faithfully sent money back home to his wife and seven children. And eventually, after the season was over, Ignacio would return home as well.

On that last trip, though, Ignacio disappeared. There was no money, and no one ever heard from him again. He left behind an impoverished wife, seven starving children and a lifetime's worth of unanswered questions.

Realizing this man, too, must have a family waiting for him back home in Mexico, Juan knelt beside him. Overhead, the broiling sun beat down on both of them, and Juan knew he had to hurry. He placed one of his own precious jugs of water well within reach of the other man's hand and closed his fingers around the handle. Then, without a word, Juan stood up and went for help.

As he walked south, he knew full well what that fool-hardy action meant and what it could cost him. He would probably be caught and deported, shipped back home without enough money to marry Carmen, the girl who was waiting for him there. He knew she would be disappointed. So was he, but he had to do it. He had no choice.

If nothing else, he owed his father that much. And for that reason, and that reason alone, only two men died that afternoon. The third one—Leon Morales—lived. Unlike Ignacio Romero, Leon returned to his family in Mexico eventually, to the little town of Santa Teresa in Sonora. He went home crippled and unable to walk but with a compelling story to tell.

When called upon to do so, Leon would relate the harrowing tale about how, as he and his grandsons had followed a wash north through the Arizona desert, they had been set upon by a *bandido* who shot them all, killing his grandsons and leaving Leon to die as well. He never tired of telling his enthralled listeners about how he had been saved that day by an angel who appeared out of nowhere, gave him water to drink, and then brought help. Leon always finished the tale by explaining how, in America, a *federale*—a *gringo federale*—had found the *bandido*. After keeping Leon in the States long enough to testify, his would-be killer had been sent off to jail.

Leon's was a good story, and he told it well. Well enough that, on long evenings in Santa Teresa's dusty cantina, a command performance of the old man's shocking adventure up north was always good for a *cerveza*. Or maybe even two.

*   *   *

July 1988

It was dark and hot and long after lights-out in the Arizona State Prison at Florence, but Andrew Carlisle was wide awake and working. Since he was blind, the dark didn't bother him. In fact, that was when he did most of his best work—after everyone else was asleep.

Careful to make no noise that might attract the attention of a passing guard, he pulled out a single sheet of paper, placed it on the clipboard, and then clamped it in place with the template he had devised and that his father's money had allowed him to have built. The template consisted of a sheet of clear plastic that was large enough to cover an eight-and-a-half-by-eleven-inch piece of paper. It was punched through with lines of small squares. In the far left-hand margin was a column of holes. By moving a peg down the side of the sheet as he worked, it was possible for Carlisle to keep track of which line he was working on. He had to be sure to keep the tip of his pencil in the proper box so as not to use the same one twice.

This process—laborious, slow, and cumbersome as it might have seemed to others—allowed Carlisle to write down his innermost thoughts with a privacy not to be had by users of the communal computers and typewriters available in the library.

One at a time he filled the squares with small capital letters. It bothered him that the system made no allowances for revisions. That reality had forced him to develop a very disciplined style of writing.

JUNE 18, 1988. AFTER YEARS OF DILIGENT SEARCHING, I BELIEVE I HAVE FINALLY FOUND A SUITABLE SUCCESSOR, ONE WHO WILL—WITH A CERTAIN AMOUNT OF GUID-ANCE—GROW TO BE A KIND OF EXTENSION OF ME; ONE WHO WILL TAKE ON MY BATTLES AND MAKE THEM HIS

OWN. IF I SHOULD SUCCEED IN MY ENDEAVOR TO CREATE
A MODERN-DAY PYGMALION, I WILL TAKE A WORTHLESS
LUMP OF CLAY AND MOLD IT INTO SOMETHING MAGNIFI-
CENT. WISH ME LUCK, DIANA. IF IT WORKS, YOU AND
YOURS WILL BE THE FIRST TO KNOW.

That said, Carlisle removed the paper from the clipboard
and stashed it with a growing stack of similar sheets. The
guards had long since grown accustomed to the fact that Andrew Carlisle kept a diary. They hardly ever asked to see it
anymore. Still he resisted the temptation to be any more specific than that, just in case some nosy guard did decide to
read through some of it.

With the diary entry made, Carlisle settled down on his
cot and tried to sleep. At first the doctor's words—his ver-
dict, really—got in the way, but gradually, as he had done
for years now, Carlisle used a daydream about Diana Ladd
to help him conjure sleep. He saw her again as she had been
that night when he forced himself on her in what should
have been the sanctuary of her own bedroom. She was one
of the last things Andrew Carlisle had seen before his vision
was stolen from him, and he reveled at the image of her
there on the bed—naked, terrified, and defeated. In those
glorious moments, except for her stubborn silence, she had
belonged wholly to him, just as all the others had—the ones
who had gone before.

The memory of that godlike moment washed over him
like a sustaining wave, carrying him along on the crest of it,
buoying him up. The only thing that would have made that
moment any better would have been if she had cried out
when he bit her, if she had whimpered and begged for
mercy. She had not done so in real life, but in Andrew
Carlisle's daydream, in these midnight recollections, she always did. Always.

Knowing no one was there to see him do so, he grasped
himself and used that powerful remembered image to sum-

mon a solitary orgasm. When it was over, as he lay with his breath coming fast and with sticky semen dribbling through his fingers, he thought of how much it felt like blood. He only wished that it was hers. It should have been. That was what he had intended. Why hadn't it worked?

As usual, in the aftermath of that remembered high came the crushing remembrance of defeat as well. The two experiences were like Siamese twins. One never came without the other.

The exact nature of his defeat—the how of it—was something that was never quite clear in Andrew Carlisle's mind, but he never allowed himself to dodge it, either. One moment she had been under his control. In those still-golden minutes in the bedroom he could have sworn he owned her very soul and that she would have done anything he said, yet somehow—a few moments later—she had overcome the temporary paralysis of her fear and had fought back. She fought him and won.

Thirteen years had passed since that night. In the intervening time what Diana Ladd had done to him on the kitchen floor of her house in Gates Pass had become the central issue of Andrew Carlisle's life. More than anything, she was the one who got away. The fact that their battle had left him blind and with a mangled arm wasn't as important as the simple fact that she had somehow escaped him.

However painful that realization might be, Andrew Carlisle never for even a moment allowed himself to forget it. She had been far tougher, far braver, and more resourceful than he had ever expected. Carlisle's proxy would have to be warned, in no uncertain terms, not to underestimate this woman. After all, look what she had done to him! He was locked away in prison for the rest of his natural life— shut up with no chance of parole while she was still out there somewhere, free to do whatever she liked.

Still courting elusive sleep, Andrew Carlisle tormented himself with wondering where Diana Ladd was at that very moment and what she might be doing. Right then, in the middle of the night, she was probably in that same little house down in Tucson, sleeping next to that asshole husband of hers, and reveling in the fact that one of her puny, stupid books had managed to edge its way onto the *New York Times* Best Sellers list.

There was a special radio station, available to Carlisle because he was blind, that provided audio editions of newspapers on a daily basis. Carlisle listened to the broadcasts every day. Recently, one of those had contained a feature article on Diana Ladd Walker and her newly released book.

"I have a husband and kids and a career I love," she had said. "Most of the time I feel as though I'm living in a dream."

Andrew Carlisle had heard those words, and they had galvanized him to action. Diana Ladd Walker was living the kind of life that had been forever denied him—one *she* had robbed him of through her own personal efforts. He felt as though every ounce of her success had been built on his own failure. That was unforgivable.

You may think it's a dream right now, he thought as he finally drifted off to sleep, *but with any kind of luck, I'll turn it into a nightmare.*

1

They say it happened long ago that the whole world was covered with water. I'itoi—*Elder Brother*—was floating around in the basket which he had made. After a time, Great Spirit came out of his basket and looked around. Everything was still covered with water, so I'itoi made himself larger and larger until shuhthagi—*the water*—reached only to his knees.

Then, while I'itoi was walking around in the water, he heard someone call. At first he paid no attention, but when the call came the fourth time, Elder Brother went to see who was shouting. And so I'itoi found Jeweth Mahkai—*Earth Medicine Man*—rejoicing because he was the first one to come out of the water.

Elder Brother said, "This is not true." He explained that he himself was first, but Jeweth Mahkai was stubborn and insisted that he was first.

Now I'itoi and Earth Medicine Man, as they were talking,

were standing in the south. They started toward the west. As they were going through the water—because there was as yet very little land—they heard someone else shouting.

Ban—*Coyote*—was the one who was making all the noise. I'itoi *went toward the sound, but Elder Brother went one way, and* Ban *went another. And so they passed each other. Coyote was shouting that he was the very first one out of the water and that he was all alone in the world.*

I'itoi *called to* Ban, *and at last they came together. Elder Brother explained to Coyote that he was not the first. And then the three—Great Spirit, Earth Medicine Man, and Coyote—started north together. As they went over the mud, I'itoi saw some very small tracks.*

Elder Brother said, "There must be somebody else around." Then they heard another voice calling. It was Bitokoi—*Big Black Beetle*—which the Mil-gahn, *the Whites, call stinkbug.* Bitokoi *told* I'itoi *that he was the very first to come out of the water.* I'itoi *did not even bother to answer him.*

And then the four—Elder Brother, Earth Medicine Man, Coyote, and Big Black Beetle—went on together toward the east because, as you remember, nawoj, *my friend, all things in nature go in fours.*

June 1996

Dolores Lanita Walker's slender brown legs glistened with sweat as she pumped the mountain bike along the narrow strip of pavement that led from her parents' house in Gates Pass to the Arizona Sonora Desert Museum several miles away. Lani wasn't due at her job at the concession stand until 9 A.M., but by going in early she had talked her way into being allowed to help with some of the other duties.

About a mile or so from the entrance, she came upon the

artist with his Subaru wagon parked off on the side of the road. He had been there every morning for a week now, standing in front of an easel or sitting on a folding chair, pad in hand, sketching away as she came whizzing past with her long hair flying out behind her like a fine black cape. In the intervening days they had grown accustomed to seeing one another.

The man had been the first to wave, but now she did, too. "How's it going?" he had asked her each morning after the first one or two.

"Fine," she'd answer, pumping hard to gain speed before the next little lump of hill.

"Come back when you can stay longer," he'd call after her. Lani would grin and nod and keep going.

This morning, though, he waved her down. "Got a minute?" he asked.

She pulled off the shoulder of the road. "Is something the matter?" she asked.

"No. I just wanted to show you something." He opened a sketch pad and held it up so Lani could see it. The picture took her breath away. It was a vivid color-pencil drawing of her, riding through the sunlight with the long early-morning shadows stretching out before her and with her hair floating on air behind her.

"That's very good," she said. "It really does look like me."

The man smiled. "It *is* you," he said. "But then, I've had plenty of time to practice."

Lani stood for a moment studying the picture. Her parents' twentieth wedding anniversary was coming up soon, in less than a week. Instinctively she knew that this picture, framed, would make the perfect anniversary present for them.

"How much would it cost to buy something like this?" she asked, wondering how far her first paycheck from the museum would stretch.

"It's not for sale," the man said.

Lani looked away, masking her disappointment with downcast eyes. "But I might consider trading for it," he added a moment later.

Lani brightened instantly. "Trading?" she asked. "Really?" But then disappointment settled in again. She was sixteen years old. What would she have to trade that this man might want?

"You're an Indian, aren't you?" he asked. Shyly, Lani nodded. "But you live here. In Tucson, I mean. Not on a reservation."

Lani nodded again. It didn't seem necessary to explain to this man that she was adopted and that her parents were Anglos. It was none of his business.

"I've tried going out to the reservation to paint several times," he told her, "but the people seem to be really suspicious. If you'd consider posing for me, just for half an hour or so some morning, I'd give you this one for free."

"For free? Really?"

"Sure."

Lani didn't have to think very long. "When would you like to do it?" she asked.

"Tomorrow morning?"

"That would work," Lani said, "but I'd have to come by about half an hour earlier than this, otherwise I'll be late for work."

The man nodded. "That's fine," he said. "I'll be here. And could I ask a favor?"

Lani, getting back on her bike, paused and gave him a questioning look. "What's that?"

"Could you wear something that's sort of . . . well, you know"—he shrugged uncomfortably—"something that looks Indian?"

Lani grinned. "How about the cowgirl shirt and hat I wore for rodeo last year? That's what Indians all wear these days—cowboy clothes."

"Whatever you decide," the man said. "I'm sure it'll be just fine."

"I have to go," she told him, putting one foot on the pedal and giving the bike a shove as she hopped on. "Or else I'll be late today, too. See you tomorrow then."

"Sure thing," he called after her, waving again as she rode away.

Once Lani was out of sight, Mitch Johnson quickly began gathering up his material and stowing it back in the car. Soon the Subaru was headed back toward Gates Pass and toward the lookout spot up over the Walker house where he would spend the rest of the morning, watching and pretending to draw.

How was that, Andy? he asked himself as he unpacked his gear once more and started limping up the steep hillside. *It worked just the way you always said it would. Like taking candy from a baby.*

The dream that awakened David Ladd shortly before sunrise on the morning he was scheduled to leave his grandmother's house in Evanston was the same dream that had been plaguing him and robbing him of sleep for weeks. It had come for the first time the night before he was to take his last law school exam—his final final as he thought of it—although he knew that the hurdle of passing the bar was still to come.

The recurring nightmare was one he'd had from time to time over the years, but the last time was so long ago that he had nearly forgotten it. In the dream he was standing alone in the dark—a terrible soul-numbing blackness without even the comfort of a single crack of light shining under the door.

He listened, waiting endlessly for what he knew must come—for the sound that would tell him the life-and-death battle had begun, but for a long time there was nothing at all from beyond that closed door but empty, breathless silence. Once there had been other living people trapped in the dark prison with him. Rita Antone had been there with him, as had the old priest, Father John. But they were both dead now—dead and gone—and Davy Ladd was truly alone.

Finally, from outside the terrible darkness, he heard a faint but familiar voice calling to him from his childhood. *"Olhoni, Olhoni."*

Olhoni! Little Orphaned Calf—his secret *Tohono O'othham* name—a name David Ladd hadn't heard spoken in years. Only Rita Antone—the beloved Indian godmother he had called Nana *Dahd*—and his sister Lani—had called him that. For years Nana *Dahd* had used Davy's Indian name only when the two of them were alone and when there was no one else to hear. Later on she used it in the presence of Davy's baby sister as well.

Once again Nana *Dahd*'s song flowed through the darkness, bolstering him, giving him courage:

"Listen to me, Little Olhoni.
Do not look at me, but do exactly as I say."

David Ladd held his breath, straining to hear once again the comforting chanted words of the *Tohono O'othham* song Rita had sung that fateful day while the life-and-death battle between his mother and the strange bald-headed man had raged outside that closed and locked root cellar door. The man who had burst into their home earlier that afternoon was *Mil-gahn*—a white, but in the song Rita had used to summon I'itoi to help them, she had called Andrew Carlisle by the word *Ohb*. In the language of the *Tohono O'othham*—the Desert People—that single word means at once both Apache and enemy.

Nana *Dahd*'s war chant had cast a powerful spell, instilling a mysterious strength in Davy and in other members of the embattled household. That strength had been enough to save them all from the *Ohb*'s evil that awful day. Davy, Rita, the priest, Davy's mother, and even the dog, *Oh'o*—Bone—had all been spared. At least, they had all lived. And at age six going on seven, *Mil-gahn* though he was, it had been easy for Davy Ladd to believe that *I'itoi*—Elder Brother—had interceded on their behalf; that the Spirit of Goodness had heard Nana *Dahd*'s desperate cry for help; that he had descended from his home on cloud-shrouded Baboquivari to help them vanquish their enemy.

Twenty years later, that was no longer quite so easy to accept. Even so, a grown-up David Ladd strained to listen and to gather strength from Rita's familiar but almost forgotten words. She had chanted the song in soft-spoken, guttural Papago—a language the evil *Ohb* hadn't been able to speak or understand. Back then Nana *Dahd*'s war song had served the dual purpose of summoning *I'itoi* to help them and also of telling a terrified little boy exactly what he had to do—what was expected of him.

But at the point where Rita's song should have been rising to a crescendo, it dwindled away to nothing. And now, with Nana *Dahd* gone, Davy was once again alone in the dark—a helpless, terrified child listening from one side of a door while on the other his mother fought for her life against the evil *Mil-gahn* intruder.

In his dream, David waited—for what seemed like hours—for the shocking roar of gunfire that would signal the beginning of the final stage of that deadly battle. But the gunshot never came. Instead, for no apparent reason, the door fell silently and inexplicably open, as though it had been unlatched by a ghost, or by a sudden stray gust of wind.

In real life, when the door had crashed open, the *Ohb* had been lying on the floor, screaming in rage and agony, with his face burned beyond recognition by a pan full of overheated bacon grease. His skin had blistered and bubbled, leaving his features horribly distorted like a strange wax mask that had been left to melt in the searing sun. Injured and bleeding, Davy's mother had stood over the injured man, still clutching the smoldering frying pan in her one good hand.

A terrified Davy had fled that awful scene. He had escaped through the slick, grease-spattered kitchen just as he had been ordered to do. Pushing open the sliding glass outside door, he had opened the way for his dog to get inside. Bone, outraged and bent on protecting his humans from the intruder, had hurtled into the room, going straight for the injured *Ohb*'s vulnerable throat.

Twenty years later in David's dream, the heavy cellar door fell open silently on an equally silent kitchen. And on the floor, instead of a defeated evil *Ohb*, Davy saw his sister. Lani hadn't even been born on the day Andrew Carlisle broke into the house in Gates Pass, and yet here she was, lying still and bloody, in the middle of the room. Without moving forward to touch her, without even emerging from the darkness of his cellar prison, David Ladd knew just from looking at her that Dolores Lanita Walker was dead.

He had awakened from the awful dream with his heart pounding and with his bedclothes soaked in sweat. He could barely breathe. For a while, he thought he was having a heart attack—that he was actually dying. Later that night, a jovial and not overly sympathetic emergency room physician told Davy that what had happened to him was an ordinary panic attack. Nothing serious at all, the doctor assured him. With the pressure of law school finals and all that, Davy was probably overstressed.

Nothing to worry about, the doctor said. He'd get over it.

The stress of those final exams was long gone. He had spent the last few weeks working around his grandmother's place, painting the things that needed painting, refinishing furniture, clearing out dead tree branches, and generally making himself useful. He did it in no small part to repay his grandmother, Astrid Ladd, for the many kindnesses she had offered him during the years he had been in Chicago going to school. The whole time he had lived there, he had stayed in the small chauffeur's apartment over his grandmother's garage.

He had hoped that a few days of hard physical labor would help relieve whatever was causing the panic attacks, but as he lay in bed, gasping for breath that early Friday morning, he knew it hadn't worked.

Brandon Walker was cutting wood. Cutting and stacking wood. Once a week—on Friday afternoons—a ramshackle old dump truck would arrive. Filled to the rim with a drying tangle of creosote, greasewood, palo verde, and mesquite, the truck would turn off Speedway, rumble down a steep incline, and then labor slowly up a rock-scattered sandy track that led to a house perched on a mountainside in Gates Pass west of Tucson, Arizona.

Out behind the house with its six-foot-high river-rock wall, the truck would disgorge another sorry load of doomed desert flora. For months now, Brandon Walker had waged a dogged one-man war, working to salvage the throwaway wood that had been bulldozed off the desert to make way for yet another thirsty golf course. He knew he was powerless to stop the burgeoning development that was eating away the beautiful Sonora Desert that he loved, but by cutting and stacking the wood, Brandon felt as though he was somehow keeping faith with the desert. In some small way he was keeping what the bulldozers destroyed from simply going to waste.

Late on those Friday afternoons, the empty dump truck would pull away, leaving behind its ruined mound of wood. Throughout the following week, Brandon would pull one log after another out of the snarl, saw it, and stack it. He had bought a gasoline-powered grinder that chewed up the smaller branches into chips. Someone had told him that those could probably be used as mulch, so each day he gathered the leavings into a growing mountain of shredded wood chips. The mound of drying chips and the stack of wood grew along the outside of the rock wall that stretched around the backyard perimeter of Brandon and Diana Ladd Walker's secluded desert compound.

The hard physical labor was good for him. He had sweated off the flab that was the natural outgrowth of four four-year terms as sheriff. His blood pressure was down, as were his triglycerides and his cholesterol. He ignored the fact that some of his neighbors thought him peculiar. During the hours when other men his age and in his position might have been out whacking endless golf balls around artificially grassy courses, Brandon fought his solitary battle with himself and with that week's messy jumble of wood, gradually bringing the dead mesquite and palo verde to order, even if he wasn't able—with a chain saw and ax—to work the same miracle on his own life.

Brandon worked on the wood in the early morning hours while the sun was still relatively cool. He put in another shift in the late afternoons and evenings, just before sunset. During the middle of the day, he slept.

It was funny that he could go into the bedroom in the late morning after a quick shower, tumble onto the bed, and fall fast asleep. At night he tossed and turned, paced and thought, and did everything but sleep. At regular bedtimes, as soon as he lay his head on the pillow, his mind snapped into overdrive, tormenting him with every perceived or imagined flaw in his life. During the day, with the sun on his back and with the sweat pouring off his face, he knew how lucky he was. Diana's increasing success meant that, after losing the election, there was no need for him to eat humble pie and go looking for another job. He'd even had offers. Roswell, New Mexico, had tried to entice him there with the job of police chief—a position he had been more than happy to turn down.

As soon as it was time to go to bed at night, however, his

cup was half empty rather than half full. In the dead of night, Diana's growing monetary success merely underscored his own overriding sense of failure, his belief that he had somehow not been good enough or provided well enough. Diana never said anything of the kind, of course. She never even hinted at it. In the cold light of day he could see that his nighttime torment was merely a replay of his mother's and his ex-wife's old blame-game tapes. At night, however, that clear-cut knowledge disappeared the moment he turned out the lights.

In the darkness he wrestled with the reality of being fifty years old and let out to pasture. On his fortieth birthday, he had counted himself as one of the luckiest men in the world. He had a wife who loved him and, according to his lights, a reasonably well-blended family—his two sons, Diana's son, Davy, and the baby, Lani. The icing on the cake had been his job. The chance to be elected sheriff had fallen into his lap in a way he hadn't anticipated, but the job had suited him. He had been damn good at it.

Now, ten years later, most of his "dream" life was gone, wiped out of existence as if it had never existed in the first place. The job had disappeared with the results of the last election. Bill Forsythe was the new Pima County sheriff now, leaving Brandon Walker as an unemployed fifty-year-old has-been. He still had Diana, of course, but there was a cool distance between them now—probably one of his own making and one he doubted they'd ever bridge again. Careerwise, she had moved beyond him—beyond anything either one of them had anticipated. She no longer needed him, certainly not the way she had in the beginning. As for the kids—the boys were pretty much lost to him. Tommy was gone—dead, most likely; Quentin was a lying, cheating, boozing ex-con; and Davy was off in Chicago being beguiled by his paternal grandmother's money and the myth of his long-dead father. In this bleak landscape, Brandon Walker's only consolation, his sole ray of sunshine, was Lani—the baby he had once argued fiercely against adopting.

Now, though, laboring over the wood, he felt the need to distance himself from her as well. She was sixteen and still dependent, but she wouldn't be for long. She had a job now and a driver's license. It was only a matter of time before she, too, would grow up and slip away from him.

And when that happened, Brandon wondered, would there be anything left for him, anything at all? Well, maybe that never-ending mountain of wood, waiting to be chopped and stacked and salvaged. There would probably always be plenty of that.

He worked until it was too hot to continue, then he went in, showered, and threw himself onto the bed. Only then, at eleven o'clock in the morning, was he able to fall asleep.

From his perch high up on the mountain, Mitch Johnson had a perfect view of the Walkers' river-rock compound in Gates Pass. He liked to think of it as a God's-eye view. If he'd had a rifle in his hand right about then instead of a damned stupid sketch pad, Brandon Walker standing out by his woodpile would have been an easy shot. Bang, bang, you're dead. But as Andy had pointed out, killing Brandon Walker wasn't the point. Destroying him was. If the United States was going to continue to survive as a nation, people who contributed to that destruction—people who helped the job-eating illegal scum—had to be destroyed themselves.

"Mr. Johnson," Andy had asked him once, early on, "why do you suppose the cat toys with the mouse?"

Mitch Johnson had already learned that Andrew Carlisle was sometimes an irascible teacher. Even his most oddball question required a thoughtful response. "I suppose because it's fun," he had answered.

"For whom?" Andy had persisted.

"Certainly not for the mouse."

"Don't be so sure. You see, in those moments, the mouse must have some moments of clarity, when it may possibly see through its own terror and imagine surviving. Continuing. There's a real beauty in that, a sort of dance. The mouse tries to escape. The cat blocks it. The mouse tries again, and the same thing happens. As long as the mouse keeps trying, it hasn't lost hope. Once it does, the cat becomes bored and simply eats it. End of story."

They lay on their bunks in silence for a while, Mitch Johnson in the upper bunk and Carlisle in the lower so he could get to the toilet more easily during the night.

Mitch didn't want to seem stupid, but he couldn't see where Andy was going on this one. "So what's the point?" he finally asked.

"Did you enjoy shooting those guys in the back?" Andy asked.

A peculiar intimacy existed between the two men that Mitch Johnson was hard-pressed to understand. If somebody else had asked that question, Mitch would have decked the guy, but because it was Andy asking, Mitch simply answered. "Yes," he said.

"But wouldn't it have been better," Andrew Carlisle asked, "if they'd had the chance to ask you—to beg you—not to do it and you did it anyway? Wouldn't that have been more fun? Have you ever done it that way?"

"What do you mean?" Mitch said. "I did it the way I did it. I shot them and that's it."

"But it doesn't have to be," Andrew Carlisle told him. "You have a mind, an imagination. All you have to do is rewrite the scenario. Change your mind and change your reality. Close your eyes and see them walking again. Only this time, instead of pulling the trigger, you call out to them. You order them on their hands and knees. It was hot, wasn't it? The middle of summer?"

"Yes, almost the end of June."

"So imagine them on their hands and knees in the sand,

with the hot earth blistering their skin. They're going to beg you not to shoot them. Plead with you to let them stand up again so they'll have the protection of their shoe leather between their skin and the sand. But if you wait, if you don't let them up off their hands and knees, eventually, they'll belong to you in the same way the mouse belongs to the cat, you see. In exactly the same way."

In the upper bunk, Mitch Johnson closed his eyes and let Andrew Carlisle's almost hypnotic voice flow over him. Mitch was right there again, standing on the bank of Brawley Wash, calling down to the wetbacks marching ahead of him.

"Stop," he shouted at them, and they did.

"Down!" he ordered. "Get down on your hands and knees." And they did that, too, all three of them groveling in the burning sand before him, all of them scraping their faces in the dirt. *This must be what it feels like to be a king,* Mitch thought. *Or maybe even a god.*

"Please," the older one said, speaking to Mitch in English rather than in Spanish. "Please, let my grandsons be. I'll do whatever you want. Just let my daughter's boys go free. Let them go."

"What would you do, old man?" Mitch asked him.

"Anything. Whatever you say."

"Put the barrel in your mouth."

For Mitch, that was such a sexually charged image that it almost broke the spell, but Andy's voice, washing over the whole scene, kept the images in play. Reaching up tentatively, the old man took the barrel of the gun and lovingly, almost reverentially, put it into his own mouth. And with the grandsons cowering there on the ground, and with the old man's eyes full on his face, Mitch Johnson pulled the trigger.

"And this time," Andrew Carlisle finished, "you can be sure the bastard is dead. What do you think?"

Mitch opened his eyes, unsure of what had happened but with the tracks of a wet dream still hot on his belly and between his legs.

"It beats jacking off, doesn't it?" Andrew Carlisle asked.

Yes, it does, Mitch meant to say, but, for some strange reason, he was already asleep.

Diana Ladd Walker was at work in her study. On that Friday morning she was supposed to be writing, working on the outline for her next book, *Den of Iniquity.* What she was doing instead was fielding phone calls. The month before her previous book, *Shadow of Death,* had won a Pulitzer. Even though the book had been out for nine months, the whirl of publicity surrounding the prize had pushed the book into numerous reprints. Not only that, it was back on the *New York Times* Best Sellers list as well, sitting at number eight, for the third week in a row.

Which is why, at a time when Diana should have been writing, she had been sucked instead back into book-promotion mode. She had left her desk and was on her way to shower when the phone rang again.

"It's me," Megan Wright announced. Megan was a publicist working for Diana's New York publisher, Sterling, Moffit, and Dodd. She was young—not more than twenty-five—but she was businesslike on the phone and brimmed with a kind of boundless energy and enthusiasm that suited her for the job.

"I'm calling with your weekend's marching orders," Megan continued. "I just wanted to double-check the schedule."

Obligingly, Diana hauled out her calendar and opened it to the proper page.

"First there's the University of Arizona Faculty Wives Tea this afternoon at two o'clock."

"I know," Diana observed dryly. "As a matter of fact, I was on my way into the bathroom to shower and dress when the phone rang."

"I'll hurry," Megan said. "And then there are the two appointments for tomorrow. I'm sorry about filling up your

Saturday, but I didn't have any choice. Tomorrow's the only time I could schedule the Monty Lazarus interview. Don't forget, he's the West Coast stringer for several different magazines, so it's an important interview. My guess is he'll be pitching the story to all of them."

"Where's that interview?" Diana asked. "I wrote down his name but not where I'm supposed to meet him."

"In the lobby of the La Paloma Hotel at noon. I don't have either an address or a map. Can you find it, or will you need a driver?"

Tucson may have been totally foreign territory to Megan, but Diana had lived in the Tucson area for more than thirty years. "Noon, La Paloma," Diana repeated as she jotted the words into the correct slot on the calendar under the name, "Monty Lazarus."

"And don't worry about a driver," Diana continued. "Believe me, I can find La Paloma on my own."

"Mr. Lazarus likes to take his own pictures, so you'll need to go prepared for a photo shoot. I warned him that he'll have to finish up no later than four, though, so you'll have time enough to get back home, change, and be at the El Dorado Country Club for the Friends of the Library banquet at six. Mrs. Durgan, your hostess for that event, called just a few minutes ago to make sure your husband will be attending. She wanted to know if she should reserve a place at the head table. Brandon is going, isn't he?"

"He'll be there," Diana said grimly. "If he isn't, I'll know the reason why."

"Good," Megan said, sounding relieved. "I told her I was pretty sure he was planning to attend."

When the phone call finally ended, Diana headed for the shower once more. On her way through the bedroom, she found Brandon sound asleep on the bed. She tiptoed by without waking him. No doubt he needed it. He barely slept at night these days, passing the nighttime hours prowling the house or pacing out on the patio. The midday naps he took between woodcutting shifts were pretty much the only decent rest he seemed to get.

Closing the door between the bathroom and bedroom, she undressed and then stood in front of the mirror, observing her reflection. She wasn't that bad looking for being a couple of years over the half-century mark. The face and body reflected back at her bore an amazing resemblance to what her mother, Iona Dade Cooper, had looked like just before she got so sick.

In the past few years Diana had put on some weight, especially around the hips. Her softly curling auburn hair had two distinct streaks of white flowing away from either temple. But her skin was still good, and with the help of a little makeup she'd look all right, not only for today's afternoon tea, but also for the photo shoot and banquet tomorrow.

Stepping into the shower, though, she was still chewing on what was going on between Brandon and her. It was too bad that if she was going to win some big prize that it had to be for *Shadow of Death,* a book Brandon had never wanted her to write in the first place. Not only that, it was unfortunate that what should have been her finest hour, the pinnacle of a writing career that spanned more than twenty years, should come at a time when Brandon, after being tossed out of office, was at his very lowest ebb.

The last month and a half, in fact, had been pure hell. She and Brandon had been at one another's throats ever since the engraved invitation had arrived, summoning them both to the awards festivities in New York.

Brandon had backed away from the gold-embossed envelope with both their names on it as though that rectangular piece of paper were a coiled rattlesnake.

"No way!" he had declared. "No way in hell! I'm not going to New York for that, not in a million years!"

"Why not? It'll be fun."

"For you, maybe. People are interested in you; they want to meet you. And while you're busy talking, someone will turn to me and say, 'What is it you do, Mr. Walker? Are you a writer, too?' And when I tell them I used to be sheriff but I don't do anything anymore, their eyes will glaze over and pretty soon they'll wander away. It's a ball doing that. I love it."

Diana had winced at the sarcasm in his voice, but she also knew the perils of playing second banana. She had felt the same way about attending political gatherings—the rubber-chicken luncheons and living room campaign coffee hours—back when Brandon had been a candidate for public office. But she had gone. She had kept her mouth shut, she had put on her good clothes and company manners, and she had gone. She had served as the proper political wife and had behaved the way political wives the world over are expected to behave.

Part of what had made that easy to do was the fact that she had believed so strongly in what Brandon Walker stood for. She had backed his plans for cleaning up the sheriff's department, for getting rid of the crooks and putting an end to the graft and corruption.

To be fair, back when she was first published, he had been there for her, as well. Those first few book tours when he had sometimes been able to join her for a few days at a time had been a ball. Back then, his going to functions with her had been easier for him because he had been more sure of his own place in the scheme of things. The ego damage associated with losing the election—from being booted out of a job he loved—seemed to have knocked the emotional pins out from under him. It was almost as though there had been a death in the family, and the grieving process had left him lost and directionless.

But to Diana's way of thinking, the main problem with the Pulitzer and everything associated with it was that the accolades were all coming to Diana over *Shadow of Death,* a book Brandon Walker had opposed from the very beginning.

"Don't bring all that stuff up again," he had warned her on the day Andrew Carlisle's letter had arrived from the Arizona State Prison. "Let sleeping dogs lie."

But she hadn't followed his advice. She had gone ahead and written the book anyway. And now, based on that, Diana Ladd Walker's stock had shot way up in the world of publishing. Sandy Hawkins, Diana's editor at Sterling, Moffit, and Dodd, was downright ecstatic. Requests for interviews and public appearances were flowing in. Meanwhile, Diana's marriage was in the toilet.

She and Brandon had argued bitterly over the trip to New York, with him citing any number of plausible but nonetheless phony excuses for not going. He didn't have a tux. With only one of them working, he couldn't see squandering all that money on his airfare. He hated being locked up in an airplane seat without enough room for his long legs. Most of all, in his opinion, Lani shouldn't be left home on her own, not with the end-of-school party season heating up.

"Why don't you say what you mean?" an exasperated Diana had demanded finally when she tired of arguing. "Why don't you just admit it? You don't want to go."

Brandon complied at once. "You're right," he had said. "I don't want to go."

"Fine!" Diana had stormed. "Suit yourself, but one of these days you're going to have to get over it, Brandon. One of these days you're going to have to realize that losing that election was not the end of the world."

She regretted her outburst almost immediately, but she had retreated to her office without an apology while Brandon had made tracks for his damned woodpile. And two weeks later, when Diana Ladd Walker flew off to New York, she had done so alone, with the quarrel between them still unresolved. A month and a half later, his role as "author consort" was still a bone of contention.

When the invitation came for her to speak at the annual

Friends of the Library banquet, there had been yet another firefight. This time, though, Diana had dug in her heels.

"Look," she had told him. "I can see your not going to the faculty tea. If I could get out of that one myself, I would. But the library banquet is something for the whole community, the community that elected you to office for sixteen years. People expect you to be there. *I* expect you to be there. We're married, Brandon. I don't want to spend my life out in public as one of those married singles."

"But I hate all that crap," he argued. "I hate standing around with a drink in my hand, looking like a sap, and listening to some little old lady talk about something I've never heard of."

"Get over it," Diana had snapped back at him. "If you were tough enough to face down armed crooks in your day, you ought to be able to stand up to any little old lady in the land."

Stepping out of the shower, Diana stood toweling her hair dry. Suddenly, out of nowhere, something her mother had told her once came back to her as clearly as if she had heard the words yesterday instead of thirty years earlier.

Iona Dade Cooper had been at home in Joseph, Oregon, dying of cancer. Diana, away at school at the University of Oregon in Eugene, had finally been forced to drop out temporarily to care for her. Diana had been sitting in the chair next to her mother's bed telling of her secret ambition not only to marry Garrison Ladd but also to become a writer.

"You can't have it all, you know," Iona had said quietly. "If you try to do too much, something is bound to suffer."

Standing in the bathroom thirty years later, Diana had to swallow a sudden lump in her throat. She remembered arguing the point with her mother back then, telling Iona passionately exactly how wrong she was.

"These are the sixties," Diana had said with the absolute conviction of a know-it-all twenty-one-year-old. "Women are moving into their own now, Mother. Everything is possible, you'll see."

Iona Dade Cooper had died a few months later without seeing anything of the kind. And Diana, now several years older than her mother had lived to be, was forced to acknowledge that Iona's assessment was one hundred percent accurate.

Mom, you were right, after all, Diana Cooper Ladd Walker admitted to herself. *You really can't have it all.*

2

Now in that long ago time the earth—*jeweth*—*was not yet firm and still as it is today. It was shaking and quivering all the time. That made it hard for the four to travel. So Earth Medicine Man*—Jeweth Mahkai*—*threw himself down and stopped the shaking of the earth. And that was the first land.*

But the land was floating around in separate pieces. So Earth Medicine Man called to the Spider Men. Totkihhud O'othham came out of the floating ground and went all over the world spinning their webs and tying the pieces of earth together. And that is how we have it today—land and water.

Then I'itoi wanted to find the center of the earth. So he sent Coyote toward the south and Big Black Beetle to the north. He said they must go as fast and as far as they could and then return to him.

Bitokoi—Big Black Beetle—was back quite a while before Ban—Coyote—returned. In this way I'itoi knew that he had not yet found the center of the earth.

Then Spirit of Goodness took Bitokoi *and* Ban *a little farther south and sent them off once more. Again Big Black Beetle came back before Coyote, so* I'itoi *moved still farther toward the south.*

On the fourth try Bitokoi *and Coyote came back to* I'itoi *at exactly the same time. In that way Elder Brother knew he was exactly in the center of the world. Because the Spirit of Goodness should be the center of all things, this was where* I'itoi *wished to be.*

And this center of all things where Elder Brother lives is called Tohono O'othham Jeweth, *which means Land of the Desert People.*

Mitch Johnson waited on the hill, watching and sketching, until Brandon Walker went inside around ten-thirty. By then he had several interesting thumbnail drawings—color studies—that he'd be able to produce if anyone ever questioned his reason for being there.

"You see, Mitch," Andy had told him years ago, "you always have to have some logical and defensible reason for being where you are and for doing whatever it is that you're supposedly doing. It's a kind of protective coloration, and it works the same way that the patterns on a rattlesnake's back allow it to blend into the rocks and shadows of the land it inhabits.

"The mask that allowed me to do that was writing. Writing takes research, you see. Calling something research gave me a ticket into places most people never have an opportunity to go. Drawing can do the same for you. You're lucky in that you have some innate ability, although, if I were you, I'd use some of the excess time we both seem to have at the moment to improve on those skills. You'll be surprised how doing so will stand you in good stead."

That was advice Mitch Johnson had been happy to follow, and he had carried it far beyond the scope of Andy's somewhat limited vision. Claiming to be an artist had made it possible to park his RV—a cumbersome and nearly new Bounder—on a patch of desert just off Coleman Road within miles of where Andrew Carlisle had estimated it would most likely be needed. The rancher he had made arrangements with had been more than happy to have six months' rent in advance and in cash, with the only stipulation being that Mitch keep the gate closed and locked.

"No problem," Mitch had told the guy. "I'm looking for privacy. Keeping the gate locked will be as much of a favor to me as it is for you."

And so, Mitch Johnson—after sorting through his catalog of fake IDs—took up residence on an electricity-equipped corner of the Lazy 4 Ranch under the name of M. Vega, artist. He was there, he told his landlord, to paint the same scenes over and over, in all their tiny variations through the changing seasons of the year.

The Bounder had been parked on the ranch for two months now. Long enough for locals to accept that he was there. He worried sometimes that he might possibly run into someone who had known him before, in that old life, so he mostly stayed away from the trading post and did all his shopping—including buying periodic canisters of butane— at stores on the far northeast side of town.

And that's where he headed that particular morning—to Tucson. If he was going to have company for a day or two, he needed to have plenty of supplies laid in—extra food and water both.

"It's a good plan, Mitch," Andy had told him. "My part is to make sure you have everything you need to pull it off and to get away afterward. Yours is to follow that plan and make it work."

When Andy's voice came to him out of the blue like that, so clearly and purposefully, it was hard to remember the man was dead. It took Mitch back to countless nighttime conversations when their quiet voices had flowed back and forth in the noisy privacy of their prison cell. That was when and where they had first crafted the plan and where they had refined it.

And now, putting that long-awaited plan into action, Mitch Johnson felt honor-bound to do it right. The emotional turmoil about to be visited upon Brandon and Diana Walker's complacent lives would make a fitting memorial for Andy Carlisle, the only real friend Mitch had ever had. It would mean far more than any marble slab Mitch might have had erected in a cemetery.

Sitting up on the mountain, watching Brandon Walker labor over his wood, Mitch wished it would be possible to burn it up, to turn all that carefully stacked wood into a spectacularly blazing inferno. But even as the thought passed through his mind, Mitch dismissed it. Doing that would be too much like firing a warning shot across a ship's bow.

Brandon Walker deserved no such advance notice from Mitch Johnson, and Diana Ladd wouldn't be getting one from Andy, either. One day their lives would be going along swimmingly, and the next day everything would turn to shit. That was one of the basic realities of life—something that happened to everyone sooner or later.

The last time Mitch saw Andrew Carlisle had been some eight months earlier. The man was too weak to walk by then, so the guard had brought him back to the cell in a wheelchair.

"Here's some company for you, Johnson," the guard said, opening the barred door and shoving the chair into the cell. "We've got so many cases of flu in the infirmary right now, the doc thought he might be better off here than there. Can you handle it?"

"It's not exactly news," Mitch told the guard. "Of course I can handle it."

The guard had left the wheelchair just inside the door.

Mitch had pushed it over next to the bunk and lifted Carlisle out of the chair and onto the narrow bed. Illness had ravaged his body so there was very little left of him. He couldn't have weighed more than a hundred and twenty pounds.

"I hear you're getting out," Carlisle croaked. "Congratulations."

Mitch shook his head. It was difficult for him to speak. He hadn't expected that he and Andy would become friends, but over the years they had. Now he felt a sudden sense of grief at the prospect of losing that friend not just to Mitch's own release, but also to death. Andrew Carlisle was clearly a dying man.

"When do you leave?" Andy asked.

"Tomorrow," Mitch said. "I'm sorry," he added. "Sorry to leave you alone after all this time."

"Oh, no," Andy told him. "Don't be sorry about leaving. I'll be out, too, before very long. They gave me two consecutive life sentences, but I'm going to fool the bastards. I'm only going to serve one."

Mitch laughed at that. One of the things he had always enjoyed was Andy's black humor.

"As for leaving me alone," Andy added cheerfully, "I spend so much time in the infirmary anymore that it hardly matters. Besides, the sooner I go, the sooner you'll be able to get our little job done and get on with your own life."

They were both quiet for a long time after that. Mitch was thinking about Andy's veiled reference to his trust fund monies. Maybe Andy was, too. Andrew Carlisle was the one who broke the silence.

"You will keep your end of the bargain, won't you, Mitch?" The voice was soft and pleading. The two men had lived side by side, sharing the same cell, for seven and a half years. In all that time, through years of terrible illness and unremitting pain, Mitch Johnson had never heard the man beg.

"Yes, Andy," Mitch answered quietly. "I gave you my word, and I intend to keep it."

"Thank you," Andrew Carlisle said. "So will I."

Mitch Johnson had known from the beginning that Andrew Carlisle was HIV positive, since that day in 1988 when Warden Clint Howell had called him into his office, sat him down in a chair, and offered him a cup of coffee. Inmates didn't usually merit that kind of hospitality, but Johnson had brains enough not to question it aloud.

"We've got a little problem here," Howell said, leaning back in his chair.

More than one, Mitch thought, but again he said nothing. "It's one I think maybe you can help us with," Howell continued.

The indiscriminate use of the words "we" and "us" reminded Mitch of his first grade teacher, Mrs. Wiggins, back home in El Paso, Texas.

"What's that?" Mitch asked, keeping his tone interested but properly deferential.

"One of our inmates has just been diagnosed HIV positive," Howell told him. "He wants you to be his cellmate."

"Like hell he does!" Mitch returned. "I'm not going anywhere near him."

"Please, Johnson," Howell pleaded. "Hear me out. He's specifically asked for you, but only if you're willing."

"Well, I'm not. Can I go now?"

"No, you can't. We're too overcrowded here for him to be left in a cell by himself, and if I put more than one HIV-positive prisoner in the same cell, then those damned bleeding-heart lawyers will be all over me like flies on shit. Cruel and unusual punishment and all that crap."

"What about cruel and unusual punishment for me?" Johnson asked.

"Do me a favor," Howell said. "Talk to him here in my office. I'll have him brought in, and the two of you can discuss the situation. After that, you decide. Wait right here."

Moments later, a guard led Andrew Carlisle into the room. Johnson had never met him before, but as soon as he saw the blind man with his one bad arm in a permanent sling, he knew who it was. Andrew Carlisle was legendary in Florence for being the best jailhouse lawyer in the joint. Other people had to look up the points of law and read them to him aloud, but when it came to writing up paperwork, no one could top him.

"Hello, Mr. Johnson," Carlisle said, as the door closed behind the departing guard.

"I won't do it," Mitch said. "Go fuck yourself."

"We're not here to discuss sexual gratification, Mr. Johnson. I asked for you specifically because I have a business proposition which I believe will be of some interest to you. I believe I can offer you something that you want."

"What's that?" Mitch Johnson asked.

"An education, for one thing," Andrew Carlisle answered calmly. "And revenge, for another."

"Revenge?"

"Against Sheriff Brandon Walker and his wife, Diana."

A brief silence followed that statement. Mitch was taken aback. He hadn't made a secret of his long-simmering hatred of Brandon Walker. The case against Mitch Johnson had been built by Walker while he was still an ambitious homicide detective in the Pima County Sheriff's Department. Sending Mitch Johnson to prison had made Walker's reputation in the local Hispanic community.

For twenty-some years Sheriff Jack DuShane's political machine had called the shots. Anglos killed Mexicans and Indians with relative impunity. The way cases were investigated dictated how they were prosecuted as well. More often than not, Anglos—especially ones who could afford to pay the freight—got off or were charged with reduced offenses. Non-Anglos usually couldn't afford the bribes.

The tide had started to turn with Andrew Carlisle's second trial. Everybody knew by then that the former professor had gotten away with murdering the drunk Indian girl, but there was nothing anyone could do about it. Except maybe use him as an example. A year later, when DuShane tried to intervene on Mitch Johnson's behalf, Walker had blown the whistle on all of it. In the process of shipping Mitch Johnson off to prison for fifteen years to life, Walker had won himself a reputation as a crusading and even-handed lawman. When the next election came around, he won office in a landslide, collecting an astonishing eighty percent of the county's non-Anglo vote in the process.

"Who told you about that?" Mitch asked finally.

Carlisle smiled. "I make it my business to know what goes on in this place. I've been keeping track of you for years, for as long as you've been here. From everything I've been able to learn about you, I'd say you're a very smart man—smart enough to know a good deal when you see one."

"What kind of a deal?"

"I may be a prisoner here," Carlisle said, "but I'm also relatively well off. I inherited my father's entire estate, you see. And since I'm not using any of the money—interest or principal—it's accruing at an amazing rate. I can show you the figures if you want. When I die, I can either leave the whole thing to charity or I can leave it to you."

"Why would you give any of it to me?"

"Because I think you'll agree to my terms."

"Which are?"

"Number one, that you agree to be my cellmate for the remainder of whatever time we both have here together."

"And number two?"

"You become my star pupil. I'm a teacher, you see, not only by training, but also by virtue of personal preference. I have a good deal of knowledge that I would like to impart to someone before I die, a philosophical legacy in addition to the monetary one. Then, once I've taught you what I know, you go out into the world and use that knowledge on the two people who are responsible for sending us both here."

"What exactly do you mean?"

Carlisle sighed. "Don't be obtuse, Mr. Johnson. Brandon Walker and his wife, Diana. Walker cost you your wife, your son, and your standing in the community. The woman who is now Walker's wife, Diana Ladd Walker, is responsible for the loss of both my sight and the use of one of my arms. Once I was locked up in here, I eventually contracted AIDS, so before long, she'll be costing me my life as well. I don't see how it could be any clearer than that. I want them to suffer, in the same way you and I are suffering."

"You want me to kill them?"

"Oh, no, Mr. Johnson. Not at all. I firmly believe that between the two of us, we'll be able to devise something much better than that, something far more imaginative."

"What's number three?"

"There is no number three, Mr. Johnson. Only numbers one and two. What do you think, or would you like to see some of the accounting figures before you make your decision? I can show you what's involved right now, although there's no way to tell how much money there will be in the long run. Obviously we have no idea how long this will take, do we?"

Again there was a long silence. "This is on the level?" Mitch asked finally.

"Absolutely," Carlisle answered. "I could hardly be more serious."

"That's all?"

"Yes."

"Then, Mr. Carlisle," Mitch Johnson said, "you've got yourself a deal."

What had started out way back then as a straight business deal had become for Mitch both a point of honor and pride. By the time he completed the project it would seem to all the world that Andrew Carlisle had somehow returned from the grave to wreak his revenge on the people who had destroyed him. It would give Andy the kind of immortality he had always craved in life.

In the meantime, Mitch Johnson would be left alone, free to walk off into the sunset and disappear. That kind of heroic image appealed to Mitch. It was one of the time-honored icons of the Old West.

He had no difficulty casting himself in the mold of one of those old-fashioned hired guns. None of them would ever have turned their backs on a friend in need, regardless of whether that needy friend happened to be dead or alive.

Neither would Mitch Johnson. After all, a promise is a promise unless, as in this case, it turned into a mission.

Gabe Ortiz, tribal chairman of the *Tohono O'othham* Nation, left Sells early in the morning for an all-day meeting with the Pima County Board of Supervisors. At issue was the county's most recent set of requirements designed to delay the next scheduled expansion of the tribe's booming casino. Gabe's appearance would be more ceremonial than anything, since most of the actual arguing would be handled by Delia Chavez Cachora, the recently appointed tribal attorney.

Gabe's main responsibility would be to sit there looking attentive and interested, which might prove difficult in view of the fact that he'd had so little sleep the night before. It was times like this when the countervailing pressures of being both tribal chairman and medicine man proved to be almost more than he could handle.

Before the blind medicine man, *S-ab Neid Pi Has*— Looks At Nothing—had died, years earlier, the canny old shaman had taught Gabe "Fat Crack" Ortiz a number of important things, including the meaning of those particular words, medicine man—*mahkai*. Looks At Nothing had explained the obligations involved as well.

As a confirmed Christian Scientist, Gabe initially had

been prepared to pass off most of what the old man said as superstitious nonsense. As the months went by, however, Looks At Nothing had taught Fat Crack to listen to the voice inside himself, to pay attention, and then to act on the resulting knowledge.

It was through using what Looks At Nothing taught him that Gabe's business and political ambitions had prospered. Most of the time the guidance that came to him was in the form of a gentle nudge, but in the case of Diana Ladd's book, it had been more like the blow of a hammer.

Wanda had bought him a copy of *Shadow of Death* at a book-signing in town. Diana had autographed it, wishing Gabe a happy birthday in her personalized inscription. And then Wanda had taken the gift-wrapped book home and kept it put away until Gabe's sixty-fifth birthday.

She had given it to him at a small family birthday party at their daughter's home in Tucson. As soon as Gabe held the book in his hand, even before he unwrapped it, he knew something was wrong. Something evil seemed to pulsate from inside the gaily wrapped package. Breaking the ribbon and tearing off the paper, a sense of dread seemed to fill the whole room, blurring the smiling faces of his children and grandchildren, obscuring Wanda's loving, watchful eyes.

"Diana signed it for you," Wanda said.

Gabe fumbled the book open to the title page and read the words that were written there in vivid red ink. "Gabe," the inscription said. "Happy Birthday. Here's a piece of our mutual history. I hope you enjoy it. Diana Ladd Walker."

"Do you like it?" Wanda asked.

"Yes." Gabe managed a weak smile, but as soon as possible, he put the book down. When the party was over and as he and Wanda were getting ready to leave, the grandkids had gathered up the presents and what was left of the birthday cake for Wanda and Gabe to take back home to Sells with them. Five-year-old Rita, the baby, had come racing to the door carrying the book. Afraid that whatever evil lurked in the book might somehow infect her, Gabe had reached down and snatched it from her hand.

Tears welled in her eyes. "I only wanted to carry it," she pouted. "I wouldn't drop it or anything. I like books."

"I know, baby," he said, bending over and giving the child a hug. "But this one is very special. Let me carry it, okay?"

"Okay," she sniffed. "Can I carry your hat then?"

For an answer, Gabe had put his huge black Stetson on her head. It had engulfed the child, falling down over her eyes, covering everything down to her lips, which suddenly burst into a wide grin.

"I can't see anything," she said.

"That's all right," Gabe had said, reaching out and taking her hand. "I'll lead you to the car."

"What's wrong?" Wanda asked, once they were in the Ford. "You got mad at Rita for just touching the book."

"I wasn't mad," Gabe returned, although his protest was useless. After all their years together, Wanda knew him far too well for him to be able to get away with lying.

"It's the book," he said. "It's dangerous. I didn't want her near it."

"How can a book be dangerous?" Wanda asked. "Rita's just a little girl. She can't even read."

Gabe did not want to argue. "It just is," he said.

"So what are you going to do?" Wanda asked. "Take the book to some other medicine man and have him shake a few feathers at it?"

With that, Wanda had squeezed her broad form against the door on the far side of the car. She had sat there with her arms crossed, staring out the window in moody silence as they started the sixty-mile drive back to Sells. It wasn't a good way to end a birthday party.

Looks At Nothing had taught Gabe Ortiz the importance of understanding something before taking any action. And so, in the week following the party, he had read the book, *Shadow of Death,* from cover to cover. It was slow going. In order to read it he had to hold it, and doing that necessitated overcoming his own revulsion. It reminded him of that long-ago day, when, as a curious child, he had reached into his Aunt Rita's medicine basket and touched the ancient scalp bundle she kept there.

Ni-thahth Rita had warned him then about the dangers of Enemy Sickness. Told him that by not showing proper respect for a scalp bundle he could bring down a curse on her—as the scalp bundle's owner—or on some member of her family. She had told him how Enemy Sickness caused terrible pains in the belly or blood in the urine, and how only a medicine man trained in the art of war chants could cure a patient suffering from that kind of illness.

It was late when Fat Crack finally finished reading. Wanda had long since fallen asleep but Gabe knew sleep would be impossible for him. He had stolen outside, and sat there on a chair in their ocotillo-walled, dirt-floored ramada. It was early summer. June. The month the *Tohono O'othham* call *Hahshani Bahithag Mashath*—saguaro-ripening month. Although daytime temperatures in the parched Arizona desert had already spiraled into triple digits, the nighttime air was chilly. But that long Thursday night, it was more than temperature that made Gabe Ortiz shiver.

It was true, he had known much of the story. In the late sixties, his cousin, Gina Antone, his Aunt Rita's only grandchild, had been murdered by a man named Andrew Carlisle. Diana Ladd, then a teacher on the reservation, had been instrumental in seeing that the killer, a once well-respected professor of creative writing at the university, had been sent to prison for the murder. Six years later, when the killer got out and came back to Tucson seeking revenge, he had come within minutes of killing both women—Diana Ladd and Rita Antone—and Diana's son, Davy, as well.

That much of the story Gabe already knew. The rest of it—Andrew Carlisle's childhood and Diana's, the various twists of fate that had put their two separate lives on a collision course—were things Fat Crack Ortiz learned only as he read Diana's book. Knowing those details as well as the background on Andrew Carlisle's other victims made Fat Crack feel worse instead of better. Nothing he read, including the knowledge that Andrew Carlisle had died of AIDS in the state penitentiary at Florence a few months earlier, did anything to dispel his terrible sense of foreboding about the book and the pain and suffering connected with it.

Gabe Ortiz was a practical man, given to down-to-earth logic. For an hour or more he approached the problem of the book's danger through the teachings of Mary Baker Eddy. When, at the end of several hours of consideration, he had made no progress, he walked back into the house. Careful not to disturb Wanda, he opened the bottom drawer of an old wooden teacher's desk he had salvaged from the school district trash heap. Inside one of the drawers he found Looks At Nothing's buckskin medicine pouch—the fringed *huashomi*—the old medicine man had worn until the day he died.

In the years since a frail Looks At Nothing had bequeathed the pouch to Gabe, he had kept it stocked with sacred tobacco, picking it at the proper time, drying, storing, and rolling it in the proper way. Gabe had carefully followed the sacred traditions of the Peace Smoke, using it sparingly but to good effect, all the while hoping that one or the other of his two sons would show some interest in learning what the medicine man had left in Gabe's care and keeping. Unfortunately, his two boys, Richard and Leo, nearly middle-aged now, were far more interested in running their tow-truck/auto repair business and playing the guitar than they were in anything else.

Back outside, seated on a white plastic chair rather than on the ground, as the wiry Looks At Nothing would have done, Gabe examined the contents of the bag—the medicine man's World War II vintage Zippo lighter and the cigarettes themselves. He had thought that he would light one of them and blow the smoke over the book, performing as he did so the sacred act of *wustana,* of blowing smoke with the hope of illuminating something. But sitting there, he realized that what was needed for *wustana* was a living, breathing patient. Here he had only an object, the book itself.

Rather than waste the sacred smoke, Fat Crack Ortiz decided to try blowing from his heart instead. He remembered Looks At Nothing telling him once that the process was so simple that even an old woman could do it.

Holding the book in his hands, he began the chant, repeating the verses four times just as he had been taught.

> *I am blowing now to see what it is that lives here,*
> *What breathing thing lies hidden in this book.*
> *There is a spirit in here that sickens those around it,*
> *That is a danger to those around it.*
> *I want to see this strength so I will know what kind of*
> *   thing it is.*
> *So I will know how to draw it out of where it is hiding*
> *And how to send it away to that other place,*
> *The place where the strength belongs.*

As Gabe did so, as he sang the words of the *kuadk*—observing the form and rhythms of the age-old chant of discernment—he began to figure it out. As time passed, he began to see the pattern. Without quite knowing how, he suddenly understood.

The evil *Ohb*—Fat Crack's Aunt Rita's enemy—was back. The wicked *Mil-gahn* man who, twenty-one years earlier, had somehow become a modern-day reincarnation of an ancient tribal enemy, was coming once again. Somehow the dreaded Apache was about to step out of the pages of Diana Ladd Walker's book and reenter their lives.

Gabe remembered reading in a newspaper article several months earlier that Andrew Carlisle was dead. That meant that if he was not coming in person, certainly the strength of the *Ohb* was coming, bringing danger to all of those people still alive who had once been connected with Diana Ladd and with Rita Antone—the woman Gabe called *Ni-thahth,* his mother's elder sister—in that other, long-ago battle. The fact that Carlisle was dead meant nothing. His spirit was still alive, still restless, and still bent on revenge.

Time passed. When Gabe at last emerged from his self-induced trance, the stars were growing pale in a slowly graying sky. Stiffly, Gabe Ortiz eased his cramped body out of the uncomfortable plastic chair. Before going back into the house to grab a few hours of sleep, he limped out to where the cars were parked and put both Looks At Nothing's deerskin pouch and Diana Ladd's offending book in the glove compartment of the tribal chairman's Ford sedan.

Once, long ago, when Looks At Nothing had first told him that Gabe had the power to be a great shaman, Gabe had teased the *Gohhim O'othham*—Old Man. He had laughed off the medicine man's prediction that one day Fat Crack, too, would be a great *mahkai*—a medicine man with a tow truck. That idea had struck him as too funny, especially since it came from a man who clung stubbornly to the old ways and who looked down on all things Anglo—with the single notable exception of that aging Zippo lighter.

Looks At Nothing had much preferred walking to riding in a truck. Gabe wondered now what the old shaman would say if he knew his deerskin pouch and sacred tobacco would be riding to town the next day in a two-year-old Crown Victoria. Looks At Nothing would probably think it was funny, Gabe thought, and so did he.

A few minutes later, still chuckling, he eased himself into bed. As he did so, Wanda stirred beside him.

"It's late," she complained. "You've been up all night."

"Yes," Gabe said, rolling his heavy body next to hers, and resting one of his hands on her shoulder. "But at least now I can sleep."

The sentence ended with a contented snore. Within minutes, Wanda fell asleep once more as well.

Lani had told the man that she would be late for work if she arrived any later than seven. That wasn't entirely true. The first two hours she spent at the museum each day, from seven to nine, were strictly voluntary. She went around on the meandering paths, armed with a trash bag and sharp-pronged stick, picking up the garbage that had been left behind by the previous day's visitors.

During those two hours, doing mindless work, she was able to watch the animals from time to time and simply to be there with them. Working by herself, without the necessity of talking with anyone else, she remembered the times she had come here with Nana *Dahd* and with her brother Davy.

Nana *Dahd*. *Dahd* itself implies nothing more than the somewhat distant relationship of godmother, but for Davy and Lani both, Rita Antone had been much more than that. Diana Ladd Walker may have owned the official title of "Mother" in the family, but she had come in only a distant second behind the Indian woman who had actually filled the role.

Ambitious and forever concentrating on her work, there was a part of Diana Ladd Walker that was always separate from both her children. While Diana labored over first a typewriter and later a computer, the child-rearing joys and responsibilities had fallen mainly on Rita's capable and loving shoulders.

By the time Lani appeared on the scene, Davy was already eleven years old and Rita's health was becoming precarious. Had Davy not been there to pitch in and help out, no doubt it would have been impossible for Nana *Dahd* to look after a busily curious toddler. In a symbiotic relationship that made outsiders wonder, the three of them—the old woman, the boy, and the baby—had made do.

Long after most males his age would have forsaken the company of women, Davy stayed around. He, more than anyone, understood what it was Nana *Dahd* was trying to do, and he was willing to help. Whenever he wasn't in school, he spent most of his waking hours helping the woman who had once been his baby-sitter care for his little sister.

When the three of them were alone together in Rita's apartment—with the old woman in her wheelchair and with Lani on her lap while Davy did his homework at the kitchen table—it seemed as though they existed in a carefully preserved bubble that was somehow outside the confines of regular time and space.

In that room they had spoken, laughed, and joked together, speaking solely in the softly guttural language of the *Tohono O'othham*. It was there Lani learned that Nana *Dahd's* childhood name had been *E Waila Kakaichu,* which means Dancing Quail. Rita Antone's dancing days were long since over, but Lani's were only beginning. The child danced constantly. Her favorite game consisted of standing in the middle of the room, twirling and pretending to be *siwuliki*— whirlwind. She would spin around and around until finally, losing her balance, she would fall laughing to the floor.

Just as Rita had given Davy his Indian name of *Olhoni*— Little Orphaned Calf—Nana *Dahd* gave Lani a special Indian name as well, one that was known only to the three of them. In the privacy of Rita's apartment, the *Tohono O'othham* child with the *Mil-gahn* name of Dolores Lanita Walker became *Mualig Siakam*. Rita told Lani that the words *mualig siakam* meant Forever Spinning.

There in Nana *Dahd's* room, working one stitch at a time, Rita taught Davy and Lani how to make baskets. Davy had been at it much longer, but Lani's tiny and surprisingly agile fingers soon surpassed her elder brother's clumsier efforts. When that happened, Davy Ladd gave up and stopped making baskets altogether.

Rita taught Davy and Lani the old stories and the medicinal lore Rita had learned from her own grandmother, from *Oks Amichuda*—Understanding Woman. Had Rita been physically able, she would have taken her charges out into the desert to show them the plants and animals she wanted them to understand. Instead, the three of them spent hours almost every weekend at the Arizona Sonora Desert Museum, with Davy pushing Nana *Dahd*'s chair along the gently graded paths and with Lani perched on the old woman's lap.

For Rita, every display in the museum was part of her comprehensive classroom. As they went from one exhibit to another, Rita would point out the various plants and tell what each was good for and when it should be picked. And on those long afternoons, if it was still wintertime, so the snakes and lizards were unable to hear and swallow the storyteller's luck, Rita would tell stories.

Each animal and plant came with its own traditional lore. Patiently, Nana *Dahd* told them all. Some tales explained the how of creation, like the spiders stitching together the floating pieces of earth. Others helped explain animal behavior, like the stories about how *I'itoi* taught the birds to build their nests or how he taught the gophers to dig their burrows underground. There were stories that did the same thing for plants, like the one about the courageous old woman who went south to rescue her grandson from the warlike Yaquis and was rewarded by being turned into the beautiful plant, the night-blooming cereus. And there were some, like the stories of how Cottontail and Quail both tricked Coyote, that were just for fun.

As the children learned the various stories, Rita had encouraged them to observe the behavior of the animals involved and to consider how the story and the animal's natural inclination came together to form the basis of the story. What was observable and what was told combined to help the children learn to make sense of their world, just as those same stories had for the *Tohono O'othham* for thousands of years.

Rita—her person, her stories, and her patient teaching—had formed the center of Lani Walker's existence from the moment the child first came to Gates Pass, from the time before she had any conscious memory. When Rita Antone died, the day before Lani's seventh birthday, a part of the child had died as well, but there on the paths of the museum the summer of her sixteenth year—wandering alone among the plants and animals that had populated Nana *Dahd*'s stories—Lani was able to recapture those fading strains of stories from her childhood and breathe life into them anew.

And each day at nine o'clock, when she finished up with one shift and had an hour to wait before the next one started, she would make sure she was near the door to the hummingbird enclosure. For it was there, of all the places in the museum, where she felt closest to Nana *Dahd*. This was where she and Davy had been with Rita on the day Lani Walker first remembered hearing Rita mention the story of *Kulani O'oks*—the great Medicine Woman of the *Tohono O'othham*.

"*Kulani,*" Lani had repeated, running the name over her tongue. "It sounds like my *Mil-gahn* name."

And Rita's warm brown face had beamed down at her in a way that told Lani she had just learned something important. Nana *Dahd* nodded. "That is why, at the time of your adoption, I asked your parents to make Lani part of your English name. *Kulani O'oks* and *Mualig Siakam* are two different names for the same person. And now that you are old enough to understand that, it is time that you heard that story as well."

Whenever Lani Walker sat in the hummingbird enclosure, all those stories seemed to flow together. *Kulani O'oks* and *Mualig Siakam* were one and the same, and so were Dolores Lanita Walker and Clemencia Escalante.

Four different people and four different names, but then

Nana *Dahd* had always taught that all things in nature go in fours.

Fat Crack and Wanda Ortiz, Rita Antone's nephew and his wife, had stopped by the Walker home in Gates Pass on their way home from Tucson that warm September day. Wanda Ortiz, after years of staying at home with three kids, had gone off to school and earned a degree in social work from the University of Arizona. Her case load focused on "at risk" children on the reservation, and she had ridden into town earlier that day in an ambulance, along with one of her young charges.

"It's too bad," Wanda said, visiting easily with her husband's wheelchair-bound aunt in Diana Walker's spacious, basket-lined living room. "She has ant bites all over her body. The doctor says she may not make it."

At seventy-one, Rita Antone could no longer walk, having lost her left leg—from the knee down—to diabetes. She spent her days mostly in the converted cook shack out behind Diana and Brandon Walker's house. The words "cook shack" hardly applied any longer. The place was cozy and snug. It had been recently renovated, making the whole thing—including a once tiny bathroom—wheelchair-accessible. Evenings Rita spent in the company of Diana and Brandon Walker or with Davy Ladd, the long-legged eleven-year-old she still sometimes called her little *Olhoni*.

On that particular evening, Brandon had been out investigating a homicide case for the Pima County Sheriff's Department. Diana excused herself to go make coffee for the unexpected guests while Davy lay sprawled on the floor, doodling in a notebook and listening to the grown-ups talk rather than doing his homework. Rita sat nearby with her *owij*—her awl—and the beginnings of a basket in hand. She frowned in concentration as a long strand of bear grass tried to escape its yucca bindings.

"Ant bites?" Rita asked.

Wanda Ortiz nodded. "She was staying with her great-grandmother down in *Nolic*. Her father's in jail and her mother ran off last spring. Over the summer, the other kids helped look after the little girl, but they're all back in school now. Yesterday afternoon, the grandmother fell asleep and the baby got out. She wandered into an ant bed, but her grandmother is so deaf, she didn't hear the baby screaming. The other kids from the village found her in the afternoon, after they came home on the bus.

"Someone brought her into the hospital at Sells last night, but she's still so sick that this morning they transferred her to TMC. I came along to handle the paperwork. By the time I finished, the ambulance had already left, so Gabe came to get me."

"How old is the baby?" Rita asked.

"Fifteen months," Wanda answered.

"And what will happen to her?"

"We'll try to find another relative to take her, I guess. If not . . ." Wanda Ortiz let the remainder of the sentence trail away unspoken.

"If not what?" Rita asked sharply. It was a tone of voice Davy had seldom heard Nana *Dahd* use. He looked up from his drawing, wondering what was wrong.

Wanda shrugged. "There's an orphanage up in Phoenix that takes children. If nobody else wants her, she might go there."

"Whose orphanage?" As Rita asked the question, she pushed the awl into the rough beginning of her new basket and set her basket-making materials aside.

"What do you mean, whose orphanage?" Wanda asked.

"Who runs it?" Rita asked.

"It's church-run," Wanda replied. "Baptist, I think. It's very nice. They only take Indian children there, not just *Tohono O'othham* children, but ones from lots of different tribes."

"But who's in charge?" Rita insisted. "Indians or Anglos?"

"Anglos, of course," Wanda said, "although they do have Indians on staff."

Diana walked back into the living room carrying a tray. "Indians on staff where?" she asked as she distributed cups of coffee. In view of the fact that Rita Antone made her home with a *Mil-gahn* family, Wanda Ortiz was a little mystified at Rita's obvious opposition to the idea of Indian children being raised by Anglos. After all, Rita had raised Davy Ladd, hadn't she?

"Running an orphanage for Indians," Wanda Ortiz told Diana. "We were talking about the little girl I brought to TMC this morning. Once she's released, if we can't find a suitable relative to take care of her, she may end up in a Baptist orphanage up in Phoenix. They're really very good with children."

"Do they teach basket-making up there?" Rita asked, peering at her nephew's wife. "And in the wintertime, do they sit around and tell *I'itoi* stories, or do they watch TV?"

"*Ni-thahth,*" Gabe objected, smiling and respectfully addressing his aunt in the formal *Tohono O'othham* manner used when referring to one's mother's older sister. "The children out on the reservation watch television, and those are kids who still live at home with their parents."

"Someone should be teaching them the stories," Rita insisted stubbornly. "Someone who still remembers how to tell them."

After that, the old woman lapsed into a moody silence. By then Rita Antone and Diana Ladd had lived together for almost a dozen years. Diana knew from the expression on the old woman's face that Rita was upset, and she quickly went about turning the conversation to less difficult topics. She wouldn't have mentioned it again, but once Gabe and Wanda left for Sells and after Davy had headed off to bed, Rita herself brought it up.

"That baby is *Hejel Wi i'thag,*" Rita Antone said softly. "She is Left Alone, just like me." Orphaned as a young child and then left widowed and with her only son dead in early middle age, Rita had been called *Hejel Wi i'thag* almost her whole life.

"And if they take her to that orphanage in Phoenix," Rita continued fiercely, "she will come back a Baptist, not *Tohono O'othham*. She will be an outsider her whole life, again just like me."

Diana could see that her friend was haunted by the specter of what might happen to this abandoned but unknown and unnamed child. "Don't worry," Diana said, hoping to comfort her. "Wanda said she was looking for someone—a blood relative—to take the baby. I'm sure she'll find someone who'll do it."

Rita Antone shook her grizzled head. "I don't think so," she said.

A week later, Fat Crack Ortiz was surprised when his Aunt Rita, who usually avoided using telephones, called him at his auto-repair shop at Sells.

"Where is she?" Rita asked without preamble.

"Where's who?" he asked.

"The baby. The one who was kissed by *Ali-chu'uchum O'othham*—by the Little People, by the ants and wasps and bees."

"It was ants, *Ni-thahth*," Fat Crack answered. "And she's still in the hospital in Tucson. She's supposed to get out tomorrow or the next day."

"Who is going to take her?" Rita asked.

"I'm not sure," Gabe hedged, even though he knew full well that Wanda's search for a suitable guardian for the child had so far come to nothing.

Rita correctly interpreted Fat Crack's evasiveness. "I want her," Rita said flatly. "Give her to me."

"But, *Ni-thahth*," Gabe objected. "After what already happened to that little girl, no one is going to be willing to hand her over to you."

"Why?" Rita asked. "Because I'm too old?"

"Yes." Fat Crack's answer was reluctant but truthful. "I suppose that's it. Once the tribal judge sees your age, she isn't going to look at anything else."

Rita refused to take no for an answer. "Give her to Diana, then," she countered. "She and Brandon Walker are young enough to take her, but I would still be here to teach her the things she needs to know."

Gabe hesitated to say what he knew to be true. "You don't understand. Diana and Brandon are Anglos, Rita. *Milgahn*. They're good friends of mine as well as friends of yours, but times have changed. No one does that anymore."

"Does what?"

"Approves those kinds of adoptions—adoptions outside the tribe."

"You mean Anglos can't adopt *Tohono O'othham* children anymore?"

"That's right," Gabe said. "And it's not just here. Tribal courts from all over the country are doing the same thing. They say that being adopted by someone outside a tribe is bad for Indian children, that they don't learn their language or their culture."

There was a long silence on the telephone line. For a moment or two Fat Crack wondered if perhaps something had gone wrong with the connection. "Even the tribal judge will see that living in a Baptist orphanage would be worse than living with us," Rita said at last. After that she said nothing more.

Through the expanding silence in the earpiece Fat Crack understood that, from sixty miles away, he had been thoroughly outmaneuvered by his aunt. Anglo or not, living with the Walkers was probably far preferable to living in a group home.

"I'll talk to Wanda," he agreed at last. "But that's all I'll do—talk. I'm not making any promises."

Mitch Johnson drove to Smith's, a grocery store on the corner of Swan and Grant. Once there, he stood in the soft-drink aisle wondering what he should buy. With one hand in the pocket of his jacket, he held one of the several vials of scopolamine between his fingers—as if for luck—while he tried to decide what to do.

What do girls that age like to drink early in the morning? he wondered. *Sodas, most likely.* He chose several different kinds—a six-pack of each. *Maybe some kind of juice.* He put two containers into his basket, one orange and one apple. And then, for good measure, he threw in a couple of cartons of chocolate milk as well. Andy had warned him against using something hot, like coffee or tea, for instance, for fear that the boiling hot liquid might somehow lessen the drug's impact.

And it did have an impact. Mitch Johnson knew that from personal experience.

One day in August of the previous year, Andrew Carlisle had returned from another brief stay in the prison infirmary holding a small glass container in his hand.

"What's that?" Mitch had asked, thinking it was probably some new kind of medicine that would be used to treat Andrew Carlisle's constantly increasing catalog of ailments.

"I've been wondering all this time exactly how you'd manage to make off with the girl. I think I've found the answer." Andy handed the glass with its colorless liquid contents over to Mitch. He opened it and took a sniff. It was odorless as well as colorless.

"I still don't know what it is," he said.

"Remember that article you were reading to me from the *Wall Street Journal* a few weeks ago? The one about the Burundianga Cocktail?"

"That's what the drug dealers down in Colombia used to relieve that diplomat of his papers and his money?"

Carlisle smiled. "That's the one," he said. "And here it is."

Over the years, Andy had clearly demonstrated to Mitch that sufficient sums of money available outside the prison could account for any amount of illegal contraband inside.

"Where did you get it?" Mitch asked.

"I have my sources," Andy answered. "And you'll find plenty of it with your supplies once you're on the outside. It isn't a controlled substance, so there were no questions asked. But it made sense to me to make a single large buy rather than a series of small ones."

"But how exactly does it work, and how much do I use?"

"That's the sixty-four-thousand-dollar question, isn't it," Andy had replied. "There may be a certain amount of trial and error involved. You should use enough that she's tractable, but you don't want to use so much that she loses consciousness or even dies as a result of an overdose."

"You're saying we should do a dry run?" Mitch asked.

"Several dry runs might be better than just one."

Mitch thought about that for a moment. Andy's health was so frail that he certainly couldn't risk taking anything out of the ordinary.

"I guess I'd better be the guinea pig then," Mitch said. "No telling what a shot of this stuff would do to you."

Andy nodded. "We won't give you that much," he said re-assuringly. "Just enough to give you a little buzz so you'll know exactly what it feels like."

"When should we do it?"

"This afternoon. You'll have a soda break with a little added kick."

That afternoon, at three o'clock, Mitch Johnson had served himself up a glass of scopolamine-laced Pepsi. They used only half the contents of that one-ounce bottle. From Mitch's point of view, it seemed as though nothing at all happened. He didn't feel any particular loss of control. He remembered climbing up on the upper bunk and lying there, feeling hot and a little flushed, waiting for the effects of the drug to hit him. The next thing he noticed was how everything around him seemed to shrink. Mitch himself grew huge, while a guard walking the corridor looked like a tiny dwarf. When Mitch came to himself again, he was eating breakfast.

"What happened to dinner?" he asked Andy irritably. "Did something happen and they skipped it?"

"You ate it," Andrew Carlisle told him.

"The hell I did. I lay down here on the bed just a little while ago . . ." Mitch stopped short. "You mean dinner came and went, the whole night passed, and I don't remember any of it?"

"That's right," Andy said. "This stuff packs a hell of a wallop, doesn't it? Since the girl is physically so much smaller than you are, you'll have to be careful not to give her too much. It makes you realize why some of those scopolamine-based cold medicines caution against using mechanical equipment, doesn't it?"

They had been silent for some time after that. Mitch Johnson was stunned. Fifteen hours of his life had disappeared, leaving him no conscious memory of them.

"Did I do or say anything stupid while I was out of it?"

"Not stupid," Andy replied. "I found it interesting rather than stupid."

"What do you mean?"

"I've always wondered whether or not those three wetbacks were the first ones. And it turns out they weren't."

Mitch shoved his tray aside. "What the hell do you mean?"

"You know what I mean, Mitch. I'm talking about the girl. The *'gook,'* I believe you called her. The one you raped and then blew to pieces with your AR-sixteen."

Mitch Johnson paled. "I never told anyone about that," he whispered hoarsely. "Not anyone at all."

"Well," Carlisle said with a shrug. "Now you've told me, but don't worry. After all, what are a few secrets between friends?"

3

After I'itoi *found the center of the world, he began making men out of mud.* Ban—Coyote—*was standing there watching.* I'itoi *told* Ban *that he could help.*

Coyote *worked with his back to* I'itoi. *As he made his men, he was laughing. Because the Spirit of Mischief is always with him,* Coyote *laughs at everything.*

After a while I'itoi—*the Spirit of Goodness—finished making his mud men and turned to see why* Coyote *was laughing. He found that* Ban *had made all his men with only one leg. But still* Coyote *continued to laugh.*

At last, when they had made enough mud men, I'itoi *told* Coyote *to listen to see which of all the mud men would be the first to speak.*

Ban *waited and listened, but nothing happened. Finally he went to* I'itoi *and said, "The mud men are not talking."*

But I'itoi *said, "Go back and listen again. Since the Spirit of Mischief is in your men, surely they will be the first to speak."*

And this was true. The first of the spirits to speak in the mud men was the Spirit of Mischief. For this reason, these men became the Ohb, *the Apaches—the enemy. According to the legends of the Desert People, the* Ohb *have always been mean and full of mischief, just the way Coyote made them.*

When all the mud men were alive, I'itoi *gathered them together and showed them where each tribe should live. The Apaches went to the mountains toward the east. The Hopis went north. The Yaquis went south. But the* Tohono O'oth-ham—*the Desert People—were told to stay in that place which is the center of things. And that is where they are today,* nawoj, *my friend, close to Baboquivari,* I'itoi's *cloud-veiled mountain.*

And all this happened on the First Day.

At four o'clock in the afternoon, Gabe Ortiz climbed into his oven-hot Crown Victoria, turned on the air-conditioning, and sat there letting the hot air blow-dry the sweat on his skin. He loosened his bola tie and tossed his Stetson into the backseat, then he leaned back and closed his eyes, waiting for the car to cool.

All the back-and-forth hassling was enough to make Gabe long for the old days, before the election, when most of his contacts with the whites, the *Mil-gahn*, had been when he towed their disabled cars or motor homes out of the sand along Highway 86 and into Tucson or Casa Grande for repairs.

Why was it that Anglo bureaucrats seemed to have no other purpose in life than seeing that things *didn't* happen? Delia Chavez Cachora was a fighter when it came to battling the guys in suits, but even she, with her Washington D.C.-bureaucrat experience, had been unable to move the county road-improvement process off dead center. Unless traffic patterns to the tribal casino could be improved, further expansion of the facility, along with expansion of the casino's money-making capability, was impossible.

Delia was bright and tough—a skilled negotiator whose verbal assertiveness belied her *Tohono O'othham* heritage. Those traits, along with her D. C. experience, were what had drawn Gabe Ortiz to her during their first interview. He was the one who had championed her application over those of several equally qualified male applicants. But the very skills that made Delia an asset as tribal attorney and helped her forward tribal business when it came to dealing with Anglo bureaucracies seemed to be working against her when it came to dealing with her fellow *Tohono O'othham*.

Gabe had heard it said that Delia Chavez Cachora sounded and acted so much like a *Mil-gahn* at times that she wasn't really "Indian" enough. She was doing the proper things—living with her aunt out at Little Tucson was certainly a step in the right direction—but Gabe knew she would need additional help. He had developed a plan to address that particular problem. Delia just didn't know about it yet, although he'd have to tell her soon.

Davy Ladd was a young man, an Anglo who had been raised by Gabe Ortiz's Aunt Rita. A recent law school graduate, Davy was due back in Tucson sometime in the next few days. By the time he arrived, Delia would have to know that Gabe had hired Davy to spend the summer months and maybe more time beyond that working as an intern in the tribal attorney's office.

Gabe thought it would be interesting to see how Delia Chavez Cachora dealt with an Anglo who spoke her supposedly native tongue far better than she did. Not only that, Gabe was looking forward to getting to know the grown-up version of his late Aunt Rita's Little Olhoni.

Next to his ear, someone tapped on the window. Gabe opened his eyes and sat up. Delia herself was standing next to his car, a concerned frown on her face. "Are you all right?" she asked when he rolled down the window.

"Just resting my eyes," he said.

"I was afraid you were sick."

Gabe shook his head. "Tired," he said with a smile. "Tired but not sick."

"Are you going straight home?" she asked. "We could stop and get something to drink."

"No, thanks," he said. "You go on ahead. I have to visit with someone on the way."

"All right," she said. "See you Monday."

As she walked away from the car, Gabe noticed she was stripping off her watch and putting it in her purse. When Gabe had asked her about it, she had told him that on weekends she tried to live on Indian time; tried to do without clocks and all the other trappings of the Anglo world, including, presumably, the evils of air conditioning, he thought as she drove past him a few minutes later with all the windows of her turbo Saab wide open.

Gabe put the now reasonably cool Ford in gear and backed out of his parking place. Instead of heading for Ajo Way and the road back to Sells, he headed north to Speedway and then west toward Gates Pass and the home of his friends, Brandon and Diana Walker.

It wasn't a trip Gabe was looking forward to because he didn't know what he was going to say. However, he knew he would have to say something. It was his responsibility.

"Brandon?"

Over the noise of the chain saw, Brandon hadn't heard the car stop outside the front of the house, nor had he noticed Gabe Ortiz materialize silently behind him. Startled by the unexpected voice, Brandon almost dropped the saw when he turned around to see who had spoken.

"Fat Crack!" he exclaimed, taking off his hat and wiping his face with the damp bandanna he wore tied around his forehead. "The way you came sneaking up behind me, it's a wonder I didn't cut off my leg. How the hell are you? What are you doing here? Would you like some iced tea or a beer?"

Now that he was tribal chairman, Fat Crack was a name Gabe Ortiz didn't hear very often anymore, not outside the confines of his immediate family. The distinctive physiognomy that had given rise to his nickname was no longer quite so visible, especially not now when he often wore a sports jacket over his ample middle. The dress-up slacks, necessary attire for the office and for meetings in town, didn't shift downward in quite the same fashion as his old Levi's had. Still, he reached down and tugged self-consciously at his belt, just to be sure his pants weren't hanging at half-mast.

"Iced tea sounds good," Gabe said.

The two men walked into and through the yard and then on inside the house. With the book fresh in his mind, Gabe looked around the kitchen. It had been completely redesigned and upgraded since the night of Andrew Carlisle's brutal attack. The wall between the root cellar, where Rita Antone and Davy Ladd had been imprisoned, had been knocked out, as had the wall between the kitchen and what had once been Rita's private quarters. The greatly enlarged kitchen now included a small informal dining area. The cabinets were new and so were the appliances, but to Gabe's heightened perceptions a ghost from that other room—the room from the book—still lingered almost palpably in the air. The damaged past permeated the room with evil in the same way the odor of a fire lingers among the ruins long after the flames themselves have been extinguished.

Acutely aware of that unseen aspect of the room, Gabe looked at the other man, trying to gauge whether or not he noticed. As Brandon bustled cheerfully around the kitchen, he seemed totally oblivious. A full pitcher of sun tea sat on the counter. He filled glasses with ice cubes from the machine in the door of the fridge, added the tea, sliced off two wedges of lemon, and passed Gabe the sugar bowl and a spoon along with the tall glass of tea and a lemon wedge.

"How are you?" Gabe asked. Spooning sugar into his tea, he was thankful Wanda wasn't there to tell him not to.

Brandon shrugged. "Can't complain. Doesn't do any good if I do. Now to what do I owe this honor?" Brandon sat down across the table from his guest. "Not some hitch with Davy's internship, I hope. He should be leaving for home within the next day or two."

Gabe took a sip of tea. "No," he said. "Everything's fine with that."

"What then?" Brandon asked.

The two men had been friends for a long time. Fighting the war with Andrew Carlisle and living through the courtroom battles that followed had turned Brandon Walker and Gabe Ortiz into unlikely comrades at arms. And their political ambitions—Gabe's within the tribe and Brandon's in the county sheriff's department—had led them along similar though different paths. Gabe had stood for election to the tribal council for the first time at almost the same time Brandon Walker took his first run at Pima County sheriff. Both of them had won, first time out.

With Gabe working in the background of tribal council deliberations and Brandon running the sheriff's department, the two men had managed to create a fairly close working relationship between tribal and county law enforcement officers. Gabe's elevation to chairman had happened only recently, after Brandon Walker had been burned at the polls and let out to pasture. With Brandon Walker no longer running the show at the sheriff's department, the spirit of cooperation that had once existed between Law and Order—the Tribal Police—and the Pima County Sheriff's Department was fast disappearing.

"Is Diana here?" Gabe asked.

Frowning, Brandon looked at his watch. When he left office, they had given him a gold watch, for Chrissakes. He hated the damn thing and everything it symbolized. He wore it all the time in the vain hope that daily doses of hard physical labor would eventually help wear it out.

"She should be home in a little while. She had to go to some kind of shindig over at the university. A tea, I think. I must have been a good boy, because she let me off on good behavior, thank God," he added with a grin.

Gabe didn't smile back. With instincts honed sharp from years of being a cop, Brandon recognized that non-smile for what it was—trouble.

"What's the matter, Gabe? Is something wrong?"

Gabe Ortiz took a deliberate sip of his tea before he answered. Convincing other people of the presence of an unseen menace had seemed so easy last night when he had been in tune with the ancient rituals of chants and singing. Now, though, the warning he had come to deliver didn't seem nearly so straightforward.

"I came to talk to you about Diana's book," he managed finally.

"Oh," Brandon Walker said. "Somehow I was afraid of that."

"You were?" Gabe asked hopefully. Perhaps he wasn't the only one with a powerful sense of foreboding.

"When she first came up with the idea for that book, I tried my best to talk her out of it," Brandon said. "I told her from the very beginning that I didn't think it was a good idea to rehash all that old stuff. Which shows how much I know. The damn thing went and won a Pulitzer. Now that it's gone into multiple printings, the publisher is turning handstands. Months after it came out, the book is back on the *New York Times* Best Sellers list and moving up." He stopped and gave his visitor a sardonic grin. "I guess I was a better sheriff than I am a literary critic—and I wasn't too hot at that."

For a moment they both sipped their tea. Brandon waited to see if Fat Crack would say what was on his mind. When nothing appeared to be forthcoming, Brandon tried priming the pump.

"So what is it about the book?" he asked. "Is there something wrong with it? Did she leave something out or put too much in? Diana's usually very good with research, but everybody screws up now and then. What's the scoop, Fat Crack? Tell me."

"Andrew Carlisle's coming back," Gabe said slowly.

Walker started involuntarily but then caught himself. "The hell he is, unless you're talking about some kind of instant replay of the Second Coming. Andrew Philip Carlisle is dead. He died a month and a half ago. In prison. Of AIDS."

"I know," Gabe replied. "I saw that in the paper. I'm not saying he's coming back himself. Maybe he's sending someone else."

"What for?"

"I don't know. To get even?"

Brandon leaned back in his chair. Most Anglos would have simply laughed the suggestions aside. Gabe was relieved that Brandon, at least, seemed to be giving the idea serious consideration.

"Most crooks talk about getting revenge, but very few ever do," he said finally. "Either in person or otherwise."

"He did before," Gabe said.

That statement brooked no argument. Brandon nodded. "So what do we do about it?"

For an answer, Gabe pulled Looks At Nothing's deerskin pouch out of his pocket. "Remember this?" he asked, opening it and removing both a cigarette and the lighter.

A single glimpse of that worn, fringed pouch threw Brandon Walker into a sea of remembrance. He waited in silence as Gabe lit one of the hand-rolled cigarettes. And once he smelled a whiff of the acrid smoke, that, too, brought back a flood of memories.

The last time Brandon had seen the pouch was the night after Davy Ladd's *Tohono O'othham* baptism. Back then the customs of the Desert People had been new and strange. The old medicine man, with help in translation from both Fat Crack and the old priest, had patiently explained some of the belief systems surrounding sickness, both Traveling Sickness—*Oimmedtham Mumkithag*—and Staying Sickness—*Kkahchim Mumkithag*.

According to the medicine man, traveling sicknesses were contagious diseases like measles, mumps, or chicken pox. They moved from person to person and from place to place, affecting everyone, Indian and Anglo alike. Traveling sicknesses could be treated by medicine men, but they also responded to the efforts of doctors, nurses, and Anglo hospitals.

Staying sicknesses, on the other hand, were believed to affect only Indians and could be cured only by medicine men. Both physical and spiritual in nature, staying sicknesses resulted from someone breaking a taboo or coming in contact with a dangerous object. By virtue of being an unbaptized baby, Davy himself had become the dangerous object that had attracted the attentions of the *Ohb*-infected Andrew Carlisle. As a cop investigating a case, Brandon had been little more than an amused outsider as he observed Diana Ladd complying with the requirements of Looks At Nothing's ritual cure.

The prescription had included seeing to it that Davy Ladd was baptized according to both Indian and Anglo custom. Father John, a frail old priest from San Xavier Mission, had fulfilled the *Mil-gahn* part of the bargain by baptizing Davy into the Catholic Church of Diana Ladd's Anglo upbringing. Looks At Nothing, aided by ceremonial singers, had baptized Davy according to the ritual of the *Tohono O'othham*. In the process the boy was given a new name. Among the *Tohono O'othham* Davy Ladd became *Edagith Gogk Je'e*— One With Two Mothers.

"But I thought you told me staying sicknesses only affect Indians," Brandon had objected.

"Don't you see?" Looks At Nothing returned. "Davy is not just an Anglo child. He has been raised by Rita as a child of her heart. Therefore he is *Tohono O'othham* as well. That's why two baptisms are necessary, Anglo and Indian both."

"I see," Brandon had said back then. Now, after years living under the same roof with Rita, Davy, and Lani, Brandon understood far more about Staying Sickness than he ever would have thought possible. For instance, Eagle Sickness comes from killing an eagle and can result in head lice or itchy hands. Owl Sickness comes from succumbing to a dream in which a ghost appears, and can result in fits or trances, dizziness, and "heart shaking." Coyote Sickness comes from killing a coyote or eating a melon a coyote has bitten into. That one can cause both itching and diarrhea in babies. Whenever one of the kids had come down with a case of diarrhea, Rita was always convinced Coyote Sickness was at fault.

Now, though, sitting in the kitchen of the house at Gates Pass, Brandon Walker smelled the smoke and was transported back to that long ago council around the hood of Fat Crack's bright red tow truck. It was at the feast after the ceremony, after Rita and Diana and Davy Ladd had all eaten the ritual gruel of white clay and crushed owl feathers. There had been four men in all—Looks At Nothing, Father John, Fat Crack, and Brandon Walker—who had gathered in that informal circle.

Brandon remembered how Looks At Nothing had pulled out his frayed leather pouch and how he had carefully removed one of his homemade cigarettes. Brandon had watched in fascination as the blind man once again used his Zippo lighter and unerringly ignited the roll of paper and tobacco. Before that, Brandon had been exposed only once to the *Tohono O'othham* custom of the Peace Smoke, one accomplished with the use of cigarettes rather than with the ceremonial pipes used by other Indian tribes. He knew, for example, that when the burning cigarette was handed to him, he was expected to take a drag, say *"Nawoj"*—which means friend or friendly gift—and then pass it along to the next man in the circle.

It had seemed to Brandon at the time that the cigarette was being passed in honor of Davy's successful baptism, but that wasn't true. The circle around the truck had a wholly separate purpose.

Only when the cigarette had gone all the way around the circle—from medicine man to priest, from tow truck driver to detective and back at last to Looks At Nothing—did Brandon Walker learn the rest.

"He is a good boy," Looks At Nothing had said quietly, clearly referring to Davy. "But I am worried about one thing. He has too many mothers and not enough fathers."

Not enough fathers? Brandon had thought to himself, standing there leaning on a tow truck fender. What the hell is that supposed to mean? And what does it have to do with me?

Obligingly, Looks At Nothing had told them.

"There are four of us," the shaman had continued. "All things in nature go in fours. Why could we not agree to be father to this fatherless boy, all four of us together? We each have things to teach, and we all have things to learn."

Brandon recalled the supreme confidence with which the medicine man had stated this position. Out of politeness, it was framed as a question, but it was nonetheless a pronouncement. No one gathered around the truck that warm summer's night in the still-eddying smoke from the old man's cigarette had nerve enough to say otherwise.

Twenty-one years had passed between then and now. Two of Davy Ladd's four fathers were dead—Father John for twenty years and Looks At Nothing for three years less than that. One of the two mothers, Rita Antone, was gone as well.

Of the six people charged by the medicine man with Davy Ladd's care and keeping, only three remained—Diana Ladd Walker, Fat Crack Ortiz, and Brandon Walker.

*   *   *

"That's the pouch that belonged to the old blind medicine man, isn't it?" Brandon asked.

Fat Crack, nodding, passed the cigarette to Brandon. *"Nawoj,"* Fat Crack said.

At Diana's insistence, Brandon Walker had quit smoking completely years ago. When he took that first drag on the ceremonial tobacco, the sharp smoke of the desert tobacco burned his throat and chest. He winced but managed to suppress a cough.

"Nawoj," he returned, passing the cigarette back to Gabe.

For a time after that, the two men smoked in utter silence. Only when Brandon with typical Anglo impatience was convinced that Fat Crack had forgotten how to speak, did Gabe Ortiz open his mouth.

"I finished reading Diana's book last night," he said at last. "It gave me a bad feeling. Finally I took the book outside and sang a *kuadk* over it."

"A what?" Brandon asked.

"Kuadk. One of the sacred chants of discernment that Looks At Nothing taught me. That's how I learned the evil *Ohb* is coming back."

Brandon frowned. "Even though he's dead."

Fat Crack nodded. "I can't see the danger, I just know it's coming."

Brandon shook his head. There was no point in arguing. "What are we supposed to do about it?" he asked.

"That's what you and I must decide."

Brandon Walker sighed. Abruptly he stood up and walked back to the counter to fetch the pitcher of tea. In the process, he seemed to shake off the effects of the smoke and all it implied.

"What do you suggest?" he asked irritably. "In case you haven't noticed, I'm not the sheriff anymore. I'm not even a deputy. There's nothing I can do. Nothing I'm *supposed* to do."

Realizing that Brandon Walker was no longer in touch with the spiritual danger, Gabe attempted to respond to the physical concerns. "Maybe you could ask the sheriff to send more patrols out this way," he suggested.

"Why? To protect us from a dead man?" Brandon Walker demanded. "Are you kidding? If I weren't a laughingstock already, I sure as hell would be once word about that leaked out. I appreciate your concern, Gabe. And I thank you for going to all the trouble of stopping by to warn us, but believe me, you're wrong. Andrew Carlisle is dead. He can't hurt anybody anymore."

"I'd better be going, then," Gabe Ortiz said.

"Don't you want to stay and see Diana? She should be home before long."

Fat Crack shook his head. If Brandon wouldn't listen to him, that meant that the evil here in the kitchen would grow stronger still. He didn't want to sit there and feel it gaining strength around him.

"I'll be late for dinner," he said. "It'll make Wanda mad."

When he stood up, his legs groaned beneath him. His joints felt stiff and old as his whole body protested the hours he had spent the night before seated in that uncomfortable molded plastic chair. Wanda had picked up a whole set of those chairs on sale from Walgreen's at the end of the previous summer. Now Gabe understood why they had been so cheap.

"Do me a favor, *nawoj,* my friend," Gabe Ortiz said, limping toward the door. "Do something for an old man."

"You're not so old," Brandon Walker objected. "But what favor?"

"Think about what I said," Gabe told him, slipping the deerskin pouch back into his pocket.. "And even if you don't believe what I said, act as though you do."

"What's that supposed to mean?"

"Be careful," Gabe answered. "You and Diana both."

Brandon nodded. "Sure," he said, not knowing if he meant it or not.

Outside, Gabe Ortiz paused with his hand touching the door handle on the Crown Victoria. "What are you going to do with all that wood out there?" he asked.

"Oh, that." Brandon shrugged. "Right now I'm just cutting it, I guess," he said. "I haven't given much thought to what we'll do with it. Burn some of it over the winter, I suppose. Why, do you know someone who needs wood?"

"The ladies up at San Xavier sure could use it," Gabe answered. "The ones who cook the popovers and chili. Most of the wood is gone from right around there. They have to haul it in. And the chips would help on the playfield down at Topawa Elementary. When it rains, that whole place down there turns to mud."

"If somebody can use it, they're welcome to it," Brandon said. "All they have to do is come pick it up."

"I'll have the tribe send out some trucks along with guys to load it."

"Sure thing," Brandon said. "They can come most anytime. I'm usually here."

As soon as Gabe Ortiz's Crown Victoria headed down the road, Brandon Walker returned to his woodpile. A reincarnated Andrew Carlisle? That was the most ridiculous thing he'd ever heard. Still, there was one point upon which Brandon Walker fully agreed with Fat Crack Ortiz—writing *Shadow of Death* had been a dangerous undertaking.

Four years earlier, on the day the letter arrived from Andrew Carlisle, Brandon Walker and Diana Ladd had already been together for seventeen years. They had come through the trials and tribulations of raising children and stepchildren. Together they had survived the long-term agonies of writing and publishing books and dealt with the complexities and hard work of running for public office. There had been difficulties, of course, but always there had been room for compromise—right up to the arrival of that damned letter. And from that time since, it seemed to him they had been locked in a downward spiral.

That was Brandon's perception, that things had been hunky-dory before the letter and had gone to hell in a handbasket afterward, although in actual fact everything wasn't absolutely perfect beforehand. They had already lost Tommy by then, and Quentin had already been sent to prison on the drunk-driving charge. But still . . .

The letter, ticking like a time bomb, had come to the house as part of a packet of publisher-forwarded fan mail. Diana had opened the envelope and read the oddly printed, handwritten letter herself before handing it to her husband.

MY DEAR MS. WALKER,

AFTER ALL THESE YEARS IT MAY SURPRISE YOU TO HEAR FROM ME AGAIN. FURTHER, IT MAY COME AS NEWS TO YOU TO KNOW THAT I HAVE RECENTLY BEEN DIAGNOSED AS SUFFERING FROM AN INEVITABLY FATAL DISEASE (AIDS). I AM WRITING TO YOU AT THIS TIME TO SEE IF YOU WOULD BE INTERESTED IN WORKING WITH ME ON A BOOK PROJECT THAT WOULD CHRONICLE THE CIRCUMSTANCES THAT BROUGHT ME TO THIS UNFORTUNATE PASS.

I HAVE ALREADY ASSEMBLED A GOOD DEAL OF INVALUABLE MATERIAL FOR SUCH A PROJECT, BUT I AM OFFENDED BY THE RULES CURRENTLY IN EFFECT THAT MAKE IT IMPOSSIBLE FOR CONVICTED CRIMINALS TO REAP ANY KIND OF FINANCIAL REWARDS FROM RECOUNTING THEIR NEFARIOUS DEEDS, INCLUDING WRITING BOOKS ABOUT SAME. BECAUSE SOMEONE SHOULD BE ALLOWED TO MAKE AN HONEST BUCK OUT OF SUCH AN UNDERTAKING, I AM WILLING TO TURN THE ENTIRE IDEA, ALONG WITH MY ACCUMULATED MATERIAL, OVER TO A CAPABLE

WRITER—WITH NO STRINGS ATTACHED—TO DO WITH AS
HE OR SHE MAY CHOOSE.

YOU ARE UNIQUELY QUALIFIED TO WRITE SUCH A
BOOK, AND I BELIEVE THAT OUR TWO DIVERGING POINTS
OF VIEW ON THE SAME STORY WOULD MAKE FOR COM-
PELLING READING, EVEN IF WE BOTH KNOW, GOING INTO
THE PROJECT, EXACTLY HOW IT WILL ALL TURN OUT.

DURING MY YEARS OF INCARCERATION HERE IN FLOR-
ENCE, I HAVE FOLLOWED YOUR FLOURISHING (PARDON
THE UNINTENTIONAL ALLITERATION) CAREER WITH MORE
THAN CASUAL INTEREST. THIS HAS BEEN DIFFICULT AT
TIMES SINCE IT TAKES TIME FOR NONFICTION WORK TO BE
TRANSLATED INTO EITHER "TALKING BOOKS" OR
BRAILLE. (AS A RELATIVE "LATECOMER" TO THE WORLD
OF BLINDNESS, BRAILLE CONTINUES TO BE SLOW-GOING
AND CUMBERSOME FOR ME.)

THE MATERIAL I NOW HAVE IN MY POSSESSION IS IN
THE FORM OF TYPED NOTES AND TAPES. I THINK, THOUGH,
SHOULD YOU DECIDE TO TAKE ON THIS PROJECT, THAT A
SERIES OF FACE-TO-FACE INTERVIEWS WOULD BE THE
MOST EFFECTIVE WAY OF KICKING THINGS OFF.

WHATEVER YOUR DECISION, PLEASE LET ME KNOW AS
SOON AS POSSIBLE IN VIEW OF THE FACT THAT WITH THIS
DISEASE TIME MAY BE FAR MORE LIMITED THAN EITHER
ONE OF US NOW SUSPECTS.

REGARDS,
ANDREW PHILIP CARLISLE

Just holding the wretched letter in his hand had made
Brandon Walker feel somehow contaminated. And angry.

"Send this thing back by return mail and tell him to shove
it up his ass," he had growled, handing the letter back to
Diana. "Where does that son of a bitch get off and how come
he has your address?"

"Andrew Carlisle always had my address," Diana reminded her husband. "Our address," she corrected. "We haven't moved, you know, not since it happened."

"Did he send it here directly?"

"No, it came in a packet from my publisher in New York."

"If you want me to, I'll call the warden and tell him not to let Carlisle send you any more letters, whether they go to New York first or not."

"I'll take care of it," Diana had said.

"You'll tell him not to write again?" Brandon asked.

"I said I'd handle it."

Looking at his wife's determined expression, Brandon suddenly understood her intention. "You're not going to write back, are you?"

Diana stood there for a moment gazing down at the letter and not answering.

"Well?" Brandon insisted impatiently. "Are you?"

"I might," she said.

"Why, for God's sake?"

"Because he's right, you know. It could be one hell of a good book. Usually it takes at least two books to tell both sides of any given story. This would have both in one. Not only that, my agent and my editor both told me years ago that anytime I was ready to write a book about what happened, Sterling, Moffit, and Dodd would jump at the chance to publish it."

"No," Brandon said.

"What do you mean, no?"

"Just what I said. N-O. Absolutely not. I don't want you anywhere near that crackpot. I don't want you writing to him. I don't want you interviewing him. I don't want you writing about him. Forget it."

"Wait a minute," Diana objected. "You can't tell me what I can and what I can't write."

"But it could be dangerous for you," Brandon said.

"Being sheriff can be dangerous, too," she told him.

"What happens when it's time for the next election and you have to decide whether or not to run for office again?"

"What about it?"

"What if I told you to forget it? What if I told you that you couldn't run for office because I said your being sheriff worried me too much? What if you couldn't run because I refused to give my permission? What then?"

"Diana," Brandon said, realizing too late that he had stepped off a cliff into forbidden territory. "It's not the same thing."

"It isn't? What's so different about it?"

"That's politics . . ."

"And I don't know anything about politics, right?"

"Diana, I—"

"Listen, Brandon Walker. I know as much or more about politics as you do about writing and publishing. And if I have the good sense to stay out of your business, I'll thank you to have the good sense to stay out of mine."

"But you'll be putting yourself at risk," Brandon ventured. "Why would you want to do that?"

"Because there are questions I still don't have answers for," Diana had replied. "I'm the only one who can ask those questions, and Andrew Carlisle is the only one who can provide the answers."

"But why stir it all up again?"

"Because I paid a hell of a price," Diana responded. "Because more than anyone else in the whole world, I've earned the right to have those damn answers. All of them."

She had left then, stalked off to her office. Within weeks—lightning speed in the world of publishing contract negotiations—the contract had come through for *Shadow of Death*, although the book hadn't had that name then. The original working title had been *A Private War*.

And it had been, in more ways than one. From then on, things had never been quite the same between Brandon and Diana.

*   *   *

Diana heard the whine of the chain saw as soon as she pulled into the carport alongside the house and switched off the Suburban's engine. Hearing the sound, she gripped the steering wheel and closed her eyes.

"Damn," she muttered. "He's at it again."

Shaking her head, Diana hurried into the house, determined to change both her clothes and her attitude. The literary tea was over, thank God. It had been murder—just the kind of stultifying ordeal Brandon had predicted it would be. Listening to the saw, Diana realized that it would have been nice if she herself had been given a choice of working on the woodpile or dealing with Edith Gailbraith, the sharp-tongued wife of the former head of the university's English Department. Compared to Edith, the tangled pile of mesquite and creosote held a certain straightforward appeal.

Edith, social daggers at the ready, had been the first one to inquire after Brandon. "How's your poor husband faring these days now that he lost the election?" she had asked.

Diana had smiled brightly. At least she hoped it was a bright smile. "He's doing fine," she said, shying away from adding the qualifying words "for a hermit." As she had learned in the past few months, being married to a hermit-in-training wasn't much fun.

"Has he found another job yet?" Edith continued.

"He isn't looking," Diana answered with a firm smile. "He doesn't really *need* another job. That's given him some time to look at his options."

"I'd watch out for him, if I were you," Edith continued. "Don't leave him out to pasture too long. American men take it so hard when they stop working. The number who die within months of retirement is just phenomenal. For too many of them, their jobs are their lives. That was certainly the case with my Harry. He mourned for months afterward.

I was afraid we were going to end up in divorce court, but he died first. He never did get over it."

Nothing like a little sweetness and light over tea and cakes, Diana thought, seeing Brandon's frenetic work on the woodpile through Edith Gailbraith's prying eyes. And lips. With unerring accuracy, Edith had zeroed in on one of Diana Ladd Walker's most vulnerable areas of concern. What exactly was going on with Brandon? And would he ever get over it?

Driving up to the house late that afternoon, she still didn't have any acceptable answers to that question. The only thing she did know for sure was that somehow cutting up the wood was helping him deal with the demons that were eating him alive. Having left Edith behind, it was easy for Diana to go back home to Gates Pass prepared to forgive and forget.

"Go change your clothes and stack some wood, Diana," she told herself. "It'll do you a world of good."

In the master bedroom of their house Diana slipped out of the smart little emerald green silk suit she had worn to the tea. She changed into jeans, boots, and a loose-fitting T-shirt. When she stopped in to pick up a pair of glasses of iced tea, she noticed the two glasses already sitting in the kitchen sink and wondered who had stopped by.

She took two newly filled glasses outside. Brandon, stacking wood now with sweat soaking through his clothing, smiled at her gratefully when she handed him his tea. "I'm from Washington," she joked. "I'm here to help."

As a victim of many hit-and-run federal bureaucrats, the quip made Brandon laugh aloud. "Good," he said. "I'll take whatever help I can get."

Without saying anything further, he handed her a piece of chopped log, which she obligingly carried to the stack. They worked together in silence for some time before Brandon somewhat warily broached the subject of the university tea. "How was it?" he asked.

Diana shrugged. "About what you'd expect," she said. "By holding it at the Arizona Historical Society instead of someplace on campus or at the president's residence, they managed to make it clear that as far as they're concerned, I'm still not quite okay."

"You can't really blame them for that," Brandon said. "Andrew Carlisle isn't exactly one of the U. of A.'s more stellar ex-professors. You can hardly expect them to be good sports about what they all have to regard as adverse publicity."

In writing *Shadow of Death,* Diana hadn't glossed over the fact that Andrew Carlisle had used his position as head of the Creative Writing Department at the University of Arizona to lure Diana's first husband, Garrison Ladd, into playing a part in a brutal torture killing. Members of the local literary community—especially ones in the university's English Department who had known Andrew Carlisle personally and who still held sway over the university's creative writing program—were shocked and appalled by his portrayal in the book. They were disgusted that a book one *Arizona Daily Sun* reviewer had dismissed as nothing more than "a poor-taste exercise in true crime" had gone on to be hailed by national critics and booksellers alike as a masterwork.

"You were absolutely right not to go," Diana added, bending over and straightening a pile of branches into a manageable armload. "The vultures were out in spades. Several of the women took great pains to tell me that although they never deign to read that kind of thing themselves, they were sure this must be quite good."

"That's big of them," Brandon said. "But it is quite good."

Diana stopped what she was doing and turned a questioning look on her husband's tanned, handsome face. "You mean you've actually read it?"

"Yes."

"When?"

"While you were off in New York. I didn't want to be the only person on the block who hadn't read the damn thing."

When she had been writing other books, Brandon had read the chapters as they came out of the computer printer. With the manuscript for *Shadow of Death* he had shown less than no interest. When the galleys came back from New York for correction, she had offered to let him read the book then, but he had said no thanks. He had made his position clear from the beginning, and nothing—not even Diana's considerable six-figure advance payment—had changed his mind.

Hurt but resigned, Diana had decided he probably never would read it. She hadn't brought up the subject again.

Now, though, standing there in the searing afternoon heat, cradling a load of branches in her arms, Diana felt some of the months of unresolved anger melt away. "You read it and you liked it?" she asked.

"I didn't say I liked it," Brandon answered, moving toward her and looking down into her eyes. "In fact, I hated it—every damned word, but that doesn't mean it wasn't good, because it is. Or should I say, not bad for a girl?" he added with a tentative smile.

The phrase "not bad for a girl" was an old familiar and private joke between them. And hearing those words of praise from Brandon Walker meant far more to Diana than any Pulitzer ever would.

With tears in her eyes, she put down her burden of wood and then let herself be pulled close in a sweaty but welcome embrace. Brandon's shirt was wet and salty against her cheeks. So were her tears.

"Thank you," she murmured, smiling up at him. "Thank you so much."

By mid-afternoon, Mitch Johnson's errands were run and he was back on the mountain, watching and waiting. The front yard of the Walker place was an unfenced jungle—a snarl of native plants and cactus—ocotillo, saguaro, and long-eared prickly pear—with a driveway curving through it. One part of the drive branched off to the side of the house, where it passed through a wrought-iron gate set in the tall river-rock wall that surrounded both sides and back of the house.

Late in the afternoon what appeared to be an almost new blue-and-silver Suburban drove through an electronically opened gate and into a carport on the side of the house. Mitch watched intently through a pair of binoculars as the woman he had come to know as Diana Ladd Walker stepped out of the vehicle and then stood watching while the gate swung shut behind the vehicle.

She probably believes those bars on that gate mean safety, Mitch thought with a laugh. *Safety and security.*

"False security, little lady," he said aloud. "Those bars don't mean a damned thing, not if somebody opens the gate and lets me in."

Using binoculars, Mitch observed Diana Ladd Walker's progress as she made her way into the house. She had to be somewhere around fifty, but even so, he had to admit she was a handsome woman, just as Andy had told him she would be. Her auburn hair was going gray around the temple. From the emerald-green suit she wore, he could see that she had kept her figure. She moved with the confident, self-satisfied grace that comes from doing what you've always wanted to do. No wonder Andrew Carlisle had hated Diana Ladd Walker's guts. So did Mitch.

A few minutes after disappearing into the house she reemerged, dressed in work clothes—jeans, a T-shirt, and hat and bringing her husband something cold to drink.

How touching, the watcher on the mountain thought. *How sweet! How stupid!*

And then, while Brandon and Diana Walker were busy with the wood, the sweet little morsel who was destined to

be dessert rode up on her mountain bike. Lani. The three unsuspecting people talked together for several minutes before
the girl went inside. Not long after that, toward sunset, Brandon and Diana went inside as well.

In the last three weeks Mitch Johnson had read *Shadow
of Death* from cover to cover three different times, gleaning
new bits of information with each repetition. Long before he
read the book, Andy had told him that the child Diana and
Brandon Walker had adopted was an Indian. What Mitch
hadn't suspected until he saw Lani in the yard and sailing
past him on her bicycle was how beautiful she would be.

That was all right. The more beautiful, the better. The
more Brandon and Diana Walker loved their daughter, the
more losing her would hurt them. After all, Mikey had been
an angelic-faced cherub when Mitch went away to prison.

"What's the worst thing about being in prison?" Andy
had asked one time early on, shortly after Mitch Johnson
had been moved into the same cell.

Mitch didn't have to think before he answered. "Losing
my son," he had said at once. "Losing Mikey."

His wife had raised so much hell that Mitch had finally
been forced to sign away his parental rights, clearing the
way for Mikey to be adopted by Larry Wraike, Lori Kiser
Johnson's second husband.

"So that's what we have to do then," Andy had said determinedly.

This was long before Mitch Johnson had taken Andrew
Carlisle's single-minded plan and made it his own. The conversation had occurred at a time when the possibility of
Mitch's being released from prison seemed so remote as to
be nothing more than a fairy tale.

"What is it we have to do?" he had asked.

"Leave Brandon Walker childless," Andy had answered.
"The same way he left you. My understanding is that one of
his sons is missing and presumed dead. That means he has
three children left—a natural son, a stepson, and an adopted

daughter. So whatever we do we'll have to be sure to take care of all three."

"How?" Mitch had asked.

"I'm not certain at the moment, Mr. Johnson," Andy responded. "But we're both quite smart, and we have plenty of time to establish a plan of attack. I'm sure we'll be able to come up with something appropriately elegant."

For eighteen years—the whole time Mitch was in prison—he sent Mikey birthday cards. Every year the envelopes had been returned unopened.

Mitch Johnson had saved those cards, every single one of them. To his way of thinking, they were only part of the price Brandon and Diana Walker would have to pay.

4

Because *everything in nature goes in fours,* nawoj, *there were four days in the beginning of things. But these four days were not like four days are today. It may have meant four years or perhaps four periods of time.*

On the Second Day I'itoi went to all the different tribes to see how they were getting along. And Great Spirit taught each tribe the kind of houses they should build.

First, I'itoi went to the Yaquis, the Hiakim, who live in the south. It was very hot in the land of the Yaquis, so he showed them how to dig into the side of a hill and to make houses that would be cool.

When Great Spirit went south, Gopher—Jewho—and Coyote—Ban—followed him because, as you remember, everything must follow the Spirit of Goodness. And while I'itoi was digging into the side of the hill to show the Hiakim how to build their houses, Gopher and Coyote stood watching. And soon, Jewho and Ban began digging as well.

Every minute or two, as they worked, they pulled their heads out of the holes they were digging to see how Elder Brother did it.

Presently I'itoi *stopped to rest. When he saw what Gopher and Coyote were doing, he laughed and said, "That is a good house for you." And that,* nawoj, *is why the gophers and coyotes have lived that same way ever since.*

Moments after Lani stepped into the house, the phone rang. "Davy!" she exclaimed, her voice alive with delight as soon as she heard her brother's greeting. "Where are you? When will you be home?"

"I'll be leaving Evanston tomorrow morning," he said. "I won't be home until sometime next week."

"In time for Mom and Dad's anniversary?" she asked.

"What day is it again?" David asked.

"Saturday," she told him. "A week from tomorrow."

"I should be there by then. Why? Is there a party or something?"

"No, but wait until you see what I'm getting them. There's a guy I met on the way to work. He's an artist. I'm going to pose for him tomorrow morning, and he's going to give me a picture."

"What kind of pose?" David asked.

"He wants me to wear something Indian," Lani said. "I'm going to wear the outfit I wore for rodeo last year."

"Oh," David Ladd said, sounding relieved. "That kind of pose."

"What kind of pose did you think?" Lani asked.

"Never mind. Is Mom there?"

"She's outside with Dad. Want me to go get her?"

"Don't bother. Just give her the message that I'm leaving in the morning, so she won't be able to reach me. Tell her I'll call from here and there along the way to let her know how I'm doing."

From the moment Lani had come to the house in Gates Pass, Davy Ladd had been the second most important person in her young life, right behind Nana *Dahd*. The bond that existed between the two went far beyond the normal connection between brother and sister. Even halfway across the continent Lani sensed something was amiss.

"What's wrong?" she asked.

David Ladd was more than a little concerned about driving cross-country alone. Under normal circumstances, it wouldn't have bothered him at all. In the course of his years of going to school at Northwestern, he had made the solo drive several times. Now, though, he was living with the possibility of another panic attack always hanging over his head. What would happen if one came over him while he was driving alone down a freeway? He had called home, looking for reassurance, but obviously the edginess in his tone had communicated itself to his little sister. That embarrassed him.

"It's no big deal," he said. "I've just been having some trouble sleeping is all."

Lani laughed. "You? Mom always said you were the world-class sleeper in the family, that you could sleep through anything."

"Not anymore," Davy replied somberly. "I guess I must be getting old." He paused. "So are things all right at home? With Mom and Dad, I mean?"

"Sure," Lani said. "Mom's getting ready to start another book, and Dad's still cutting up wood like mad."

"And how about you?" Davy added. "How are things going with the new job?"

"It's great," Lani answered. "There's that hour in the morning, between shifts . . ." She stopped. "Hey, maybe when you're back here, you could come over to the museum in the afternoons sometimes. I can get you in for free. The two of us could spend the afternoon there together, just like we used to, with Nana *Dahd*."

"I'd like that, *Mualig Siakam*," David Ladd said softly,

drifting back into the world of their childhood names and squeezing the words out over an unexpected lump that suddenly rose in his throat. "I'd like that a lot."

"Mr. Walker?"

Quentin Walker, slouched in front of a beer on his customary stool, was drinking his way toward the end of Happy Hour at El Gato Loco, a dive of a workingman's bar just east of the freeway on West Grant Road in Tucson. At the sound of his own name, one Quentin didn't necessarily bandy about among the tough customers of El Gato, Quentin swung around on his stool and studied the newcomer over the rim of his draft beer.

"Yeah," he said without enthusiasm. "That's me."

"Long time no see."

Quentin was more than moderately drunk. He had been sitting at the smoke-filled bar since five, working his way through his usual TGIF routine—shots of bourbon with beer chasers. He squinted up at the newcomer, a tall, spare man who, even in the shadowy gloom of the nighttime bar, still wore sunglasses and a baseball cap pulled low on his forehead. Only when the man finally reached up and removed the sunglasses did recognition finally dawn.

"Why, Mitch Johnson!" Quentin exclaimed. "How the hell are you?"

"I'm out, same as you," Mitch answered with a grin as he settled on the next stool. "Which means I'm fine. You?"

Quentin shrugged. "Okay, I guess. What'll you have to drink?"

"A beer," Mitch said. "Bud's okay."

Quentin signaled the bartender, who brought two beers and another shot as well. When Mitch paid for all three drinks, Quentin nodded his thanks. He hadn't really planned on another. By the time Happy Hour finished at seven, he was usually juiced enough that he could stagger the three blocks up the street to his grubby apartment. There, if he was lucky and drunk enough both, he'd fall into bed and sleep through the night. Maybe it was just the geography of it, of being back so near to where it had all happened. Whatever the cause, in the months since he'd left prison and returned to Tucson, sleep without the benefit of booze was a virtual impossibility. He went to bed more or less drunk every night. That was the only thing that held his particular set of demons at bay.

"I heard about Andy," Quentin said. "Read about it in the paper, that he died, I mean. It's too bad . . ."

"I'm sure he was more than ready to go," Mitch replied. "He'd been sick for a long time. He was in a lot of pain. I think he had suffered enough."

Quentin cast a bleary, questioning stare at the man seated next to him. Mitch had seen that look before and understood it. He had seen it on the faces of countless guards and fellow prisoners. They were all searching his face for signs of the awful lesions that had made Andrew Carlisle's grotesque face that much worse toward the end. Everyone was waiting to see when the same visible marks of AIDS—symptoms of his impending death—would show up on Mitch's body as well. For all of them—guards and prisoners alike—it was a foregone conclusion that the telltale marks of Kaposi's sarcoma would inevitably appear.

Mitch alone knew that those conclusions were wrong. He and Andy Carlisle had been cell mates and friends for seven and a half celibate years. Although the rest of the prison population may have thought otherwise, their relationship had been intellectual rather than sexual. Originally there had been some of the trappings of teacher and student, but eventually that had evolved into one of fully equal co-conspirators—with the two of them aligned against the universe.

Their long-term interdependence and mutual interests had merged into a closeness that, outside prison, might well have been mistaken for a kind of love. And in a way, it was.

It had been a private joke between them that the universal presumption of physical intimacy between them had given Mitch Johnson a certain kind of protection from attack that he had very much appreciated. Originally that physical security had meant far more to Mitch than Andrew Carlisle's promised monetary legacy. Once the former professor was in the picture, no one ever again attempted to mess with Mitch Johnson, no one at all.

"Believe it or not, still no symptoms, if that's what you're looking for," Mitch said, answering Quentin's unasked question.

Embarrassed, Quentin's eyes dodged away from Mitch's unflinching gaze. "Sorry," he mumbled.

"It's okay," Mitch said.

For a time the two men were silent while Quentin stared moodily into his beer. "I didn't mean to insult you . . ."

"Forget it," Mitch said. "It's nothing. I'm used to it by now."

Quentin shook his head. "You two were the only ones up there who ever helped me, you know," he muttered. "You and Andy. And of all the people there, you two should have been the very last ones. I mean, with everything my family did to you . . ."

"It's all water under the bridge, Quentin," Mitch reassured him. "That was then, and this is now."

"But you don't know how bad it was for me," Quentin continued, undeterred. "That first year after I got sent up was a nightmare. I was young and stupid and the son of a sheriff, for God's sake, and I thought I was so tough. But I wasn't, not nearly tough enough. Everybody in the joint was after my ass, or worse. Those guys had me six ways to Sunday. They turned me into nothing but a piece of meat." He shuddered, remembering.

"If you and Andy hadn't taken me under your wings, I don't know what would have happened to me. I'd probably be dead by now."

"Don't give me any of the credit," Mitch cautioned. "It was Andy's idea, not mine."

"But why did he do it? I've always wondered about that. All he had to do was put out the word that I belonged to him and that was it. After that nobody else ever touched me. I was scared shitless that he would . . . that someday he'd make a demand and I'd have to come across, but he never did."

"No," Mitch agreed. "Andy wasn't like that. That's the part nobody understood about him."

"Not even with you?" Quentin asked.

"No, not even with me."

"So why then?" Quentin continued. "Why did he protect me without demanding anything in return?"

"Because that's the way he was," Mitch answered. "Because Andrew Carlisle was a remarkable man."

"It's the nicest thing anybody ever did for me." Quentin Walker's blood alcohol level had taken him to the edge of maudlin. He ducked his head and swiped tears from his eyes.

Mitch looked away and pretended not to notice. "He helped me the same way he did you," he said quietly. "He taught me how to survive, no matter what. In the end, he was the one who gave me a reason to go on living."

"Hell of a guy," Quentin murmured, raising his beer glass in a toast. "Here's to Andy. May he rest in peace."

Again they were both silent for a moment. "I suppose you've read your stepmother's book about him?" Mitch said finally.

Quentin Walker scowled into his glass. "Are you kidding? Whatever that bitch has to say about him, I'm not interested. Just because she had a problem with Andrew Carlisle doesn't mean I did, too."

Mitch clicked his tongue. "Your stepmother may be famous, but it doesn't sound as though she's one of your favorite people."

Quentin shook his head. "Are you kidding? She's got my

dad wound so tight around her little finger, it's a wonder the man can even breathe on his own."

"One of those blended families that isn't quite working," Mitch Johnson observed.

Quentin Walker had come back to Tucson from prison to a kind of internal exile. He was right there in town with them, but he wanted nothing whatever to do with Brandon Walker and his "second" family. He had seen his mother a few times, but the second time he hit Janie Walker Fellows Hitchcock up for a loan, Quentin's goody-goody half-brother, Brian Fellows, had barred the door. Now Quentin was only allowed to speak to his mother in person and in the presence of either her nurse or of Brian himself.

Working construction, Quentin had developed a reputation as a loner. He caught rides to and from work with various coworkers, but having discovered how people reacted to the news that he was fresh out of the slammer, he now kept that information strictly to himself. He resisted all suggestions of possible friendship and relied on various neighborhood bartenders when he needed a shoulder to cry on.

In all those lonely months, Mitch Johnson's was the first truly friendly face he had encountered. Here at last was someone who, however distant, qualified as a friend; someone who could be counted on to understand the depths of Quentin's own miserable existence. Here was a kindred spirit, an ex-con himself, who didn't automatically regard Quentin as some kind of repulsive monster. Grateful beyond measure, the younger man warmed to this prison acquaintance in the same boozy way he might have approached an old classmate at a high school reunion.

For months, for years, in fact, Quentin had kept his feelings locked behind a dam of self-pity. Now, as the floodgates opened, he spilled out his sad tale, wallowing in the injustice of it all.

"Tommy and me didn't get blended," Quentin replied bitterly. "Sliced and diced is more like it. Or else pureed right out of existence."

"Tommy's your brother then?" Mitch Johnson asked.

Quentin considered for a moment before he answered. "He was my little brother. The two of us always ended up taking a backseat to Davy, my stepmother's kid, and even to Lani, once she came along. They got everything, and we got nothing."

"Lani's the Indian girl your dad and stepmother adopted?"

Quentin frowned. "How did you know that?"

"It's in the book," Mitch said quickly. "In your stepmother's book. You're all in it. You said Tommy *was* your little brother. I don't remember the book saying anything about him being dead."

"Tommy's missing," Quentin answered firmly. "He's been missing for years. He disappeared between his freshman and sophomore years in high school. After all this time, I suppose he's dead. Nobody's heard from him since."

Quentin ducked his head and took another quick sip of beer. "Sorry," he added. "I didn't mean to end up spilling out all this family crap."

"It's okay," Mitch returned. "Families are like that, especially for people like us. All you have to do is screw up once and then you find out the whole idea of 'unconditional love' is a crock of shit. The people who are supposed to love you usually turn out to be the ones who break your heart. That's why friends are so important. A lot of times, friends are it. They're all you end up with."

Once again Quentin gave Mitch a searching, sidelong look. "You mean you're in the same boat?"

Mitch nodded. "Pretty much," he said. "If it's any consolation, there's a whole lot of that going around."

"As in misery loves company?"

"More or less."

Quentin gave a bleak laugh and lifted his almost empty glass. "Here's to friends, then," he said.

"To friends," Mitch agreed, touching his still almost full

glass to Quentin's nearly empty one. Quentin raised one finger and called for another beer.

"So what are you up to these days?" Quentin asked as they waited for the bartender to deliver the order.

"For the last couple of months," Mitch Johnson said quietly, "I've been looking for you."

"Looking for me?" Quentin asked, as though he couldn't quite believe it.

Mitch nodded. "I probably wouldn't have found you now if it hadn't been for your mother."

"Which one, my stepmother or my real mother?"

"Your biological mother," Mitch answered.

"You mean you actually made it past the screen and talked to her?"

"What screen?"

"My brother, Brian. My half-brother. He doesn't let me anywhere near Mom if he can help it. He claims I upset her. What he really means is she might end up slipping me some cash. Brian wants to keep all that for himself."

"Your brother must not have been home," Mitch replied, "because I talked to her directly. She's the one who told me where you were living."

"You still haven't told me how come you were looking for me in the first place."

"Andy told me once that you claimed to have found some pottery—some Indian pottery—out on the reservation. Is that true?"

Quentin had been chatting easily enough. Now, though, he pulled back. "What if it is?" he asked.

Mitch ignored the sudden shift in mood. "One of the things Andy did for me before he died," Mitch continued, "was to give me the benefit of some of his contacts. I may have found a possible buyer for those pots of yours—if they're legit, that is."

The conversation ground to a momentary halt. "How much money?" Quentin asked finally, looking up.

Mitch shrugged. "That depends on quality and quantity of the merchandise, of course. But before my buyer will deal on any pots, he wants me to take a look at them. He wants me to see the pots as well as where you found them."

Before Mitch could even finish the sentence, Quentin Walker was already shaking his head. "No way!" he said. "No way in hell! I can maybe bring them out for you to see them, but you can't go there to look at them. It's not possible."

"Why not?"

"You just can't, that's all."

"But I can make it worth your while," Mitch said.

Reaching into his pocket, he pulled out his wallet. He removed several bills and laid them on the bar. "Believe me, Quentin, there's a lot more where this came from. It's our chance to make some big bucks."

Quentin looked at the money blankly for some time, as though lost in thought. "What's this?" he asked at last.

"What does it look like?" Mitch Johnson smiled. "It's a small down payment, Quentin. But remember, seeing the material on site is part of the deal. This is the first half. You get the same amount as soon as you show me the spot. After that, it's a sixty-forty split of whatever my buyer pays."

Mitch knew very well the kind of hand-to-hand existence Quentin Walker had lived since being released from prison. He had expected the man to leap at the opportunity to make some fast money. Mitch found Quentin's apparent reticence somewhat surprising. He waited impatiently while the younger man stared down at the bills without touching them.

"Drywalling money's that good then?" Mitch asked in an effort to move things forward.

Tentatively, almost as if afraid they might bite, Quentin Walker reached out and moved the bills closer to him. He leaned down and examined them in the dim light of the bar. An unfamiliar picture stared back at him from the topmost one. Quentin may not have recognized Grover Cleveland's likeness right off the bat, but the numbers in the corner of the bill were easily identifiable—a one and three zeros.

"There's more where that came from."

Not quite believing what he was seeing, Quentin thumbed through the other bills. "Five thousand dollars?" he mouthed silently.

Mitch nodded. Quentin glanced furtively around the bar. Most of the customers were engrossed in the San Diego Padres baseball game blaring from the television set at the far end of the bar. As the bartender pulled himself away from the game and started toward them with the next round, Quentin snatched the bills off the counter and stuffed them into his shirt pocket.

Watching him, Mitch suppressed a sigh of relief. The surge of power he felt was almost sexual in nature. It reminded him of that first time he had invited Lori Kiser to go on a date—a picnic in Sabino Canyon. She had said yes, even though they both knew at the time that she was saying yes to far more than just a picnic. There had been an implicit understanding in her saying yes that day, in the way she had blushed when she answered. Her yes was to the picnic, but it was also to something else. To going to bed with him, probably before the day was over. They had gone on the picnic. Mitch had taken a blanket along, just in case, and he had been absolutely right.

Sitting in the bar with Quentin Walker, Mitch sensed that this was the same thing. By taking the money, Quentin knew he was agreeing to break the law. Again. What he couldn't possibly know was exactly which laws he would end up breaking.

"When do you want to go?" Quentin was asking.

Now it was Mitch's turn to pull himself out of a reverie in order to answer. "How about tomorrow evening?"

He forced himself to ask the question casually, even though he knew from his scheduling discussion with Megan in New York that this was the one time when he could be reasonably sure that Brandon and Diana Walker were going to a banquet together. That meant they would both be away from the house for a predictable period of time.

Already more than a little drunk, Quentin tried to think his way through all the various ramifications. There were risks involved in selling the pottery, but that much money— ten thousand tax-free dollars—almost made the risks worthwhile. At least, it made them seem far less significant.

"I suppose that would work," Quentin said. "In fact, it'll probably be better if we go there in the dark. Fewer people will see us if we go then. This place is a secret, you know. I want to keep it that way. Not only that, it won't be nearly as hot."

"All right," Mitch agreed. "What time?"

"Five?"

"I already have another afternoon appointment. Five may be pushing it. Let's make it six. Where should we meet?"

"Here," Quentin said. "I don't have wheels at the moment."

"No problem," Mitch assured him. "Meet me out front. You can ride with me." He stood up and staggered slightly, waiting for his permanently damaged knee to steady under his weight.

Quentin noticed and seemed to relax. "At least I'm not the only one who's had one too many."

"I guess not," Mitch said agreeably. "See you tomorrow."

He limped outside and climbed into his waiting Subaru. He sat there for a few moments, eyeing the bar's vivid neon lights and thinking. Originally the plan had simply been to do the girl in her parents' house and to leave a drunken Quentin there to take the blame. In that basic plan, the pots had been intended as nothing more than bait, something off the wall enough to dupe Quentin into going along with the program.

In the months since Mitch had been out of prison, however, he had been doing some research. He had learned that these pots—if they actually existed—were probably worth a fortune in their own right. And if he could have Quentin Walker and his pots as well, why not go for broke?

The original plan had been a perfectly good one, and it gave every indication of working in a totally predictable fashion. That didn't mean, however, that it couldn't be improved upon. After all, Andy hadn't left Mitch so much money that he couldn't do with a little more.

See you tomorrow, sucker, Mitch thought, as he turned the key in the ignition. *We'll have so much fun that you won't be able to believe it.*

Once Mitch Johnson left the bar, Quentin Walker wasted no time in summoning the bartender once again. "Let me have one for the road," he said. "Jack Daniels on ice. A double."

"Why the sudden change?" the bartender asked. "Did you win the lottery or something?"

"Damn near," Quentin replied, trying his best not to sound too enthusiastic. He patted his shirt pocket, checking to make sure the five bills were still there. They rustled crisply beneath his hand. He hadn't dreamed them, then; hadn't made them up. He hadn't made up Mitch Johnson, either.

The money was good. In fact, the money was great, better than he would have dreamed possible. The only problem was taking Mitch Johnson up to the cave.

The prospect of doing that left Quentin almost sick with fear. There must be a way around it, he thought as the bartender delivered his next drink. There just has to be. All he needed was a good solid shot of whiskey to clear his head.

Not long after that, Quentin left the bar. He was afraid that if he stayed around too long, he might shoot his mouth off and tell somebody about the money. In this neighborhood, walking around with a wad of money on you was almost as bad as being handed a death warrant.

Glancing warily over his shoulder, Quentin staggered the block and a half to his alley-fronting apartment. It would have been a crying shame if somebody had hit him over the head and rolled him on his way home.

A hell of a crying shame!

Brandon waited until he and Diana were getting ready for bed before he brought up the subject of Fat Crack's visit. They had been having so much fun together out chopping and stacking wood that he hadn't wanted to spoil things by bringing it up. And then again, during dinner, he hadn't wanted to mention anything at all about Andrew Carlisle in front of Lani.

He was just gearing up to say something when Diana beat him to the punch. "What did Fat Crack want?" she asked.

"It drives me crazy when you do that," Brandon told her.

"When I do what?"

"When you read my mind. I was about to tell you, and then you asked me before I had a chance to spit out the words."

"Well?"

Brandon Walker took a deep breath. "He came to talk to us—to me, really—about Andrew Carlisle."

Diana finished slipping her nightgown on over her head. "What about Andrew Carlisle?"

"Fat Crack says he's coming back."

"Andrew Carlisle is dead."

"That's exactly what I tried to tell Fat Crack when he was here," Brandon explained. "It didn't make any difference. He says he's read your book and it convinced him that, dead or not, Andrew Carlisle's still after us. That he's after you."

"That's ridiculous," Diana said at once. "It doesn't make any sense."

"Maybe not, but I can tell you Fat Crack is serious as hell about this. He wanted me to call up the department and ask Bill Forsythe to send more patrols out this way."

"To protect us from a dead man," Diana said.

"Right."

"What did you tell him?"

"That Bill Forsythe would laugh himself silly at the very idea."

"Good, because that's exactly what would happen."

"But still," Brandon cautioned, "maybe it would be better if you didn't run around by yourself too much for the next little while. What are you doing tomorrow?"

"I have that interview, the one New York set up out at La Paloma, but first I go to the beauty shop for hair, nails, and makeup. There's a photo shoot along with the interview. And then in the evening, there's the dinner. You're already going to that."

"If you want me to, I'll be happy to go along in the morning as well," Brandon offered.

"To the beauty shop and the interview?" Diana asked incredulously. "Have you lost your marbles?"

"I love you, Diana," Brandon said. "Sure it sounds crazy, but Fat Crack scared the hell out of me. If anything happened to you . . ."

"Nothing's going to happen," Diana said firmly. "And if you wouldn't go with me to the damn Pulitzer banquet, you sure as hell are not going to come hold my hand in the beauty shop or bird-dog me through an interview. That's final."

"But—"

"No buts," she said, shaking her head. "I could have used you at the ceremony, but the beauty shop is absolutely off limits. I'd say that's true for both of you," she added with a smile. "You wouldn't be caught dead there, and neither would Andrew Carlisle."

*   *   *

Back home in his RV on Coleman Road, Mitch Johnson tried to sleep but couldn't. He was too excited. He felt like a little kid again, and thinking Christmas Eve would never end, that morning would never come, and it would never be time to unwrap the few presents that his impoverished parents had somehow managed to put under their scrawny tree.

His own son, Mikey—Michael Wraike, as he was now called—had never known the kind of grinding poverty that had shaped his biological father. Raised in the affluence provided by his hotshot developer stepfather, Mike was now a tall, handsome, rangy kid, a student at the University of Arizona, who had attended his stepfather's funeral service with no idea that his natural father—his *real* father, as Mitch liked to think of himself—was standing in the fifth row only a few yards away.

Mitch had known that going to the funeral was risky, especially since Lori's relatives would be there right along with her dead husband's. But using the makeup techniques Andy had taught him, Mitch had taken great pains to disguise himself. Obviously it had worked. He had held his breath when Lori's Great Aunt Aggie had plopped her ample butt down on the pew beside him.

Even though being so near her made him nervous as hell, he nonetheless had to smile to himself at the realization that after years of good living, Lori had gone to fat as well, just like her well-fed auntie.

Aunt Aggie had given Mitch the benefit of one of her cursory and universally disapproving glances. Then, with no hint of recognition, she had sighed and settled back in the pew, turning her attention to the beginning of the service.

Larry Wraike's funeral was, of course, a closed-casket affair. That may have been a surprise to Aunt Aggie and a few of the other attendees. It was no surprise to Mitch Johnson. He had made a very conscious effort to make sure that would be the case.

* * *

"Greedy targets are easy targets," Andy had told him once. In Larry Wraike's case, that had proved absolutely true. Using a simple electronic device that altered his voice, Mitch had called his wife's second husband at his plush office at Stone and Pennington in Tucson to give him some unwelcome news.

"The problem is, Mr. Wraike, that the land you've developed wasn't yours in the first place."

"Now wait just a goddamned minute here!" Larry had sputtered. "I don't know who the hell you think you are, but—"

"I think you'd better hear me out," Mitch interrupted. "As I understand it, there's been a mistake of some kind, back in D.C. Kiser Ranch Estates is actually supposed to be part of the reservation."

"But that's impossible. It's been in my wife's family for years."

"Illegally," Mitch said.

"But the Kiser land isn't anywhere near the reservation. This doesn't make sense."

"Since when does anything that happens in Washington have to make sense? Here's the deal. A few people out on the reservation—a very few—are aware of this situation. And they're prepared to forget it—for a price, that is."

"For a price?" Wraike protested. "They can't do that. That's blackmail!"

"My principals would prefer you didn't call it blackmail," Mitch Johnson said smoothly. "They'd like me to meet with you to discuss a possible settlement. If I were you, in advance of that meeting, I'd make damned sure I didn't mention a word of this to a soul."

There was a long silence on the phone. "A meeting where?" Wraike asked at last, and Mitch Johnson knew he had him.

* * *

They had met in a darkened bar in Nogales, Arizona. It had been an easy thing to slip a dose of scopolamine into his drink. Larry was so upset at the thought of losing his real estate empire that he never suspected a thing, never saw through Mitch's simple disguise that made a much older man out of a middle-aged one.

It was only later when the makeup was gone and as the drug started to wear off that he recognized who Mitch was. Even then Wraike didn't tumble to the full extent of his danger.

That was something Mitch regretted now, as he sat looking up at the stars over Kitt Peak. He had rushed things. He hadn't made sure Larry Wraike was fully aware of what was going on before it happened. Mitch had only himself to blame that he hadn't taken time enough to savor the moment.

"So whaddya want, Mitch? Money?" Larry had asked. "I have plenty of that. We can make a deal."

Mitch shook his head. "No deals," he said.

Larry Wraike's mumbled, half-drugged offer of a deal constituted his last words. Moments later, Mitch shoved a fist-sized gag into the man's mouth. Looking down at his trussed and helpless victim, Mitch peeled off his own clothes and set them out of harm's way. That was another piece of Andy's sage advice. No sense in getting blood anywhere it wouldn't be easy to wash off.

When Mitch turned back to the bed, he was holding the knife. As soon as he saw it, Larry's eyes bulged with fear. He thrashed on the bed, trying to get loose, but Mitch's expert knots held firm. It would have been fun to tease him with the knife for a while, to prick the son of a bitch here and there, just to get his attention.

That was where the scheduling problem came in. Without realizing how long it would take for the drug to wear off, Mitch had hired a young prostitute to show up later in the afternoon. Now her scheduled arrival was less than an hour away. By the time she showed up and let herself in with the room key Mitch had thoughtfully provided, Mitch had to be finished with Wraike—finished, cleaned up, and long gone.

"It can be a beautiful thing if you do it right," Andy had said. "It's almost like a dance. All you have to do is touch them with the tip of the knife, and you can watch their flesh try to crawl away from it. A knife has far more nuances than a gun.

"Given your history, I can understand your peculiar fascination with what an exploding shell can do to the human anatomy. But let me ask you this: When you shoved the barrel of your rifle up that little gook girl's twat, you couldn't feel her heart beating, could you?"

Still shocked that Andy had used the effects of the drug dose to trick him into revealing his darkest secret, Mitch Johnson had shaken his head.

"I didn't think so. With the tip of a knife, though, if you hold it right here in the hollow of someone's neck, you can feel their pulse," Carlisle said. "It comes right up through the handle with a vibration that's so faint you can barely feel it. And the more scared they are, the better you can feel it. There's nothing quite like it," he had added, twisting his distorted lips into what could only have been a smile of remembrance.

"There's nothing like it at all. And then, after you let them know that you own them, that there's nothing they can do, that's when it gets personal. You stand there and you're God, and all you have to decide is where to cut them, where to draw the first blood. Just wait," he added. "You won't believe how great it feels."

"Like getting your rocks off?" Mitch asked.

"No," Andy Carlisle had said. "Better than that. Much better."

And so, with his rival lying naked on the bed, Mitch tried touching the tip of the knife against the hollow at the base of

Larry Wraike's throat. The thrashing stopped. Larry lay there still as death beneath the weight of the knife. The only thing that moved were his eyes. They swung back and forth between Mitch's face and the slightly trembling blade.

Mitch held the knife delicately. The vibration that came through the bone handle reminded him of a time long ago when, as a twelve-year-old, he had plucked a tiny baby bird out of a nest. He had held it in the palm of his hand for several minutes, feeling the frantic beating of its heart and wings against his skin. He didn't remember how long he held it. What he did remember was that eventually the damned thing pecked him, bit him so hard that it drew blood. When that happened, he simply closed his fist around it, crushing out that little bit of life as if it had never existed.

That had been a very clear and simplified lesson in the ethics of crime and punishment. The bird had hurt him, so he killed it. This was the same thing.

Moving the tip of the knife away from Wraike's throat, Mitch was gratified to see the man's heartfelt sigh of relief. As the stark tension drained out of Larry's body, Mitch felt a sudden stiffening in his own. He almost laughed aloud at the sensation. Some idiot psychology major had once done a series of interviews at the prison, asking some of the more violent offenders if there was any correlation for them between sex and violence.

If Mitch ever ran into that broad again, he'd have to be sure to tell her that for him the answer was a definite yes.

"You do know why I'm doing this, don't you?" he asked.

Larry shook his head frantically.

"Would you like me to tell you?"

This time Larry's answering nod was equally frantic. Mitch wasn't so much interested in having this one-sided conversation as he was in stretching the moment. He could not, in his whole life, ever remember having anyone listen to him with quite such rapt attention.

"You cheated me," Mitch said with no particular animosity. By the time they reached that point, Mitch Johnson had moved far beyond anger. He was simply delivering information, allowing Larry to understand the gravity of his mistake. Maybe, in another lifetime, he wouldn't make the same fatal error a second time.

"The deal was all set," Mitch continued reasonably. "All either one of us had to do was wait for old man Kiser to kick off. He was already sick, so it wouldn't have taken long. Once he did, we both would have made out like bandits. Instead, you waited until I was locked up and then you moved in and took your share and mine as well. To top it all off, you ended up fucking my wife, too. That wasn't a nice thing to do, Larry. It just wasn't right."

Around the gag and behind it, Larry's lips and tongue tried vainly to form words. He might have been agreeing with Mitch's assessment. He might even have been trying to say he was sorry, but as far as Mitch was concerned, it was far too late for apologies. After eighteen years, sorry didn't exactly cut it.

In the end it was the sexual injustice of Larry Wraike's actions that ruled the day. That, even more than the money, dictated the final result. That was why the first cut—the one that bled the most—was directly between Larry Wraike's legs. Mitch stood back and watched for a while, watched the man writhe and squirm and bleed and try to scream. And then, when Mitch lost interest in that, just as he had with the bird, and because he was worried about the time element, he went ahead and finished him off.

Larry Wraike was dead long before Mitch took the knife and began carving up his face. Andy would have called that gratuitous. It might even have been more than Andy himself would have done. If so, it was a way for Mitch to prove to himself that he had graduated, that he had moved beyond being Andrew Carlisle's student. He was, in fact, a talented killer in his own right, out to get a little of his own back from those who had wronged him in the past.

It took only a matter of seconds to mangle Larry Wraike's face. Afterward, while Mitch was showering, he laughed to think of Lori being called into a coroner's office to identify the bloody remains. Other than Lori and a few cops, not many people would see what he had done, but the thought of Lori seeing her husband that way made Mitch happy.

She was, after all, the only one who mattered.

As expected, Mitch himself was miles away from the motel when the teenaged prostitute from the other side of the border let herself into the room and discovered the body. Despite her frenzied screams and her subsequent protestations of innocence, she and her pimp would be going on trial soon, down in Santa Cruz County, for the savage murder of Larry Wraike.

Mitch Johnson had made it back to his RV on Coleman Road without any questions asked. And if any homicide cops from Nogales ever went looking for the old man who had met with the victim in a bar a few hours before his death, they never had any luck finding him.

Nope, as far as Larry Wraike was concerned, Mitch Johnson got away clean.

More relaxed now, Mitch stood up, stretched, and went inside, but he still didn't feel like sleeping. Instead, he took out a sketchbook and went to work.

"What was the author's name again?" Noreen Kennedy, the prison librarian, had asked.

"Nicolaïdes," Mitch Johnson answered. "He's Greek."

"And the name of the book?"

The Natural Way to Draw.

Noreen was a firm believer in the importance of rehabilitation. "You're studying art, then?" she asked.

Mitch smiled diffidently. "I've always been interested in art," he said. "But there was never enough time to do anything about it. Now I've got nothing but time. This book is supposed to be the best there is."

The book arrived eventually, courtesy of an inter-library loan. And it was every bit as good as Mitch had been told it would be. With a pencil and a cheap sketchbook, he went to work doing the exercises. The book contained a year-long course of study. Unfortunately, the checkout period was limited to two weeks.

"Could you order it for me again, Mrs. Kennedy?" he asked, the day he returned it to the library. "In two weeks' time, I barely got started. What I really need is my own copy."

"I don't know," she said. "I'll see what I can do."

It was a month before Mitch received a summons to the library. Noreen Kennedy, who was almost as wide as she was tall, smiled broadly at him. "You'll never guess what I found," she said, holding up a shabby volume Mitch instantly recognized as a much-used copy of the Nicolaïdes book.

"I got it from a used-book dealer in Phoenix who's an old friend of mine," she said. "We went to Library School together. Jack said he's had it in inventory for years and he only charged me five bucks. Can you afford to buy it, or should I just go ahead and put it in the collection?"

"I'd really like to have my own copy, if you don't mind," Mitch said.

"I thought you would," Noreen said, handing it over.

The book had been a godsend. When Mitch was sketching, the hours seemed to fly by. As the months went past, it was easy to recognize the increasing skill in the way he executed the exercises. While he sketched, Andrew Carlisle talked. It was as though he had an almost physical need to share his exploits with someone. Mitch Johnson became Andy's chosen vessel.

Andy's bragging about the tapes was how Mitch first heard about them. At first it made him uneasy that Andy had taken such pains to make a record of all he had done, but in the long run, Mitch realized that recordings were just that—mechanical reproductions. They didn't allow for any artistic license. Painting did.

There was a locked storage unit under the bed in the Bounder. In it were two 18-by-24-inch canvases. Each oil painting was of Larry Wraike, one before and one after. The first was of a moderately handsome overfed businessman in a well-pressed suit, the kind of dully representative portrait that an overly proud wife might have commissioned in honor of some special occasion. An art critic seeing the second painting would have assumed, mistakenly, that this was an imaginative rendition of a soul in torment.

Only Mitch Johnson knew that that one, too, was fully representational. He thought of them as a matched pair—"Larry Wraike Before" and "Larry Wraike After."

Half an hour after returning to the RV, when he held the unfinished drawing up to a mirror to examine it, the artist was pleased with the likeness. Anyone who knew Quentin Walker would have recognized him. The picture showed him sitting slump-shouldered, his elbows resting on the bar, his eyes morosely focused on the beer in the bottom of the glass in front of him. Quentin Walker Before.

Looking at the picture, though, Mitch Johnson realized something else about it—something he had never noticed before that moment—how very much the son resembled the father. That hadn't been nearly so apparent when Quentin first showed up in Florence as it was now. He had come to prison as nothing but a punk kid. The hard years in between had matured and hardened him into what Brandon Walker had been when Mitch first knew him.

"Well, I'll be damned!" Mitch said to the picture reflected back from the mirror. "If you aren't your daddy's spitting image, Mr. Quentin Walker. Imagine that!"

5

They say it happened long ago that the weather grew very hot—the hottest year the Tohono O'othham had ever known. And all this happened in the hottest part of that year.

For many weeks the Indians and the animals had looked at the sky, hoping to find one cloud that would show them that Chewagi O'othham—*Cloud Man*—was still alive. There was not a cloud.

The water holes had been dry for a long time. The Desert People had gone far away to find water. The coyotes had followed the Indians. The wolves and foxes had gone into the mountains. All the birds had left. Even Kakaichu—*Quail*—who seldom leaves his own land, was forced to go away.

Gohhim Chuk—*Lame Jackrabbit*—had found a little shade. It was not much, just enough to keep him from burning. The tips of his ears and his tail were already burned black. And that, nawoj, *is why that particular kind of jackrabbit—chuk chuhwi—is marked that same way, even today.*

As Gohhim Chuk—*Lame Jackrabbit*—lay panting in his little bit of shade, he was wondering how he would manage the few days' journey to a cooler place. Then he saw Nuhwi—*Buzzard*—flying over him.

Now it is the law of the desert to live and let live, that one should only kill in self-defense or to keep from starving. The animals forget this law sometimes when their stomachs are full and when there is plenty of water, but when the earth burns and when everyone is in danger, the law is always re-membered. So Lame Jackrabbit did not run away when he saw Buzzard circling down over him. Buzzard knew the law of the desert as well as Lame Jackrabbit did.

Nuhwi *flew in circles, lower and lower. When he was low enough, he called to Lame Jackrabbit.* "I have seen some-thing very odd back in the desert," Nuhwi *said. When he was high up over the part of the desert which was burned bare, he told Lame Jackrabbit, he saw on the ground a black place that seemed to be in motion. He had circled down hoping it was water. But it was only a great crowd of* Ali-chu'uchum O'othham, *the Little People.*

As you know, nawoj, *my friend, the Little People are the bees and flies and insects of all kinds. Buzzard said these Lit-tle People were swarming around something on the ground. He said* Nuhwi *and* Gohhim Chuk *must carry the news to-gether because it might help someone. It is also the law of the desert that you must always help anyone in trouble.*

Lame Jackrabbit agreed that what Buzzard had seen was very strange. Little People usually leave early when the water goes away. Lame Jackrabbit said he would carry the news.

But Gohhim Chuk, *whose ears and tail were burned black, being lame, could not travel very well. So he found Coyote and told him what* Nuhwi—*Buzzard*—*had seen.*

Ban—*Coyote*—*was puzzled too. He said he would*

carry the message on to the Tohono O'othham—*the Desert People.*

It was still dark when Lani's alarm buzzed in her ear. She turned it off quickly and then hurried into the bathroom to shower. Standing in front of the steamy mirror, she used a brush and hair dryer to style her shoulder-length hair. How long would it take, she wondered, for her hair to grow back out to the length it had been back in eighth grade, before she had cut it?

From first grade on, Lani Walker and Jessica Carpenter had been good friends. By the time they reached Maxwell Junior High, the two girls made a striking pair. Lani's jet-black waist-length hair and bronze complexion were in sharp contrast to Jessie's equally long white-blond hair and fair skin. Because they were always together, some of the other kids teasingly called them twins.

Their entry into eighth grade came at a time when Lani Walker needed a faithful ally. For one thing, Rita was gone. She had been dead for years, but Lani still missed her. When coping with the surprising changes in her own body or when faced with difficulties at home or in school, Lani still longed for the comfort of Nana *Dahd's* patient guidance. And there were difficulties at home. In fact, the whole Walker household seemed to be in a state of constant upheaval. Things had started going bad when her older stepbrother, Quentin, had been sent to prison as a result of a fatality drunk-driving accident.

Lani had been too young to realize all that was happening when Tommy disappeared, but she had watched her grim-faced parents deal with the first Quentin crisis. She had been at the far end of the living room working on a basket the night after Quentin Walker was sentenced for the drunk-driving conviction. Brandon had come into the house, shambled over to the couch, slumped down on it, and buried his face in his hands.

"Five years," he had groaned. "On the one hand it seems like a long time and yet it's nothing. He killed three people, for God's sake! How can a five-year sentence make up for that, especially when he'll probably be out in three?"

"That's what the law says," Diana returned, but Brandon remained unconvinced and uncomforted.

"Judge Davis could have given him more if he had wanted to. I can't help thinking that it's because I'm the sheriff . . ."

"Brandon, you have to let go of that," Diana said. "First you blame yourself for Quentin being a drunk, and now you're taking responsibility for the judge's sentence. Quentin did what he did and so did the judge. Neither one of those results has anything at all to do with you."

Lani had put her basket aside and hurried over to the couch, where she snuggled up next to her father. "It's not your fault, Daddy," she said confidently, taking one of his hands in both of hers. "You didn't do it."

"See there?" Diana had smiled. "If Lani's smart enough to see it at her age, what's the matter with you?"

"Stubborn, maybe?" Brandon had returned with a weak smile of his own.

"Not stubborn maybe," Diana answered. "Stubborn for sure."

So the family had weathered that crisis in fairly good shape. The next one, when it came, was far worse. As near as Lani could tell, it all started about the time the letter arrived from a man named Andrew Carlisle, the same person Nana *Dahd* had always referred to as the evil *Ohb*. Within months, Diana was working on a book project with Andrew Carlisle while Brandon stalked in and out of the house in wounded silence.

Lani was hard-pressed to understand how the very mention of Carlisle's name was able to cause a fight, but from a teenager's point of view, that wasn't all bad. The growing wedge between her parents allowed Lani Walker to play both ends against the middle. She was able to get away with things her older brother Davy never could have.

It was during the summer when Lani turned thirteen that the next scandal surfaced concerning Quentin Walker. Still imprisoned at Florence, he was the subject of a new investigation. He was suspected of being involved in a complex protection racket that had its origins inside the prison walls. By the time school started at the end of the summer, a sharp-eyed defense attorney had gotten Quentin off on a technicality, but all of Tucson was abuzz with speculation about Brandon Walker's possible involvement with his son's plot.

The whole mess was just surfacing in the media the week Lani Walker started eighth grade. At home the inflammatory newspaper headlines and television news broadcasts were easy to ignore. All Lani had to do was to skip reading the paper or turn off the TV. At school that strategy didn't work.

"Your father's a crook." Danny Jenkins, the chief bully of Maxwell Junior High, whispered in Lani's ear as the yellow school bus rumbled down the road. "You wait and see. Before long, he'll end up in prison, too, just like his son."

Lani had turned to face her tormentor. Red-haired, red-necked, and pugnacious, Danny had made Lani's life miserable from the moment he had first shown up in Tucson two years earlier after moving there from Mobile, Alabama.

"No, he won't!" Lani hissed furiously.

"Will, too."

"Prove it."

"Why should I? It says so on TV. That means it's true, doesn't it?"

"No, it doesn't, *s-koshwa*—stupid," she spat back at him. "It just means you're too dumb to turn off the set."

"Wait a minute. What did you call me?"

"Nothing," she muttered.

She turned away, thinking that if she ignored him, that would be the end of it. Instead, he grabbed a handful of her hair and yanked it hard enough that the back of her head bounced off the top of the seat. Tears sprang to her eyes.

"Leave her alone, Danny," Jessica Carpenter ordered. "You're hurting her."

"She called me a name—some shitty Indian name. I want to know what it was."

Lani, with her head pulled tight against the back of the seat, clamped her lips shut. But just because Lani stayed quiet, didn't mean Jessica Carpenter would.

"I'm telling," Jessica yelled. "Driver, driver! Danny Jenkins is pulling Lani's hair."

The driver didn't bother looking over her shoulder. "Knock it off, Danny," she said. "Stop it right now or you're walking."

"But she called me a name," Danny protested. "It sounded bad. Koshi something."

"I don't care what she called you. I said knock it off."

Danny had let go of Lani's hair, but that still wasn't the end of it. "Why don't you go back to the reservation, squaw," he snarled after her as they stepped off the bus. "Why don't you go back to where you belong?"

She turned on him, eyes flashing. "Why don't you?" she demanded. "The Indians were here first."

Nobody liked Danny Jenkins much, although over time his flailing fists had earned him a certain grudging respect. But now, the kids who overheard Lani's retort laughed and applauded.

"You really told him," Jessica said approvingly later on their way to class. "He's such a jerk."

Going home that afternoon, Lani and Jessica chose seats as far from Danny as possible, but after the bus pulled out of the parking lot, he bribed the girl sitting behind Lani to trade places. When Lani and Jessica got off the bus twenty minutes later, they found that a huge wad of bubblegum had been plastered into Lani's hair.

They went into the bathroom at Jessica's house. For an hour, the two of them struggled to comb out the gum, but combing didn't work.

"It's just getting worse," Jessica said finally, giving up. "Let's call your mother. Maybe she'll know what to do."

Lani shook her head. "Mom and Dad have enough to worry about right now. Bring me the scissors."

"Scissors," Jessie echoed. "What are you going to do?"

"Cut it off."

"You can't do that," Jessie protested. "Your hair's so long and pretty . . ."

"Yes, I can," Lani told her friend determinedly. "And I will. It's my hair."

In the end Jessica helped wield the scissors. She cut the hair off in what was supposed to be a straight line, right at the base of Lani's neck.

"How does it look?" Lani asked as Jessica stepped back to eye her handiwork.

Jessie made a face. "Not that good," she admitted. "It's still a little crooked."

"That's all right," Lani said. "It'll grow out."

"So will mine," Jessie said, handing Lani the scissors.

For a moment, Lani didn't understand. "What do you mean?"

"Cut mine, too. People tease us about being twins. This way, we still will be."

"But what will your mother say?" Lani asked.

"The same thing yours does," Jessica returned.

Fifteen minutes later, Jessie Carpenter's hair was the same ragged length as Lani's. Before they left the bathroom, Lani gathered up all the cuttings into a plastic trash bag. Instead of putting the bag in the garbage, however, she loaded it into her backpack along with her books.

"What are you doing?" Jessica asked.

"I'm going to take it home and use it to make a basket."

"Really? Out of hair?"

Lani nodded. "Nana *Dahd* showed me once how to make horsehair baskets. This will be an *o'othham wopo hashda*—people-hair basket."

Hair had been the main topic of conversation that night at both the Walker household and at the Carpenters' just up the road.

"Whatever happened to your hair?" Brandon Walker demanded. "It looks like you got it caught in the paper cutter at school."

"It was too long," Lani answered quietly. "I decided to cut it off. Jessie cut hers, too."

"You cut it yourself?"

Lani shrugged. "Jessie cut mine and I cut hers."

Silenced by a reproving look from Diana, Brandon shook his head and let the subject drop, subsiding into a gloomy silence.

The next day was Saturday. With the enthusiastic approval of Rochelle Carpenter, Jessie's mother, Diana collected both girls and took them to her beauty shop in town to repair the damage.

"You both look much better now," Diana had told them on the way back home. "What I don't understand is why, if you both wanted haircuts, you didn't say something in the first place instead of cutting it off yourselves."

Jessie kept quiet, waiting to see how Lani would answer. "We just decided to, that's all," she said.

Since Lani didn't explain anything more about the fight on the bus, neither did Jessie. As for Diana, she was so accustomed to the vagaries of teenagers that she let the matter drop.

Several weeks later, Lani emerged from her bedroom carrying a small flat disk of a basket about the size of a silver dollar. Diana Ladd had spent thirty years on and around the reservation. Over those years she had become something of an expert on *Tohono O'othham* basketry and she recognized that her daughter, Rita Antone's star pupil, was especially skilled. As soon as Diana saw this new miniature basket, she immediately recognized the quality of the workmanship in the delicate pale-yellow Papago maze set against a jet-black background.

"I didn't know you ever made baskets like this," Diana said, examining the piece. "Where did you get the horse-hair?"

"It's not horsehair," Lani answered. "It's made from Jessie's hair and from mine. I'm making two of them, one for each of us to wear. I'm going to give Jessie hers for her birthday."

Diana looked at her daughter. "Is that why you cut your hair, to make the baskets?"

Lani laughed and shook her head. "No," she said, "I'm making the baskets because we cut our hair."

"Oh," Diana said, although she still wasn't entirely sure what Lani meant.

It was another month before Jessie's maze was finished as well. Each of the baskets had a tiny golden safety pin fastened to the back side. Lani strung a leather thong through each of the pins, tied her necklace around her neck, and then went to Jessica's house carrying the other basket in a tiny white jeweler's box she had begged from Diana.

"It's beautiful," Jessie said, staring down at the necklace. "What does it mean?"

"It means that we're friends," Lani answered. "I made the two baskets just alike so we can still be twins whenever we wear them."

"I know that we're friends," Jessie giggled. "But the de-sign. What does that mean?"

"It's a sacred symbol," Lani explained. "The man in the maze is *I'itoi*—Elder Brother. He comes from the center of the earth. The maze spreads out from the center in each of the four directions."

In the years since then, the black-and-gold disk had become something of a talisman for Lani Walker. She called it her *kushpo ho'oma*—her hair charm. The original leather thong had been replaced several times over. Now when she wore it, the basket dangled from a slender gold chain Lani's parents had given her on the occasion of her sixteenth birthday.

The people-hair charm served as a reminder that some people were good and some were bad. Lani didn't wear it every day, only on special occasions—only when she needed to. There were times when she was nervous or worried about something—as on the day she went to the museum to apply for the job, for instance—that she made sure the necklace went with her.

Having the basket dangling around her neck seemed to give her luck. Every once in a while, she would run her fingertips across the finely woven face of the maze. Just touching the smooth texture seemed to calm her somehow. In a way Lani couldn't quite explain, the tiny basket made her feel more secure—almost as if it summoned Nana *Dahd*'s spirit back and brought the old basket maker close to her once more.

Coming out of the bathroom with her hair sleek and dry, Lani looked at the clothing she had laid out on a chair the night before—the lushly flowered Western shirt with pearl-covered snaps, a fairly new pair of jeans, shiny boots, and a fawn-colored cowboy hat. Walking past the chair, Lani went to her dresser and opened her jewelry box. She smiled as the first few bars of "When You Wish Upon a Star" tinkled into the room.

Taking her treasured maze necklace from its place of honor, she fastened it around her throat.

Mr. Vega—that was the name the artist had signed in the bottom right-hand corner of the sketch, (M. Vega)—had asked her to wear something Indian. Of all the things Lani Walker owned, her *o'othham wopo hashda*—people-hair basket—was more purely "Indian" than anything else.

Mr. Vega might not know that, but Lani did, and that's what counted.

David Ladd was still reeling from the effects of yet another panic attack that Saturday morning as he finished packing his things into his new Jeep Cherokee for the long road trip back to Arizona. Even though it was a bald-faced lie, he had told his grandmother, Astrid Ladd, that he wanted to get an early start that morning.

As expected, Astrid came out of the main house to watch the loading process. She stood in the driveway between the main house and the carriage house, leaning on her cane and shaking her head as he closed the rear hatch on his carefully packed load.

"All done?"

Davy nodded. "I should probably hit the road pretty soon."

"This early?" Astrid objected. "You can't do that. I wanted to take you to the club one last time before you go. Not only that, if you're going to be driving all that way by yourself, it's important for you to keep up your strength. You should start out with a decent breakfast under your belt."

What David knew but didn't mention to Astrid right then was that on the first day of his trip he would be driving only as far as downtown Chicago. There, just off North Michigan Avenue on Pearson, he and Candace Waverly—his girlfriend of six months' standing—planned to spend their farewell night ensconced in a deluxe suite at the Ritz Carlton. It was a graduation gift from Candace to Davy, compliments of the Gold AmEx card Richard Waverly provided for his darling daughter.

"Sure, Grandma," David said, accepting his grandmother's invitation gracefully, as he had known in advance that he would. "I suppose I can stay long enough to have breakfast," he added.

Evanston, the town, is dry. Evanston, the golf club—

across the line in Skokie—is definitely wet. That was the other thing David Ladd was both smart and discreet enough not to mention. The reason Astrid Ladd wanted to have breakfast at the golf club—which she did several times a week—had less to do with the quality of the food than it did with the inevitable Bloody Mary or two that would accompany her order of eggs Benedict.

At seventy-eight, Astrid Ladd was old enough to still observe the strictures against solitary drinking. According to her long-held beliefs, only problem drinkers drank alone. Astrid and her late husband, Garrison Walther Ladd II, had been part of the fashionable drinking set their whole married life. Living in a dry town, they had done their drinking at home, in other people's homes or in private clubs. David's grandfather had been dead for five years now. He had hemorrhaged to death, dying as a result of esophageal varices which were most likely related to all those years of social drinking.

With her husband and best tippling buddy gone, Astrid Ladd still wanted to drink, but she was terrified of being caught in the very unladylike trap of drinking alone. As a consequence, she spent her days plotting a vigorously active social calendar that usually involved suckering some poor unsuspecting chump into driving her out to the club early for her daily ration of grog. Later on, she would prevail on somebody else to chauffeur her home.

On this hazy, and already hot summer morning in early June, David Ladd drove both ways. Leaving behind his upstairs carriage house apartment with its magnificent view of Lake Michigan, he pulled up to the side entrance of his grandmother's oversized mansion in Astrid's aging but equally oversized 1988 DeVille. She came out onto the porch and stood waiting, leaning heavily on her cane, while David hustled out of the car and helped her into the rider's side.

"I can't believe you're done with school already," Astrid said as he eased her into the leather seat. "Three whole years! The time just flew by, didn't it? I'm going to miss you desperately, Davy. You don't know how much."

Actually, Davy did know. The drafty old house was far too big for Astrid. In fact, most of the upstairs and part of the ground floor had been closed off for years, since long before Davy appeared on the scene. Several times during his sojourn at Northwestern, David Ladd had hinted to his grandmother that maybe it was time for her to consider unloading the family home. He suggested that she might enjoy moving into a more reasonably sized condo, one that didn't require nearly as much upkeep. Astrid had dismissed the idea out of hand, and after the second rejection Davy hadn't mentioned it again.

"And I'm going to miss that lovely Candace," Astrid continued. "I probably shouldn't, but I can't help thinking of her as a granddaughter."

That wasn't news. Astrid Ladd had never been one to keep her feelings or opinions to herself. Her unbridled enthusiasm for Candace Waverly—of the Oak Park Waverlys, as Astrid was fond of adding when introducing Candace and Davy to one of her upscale friends—was also well known.

"I'm going to miss her, too," David managed.

"How much?"

"What do you mean, how much?"

"You know what I mean," Astrid said slyly. "Are you or are you not going to give her a ring before you leave town?"

Astrid Ladd had promised her grandson a free ride at Northwestern's law school if he wanted to go there to study. That "free ride" had included everything—tuition, books, living expenses, food, a place to stay, laundry privileges, and even a car—but it had been far from free. The cost had come in terms of three years spent living his life under Astrid Ladd's watchful scrutiny, under her eye, ear, and thumb. Astrid's far too conscientious mothering as well as Chicago's uncompromising weather—summer and winter both—were the main reasons David Ladd was anxious to go back home to Arizona.

Candace Waverly was the single reason he wanted to stay in Chicago.

"No, Grandma," he said. "No ring. We're not ready for that yet."

"But you told me that you're . . . what did you call it?"

"Going out," David supplied. "But that doesn't mean we're serious."

"I wish it did," Astrid said wistfully. "Because I'm willing to help, you know."

Davy kept his eyes on the road. "Grandma," he said patiently, "you already put me through law school. And you just gave me a Jeep Grand Cherokee for graduation. How much more help could you be?"

"You'd be surprised, Davy," Astrid Ladd said determinedly. "There are one or two more things I could do."

"Grandma, believe me, you've done enough."

They turned off Sheridan Road onto Dempster. Astrid waited until they stopped for a light. "Hold out your hand," she commanded.

Sighing, David Ladd obeyed. With a deft twist, Astrid removed a knuckle-sized diamond ring from her finger and dropped it into the palm of her grandson's hand. "You could give Candace this," she said.

"That's your engagement ring, Grandma," Davy protested. "I can't take that." He tried returning it to her. Astrid took it, but instead of keeping it, she leaned over and dropped it into his shirt pocket.

"Why not?" she returned. "Who else is there? You're my grandson and my only living heir. Who else would I leave it to but you? That's why I don't want to sell the house, either. I plan to give it to you and Candace as a wedding present, you see."

Her voice broke. She sounded close to tears. With a lump in his own throat, David almost drove the DeVille into a passing truck. "You can't be serious, Grandma," he protested.

"I'm serious as can be, Davy. If you pass the bar in Illinois and go into practice, in five years, you'll make partner, especially with Richard Waverly's connections. You and Candace will need an address like mine to help establish your place in the community. You'll need to fix it up some, decorate it to suit you and all that, but that'll be a lot less expensive than buying new."

"Grandmother," David Ladd said carefully, wanting to be firm, but not wanting to hurt her feelings. "I don't want to practice law here. I want to go home, to Arizona."

Astrid tossed her head. "I can't imagine why," she said crossly. "I don't know how regular people can tolerate living in that godforsaken place. I remember when your grandfather Garrison and I went out there for your father's memorial service—it wasn't even a funeral, mind you. It was so ungodly hot. I don't know when I've ever been more miserable."

It would have been simple to talk about the weather. David Ladd was an expert on that. He had suffered more from both heat and cold during his three years in Illinois than he could ever remember enduring in the desert back home. Although this was only the second week of June, Chicago was already soldiering through the first real heat wave of summer.

During the previous week, afternoon daytime temperatures had hovered in the mid-nineties with humidity much the same—mid-nineties. And although the humidity was that high, the weather forecasts held no hope of rain or relief. Davy was looking forward to Arizona. At least there, the heat was honest. When the summer rainstorms came, evening temperatures could drop as much as twenty degrees in a matter of minutes. In Chicago, the sweltering, smothering heat never let up. And rain, when it came, seemed to make things worse, not better.

At that moment, however, David Ladd couldn't afford the luxury of a digression into weather. His grandmother had issued a serious challenge, one that had to be met head-on.

"It's a wonderful offer, Grandma," he said at last. "It really is, and it's a wonderful house. But I can't see myself living there."

"You can't?" She sounded shocked. "Why not?"

"Because it wouldn't ever be really mine," David answered. "I wouldn't feel like I had earned it."

"That's not it," Astrid said sharply. "It's because of your mother, isn't it? Diana has always resented me, and now she's turned you against me, too."

"That's not true, Grandmother. Not at all."

David turned into the club entrance and then stopped at the front door to let Astrid out. The place wasn't all that full, so there were plenty of parking places. Even so, by the time he made it into the dining room, Astrid had already finished her first Bloody Mary and had started on the second.

David Ladd sighed. For a farewell celebration, it was not an auspicious beginning.

Lani Walker left a note for her parents on the kitchen table. "Have fun at the banquet. Remember, Jess and I are going to that dueling bands concert at the Community Center tonight. Her parents are giving us a ride both to and from. I shouldn't be too late, but don't wake me for breakfast. Tomorrow's my day off."

The Tucson Mountains loomed in deep shadows against a rosy sky when Lani rode her bike up to Mr. Vega's parking place. She had worried overnight that maybe he wouldn't show up, but he was there with his easel already set up by the time she braked the mountain bike next to his station wagon.

"Nice hat," he said. "And nice shirt, too, but you're right. Those clothes make you look more like a cowgirl than an Indian."

"Hardly anybody wears feathers anymore," Lani told him. "And most of the people who go around in leather ride motorcycles."

"Point taken," he said, with a mock salute. "I think maybe I'll have you sit over here on this rock with the saguaro in the background. By the way, do you want anything to drink before we get started? I brought along orange juice just in case you didn't have time for breakfast."

Lani took off her hat and smoothed her windblown hair. "Some orange juice would be great," she said. She settled onto the rock and tried to get comfortable while he brought her a glass of juice.

"What do I need to do?" she asked.

"Relax and try to look natural," he said.

"That's a lot easier said than done," Lani said, taking a long drink of the juice, hoping it would settle her nerves. "I don't like having my picture taken, either. That might be part of what was wrong with the kids you tried to draw out on the reservation. When the white man first came west and tried taking pictures of Indians, people believed that the photographer would somehow end up capturing their spirits."

"No kidding." Mr. Vega was busily sketching with a stick of charcoal now, pausing every few moments and studying Lani's face. "And you're saying that some people out on the reservation still believe that's true?"

"Probably some of them do," she said.

Lani had no idea how much time passed. She was aware of a sudden buzzing in her head, like the angry hum of thousands of bees. Her first thought was that she was dreaming, that something had brought to mind the old story of *Mualig Siakam*.

"Mr. Vega," she said, reaching out to steady herself as the mountains around her spun in a dizzying circle.

"What's the matter?" he asked. Mr. Vega left his easel and walked toward her.

"I don't know," she said. "I feel strange, like I can't sit up, like I'm going to fall over. And hot, too."

"Here," he said, reaching out to her. "Let me help you."

The last thing Lani felt was Mr. Vega's arms closing

tightly around her and lifting her off the ground. Weaker than she could ever remember feeling in her life, Lani let her head drop heavily against his chest.

"I don't know what's the matter with me," she mumbled. "I'm so tired, so sleepy."

"You're okay," Mr. Vega said soothingly as he carried her toward the back of the Subaru. "You close your eyes and relax now, Lani. Everything's going to be just fine."

He knows my name, Lani thought. *How come he knows my name? Did I tell him?*

She couldn't remember telling him, but she must have. How else would he have known?

Thirsty as hell, Manny Chavez woke up under a mesquite tree. Fighting his way through an alcohol-induced fog, he sat up and tried to figure out where he was. He remembered stopping off at the trading post at Three Points sometime after dark. He had gone there with a terrible thirst and the remains of his paycheck. Now the sun was high overhead, but the thirst remained.

The rockbound walls of Baboquivari rose up out of the desert far to the south while Kitt Peak was directly at his back a few miles away across the desert. From the looks of the mountain looming over him, Manny figured he was probably somewhere off Coleman Road.

Frowning, he tried to remember how he had come to be there. He had ridden to Three Points with his son, Eddie, and some of Eddie's friends. They had bought some beer—several cases—and some Big Red fortified wine—and then they had gone off somewhere in the desert, off the reservation rather than on it, to drink it in peace. Now that Delia, Manny's daughter, had returned to the reservation, Manny could no longer afford to be picked up by Law and Order. Delia had come to the jail and bailed him out once, but Manny's pride still writhed in shame at the name she had called him.

"Nawmk!" she had spat at him. "Drunkard!"

Delia had been away from the reservation for so long that he was surprised she still remembered any of the language. But that particular word was probably indelibly printed in Delia's brain, imprinted there by Ellie, Delia's mother.

Feeling a lump under him, Manny rolled over and was relieved to find that a pint bottle—still half-full—lingered in his hip pocket. He unscrewed the top and took a long swig, hoping that the wine would help clear his head. It didn't, but at least it did help slake his thirst. Struggling to his feet, he walked out to a small clearing where mounds of empty cans and bottles as well as the deep impressions of tire tracks told him where Eddie's truck had been parked.

Unfortunately, it wasn't there anymore. For some reason, Eddie and his friends had taken off, leaving Manny alone. In the early morning cool, the desert was very still. Far to the north, he could hear the occasional whine of rubber tires on pavement. From the sounds of distant vehicles speeding by, it probably meant the highway wasn't all that far, especially not as the crow flies. Striking out across the low-lying desert, Manny headed for Highway 86.

Once he hit that, someone was bound to pick him up and give him a ride back home to Sells. There he'd be able to find Eddie and ask him why he had taken off and left Manny there alone. It wasn't a nice thing for a son to do to his father, even if the father did happen to be drunk.

Quentin Walker woke up fairly early that Saturday morning, hung over as hell and in a state of blind panic. What if someone had broken into his rented room overnight and stolen the money? Or worse, what if the money didn't exist at all? What if it was a figment of his imagination—a drunken delusion of some kind? Thinking about it, though, Quentin didn't believe he had been *that* drunk when Mitch Johnson showed up in the bar looking for him.

And it turned out the money was there after all, still hidden in the toe of his mud-spattered work boots, exactly where Quentin had left it before going to bed. He took the bills out and examined them again. One by one he held them up to the light from the grimy bedroom window. There was nothing about the bills that smacked of counterfeit. The vertical, copy-proof strip was there—the one feds had announced they were putting in bills to counter the counterfeiters.

Quentin's inspection proved that the bills were real enough, but they also posed a real dilemma. Existing from paycheck to paycheck as he did, Quentin Walker had no bank account. Somebody who dressed and looked the way he did couldn't very well walk into the nearest Wells Fargo bank branch and make a five-thousand-dollar deposit with five bills. If somebody like him turned up in a bank with that kind of money, the teller was bound to notice and remember. While he was there or after he left, people would wonder and ask questions. Pretty soon, his parole officer would be asking questions, too.

On a week-to-week basis, Quenton cashed his paychecks in the bars he frequented—usually ones in his immediate neighborhood—places he could walk to. Quentin had lost both his pickup truck and his driver's license in the aftermath of that damned DWI accident that had landed him in the state prison.

Cashing a paycheck was one thing, but nobody in a bar was going to fork over change for a thousand-dollar bill. Besides, even if they had that kind of cash in a safe, changing the money in a bar in that marginal neighborhood was far too risky. Somebody might see what was going on and decide to relieve him of the cash the moment he stepped back outside. Quentin Walker knew too well that not all bartenders were honest.

Unable to decide how to proceed, Quentin stood for some time holding the bills in his hand. Finally he stuffed them into his pocket and then moved from the tiny bedroom of his furnished apartment to the equally tiny kitchen. He opened the refrigerator and took out the remainder of the loaf of bread that he kept there to protect it from marauding cock-roaches. There were only two slices of bread left in the loaf. His first instinct was to throw them out. He had the two dried crusts in his hand and was ready to drop them in the garbage when he realized what a mistake that would be. The slices of bread themselves were the makings of the perfect hiding place.

Quentin took the bills out of his pocket and placed them between the two slices of bread, folding them small enough so no pieces of paper showed on the outside of the bread. Then he put his freshly assembled money sandwich back in-side the plastic bread bag. Convinced that his hiding place was absolutely brilliant, he shoved the plastic bag into the small frost-filled freezer compartment of his refrigerator and shut the door.

Enormously pleased with himself, Quentin left the apart-ment, locked the door, and then walked as far as the Mc-Donald's on the other side of the freeway. There, he splurged on breakfast. He treated himself to coffee, orange juice, and two Egg McMuffins.

Over breakfast, Quentin's worries about taking Mitch Johnson to the cave surfaced once again with a vengeance. If he had still owned his truck, it wouldn't have been a prob-lem. He could simply have driven out to the cave well in ad-vance and checked things out for himself. If there was a problem, he could take care of it . . .

The answer came to him like a bolt out of the blue. He could buy a car. One of the major roadblocks to buying a car had always been a chronic lack of money. In order to buy a car on time—in order to get a loan—it was neces-sary to show proof of insurance. Without it, no bank in the universe would even let him drive an uninsured car off the lot. With his driving record, car insurance was something else Quentin Walker didn't have and wasn't likely to get.

But now he had the money—as much or even more than he would need—to buy a car. And if he was paying cash for something like that, the people at the dealership probably wouldn't even blink at the thousand-dollar bills, as long as the total amount was less than the ten-thousand-dollar limit that would cause all kinds of scrutiny.

With growing excitement Quentin paged through the automotive section of an abandoned *Arizona Sun* he grabbed off a neighboring table. He wanted to find something that would be rugged enough to suit his needs and cheap enough to fit his budget. He circled three that seemed like possibilities—an '87 Suzuki Samurai soft-top, a rebuilt 1980 Ford Bronco, and a '77 GMC Suburban—all of them in the thirty-five-hundred range. That would just about do it—use up his little windfall, leave him some change, and get him some wheels all at the same time.

By the time he headed back to his apartment to shower, the day had taken on a whole new promise. He was finally going to have something to show for all his years of struggle. And if he ever ran into either of his so-called brothers again—Davy Ladd or Brian Fellows—he would tell them both to go piss up a rope.

Diana was lying awake in bed when she heard the side gate open and close as Lani mounted her bike and left for work. Glancing at the bedside clock, Diana was surprised by how early it was—just barely five-thirty. Why was Lani leaving for work so early when her volunteer shift didn't start until seven?

Next to her, Brandon seemed to be sleeping peacefully for a change, so Diana was careful not to wake him as she crept out of bed herself. Wrapping a robe around her, she padded silently down the tiled hallway, through the living room, and into the kitchen to start a pot of coffee. She found Lani's note on the kitchen table.

Diana read it and tossed it back on the table. She didn't remember any discussion about Lani's going to a concert. That meant Lani had asked her father for permission rather than her mother. But then why wouldn't she? Despite Brandon's tough-guy act and protestations to the contrary, the girl had had him buffaloed from the very beginning.

"Being foster parents is one thing," he had told his wife the night before Clemencia Escalante was due to arrive at their house after being released from Tucson Medical Center. "Obviously the poor little kid needs help, and I don't mind pitching in. But just because Rita managed to bend the rules enough to have Clemencia placed with us on a foster child basis doesn't mean it's going to lead to a permanent adoption. It won't, you know. It'll never fly."

"But Rita wants her," Diana said.

"Regardless of what Rita wants, she's seventy years old right this minute," Brandon pointed out, taking refuge in what seemed to him to be obvious logic. "And considering it was neglect from an elderly grandparent that sent the poor little tyke to the hospital in the first place, nobody in the child welfare system is going to approve of Rita as an adoptive parent."

"I wasn't talking about Rita adopting her," Diana said quietly. "I was talking about us."

Brandon dropped his newspaper. "Us?" he echoed.

Diana nodded. "It's the only way Rita will ever be able to have her."

"But Diana," Brandon argued. "How long do you think Rita will be around? She already has health problems. In the long run, that little girl will end up being our sole responsibility."

"So?" Diana answered with a shrug. "Is that such an awful prospect?"

Brandon frowned. "That depends. With your work and my work, and with the three kids we already have, it seems to me that our lives are complicated enough. Why add another child into the mix?"

"We have yours, and we have mine," Diana returned quietly. "We don't have any that are ours—yours and mine together."

"A toddler?" Brandon said. He shook his head, but Diana could see he was weakening. "Are you sure you could stand having one of those underfoot again?"

Diana smiled. "I think I could stand it. I can tell you that I much prefer toddlers to teenagers."

"In case you haven't noticed, most toddlers turn into teenagers eventually."

"But there are a few good years before that happens."

"A few," Brandon conceded.

"And Rita says she'll handle most of the child-care duties. She really wants this little girl, Brandon. It's all she's talked about for days—about how much she could teach her. It's as though she wants to pour everything into Clemencia that she was never able to share with her own granddaughter."

"Diana, replacing one child with another doesn't work. It isn't healthy."

For the space of several minutes, Diana was silent. "Living your life with a hole in it isn't healthy, either," she said finally. "Garrison Ladd and Andrew Carlisle put that hole in Rita's life, Brandon. Maybe you don't feel any responsibility for Gina Antone's death, but I do. And now I have an opportunity to do something about it."

"And it's something you really want to do? Something you want us to do?"

"Yes."

Again there was a long period of silence. "I guess we'll have to see," he said finally. "I'll bet it doesn't matter one way or the other what we decide because I still don't think the tribal court will go for it."

"But we can try?"

"Diana," he said, "you do whatever you want. I'll back you either way."

Brandon made a point to come home from work early the next afternoon when Wanda Ortiz arrived with Clemencia. Diana went to answer the door, leaving Brandon and Rita in the living room. Brandon was sitting on the couch and Rita was in her wheelchair when Wanda carried the screaming child into the room.

"She's been crying ever since we left the hospital," Wanda said apologetically, setting the weeping child down in the middle of the room. "Too many strangers, I guess."

Clemencia Escalante looked awful. Most of her woefully thin body was covered with scabs from hundreds of ant bites. A few of those had become infected and were still bandaged. She stood in the middle of the room, sobbing, with fat tears dripping off her chin and falling onto the floor. She turned in a circle, looking from one unfamiliar face to another. When her eyes finally settled on Rita, she stopped.

"*Ihab*—here," Rita crooned softly, crooking her finger. "Come here, little one."

Still crying but with her attention now riveted on Rita's kind but wrinkled face, Clemencia took a tentative step forward.

"Come here," Rita said again.

Suddenly the room was deathly quiet. For a moment Diana thought that the child was simply pausing long enough to catch her breath and that another ear-splitting shriek would soon follow. Instead, Clemencia suddenly darted across the room, throwing herself toward Rita with so much force that the wheelchair rocked back and forth on its braked wheels. Without another sound, Clemencia clambered into Rita's lap, burying her face in the swell of the old woman's ample breasts. There the child settled in, clinging desperately to the folds of Rita's dress with two tiny knotted fists.

Shaking his head in wonder, Brandon Walker looked from the now silent child to his wife. "Well," he said with a shrug, squinting so the tears in his eyes didn't show too much. "It looks as though I don't stand a chance, do I?"

And he didn't. From that moment on, the child named Clemencia Escalante who would one day be known as Dolores Lanita Walker owned Brandon Walker's heart and soul.

6

After traveling a long way, Coyote reached a village where there was a little water. While Ban was hunting for a drink, an old Indian saw him. Old Limping Man—this Gohhim O'othham—still talked the speech all I'itoi's people understood. So Coyote told him what Buzzard had seen in that part of the desert which was so badly burned.

Old Limping Man told the people of the village. That night the people held a council to decide what they should do. They feared that someone had been left behind in the burning desert.

In the morning, Gohhim O'othham and a young man started back over the desert with some water. They traveled only a little way after Tash—the sun—came up. Through the heat of the day they rested. When Sun went down in the west, they went on.

The first day there were kukui u'us—mesquite trees, but the trees had very few leaves, and those were very dry.

The next day it was hotter. There were no trees of any kind, only shegoi—*greasewood bushes. The greasewood bushes were almost white from dryness.*

The third day they found nothing but a few dry sticks of melhog—*the ocotillo—and some prickly pears—*nahkag.

The fourth day there seemed to be nothing left at all but rocks. And the rocks were very hot.

The two men did not drink the water which they carried. They mixed only a little of the water with their hahki—*a parched roasted wheat which the* Mil-gahn, *the Whites, call pinole. This is the food of the Desert People when they are traveling. While they were mixing their pinole on the morning of the fourth day, Old Limping Man looked up and saw Coyote running toward them and calling for help.*

The carpenter who had helped refit the Bounder had questioned why Mitch needed a complex trundle-bed/storage unit that would roll in and out of the locker under the regular bed. "It's for my grandson," Mitch had explained. "He goes fishing with me sometimes, and he likes to sleep in the same kind of bed he has at home."

"Oh," the carpenter had grunted. The man had gone ahead and made the bed to specs, tiny four-posters and all, and now, for the first time, Mitch was going to get to use it. Leaving Lani Walker asleep on the bed above for a moment, he pulled the trundle bed out of the storage space and locked the four casters in place. Then, with the bed ready and waiting, Mitch turned his attention to the girl.

She was limp but pliable under his hands. Undressing her reminded him of undressing Mikey when he'd fall asleep on his way home from shopping or eating dinner in town. One arm at a time, he took off first her shirt and then the delicate white bra. The boots were harder. He had to grip her leg and pull in one direction with one hand and then pry off the boot with the other. On her feet were a pair of white socks. Mitch was glad to see that her toenails weren't painted. That would have spoiled it somehow in a way he never would have been able to explain. After the socks came the jeans and the chaste white panties. Only when she was completely naked, did he ease her down onto the lower bed.

Just as he had known it would be, that was a critical moment. He wanted her so badly right then that he could almost taste it. His own pants seemed ready to burst, but he knew better. That was the mistake Andy had made. Mitch Johnson was smart enough not to fall into the same trap.

"I've spent years wondering about it," Mitch remembered Andy saying time and again. "I had her under control and then I lost it."

You lost control because you fucked her, you stupid jerk, Mitch wanted to shout. How could anyone as smart as Andy be so damned dumb? Why couldn't he see that what he had done to Diana Ladd had made her mad enough to fight back? In doing that, Andy had lost his own concentration, let down his guard, and allowed his victim to find an opening.

But if Andy wasn't brainy enough to figure all that out for himself, if he had such a blind spot that he couldn't see it, who was Mitch to tell him? After all, students—properly subservient students—didn't tell their teachers which way was up, especially not if their teachers were as potentially dangerous as Andrew Philip Carlisle.

In her dream Lani was little again—four or five years old. Her mother had just dropped Nana *Dahd,* Davy, and Lani off in the parking lot of the Arizona Sonora Desert Museum. Davy was pushing Rita's chair while Lani sat perched on Nana *Dahd's* lap.

It was a chill, blustery afternoon in February, the month the *Tohono O'othham* call *Kohmagi Mashad*—the gray month. Davy, along with other Tucson-area schoolchildren, was out of school for the annual rodeo break, but as they came through the parking lot, they wheeled past several empty school buses.

"You see those buses?" Nana *Dahd* asked. "They're from Turtle Wedged, the village the *Mil-gahn* call Sells. Most of the children from there are *Tohono O'othham*, just like you."

Not accustomed to seeing that many "children like her" together in one place, Lani had observed the moving groups of schoolkids with considerable interest and curiosity. They were mostly being herded about by several Anglo teachers as well as by docents from the museum itself.

They were in the hummingbird enclosure when Nana *Dahd* began telling the story of the other *Mualig Siakam*, the abandoned woman who would eventually become *Kulani O'oks*—the great medicine woman of the *Tohono O'othham*. As Nana *Dahd* began telling the tale, one of the schoolchildren—a little girl only a year or two older than Lani—slipped away from the group she was with and stopped to listen. Drawn by the magic of a story told in her own language, she stood transfixed and wide-eyed beside Nana *Dahd*'s wheelchair as the tale unfolded. Rita had only gotten as far as the part where Coyote came crying to the two men for help when a shrill-voiced *Mil-gahn* teacher, her face distorted by anger, came marching back to retrieve the little girl.

"What do you think you're doing?" the teacher shouted. Her loud voice sent the brightly colored hummingbirds scattering in all directions. "We're supposed to leave soon," the woman continued. "What would have happened if we had lost you and you missed the bus? How would you have gotten back home?"

Instead of turning to follow the teacher, the child reached out and took hold of Nana *Dahd*'s chair, firmly attaching herself to the arm of it and showing that she didn't want to leave. "I want to hear the rest of the story," the little girl whispered in Rita's ear. "I want to hear about *Mualig Siakam*."

"Well?" the teacher demanded impatiently. "Are you coming or not? You must keep up with the others."

As the woman grasped the child by the shoulder, Nana *Dahd* stopped in mid-story and glanced up at the woman's outraged face. "You'd better go," she warned the little girl in *Tohono O'othham.*

But the little girl deftly dodged away from the teacher's reaching hand. "Are you *Nihu'uli?*" she asked, taking one of Rita's parchmentlike hands into her own small brown one. "Are you my grandmother?"

Lani never forgot the wonderfully happy smile that suffused Nana *Dahd*'s worn face as she pressed her other hand on top of that unknown child's tiny one.

"Are you?" the little girl persisted just as the teacher's fingers closed determinedly on her shoulder and pulled her away. With a vicious shake, the woman started back up the trail, dragging the resisting child after her and glaring over her shoulder at the old woman who had so inconveniently waylaid her charge.

Rita glanced from Davy's face to Lani's. "*Heu'u*—Yes," she called after the child in *Tohono O'othham.* "*Ni-mohsi.* You are my grandchild, my daughter's child."

Confused, Lani frowned. "But I didn't think you had any daughters," she objected.

"I didn't used to, but I do now." Rita laughed. She gathered Lani in her arms and held her close. "Now I seem to have several."

The dream ended. Lani tried to waken, but she was too tired, her eyelids too heavy to lift. She seemed to be in her bed, but when she tried to move her arms, they wouldn't budge, either. And then, since there was nothing else to do, she simply allowed herself to drift back to sleep.

Breakfast took time. It was almost eleven by the time David was actually ready to leave the house. Predictably, his leave-taking was a tearful, maudlin affair. Yes, Astrid Ladd was genuinely sorry to see him go, but she was also half-lit from the three stiff drinks she had downed with breakfast.

David knew his grandmother drank too much, but he didn't hassle her about it. Had she been as falling down drunk as some of the Indians hanging around the trading post at Three Points, David Ladd still wouldn't have mentioned it. Over the years, Rita Antone had schooled her *Olhoni* in the niceties of proper behavior. Among the *Tohono O'othham*, young people were taught to respect their elders, not to question or criticize them. If Astrid Ladd wanted to stay smashed much of the time, that was her business, not his.

"Promise me that you'll come back and see me," Astrid said, with her lower lip trembling.

"Of course I will, Grandma."

"At Christmas?"

"I don't know."

"Next summer then?"

"Maybe."

Astrid shook her head hopelessly and began to cry in earnest. "See there? I'll probably never lay eyes on you again."

"You will, Grandma," he promised. "Please don't cry. I have to go."

She was still weeping and waving from the porch when David turned left onto Sheridan and headed south. He didn't go far—only as far as the parking lot of Calvary Cemetery, where both David Ladd's father and grandfather were buried. He rummaged in the backseat and brought out the two small wreaths of fresh flowers he had bought two days ago and kept in the refrigerator of his apartment until that morning.

Knowing the route to the Ladd family plot, he easily threaded his way through the trackless forest of ornate headstones and mausoleums. He didn't much like this cemetery. It was too big, too green, too gaudy, and full of huge chunks of marble and granite. Davy had grown up attending funerals on the parched earth and among the simple white wooden crosses of reservation cemeteries. The first funeral he actually remembered was Father John's.

A *Mil-gahn* and a Jesuit priest, Father John was in his eighties and already retired when Davy first met him. He had been there, in the house at Gates Pass and imprisoned in the root cellar along with Rita and Davy, on the day of the battle with the evil *Ohb*. Father John had died a little more than a year later.

In all the hubbub of preparation for Diana Ladd's wedding to Brandon Walker, no one had noticed how badly Father John was failing. And that was exactly as he had intended. The aged priest had agreed to perform the ceremony, and he used all his strength to ensure that nothing marred the joy of the happy young couple on their wedding day. Of all the people gathered at San Xavier for the morning ceremony, only Rita had sensed what performing the ceremony was costing the old priest in terms of physical exertion and vitality.

Honoring his silence, she too, had kept quiet about it—at least to most of the bridal party. But not to Davy.

"Watch out for Father John, *Olhoni,*" Nana *Dahd* murmured as she straightened the boy's tie and smoothed his tuxedo in preparation to Davy's walking his mother down the aisle. "If he looks too tired, come and get me right away."

The admonition puzzled Davy. "Is Father John sick?"

"He's old," Rita answered. "He's an old, old man."

"Is he going to die?" Davy asked.

"We're all going to die sometime," she had answered.

"Even you?"

She smiled. "Even me."

But Father John had made it through the wedding mass

with flying colors. He died three days later, while Brandon and Diana Walker were still in Mazatlán on their honeymoon. The frantic barking of Davy's dog, Bone, had awakened Davy in the middle of the night.

Keeping the dog with him for protection as he peered out through a front window, Davy saw a man climbing out of a big black car parked in the driveway. As soon as the man stepped up onto the porch, Davy recognized Father Damien, the young priest from San Xavier.

Even Davy knew that having a priest come to the house in the middle of the night could not mean good news. He hurried to the door. "What's wrong?" he demanded through the still-closed door as the priest's finger moved toward the button on the bell.

"I'm looking for someone named Rita Antone," Father Damien said hesitantly, as though he wasn't quite sure whether or not his information was correct. "Does she live here?"

"What is it, Davy?" Rita asked, materializing silently out of the darkness at the back of the house.

"It's Father Damien," Davy answered. "He's looking for you."

Nana *Dahd* unlocked the dead bolt and opened the door. "I'm Rita," she said.

The priest looked relieved. "It's Father John, Mrs. Antone," he said apologetically. "I'm sorry to bother you at this hour of the night, but he's very ill. He's asking for you."

Rita nodded. "Get dressed right away, Davy," she said. "We must hurry."

They left the house a few minutes later. There was never any question of Davy's staying at the house by himself. Ever since Andrew Carlisle had burst into the house on that summer afternoon, there had been an unspoken understanding between Rita and Diana that Davy was not to be left alone. On their way to town, Rita rode in the front seat with the priest while Davy huddled in the back.

"Where is he?" Nana *Dahd* asked.

"He was at Saint Mary's," the priest answered. "In the intensive care unit, but this afternoon he made them let him out. He's back at the rectory."

At the mission, Rita took Davy by the hand and dragged him with her as Father Damien led the way. They found Father John sitting propped up on a mound of pillows in a small, cell-like room. He lifted one feeble hand in greeting. On the white chenille bedspread where his hand had rested lay Father John's rosary—his *losalo*—with its black shiny beads and olive wood crucifix.

Davy Ladd was an Anglo—a *Mil-gahn*—but he had been properly raised—brought up in the Indian way. He melted quietly into the background while Rita sank down on the hard-backed chair beside the dying man's bed. Out of sight in the shadowy far corner of the room, Davy sat cross-legged and listened to the murmured conversation, hanging on every mysterious word.

"Thank you for coming, Dancing Quail," Father John whispered. His voice was very weak. He wheezed when he spoke. The air rustled in his throat like winter wind whispering through sun-dried grass.

"You should have called," Rita chided gently. "I would have come sooner."

Father John shook his head. "They wouldn't let me. I was in intensive care. Only relatives . . ."

Rita nodded and then waited patiently, letting Father John rest awhile before he continued. "I wanted to ask your forgiveness," he said. "Please."

"I forgave you long ago," she returned. "When you agreed to help us with the evil *Ohb*, I forgave you then."

"Thank you," he said. "Thank you so much."

There was another long period of silence. Nodding, Davy almost drifted off to sleep before Father John's voice startled him awake once more.

"Please tell me about your son," the old man said quietly.

"The one who disappeared in Korea. His name was Gordon, I believe. Was that the child? Was he my son?"

Rita shook her head. There was a small reading lamp on the table beside Father John's bed. The dim light from that caught the two tracks of tears meandering down Rita's broad wrinkled cheeks.

"No," she answered. "I lost that baby in California. When I was real sick, a bad doctor took the baby from me before it was time."

There was a sharp intake of breath from the man on the bed, followed by a fit of coughing. "A boy or a girl?" Father John asked at last when he could speak once more.

"I don't know," Rita said. "I never saw it. They put me to sleep. When I woke up, the baby was gone."

"When I heard about the murder, I assumed Gina was . . ."

Again Rita shook her head. "No. Gina was my husband Gordon's granddaughter, not yours. Gordon took care of me when I was sick in California that time when I lost the baby. If it hadn't been for him, I would have died, too. Gordon was a good man. He was a good husband who gave me a good son."

"Gordon Antone." Father John said the name carefully, as if testing the feel of the words on his lips. "Someone else I must pray for."

"Rest now," Rita said. "Try to get some sleep."

Instead Father John reached out, picked up the rosary, and then dropped it into the palm of Rita's hand before closing her fingers over it.

"Keep this for me," he urged. "I have used it to pray for you every day for all these years. I won't need it any longer."

Without a word, Rita slipped the beads and crucifix into her pocket. Father John drifted off to sleep then. Eventually, so did Davy. When he awakened the next morning, the room was chilly, but Davy himself was warm. Overnight someone had put a pillow under his head and had covered him with a blanket. Rita, with her chin resting on her collarbone, still sat stolidly in the chair beside Father John's bed, dozing. She woke up a few minutes later. The priest did not.

At age seven, this was Davy Ladd's first personal experience with death. He had thought it would be scary, but somehow it wasn't. He knew instinctively that in the room that night he had shared something beautiful with those two people, something important, although it would be years before he finally figured out exactly what it was.

In the three years David Ladd had been in Chicago, he had come to Calvary Cemetery often in hopes of establishing some kind of connection between himself and the names etched into the marble monuments of the Ladd family plot. The worldly remains of Garrison Walther Ladd II and III lay on either side of a headstone bearing his grandmother's name. The only difference between Astrid's grave marker and the other two was the lack of a date.

Respectfully, David put the wreath on his grandfather's grave first. He had come to Chicago several times to visit his grandparents, first as a youngster and later as a teenager, flying out by himself over holidays along with all those other children being shuttled between custodial and non-custodial parents during school vacations. The flight attendants who had been designated to transfer him from plane to plane or from plane to the Ladds had always assumed that Davy was the product of a cross-country divorce. And some of the time he had gone along with that fiction, making up stories about where his father lived and what he did for a living. That was easier and far more fun than telling people the truth—that his father was dead.

Finished with his grandfather's grave, David turned to his father's. Breakfast with Astrid had lessened the impact of the latest visitation of the recurring dream. Vivid and disturbing, it had come to him every night for over a week now.

Each time it came, he awakened the moment he saw his sister's lifeless body in the middle of the kitchen floor. And when his eyes opened, his body would launch off, sweating and trembling, into yet another panic attack.

Night after night, the two events came together like a pair of evil twins—first the dream and then the panic attack. One followed the other as inevitably as night follows day. Davy went to bed at night almost as sick with dread at what was bound to come as he would be later when it did. As the days and virtually sleepless nights went by, anticipating the attacks became almost as shattering as the attacks themselves.

Up to that moment in the cemetery, the attacks themselves had always happened at night, in the privacy of his own room and always preceded by the dream. But right then, kneeling beside the marker bearing the name of Garrison Walther Ladd III, David felt his pulse begin to quicken. Moments later, his heart was hammering in his chest, knocking his ribs so hard that he could barely breathe. His hands began to tingle. He felt dizzy.

Not trusting his ability to remain upright, David sank down on the ground next to his father's headstone and leaned against it for support. He tried to pray. As a child, the old priest, Father John, had taught him about the Father, the Son, and the Holy Ghost. And Rita had taught him about *I'itoi*.

But right then, in Davy's hour of need, there in the hot, still air of that Chicago cemetery, all he could hear through the trees was the sound of traffic buzzing by on Lake Shore Drive. From where Davy sat, both Heavenly Father and Elder Brother seemed impossibly remote.

David had no idea how long the attack lasted. Eventually his breathing steadied and his heartbeat returned to normal. Weak and queasy, he returned to himself bathed in his own rank sweat.

Nothing to worry about, the doctor had said after running all those tests weeks before. After learning that Davy was about to embark on a cross-country drive, the emergency room physician had declined to prescribe any sedatives or tranquilizers that might have caused drowsiness.

"If you're still having difficulties when you get back home to Arizona," the doctor had told him, "you should consult with your family physician."

If I get home, David Ladd thought. What if one of these spells came over him in the middle of a freeway somewhere when he was driving by himself? What would happen then?

David staggered to his feet. Still somewhat unsteady, he stood for some time, staring down at his father's grave. This was one of the reasons he had come to Evanston in the first place, one of the reasons he had accepted his grandmother's generous offer and applied to Northwestern. He had hoped that by coming here, he might somehow come to understand his father's side of the story. After all, he had grown up and spent most of his life hearing his mother's version of those long-ago events.

But the laudatory tales about Davy's father that his grandmother told him were no help. Davy sensed that there was no more truth in them than there had been in his own mother's clipped, bare-bones answers in the face of her son's never-ending curiosity. And as for visiting the grave itself? That had told him less than nothing.

Shaking his head, David Ladd turned and walked away, wondering what to do with the solitary hours before the three-o'clock check-in time at the hotel. But by the time he reached the car, he had an answer.

Almost without thinking, he drove to the Field Museum of Natural History. There he wandered slowly through galleries of lighted displays that told the stories, one after another, of vanished and vanquished Native American cultures.

David Ladd blended into the throngs of tourists that surged like herds of grazing buffalo through the museum's long hallways. Most were Anglos of one kind or another, with their loud voices and bulging bellies. For most the displays were clearly something foreign and outside their own experience. A few of the visitors were Indian. They came to the displays with a sense of understanding and a reverence that here, at least, their past still existed.

And standing in the midst of all those different people, David Ladd felt doubly alone. Cheated, almost. He was a blond-haired, blue-eyed outsider. He felt no connection, no sense of brotherhood, with the *Mil-gahn* tourists with their Bermuda-shorts-clad legs and their ill-behaved children. But here in this place, he felt no connection to The People—to the Indians—either.

Then, almost as though she were standing beside him, he heard Rita Antone's voice once more, speaking to him out of the distant past. She sat at a kitchen table with the fragrant, newly dried bear grass and yucca laid out on the table. There was a fistful of grass in one hand. Her awl—her *owij*—was poised but still in her other hand. The raw materials for Rita's next basket lay arrayed on the table, but the old woman's real workbench was forever her ample, apron-covered lap.

"The center must be very strong, *Olhoni,*" she had said, "or the basket will be no good."

Whenever Rita had started a basket, she always said something like that. The words reminded him of the words that usually accompanied taking the Holy Sacrament. The words were almost always the same, and yet they were always different.

With tears misting his eyes, David Ladd fled the museum. *I have lost the center of my basket,* he thought despairingly. *I don't know who I am.*

With Lani Walker there in the Bounder with him, Mitch tried to keep Andy's failure clearly at the forefront of his mind.

Much as he wanted her, much as he physically ached to use that slender body, he was equally determined to deny himself the pleasure. Andrew Carlisle had allowed his base nature to overwhelm his intellect. Mitch Johnson had no intention of making the same mistake.

Watching Lani sleeping peacefully on the bed, Mitch's physical need for her was so great that he forced himself to turn his back on her and walk away. That was the only reasonable thing to do—put some distance between himself and what he knew to be an invitation to disaster.

For a time he busied himself with his art materials, setting up his easel and getting out his paper. He waited until he was once more fully under control before he turned to look at her once again, before he allowed himself to gaze down at her. Her long dark lashes rested softly on bronze cheeks. It surprised him to notice, for the first time, that here and there on the bronze skin of her body were occasional light spots, reverse freckles, almost. He wondered vaguely what might have caused those blemishes, but he didn't worry about them long. It was time to tie her, to use the four matching, richly colored teal-and-burgundy scarves he had bought for that precise purpose.

He had bought them in four separate stores, paying for them in cash. "It's for my mother's birthday," he had told the first saleslady, who waited on him at Park Mall. "For my Aunt Gertrude's eightieth," he told the second one in a store at El Con. "For my next-door neighbor," he explained, smiling at the third salesclerk in the first store in Tucson Mall. "She takes care of my two dogs when I'm out of town." By the fourth store Mitch was running out of imagination. It was back to his mother's birthday.

As an artist, Mitch Johnson possibly could have done without the scarves altogether and painted them in later from either memory or imagination. But when it came to this particular picture, Mitch Johnson was a perfectionist. He wanted to do it right. He took care to arrange the scarves properly, so that it was clear they were restraints, holding the girl against her will, but beautiful restraints nonetheless. He arranged the loose ends of the scarves in drapes and folds around her as an opulent counterpoint to the naked simplicity of the girl's body. Contrast, of course, is everything.

He also spent a considerable period of time creating just the right angle and perspective. For that he finally settled on three pillows. Two he used to raise her head and neck enough so that both her face and that funny necklace at the base of her throat were clearly visible. The third pillow went under her buttocks, raising her hips high enough so that what lay between her spread legs was fully visible. To Mitch, anyway.

That was the whole tantalizing wonder of this particular pose. Had Mitch been an ancient Greek sculptor, he would have opted for the use of fig leaves, perhaps. The painters of the Renaissance had gone in for the strategic drape of robes to conceal what shouldn't be seen. Mitch was a purist. He wanted to use the girl's own body to create the desired illusion. Nicolaïdes had taught him to look for edges and to draw those.

Afraid the shock of cold water might awaken her, he dampened his fingers with warm water from the tap. Then he petted the wild tangle of soft black pubic hair, teasing and coaxing it into place. He used the hair itself to create a concealing veil until it curved around and over what he wanted to hide from any other casual viewers if not from himself. No one else would be able to see under it, but any person viewing the picture would know unerringly that the artist himself had drunk his fill.

His hand still reeked with the heady, musky smell of her when, weak-kneed, he returned to his easel and began to work on the quick gesture sketch, using broad lines and circles to capture the general form of her.

As the charcoal scraped comfortingly across the paper, he felt himself settling down once more. As he worked, the chorus of an old Sunday-school hymn came unbidden to his mind. "Yield not to temptation, for yielding is sin." Smiling to himself, he sang as many of the words as he was able to remember.

The strange combination of drawing and humming didn't amount to quite the same thing as taking a cold shower, but the physical effect on his body was much the same. At least his damned persistent hard-on went away, enough so that he was able to concentrate on what he was doing.

David Ladd left the Field Museum and went directly to the Ritz. Carrying one small suitcase, he left the car with the attendant and walked inside. He figured he was still too early to check in, but Candace had told him to stop by the concierge desk to check for a message whenever he arrived.

"Why, Mr. Ladd," the concierge said with a welcoming smile. "Welcome to the Ritz. I'm so glad you could join us today. Your wife left a note here for you and asked that I give it to you as soon as you arrived."

His wife? Blushing furiously, David took the note and retreated to a chair at the far end of the lobby before he tore open the envelope. Inside were a note and a room key.

David,

I had some last-minute shopping to do. I'll be back as soon as I can. Our room is 1712. See you there.

> *Love,*
> *Candace*

So he already was checked in. Pocketing the note and palming the key, David headed upstairs. Leave it to Candace to figure a way around those 3 P.M. check-in rules, he thought with a rueful grin, but he was supremely grateful.

Not only was he emotionally drained by his dealings with Astrid Garrison and his trip to the museum, he was rummy from days of almost no sleep.

Upon entering the room, he was surprised to see four suitcases, two arranged on the bed as well as one on each of the room's two folding metal luggage racks. Four suitcases did seem a little much for an overnight at the Ritz, especially since the bathroom was already fully stocked with robes, hair dryer, and a selection of toiletries. Evidently the female side of the Oak Park Waverlys didn't believe in traveling light.

Hoping he had time for a quick nap, he closed the blackout curtains and then undressed. Before stripping off his shirt, he discovered Astrid's diamond engagement ring still lurking in his pocket. He had meant to give the ring back to his grandmother before he left, but he had forgotten.

Shaking his head, he put the ring on the nightstand along with his watch. He thought about leaving a wake-up call so he could be showered and dressed before Candace's arrival. In the end he decided to sleep until he woke up or Candace arrived, whichever came first. Lying down on the bed, he tried to relax, but that wasn't easy. He was smitten by an attack of conscience.

If you don't want to marry her, he thought, then what the hell are you doing here?

Hopefully screwing your brains out was the short answer, he decided, grinning ruefully up at the darkened ceiling overhead. But for that—for plain old getting your rocks off—most any place would do, from Motel 6 up. The Ritz had been Candace's idea. And even if Candace had sold him on the proposition that this special night on the town was both a graduation and a going-away gift from her, he had the distinct feeling that Candace's daddy's law firm was actually picking up the tab.

Despite Astrid Ladd's none-too-subtle lobbying, things weren't all sweetness and light between David Garrison Ladd and Candace Eugenia Waverly.

They had met the previous December, when they had both been participants in what they still laughingly referred to as the wedding from hell. Candace had been maid of honor and David best man at a pre-Christmas wedding that had fallen victim to an unseasonal but vicious mid-December blizzard. The storm had stalled prospective guests—including most of the groom's family—at airports all over the country while O'Hare and Midway airports were shut down for four solid hours.

As "best" people, Candace and David had both had their hands full. Candace had been stuck baby-sitting a somewhat hysterical bride and her mostly hysterical mother while David was closeted with an exceedingly nervous groom who had been close to bagging the whole idea well *before* the snow started falling. By the time they finally made it through the wedding, the maid of honor and best man were comrades-in-arms.

From that beginning, it was a simple step for Candace to invite her new friend to her parents' traditional Christmas party the following week—the night before David Ladd was due to fly home to spend his winter vacation with his family in Tucson.

The prospect of meeting the Oak Park Waverlys—as Astrid Ladd soon took to calling them—wasn't nearly as daunting to David Ladd as it would have been had he gone straight there from his mother's and stepfather's place in Gates Pass. Following Candace's directions through the still ice-rutted streets, he arrived at a house that was much the same size as his grandmother's lakeshore mansion, only this one was alive with lights visible in every window of all three floors.

The gateposts at the end of a long curving drive glowed a holiday welcome with hundreds of white Christmas lights. The house itself was outlined with thousands more. Handing his Jeep off to a valet-parking attendant, David rang the doorbell. One glimpse of the tux-clad butler who opened the door and relieved arriving guests of their coats made David more than happy that he'd gone to the trouble of renting a tuxedo himself.

For fifteen or twenty interminable minutes he was there on his own, trying to make acceptable small talk with people he had never met and most likely would never see again. Just when he was ready to bolt back the way he had come, Candace appeared in a slick, low-cut red dress with a slit that came halfway up her thigh.

"I see somebody put a drink in your hand," she said. "Have you tried the buffet?"

"I was waiting for you. Are you hungry?"

Candace made a face. "Not really. Mother uses the same caterer every year, although I've never quite figured out why. The food reminds me of those breakfast sausages they serve at hotels in England. They look great but they taste like they're made of sawdust."

David couldn't help laughing at that. Encouraged by an appreciative audience, Candace continued. "My two older sisters and I learned early on to load up a plate and carry it around awhile just to keep peace in the family. I suggest you do the same, but you don't have to eat it. Later on, we'll go up to my room and order a pizza."

"Order a pizza?" David echoed.

"Sure. I have my own entrance. The delivery people know to bring it there instead of to the front door. My sisters and I have been doing it for years."

"Your parents have never figured it out?"

Candace grinned at him conspiratorially from behind her champagne flute. "Never. Come on. I'll introduce you to my folks, but don't breathe a word about the pizza. If you do, I won't let you have any."

It turned out there was a whole lot more waiting for David Ladd in Candace Waverly's upstairs room than a thin-crust pepperoni and cheese. For one thing, it wasn't a room at all, but a three-room suite, complete with bedroom, sitting room, and Jacuzzi-equipped bath. And Candace Waverly wasn't particularly interested in staying in the sitting room.

David Ladd had taken his time with school, changing majors several times before finally finishing his BA and deciding on law school. At twenty-seven, he certainly wasn't a virgin, but he hadn't encountered anyone like Candace Eugenia Waverly, either. Slipping out of her bright red dress along the way, she led him into her bedroom. Davy was still nervously fumbling with his cuff links when a naked Candace stepped forward to help him and to drag him, unprotesting, into her bed. Two frenetic hours later, she sat up in bed, propped herself upright on a mound of pillows, and matter-of-factly reached out for the phone to order a pizza. By then David Ladd had experienced several exotic sexual activities he had previously only imagined. Or read about.

Candace might look delicate and ladylike, but in bed she was anything but, and in the six months since, David Ladd had found himself deeply in lust if not in love. He and Candace spent a good deal of time together—as much as possible, considering his course load. And because of Astrid Garrison's prying eyes, most of their fun and games had happened in Candace's chaste-appearing bedroom.

The sex had been great. The problem was, David Ladd still didn't feel as though he was remotely in love. During the last few weeks, tension had been building as Candace Waverly dug in her heels over David's stated plan of returning to Tucson to go to work.

"I don't see why you're taking this internship out on an Indian reservation," she had pouted one day early in May as the two of them sat sipping late-evening lattés in downtown Evanston's Starbucks.

With an important paper due in two days, this wasn't exactly the time for Davy to work his way around such a complex issue. Candace already knew that David's sixteen-year-old sister was adopted and that she was a full-blooded Native American. School-trained as a disciple of cultural diversity, Candace hadn't batted an eyelash when David had given her that bit of information, but she had cautioned him that he maybe ought not mention it to her folks. Like the secret Christmas-party pizza, as well as some of the other things that went on in Candace's upstairs bedroom—this was something Candace's mother might be better off not knowing, and it made David Ladd wonder if the elder Waverlys of Oak Park might be somewhat bigoted when it came to dealing with Indians.

Maybe Candace was, too, for that matter, he thought as he grappled with how to make her understand exactly what the internship meant to him. Should he try to tell her about Nana *Dahd*? By working on the reservation he hoped, in some small way, to repay Rita Antone for all she had done for him, all she had meant to him, but the words to explain that refused to bubble to the surface.

"I'm smart," he said at last, knowing it sounded limp and probably stupid as well. "I speak the language, and I think I can make a contribution."

"You mean make a contribution like people do in the Peace Corps?"

It wasn't at all like the Peace Corps, but David didn't know where to begin explaining that, either. Peace Corps volunteers, armed with the very best intentions, went off and spent a few years of their lives ministering to the unfortunate before returning to their real homes, jobs, and lives. As far as David Ladd was concerned, the people on the *Tohono O'othham*, with all their history and tradition, were in his blood. They were a part of him. He had learned about them at Rita's knee and in the teachings of both Looks At Nothing and Fat Crack. They were his real life far more than the years of exile in Evanston had ever been.

"But what kind of a job would the internship lead to?" Candace had continued. "Is there any kind of career path? And do they pay anything?"

At twenty-five, Candace was two years younger than

David. She had a good job in Human Resources at her father's firm—a job that probably paid far better than anything she could have found on her own with nothing more than a BS in psychology. Out of school for four years herself, she talked about someday returning to school for a graduate degree. In the meantime, she still lived at home and drove the bright red Integra her parents had given her for Christmas to replace the Ford Mustang convertible that had been her college-graduation present. The kind of grinding poverty that existed on the *Tohono O'othham* was so far outside the realm of Candace Waverly's sheltered Oak Park existence that there was no basis for common ground. Had David Ladd attempted to explain it to her, she probably still wouldn't have understood.

"The tribe doesn't pay much," David allowed with a short laugh. "And I doubt there's much room for advancement."

"But would you make enough to start a family?" she asked.

That sobered him instantly. "Probably not," he said.

"Well then," Candace continued in a tone that sounded as though there was no further basis for discussion. "Daddy will be glad to give you a job. I know because I already asked him. He's always looking for smart young men."

"But, Candace," David had objected. "I don't want to work in Chicago. I want to go home—to Tucson."

"But what's there?" she had shot back at him. "And what would I do for a job? Nobody knows me there."

Behind them, the espresso machine had hissed a noisy cloud of steam into the air. The sound reminded David Ladd of quicksand pulling someone under. No doubt he should have made a clean break of it right then, but the paper was due and finals were bearing down on him and he didn't want to provoke a confrontation.

"I'll think about it," he said. "I'll think it over and let you know."

"You goddamned gutless wonder," he berated himself now, lying there on the bed in the darkened room at the Ritz Carlton.

Honesty's the best policy.

*　　*　　*

Honesty's the best policy. Growing up, those were words he'd heard early and often from his stepfather. He had been only seven the first time he had heard them spoken, but he remembered the incident as clearly as if it had happened yesterday.

"That old lady's not just an Indian," his stepbrother had shouted. "She's a witch."

From the very beginning, Quentin Walker was always able to get Davy's goat, and there was nothing that drove the younger boy wild faster than someone saying bad things about Rita Antone.

"She is not."

"Is to. And I can prove it."

"How?"

"Look."

Quentin pulled something black out of his pocket. As soon as Davy saw it, he recognized the scrap of black hair. He knew what it was and where it had come from.

In the bottom drawer of the dresser in her room, Nana *Dahd* kept her precious medicine basket. Rita had told Davy the story a hundred times about how her grandmother, Understanding Woman, had given Rita the basket to take with her when the tribal policeman carted her off to boarding school. Back then she had been a little girl named Dancing Quail. Davy had wept at the part of the story where, on the terrifying train trip between Tucson and Phoenix, clinging to the roof of the moving train, Dancing Quail had lost the precious spirit rock, a geode, that Understanding Woman had given her granddaughter to protect her on the journey. Not only was the rock lost, but later, once she arrived in Phoenix, the basket itself had been confiscated by school matrons who had a ready market for such profitable artifacts. Years later, when Rita was sent from the reservation in disgrace, *Oks Amichuda* once again gave Rita a basket to take with her. This one, although far inferior to the first, nonetheless contained yet another spirit rock, a child's fist-sized chunk from that same geode.

Years later, working as a domestic in a *Mil-gahn* house in Phoenix, Rita had stumbled across that original medicine basket, complete with all its contents, sitting in a glass display case. On the night she fled the house for faraway California, Rita had exchanged the one basket for the other.

Having heard the stories countless times, David recognized at once that the hank of human hair in Quentin's hand was one of Rita's medicine-basket treasures—her great-grandfather's scalp bundle.

"You shouldn't have that. Nobody's supposed to touch it," Davy said. "Put it back."

"What's she going to do to me if I touch it?" Quentin taunted. "Turn me into a toad?"

"I said put it back."

"Who's gonna make me?"

Quentin was four years older than Davy and almost twice as big, but Davy flew at him with such ferocity that the older boy was caught off-guard. He fell down, cracking his head on the rock wall behind him while Davy pummeled his unprotected face with flailing fists. Once Quentin recovered from the initial shock, the fight was short but brutal. Davy took the brunt of the physical damage. When the battle was over, his nose was bloody, his shirt had been torn to pieces, and one bottom tooth dangled by a thread.

Brandon had arrived in time to put an end to the hostilities. He lined all four boys up in order of size. His own sons, Quentin and Tommy, were at the head of the line, followed by Davy and then by Brian Fellows, Quentin and Tommy's half-brother.

Janie, Brandon Walker's first wife, had been three months pregnant with Brian when she divorced Brandon in order to marry Don Fellows, Brian's father. Janie's second marriage didn't last any longer than her first one had. Don Fellows disappeared into the woodwork when Brian was three. By the time Brian was four, he would come and stand forlornly on the porch, watching whenever Brandon came by to take his own sons for an outing.

Over time, that lost, affection-starved look had worn down Brandon Walker's resistance. By the time Davy appeared on the scene, Brian came along with Quentin and Tommy as often as not. Brian was a few months younger than Davy. He was small for his age and still prone to wetting the bed. Quentin and Tommy jeeringly called him "the baby." Brandon Walker often referred to him as "the little guy."

"All right now," Brandon Walker growled on the day of the fight over the medicine basket. "Tell me what happened, and remember, honesty's the best policy. I want the truth."

"I was trying to help him learn to ride my bike," Quentin said. "The big one, not the one with training wheels. He fell, and so did I. The bike landed on top of me."

The lie came so easily to Quentin's lips that the two younger boys, Brian and Davy, looked at one another in shocked amazement. Meanwhile Brandon moved down the line to his second son. "Is that right, Tommy? Remember, what I want from you is the truth."

Tommy nodded. "Yup," he said. "That's what happened."

Next Brandon leveled his gaze on Davy. "What do you have to say, young man?"

Davy shrugged his scraped shoulder and hung his head. "Nothing," he said.

"And you, Brian?"

"Nothing, too," he said.

Convinced he still didn't have a straight answer but unable to crack the four boys' united front, Brandon turned back to Davy. "Do me a favor, Davy. Stick with the training wheels for a while, son. Thank God that's only a baby tooth. If it were a permanent one, your mother would kill us both. Go see Rita. She'll help clean you up."

The last thing Davy wanted to do was see Rita right then. Part of him wanted to tell her what had happened. But he didn't know what to say. For a week he kept quiet, watching Nana *Dahd*'s broad features for any sign that she had discovered her loss.

The next weekend, when the three boys again came to visit, Brandon took the two older boys to see *Rocky,* a movie that was deemed too old for Brian and Davy.

As soon as the two younger boys were left alone in Davy's room, Brian Fellows unzipped his knapsack. "Look," he whispered, emptying the contents of his bag out onto the bottom bunk.

On top of the heap were the extra clothes Brian always had to bring along in case he had an accident. But underneath the clothing, scattered on the bedspread, lay a collection of items most people would have dismissed as little-boy junk— the denuded spine of a feather; a shard of pottery with the faint figure of a turtle etched into the red clay; a chunk of rock, gray on one side and covered with lavender crystals on the other; the hank of long black hair; Rita's *owij*—her basket-making awl; Rita's lost son's Purple Heart. Last of all, Davy spied Father John's *losalo*—the string of rosary beads—that the old man had given Rita the night he died.

For a moment Davy gazed in wondering, hushed silence at the medicine basket's missing treasures. "Where did you get them?" he asked finally.

"I stole them," Brian said casually. "Quentin had them hidden in his sock drawer, and I stole them back."

"When he finds out, he'll kill you."

"No, he won't," Brian answered. "He'll only beat me up. He does that all the time. It's no big deal."

For the first time in his life, Davy Ladd realized he had a friend, a real one—a friend whose name wasn't Rita.

"But Tommy and Quentin are so mean," Davy said. "Aren't you afraid of them?"

"Not really," Brian replied with a cheerful shrug. "They're so afraid of getting caught, they never hurt me enough so it shows."

7

Coyote had listened to the council in the village before Old Limping Man and Young Man started on their journey across the desert. Ban had decided that anything important enough to take men back into the burning lands was worth examining. When Coyote's stomach is full of food and water, his curiosity is very active. So Ban had gone ahead of the two men to find out for himself what it was that Buzzard had seen and Jackrabbit had told him about.

But now in that burning desert, Coyote was running for his life. The Ali-chu'uchum O'othham—*the Little People*— were after him—the bees, flies, ants, wasps, and insects of all kinds. Gohhim O'othham—*Old Limping Man*—could still speak the language of I'itoi which all the animals and all the Little People understand. He called out to the Pa-nahl—*the Bees*—and to the Wihpsh—*the Wasps*—to ask what was the trouble.

The Little People were very angry, but they stopped. They

told Gohhim O'othham *that the two men must go with them and that they must keep Coyote away. But there was no danger from Coyote anymore.* Ban *was too busy rubbing his sore nose in the dirt.*

And so the two men—Old Limping Man and Young Man—followed Ali-chu'uchum—*the Little People. After a time the men saw a strange cloud made up of the flying ones—the bees and flies and wasps. They looked down and saw the ground covered with moving specks. And the moving specks were ants of all kinds—big and little, brown and black.*

The word of the coming of the men became known. The cloud of Little People spread out and parted. Then the men saw a woman lying with her eyes closed. The woman was being kissed by the wings of hundreds of bees. They were fanning her and keeping her cool, and all the while Panahl—*the Bees—were singing very softly.*

At first the men were afraid. They knew that while the Little People are very, very wise, they are also very quick-tempered. But Old Man listened to the song the bees were singing. The song was a prayer for help for this woman who was their friend. So the two men went to the woman and gave her water.

The woman moved and spoke, but the men could not understand what she said. She did not open her eyes. They gave her pinole and water. Then they raised her up and began the return trip to the distant village.

Driving to his appointment, Mitch Johnson couldn't help gloating. All morning long he had made a conscious effort not to rush, even though the clock had been ticking inevitably toward his scheduled appointment with Diana Ladd Walker. Gradually—vaguely, at first—the girl's form had taken shape on the paper. The perspective was masterful—graphic without being anatomical. He wanted her to be sexy in this one. The dissection part, the one that peeled away the outside layers—would come later.

For Mitch, one of the most difficult aspects of the drawing came when it was time to detail the girl's softly rising and falling chest. With Lani sound asleep, the virginal breasts had gone so soft and flaccid they were almost flat. The only solution for that was for Mitch to touch them and caress the nipples until they stood at attention. The difficulty and thrill of that was bringing the body to wakeful attention without necessarily disturbing the girl. If she had awakened and started struggling and fighting right then, it might have done irreparable harm to the pose. It would have spoiled the whole mood, destroyed the magic exhilaration of creation.

But of course, the full force of the drug was still upon her, and she hadn't awakened. Lying there still as death, she had stirred only slightly beneath his touch, an unconscious half-smile on her lips as though, even in sleep, Mitch's tender caress on her body somehow pleasured her. That almost drove him crazy. Breathing hard, Mitch once again retreated to the safety of his easel, forcing himself to regard her inviting body as an artistic challenge, as an enticing morsel to be avoided at all costs rather than as defenseless territory begging to be conquered and exploited.

And the fact that he could do that—put her on paper without giving in to the raging river of temptation—left him with a feeling of power and incredible superiority. Touching her body without immediately tearing into it was something Andy Carlisle never could have done. Mitch had the pleasure of knowing right then that he was a better man than his teacher. Godlike, Andy had tried to mold Mitch in his own image, but in this instance the created had moved beyond his creator.

After the breasts it had been time to do the face and hair. If anything, he wished the girl's hair had been a little longer than it was. That way the dark edge of the hair would have concealed some of the breasts rather than simply falling across the shoulders. But that couldn't be helped. This was to be a study of the actual girl, and so he copied the line of hair exactly as it presented itself.

The final item on his morning's agenda had been the necklace. Mitch had been around Tucson long enough to know that the maze design on her necklace had something to do with Indians, but he wasn't exactly sure what. He took great pains to see that he got it right, that he copied it exactly. You never could tell when . . .

As soon as the thought came to mind, it had left him shivering. That was a way to top Andy's tapes, something Andy never would have conceived of. Andy had talked a good game—murder as art—but he wouldn't have had the skill to execute such a breathtaking idea.

Mitch would re-create the design on the flat plane of the girl's belly, carving it into her flesh so that slowly oozing blood would be the actual ink. That meant Mitch would have to do that final act while the girl was still alive—maybe drugged again so she wouldn't move and mess things up. One question in Mitch's mind was whether or not, working free-hand with an X-Acto knife, he would be able to get the nested concentric circles right. The other difficulty would be placement. The most artistically unifying concept would be to use that fine little belly button of hers as the head of the man in the maze.

That would see Andy's goddamned tapes and raise him one better.

It was on that note that he walked into the hotel to meet with Lani Walker's mother.

With her hair, nails, and makeup all professionally attended to, Diana Ladd Walker headed for La Paloma and the scheduled Monty Lazarus interview. His wasn't a byline she recognized, but that didn't mean anything. The magazines he wrote for were name brand, and Megan had been delighted to schedule an interview with him.

As Diana wended her way through Tucson's relatively light summertime traffic, she smiled at the idea that she was going to a fashionable hotel to be interviewed by a reporter with a national audience. As a general rule, interviews were something to be endured rather than enjoyed. Still, considering Diana's humble origins, the very fact that she was being interviewed at all had to count as its own peculiar miracle.

Diana Cooper Ladd Walker had spent her early life in the clean but shabby caretaker's quarters at the garbage dump back in Joseph, Oregon. Diana's mother had scrubbed and fussed and worked to keep the place up, but it had remained indelibly "the old Stevens place"—a run-down one-house slum that was theirs to use only as long as Max Cooper managed to hang on to his unenviable position as Joseph's garbageman.

The job was anything but glamorous. Other than the house, it paid little more than a pittance, but it kept a roof over their heads. With a marginally motivated and often drunk husband, it was the best Iona Dade Cooper could hope for. Max kept both the job and the house for years—far longer than anyone expected—but only because Iona carried more than her share of the load. Max owned the official title of garbageman. Iona did most of the work—his and hers both.

As a child Diana hadn't been blessed with many friends. The few she did have usually found dozens of excuses to explain why they could never come play at her house. For years Diana had searched for ways to make her house more acceptable, more welcoming.

Once when she was ten or so, she had sat at the kitchen table after dinner, poring through the exotic pages of one of the several Sears and Roebuck catalogs that came to the house each year with her mother's name on them.

"Look at these," Diana had said, pointing to a set of sheer, frilly pink curtains. The curtains could be purchased as part of a set along with a matching bedspread. "Wouldn't those look nice in my bedroom?"

Diana's question had been intended for her mother's ears, but at that precise moment, Iona had stepped across the kitchen to the pantry where she was just taking off her apron. Before she could finish hanging up her apron and return to the table, Max Cooper had banged down his beer bottle and then leaned toward Diana. He peered over her shoulder, glowering at the page in the catalog.

"Won't matter none," he announced morosely. With a quick jab, he grabbed the catalog out of Diana's hand and dropped it into Iona's box of kitchen firewood. "Curtains or no, you can't make a silk purse out of a sow's ear. And all those hoity-toity girls from school still won't have nothin' to do with you. You know what they say," he added with a leer. "Once a garbageman's daughter, always a garbageman's daughter."

He had leaned back on his chair then, watching to see if she would try to rescue the catalog from the trash heap which, of course, she did not. Even at that age, she already knew better than to give Max Cooper's meanness the kind of satisfaction he wanted.

In the books Diana had devoured every day—fictional stories peopled by the likes of Nancy Drew and Judy Bolton and the Dana girls—the heroines had slick rooms, speedy little roadsters, loving parents, and enough money to do whatever they liked. If they wanted something, they bought it themselves or some nice relative gave it to them. Diana Cooper's life wasn't like that. She never had a matching set of curtains, sheets, and pillowcases until after she had been married and widowed and was living alone in the little rock house in Gates Pass.

She had left the catalog where her father threw it, but she had never forgotten what he had done. And she had never forgiven him either.

Now, driving toward her interview with Monty Lazarus, Diana Ladd Walker was struck once more by how far she had come from those bad old days. It was a long way from the garbageman's house in Joseph, Oregon, to the lobby of the La Paloma in Tucson, Arizona. A damned long way.

When she pulled into the covered driveway in front of the hotel, a valet-parking attendant stepped forward to open the door and claim her car. "Are you checking in?" he asked, helping her out of the seat.

"No," she said. "I'm here for a meeting."

"Very good," he said, handing her a claim ticket.

She stood for a moment watching as he took the Suburban and drove it out of sight. The miracle was that she didn't feel as though she were out of her league or that she had somehow overreached herself. No, she was here at a first-class hotel, and she felt totally at ease.

Smiling, Diana smoothed her dress and started inside, nodding a thank-you to the attendant who opened the door.

Not only was it a long way from Joseph to here, she thought, but every single step had been worth it.

As she entered the room a tall, gaunt-looking man with a headful of bushy red hair, slightly stooped shoulders, and an engaging grin rose and came toward her. "Mrs. Walker?" he asked.

Diana nodded and held out her hand. "Mr. Lazarus?" she asked.

"That's right," he said with a courtly bow. "Monty Lazarus at your service." He led her toward a low, comfortable-looking couch. "I've managed to corral this little seating area for just the two of us. I thought it might be nicer for talking than the restaurant would be. Would you care for a drink?"

"A glass of wine might be nice. A drink sometimes helps take the edge off."

"In other words, you're not looking forward to this."

She smiled and shook her head. "About as much as I look forward to having a root canal," she told him.

For some strange reason, that answer seemed to tickle his funny bone. Monty Lazarus laughed aloud.

"The lobby bar isn't open yet," he said. "You hang on

right here. If you'll excuse me for a few seconds, I'll go get you that glass of wine, then I'll do my best to make this as painless an interview as possible."

Diana sat back, closed her eyes, and waited, forcing herself to relax, to forget how nervous being on the subjective side of an interview always made her feel.

"Have you ever been to a bullfight?" Andy had asked Mitch once.

"A long time ago," Mitch answered. "Down in Nogales back in the early seventies. Lori and I went together. I wasn't especially impressed."

"The Nogales ring wasn't noted for the quality of its fights," Andy replied. "It's like small-town sports everywhere. The bush leagues. You get the young guys who aren't quite good enough to make it in the majors and a few major-league has-beens that aren't tough enough to cut the mustard anymore. But bullfighting, if it's done right, is a thing of beauty.

"The bullfighter has to be able to kill. That goes without saying, but the art of it is all in the capework, in the bullfighter controlling the drama with his cape. The whole point is to bring the bull's horns so close that physical injury or even death are less than a fraction of an inch away and yet, when the fight is over the bull is always dead, and usually, the bullfighter walks away unscathed. It's fascinating to watch."

Mitch Johnson remembered every word of that conversation, and he had taken them all to heart. This was his capework, then. He had set up the interview and the whole Monty Lazarus fabrication just to prove to himself that he could do it, that he could take the girl, do whatever he wanted with her, and still talk to her mother with complete impunity. There was power in that.

Mitch stood at the bar waiting for the bartender to finish

dealing with some kind of inventory issue. Even that slight suspension in the action was annoying. Now that the interview was about to begin, his whole body was alive with anticipation. The moment when Diana Ladd Walker had come across the room toward him was already one of the high points of his life. He would never forget the cordial smile on her face as he rose to meet her or the way she had held out her hand in greeting. The touch of her fingers had been absolutely electrifying because, like the poor, unfortunate bull, Diana Ladd Walker didn't suspect a thing.

She had no idea that her precious daughter belonged to the man whose hand she was shaking. She didn't have a glimmer that he had spent almost the entire morning with Lani Walker spread out before him as a visual feast for his sole enjoyment. The girl was his, both physically and artistically. Lani was a prisoner of his charcoal and paper as surely as her hands and feet were secured to the trundle bed's sturdy little corner posts. Diana Ladd Walker had no idea that her interviewer had spent several delightful morning hours being alternately tortured and exhilarated by the process of re-creating that delectably innocent body on paper; that, by controlling his aching to take Lani—because it would have been so easy to do so—he had reveled in the rational victory of denying that physical craving, that fundamental bodily urge. So far Mitch's violation of Lani Walker had been mainly intellectual, but that wouldn't last forever.

"Sorry about the delay, sir," the bartender said. "Can I help you now?"

"A glass of chardonnay for the lady," Mitch Johnson said. "And a glass of tonic with lime for me."

For the first half hour of the Monty Lazarus interview, the questions followed such a well-worn track that Diana could have given the answers in her sleep.

"How long have you been writing?" he asked.

"Twenty-five years, give or take."

"You must have studied writing in school, right?"

Diana shook her head. "No," she said. "I applied for the creative writing program here at the university, but I wasn't admitted. I became a teacher instead."

"That's right," Monty said. "I remember something about that from the book. Your husband was admitted using material you had actually written while you weren't allowed in, and Andrew Carlisle turned out to be the instructor."

Diana nodded. There didn't seem to be anything to add.

"Did you and he ever talk about that?" Monty asked.

"About what?"

"About the fact that he had admitted the wrong student, that he had given your place to someone who turned out to have far less talent."

"We never discussed it," Diana said. "There wasn't any need. After all, I won, didn't I?"

"What do you mean by that?"

"Professor Carlisle didn't let me into his class, but I got to be a writer anyway."

"Where did you go to school?"

"The University of Oregon," she answered. "I got my M.Ed. from the University of Arizona."

Monty Lazarus continued to ask questions that reeked of numbing familiarity. Diana had answered the same questions dozens of times before, including two weeks earlier on *The Today Show.*

"How did you sell your first book?"

"I submitted it to an agent I met at a writer's conference up in Phoenix."

"And how long have you been writing full-time?"

"Until I married my husband Brandon, my second husband, I had a full-time teaching job out on the reservation and only wrote during the summers. That's *Tohono O'oth-ham*—spelled T-O-H-O-N-O new word O'-O-T-H-H-A-M, by the way. The school where I taught is in Topawa, south of

Sells, about seventy or so miles from here. After Brandon and I married, I cut back to substitute teaching. I did that for about three years, and I've been writing full-time ever since."

As Diana went through the motions of answering the questions, it occurred to her that if Monty Lazarus had actually read her book, he would have known the answers to some of those questions without having to ask. She remembered dealing with many of them as part of the "back" story in *Shadow of Death*.

She bit back the temptation of mentioning to her interviewer that it might have been a good idea for him to do his homework. It wasn't at all smart to tell an interviewer how to do his job, not unless she wanted a hatchet job to appear in the periodical in question. Instead, Diana Ladd Walker answered the questions with as much poise and humor as she could muster.

Having filled several pages with cryptic notes, Monty Lazarus finally put down his pen. "Okay," he said. "Enough of that. Now, let's turn to the more personal stuff.

"Where do you live?"

"Gates Pass, west of Tucson."

"For how long?"

"Since 1969. I moved there right after my first husband died. Brandon Walker came to live there after we got married in 1976."

"Where were you from originally?"

"Joseph, Oregon," she said. "My father ran the town garbage dump. We lived in the caretaker's house the whole time I was growing up."

"So yours is pretty much one of those Horatio Alger stories," Monty Lazarus offered.

Diana smiled. "You could say so."

"And do you have children?"

"Yes."

For the first time in the whole interview, she felt suddenly wary and uneasy. That was stupid, because she had answered all these same questions time and again. She took a deep breath.

"In 1975 I was a widow raising an only son, a six-year-old child. In 1976, Brandon and I married. He had two children, two sons. In 1980 we adopted a fourth child, our daughter, Lani."

"Four," Monty Lazarus repeated. "And where are they all now?"

Maybe knowing that question would automatically follow the first one was the source of some of her anxiety. She opted for putting all the cards on the table at once.

"The two older boys were Brandon's. My one stepson disappeared years ago while he was still in high school."

"He ran away from home?"

"Yes. At this point, he's missing and presumed dead. His older brother got himself in trouble and ended up in prison in Florence. I believe he's out now, but I have no idea where he's living. We don't exactly stay in touch. The two younger ones, my son David, and our daughter, Lani, are fine. David just graduated from law school in Chicago, and Lani is a junior at University High School right here in Tucson."

Monty shook his head sympathetically. "It's tough," he said. "Raising kids is always a crapshoot. So it sounds as though you're running about fifty-fifty in the motherhood department."

"I guess so," Diana agreed. Fifty-fifty wasn't a score she was proud of. She would have liked to do better.

Monty Lazarus glanced down at his watch. "Yikes," he exclaimed. "We've been at this for over an hour. I'll go flag down a waitress. Can I get you anything? Another glass of wine, maybe?"

Diana shook her head. "I'd better switch to iced tea," she said. "No sugar, but extra lemon."

*   *   *

As Monty Lazarus sauntered away, Diana was left mulling his sardonic words about raising kids. Crapshoot. That just about covered it.

Tommy, Brandon's younger son, had walked out of their lives one summer afternoon between his freshman and sophomore years in high school. Over the years they had gradually come to terms with the idea that Tommy was probably dead—he had to be. The situation with Quentin wasn't nearly as clear-cut. Diana sometimes thought they would have been better off if Quentin had died as well.

The moment she met Quentin Walker, Diana recognized he was both smart and mean. Even as a ten-year-old, his conversation had shown intermittent flashes of intellectual brilliance. No, lack of brainpower had never been one of Quentin's problems. Curbing his tongue was, his tongue and his temper. He was manipulative and arrogant, angry and unforgiving. Not only that, by the time he was in high school, he had already developed a severe drinking problem.

Five years earlier, he had been driving drunk. He had crashed his four-wheel-drive pickup into a compact car, a Chevette, killing the woman driver and her two-year-old child. As if that weren't bad enough, the woman was six months pregnant. The baby was taken alive from his dead mother's womb, but he, too, had died three days later.

Brandon was still sheriff at the time of the trial, and the whole ordeal had been a nightmare for him. Not that he was responsible. Quentin was an adult and had to deal with his own difficulties. Brandon Walker's whole life had been committed to law and order, yet here was his son, a repeat drunk-driving offender, who had blithely killed three people. And when the judge had shipped Brandon Walker's son off to Florence for five years on two counts of vehicular homicide (the dead unborn fetus didn't count), it had almost broken Brandon's heart. It had seemed at the time that things couldn't get any worse. And then they did.

Three years and a half years after he was locked up,

shortly after Diana had started work on *Shadow of Death,* Brandon had come home from work and told her the latest bad news in the Quentin Walker department.

The moment Diana caught a glimpse of his face as Brandon stumbled into the house, she knew something was terribly wrong. His face was so gray she initially thought he might be having a heart attack.

"What's happened?" she had asked, hurrying to his side. "What's going on?"

Shaking his head, he walked past her proffered embrace, opened the refrigerator door, pulled out a pair of beers—one for each of them. He sank down beside the kitchen table and buried his face in his hands. Concerned, Diana sat down beside him.

"Brandon, tell me. What is it?"

"Quentin," he groaned. "Quentin again."

"What's he done now?"

"He's hooked up with a gang of extortionists up in Florence," Brandon answered. "They've been operating out of the prison, supposedly accepting bribes on my behalf. It's a protection racket. They've been telling people that if they don't pay up, something bad is going to happen to their building or business, without any cops being there to take care of things. In other words, if the marks don't fork over, they don't get any patrol coverage."

"But that's outrageous!" Diana exclaimed. "They're claiming you're behind it?"

"That's right."

"But that's the whole reason you were elected in the first place," Diana protested. "To clean things up and put an end to that kind of crap."

"Right." Brandon, staring into the depths of his beer bottle, answered without looking Diana in the eye.

"How did you find out?"

"Hank Maddern told me."

"Hank!" Diana echoed. "He's been retired for years. How did he find out?"

"One of the deputies—Hank wouldn't say which one—went to him with it and asked for advice as to what he should do about it. The deputy evidently thought *I* was in on it." Brandon's voice cracked with emotion. It took a minute or so before he could continue.

"Considering the well-known history of graft and corruption during Sheriff DuShane's watch, you can hardly blame the guy for thinking that. Thankfully, Hank and I go back a long way. He came straight to me with it."

"What are you going to do?"

Brandon sighed. "I already did it," he said. "I went straight to Internal Affairs and told them to check it out on the off chance that some of my officers are involved. I told them I'll cooperate in any way necessary, and that they should do whatever it takes to get to the bottom of it."

"What'll happen to Quentin?" Diana asked.

Brandon shook his head. "We're talking felonious activity, Diana. If the prosecutor gets a conviction, he'll spend a couple more years in prison. And when you're already in the slammer, what's another year or two? He won't give a damn, but it's going to be hell for us. Our lives will have to be an open book. We'll have to turn over all our bank records. The investigators will want to know just exactly how much money came in, where it came from, and where it's gone. I told them to have a ball. We've got nothing to hide."

In the bleak silence that followed that last statement, Brandon Walker slipped lower in his chair, leaning his weight against an arm that had dropped onto the table. "No matter what we did for that kid, it was never enough."

Diana reached out and put one hand over her husband's. "I'm sorry," she said.

He nodded. "I know," he murmured. "Me, too."

"It's not your fault, Brandon," Diana said. "You did everything you could."

He looked up at her then, his eyes full of hurt and outrage. And tears. "But he's my son, for Chrissakes!" he croaked. "How the hell could my own son do this to me? How could he go against everything I've ever stood for and believed in?"

"Quentin isn't you," she said. "He made his own choices . . ."

"All of them bad," Brandon interjected.

". . . and once again, he's going to have to suffer the consequences."

Even as Diana uttered the too pat words, she knew they were a cop-out. She was hurt, too, but the real agony belonged solely to Brandon. After all, Quentin was his son. With Tommy evidently out of the picture for good, Quentin was the only "real" son Brandon Walker had left, which made the betrayal that much worse.

For years they had listened while Janie, Brandon's ex-wife, made one excuse after another about why Quentin and Tommy were the way they were. In Janie's opinion, the critical missing ingredient had always been Brandon's fault and responsibility, one way or the other, although whenever Brandon had tried to exert any influence on the kids, Janie had continually run interference. Any attempt on Brandon's part to discipline the boys had met with implacable resistance from their mother. Diana had seen from the beginning that it was a lose/lose situation all the way around.

"Can you imagine what Janie's going to say when she gets wind of this? She's going to blame me totally, just like she did with the accident."

"You're the sheriff," Diana had said. "You have to do your job. Remember, Quentin's a big boy now—a grown-up. If he's turned himself into a criminal, then it's on his head, not yours."

But that wasn't entirely true. Quentin was the one who was prosecuted for his part in the extortion scheme, and a slick lawyer got him off but when the next election came around, Brandon Walker lost. His opponent, Bill Forsythe, managed to imply that there had to be some connection between Quentin's illegal but unproven activities and his father, the sheriff.

Diana thought that Brandon could have and should have fought back harder against the Forsythe campaign of character assassination, but somehow his heart wasn't in it. When the fight ended in defeat, he retreated into the Gates Pass house and lived in virtual seclusion while focusing all his energies and frustration on cutting and stacking wood.

Monty Lazarus returned to Diana trailed by a waitress bearing a tray laden with glasses of iced tea as well as a bowl of salsa and a basket of chips.

"I thought I'd order a little food—something to keep up our strength." He grinned. "Now where were we? Oh, that's right. You were telling me about your daughter. University High School. That's a prep school of some kind, isn't it?"

Diana nodded.

"So she must be smart."

"Yes. She hopes to study medicine someday."

"And pretty?"

Once again she felt that vague sense of unease, but she shook it off.

"I suppose some people would say so," Diana said dismissively. "But aren't we getting a little off track?"

"You're right," Monty Lazarus said. "Have some chips and salsa. When I'm hungry, my mind tends to wander."

Buying the car had been fun for Quentin Walker. Early on he had settled on a faded orange, '79 Ford Bronco 4-by-4 XLT, with alloy wheels, a cassette deck, towing package, a newly rebuilt 302 engine, and a slight lift. He'd had to go through the usual car-buying bullshit with that cocky bastard of a salesman who acted like he was working for a Cadillac dealership instead of hawking beaters at a South Tucson joint called Can Do Deals Used Cars.

Winston Morris, in his smooth, double-breasted khaki-colored suit and tie, had taken one look at Quentin's mud-spattered boots and figured him for some kind of low-life without a penny to his name. Quentin had willingly put up with all the crap, waiting for the inevitable moment when Winston would finally get around to saying, "What's it going to take to put you in this car today?"

Quentin had leaned back in his chair and casually crossed one leg over the other. "You've got it listed at forty-two hundred. I'll give you thirty-five, take it or leave it."

The sad look that came over Winston's face was as predictable as his initial closing question. "You can't be serious. We're in this business to sell cars, not give them away."

But when Quentin got up to leave, the bargaining had begun in earnest. Quentin ended up paying thirty-six fifty. But the most fun came when the dickering was done and Winston had said, "How do you intend to pay for this?"

That was the supreme moment, the one Quentin had been salivating over all morning. Nonchalantly, he had reached for his wallet and opened it. One by one he drew out four of the thousand-dollar bills and laid them down on the desk in front of the salesman. "You can give me change, can't you?"

The look on Winston's face as he scooped up the four bills had been well worth the price of admission. He had taken the money and disappeared into his sales manager's office. He was in there for a long time. No doubt, everybody there was busy trying to figure out whether or not the money was counterfeit. Eventually, though, he came back out and finished up the paperwork.

Leaving the lot, Quentin still felt good. After not driving a car for six years, it was strange to be back behind the wheel again, odd to be in his own vehicle. Knowing what would most likely be waiting for him in the desert, he stopped at a grocery store and picked up a six-pack of beer, a flashlight, and several spare batteries, as well as a large box—an empty toilet-paper box. Then he headed out of town.

The good mood lasted for a few miles more, but as soon as he crossed the pass and could see the mountain ahead of him, a pall of gloom settled over him. He popped open the first can and took a sip of beer, hoping to hold off the blanket of despair that was closing in on him.

If only his father hadn't made him take Davy out to the *charco* that day. Then, none of the rest of it would have happened.

"Do I have to?" Quentin had whined to his father on the phone. "Me and Tommy have better things to do today than haul Davy Ladd out into the desert to put a bunch of plastic flowers on something that isn't even a grave."

"Listen here, young man," Brandon Walker said. "We're not talking options here. Where did you get that car you're driving?"

"From Grandma," Quentin conceded grudgingly. "You bought it for us from Grandma Walker."

"That's right. Diana and I *both* bought it for you," Brandon corrected. "As long as we're paying for gas and insurance, you'd better straighten up and help out when required to do so. Is that clear?"

"I guess," Quentin said. "But do we have to do it today?"

"Yes. Today is the anniversary of Gina Antone's death. Rita's too busy with Lani to take care of the shrine herself and it would be too hard on her anyway, so Davy's agreed to do it for her. It's very important to Rita that the work be done today."

"Well, I'm not doing any of it."

"Nobody's asking you to. Davy will do whatever needs doing. Brian will probably help out too, if he can come along." Now that Quentin was being slightly more agreeable, Brandon was willing to be conciliatory as well. "I'll send along enough money so the four of you can stop off at the trading post and have a hamburger or a burrito on your way back. How does that sound?"

"Okay, I guess," Quentin said.

Showing off, Quentin had driven the aging '68 New Yorker like a maniac on the way out to the reservation. Tommy was game for anything, but Quentin was waiting to see if he could scare either Davy or Brian into telling him to slow down. Neither one of them said a word. The bad part came, though, when they turned off Coleman Road and headed for the *charco*.

Quentin was still going too fast when they came around a blind curve that concealed a sandy wash. He jammed on the brakes. Seconds later, the Chrysler was mired in sand up to its hubcaps. By then they were only half a mile or so away from the *charco* and the shrine. Brian and Davy had set off with their flowers and candles. Meantime, Quentin left Tommy to watch the car while he hiked out to the highway to find someone to pull the Chrysler out of the sand.

That took time. He was gone over an hour. When he came back with a guy with a four-wheel-drive pickup and a chain, Tommy was nowhere to be found. The car was out of the sand, the guy with the pickup was long gone, and Brian and Davy were back from doing their shrine duties before Tommy finally showed up.

"Where the hell have you been?" Quentin growled.

"I got bored," Tommy told him. "But you'll never guess what I found. There's a cave up there," he said, pointing back up the flank of Kitt Peak. "It's a big one. I tried going inside, but when it got too dark, I came back." He wrenched open the passenger door, opened the glove box, and took out the flashlight Brandon Walker insisted they keep there in case of trouble.

"Come on," he said. "I'll show you."

"We can't do that," Davy said.

"Can't do what?"

"Go in the caves on *Ioligam,*" Davy told him.

"Why not?"

"Because they belong to the Indians. They're sacred."

"That's bullshit and you know it!" Tommy said. "Caves belong to everybody. What about Colossal Cave? What about Carlsbad Caverns? Besides, it's Kitt Peak anyway, not 'chewing gum.' "

"Ioligam," Davy repeated, but by then Tommy was already headed back up the mountain. Quentin paused for a moment. He himself wasn't wild about exploring caves, but the idea of doing something Davy was against proved to be too much of a temptation. "If Tommy's going, I'm going," he said. With that, Quentin set off after his brother.

"Why are the caves sacred?" Brian asked as he and Davy trudged reluctantly up the mountain after the others.

"Nana *Dahd* told me that it's because that's where *I'itoi* goes for summer vacation," Davy answered. "But Looks At Nothing told me once that back when the Apaches attacked the village that used to be here, the village called Rattlesnake Skull, the only people who lived were some little kids who hid out in a cave. Later on, the *Tohono O'othham* found out that one of the girls from Rattlesnake Skull had betrayed her people to the *Ohb.* Some hunters went looking for her. When they found her, they brought her back and shut her up in one of the caves on the mountain to die."

With three older brothers, Brian Fellows was used to having his leg pulled. "Is that the truth or is that just a story?" he asked.

Davy Ladd shrugged. "I don't know," he said. "Looks At Nothing told it like it was the truth, but maybe it is just a story."

They had followed the older boys to the entrance of the cave and then waited outside until the flashlight gave out, forcing Tommy and Quentin to emerge.

"It's beautiful in there," a gleeful Tommy reported. "Unbelievable! It's too bad you're both chickens."

"We're not chickens," Davy said quietly.

Quentin laughed. "Yes, you are. Come on, chicky-chicky. Let's go have that hamburger. I'm starved."

During the next couple of weeks, Tommy had persuaded Quentin to spend every spare moment exploring the cave. When they ran out of money for gas and flashlight batteries, they stole bills from their mother's purse. And even Quentin was forced to agree it was worth it. The cave was magnificent—magnificent and awful at the same time. It was so much more than either of them had imagined and yet it was terribly frustrating. They had found something wonderful and amazing, beautiful beyond all imagining. Gleaming wet stalactites hung down like thousands of rocky icicles. Stalagmites rose up out of watery pools like so many gray looming ghosts. Here and there, pieces of crystal reflected back light like a thousand winking eyes. Tommy was dying to share their discovery.

"You know what'll happen if anybody finds out," Quentin had warned his brother. "They'll kick our asses out of there and we'll never get to go back."

"Will they ever open it up? Maybe charge admission like they do at Colossal Cave?"

"Don't be stupid, Tommy. You heard what Davy said. It's sacred or something."

It wasn't the first time Quentin and Tommy had squared off against the rest of the world. The two of them had been keeping secrets—some worse than others—all their lives. They were used to it, and they kept this one, too.

Three weeks after finding the cave, they ventured far enough inside the first chamber to locate the narrow passage that led to the second. The first room had been so rough and wet that it was almost impossible to walk in it. Starting in the passage, the second one seemed dryer, and it had a dirt floor, as though someone had gone to the trouble of covering the rough surface so it would be easier to walk on it.

Inside the second chamber they had discovered the rock slide barring most of what had once been a second entrance to the cavern. And over against the far wall, much to both their horror and fascination, they had found the scattered pieces of a human skeleton.

"Hey, look at this?" Tommy said, picking up a bone and flinging it across the cave. "Maybe they left this guy here to guard these pots and to cast a spell over anybody who tries to take them."

Tommy Walker's imagination and his fascination with magic had always outstripped his older brother's. "Shut up, Tommy," Quentin said. "And leave those bones alone. What if they still carry some kind of disease or something?"

Shrugging, Tommy leaned down and picked up the first pot that came to hand. In the orange glow from the flashlight it looked gray or maybe beige. A black crosshatch pattern had been incised into the surface.

"I'll bet something like this would be worth a lot of money," he said thoughtfully. "How about if we take it to the museum over at the university and try to unload it? Whaddya think of that idea?"

"It might work," Quentin had agreed. "With all the gas we're buying these days, our budget could use a little help."

Together they had discussed which pot might best serve their immediate monetary purposes, settling eventually on the one Tommy had picked up in the first place. Carrying the pot in one hand and his flashlight in the other, Tommy had started back toward the main cavern. Quentin was several feet behind him, so he never saw exactly what happened. All he knew was he heard a noise, like something falling. He also heard the pot breaking into what sounded like a million pieces. When he came around the corner, Tommy was nowhere in sight.

"Tommy," he yelled. "What happened? Where'd you go?"

For an answer, he heard only dead silence, broken occasionally by the drip of water.

"Tommy, come on now. Don't play games," Quentin said, fighting back a sudden surge of fear. "This is no time for jokes. We have to get out of here and head home. It's getting late."

But still there was no answer. None at all.

Slowly, carefully, Quentin had begun to search the area. After ten minutes or so, he found the hole, almost killing himself in the process. Just off the path they had used to get to the passage, there was something that looked like a shadow. But when Quentin shone his light that way he found instead a shaft, some twenty feet deep, with Tommy lying still as death at the bottom with his feet in a murky pool of water.

"Tommy!" Quentin shouted again. "Are you all right? Can you hear me?" But Tommy Walker didn't answer and didn't move.

Terrified, Quentin raced out of the cave. In honor of their spelunking adventures, the two boys had managed to amass a fair collection of discarded rope. Gathering an armload of rope, Quentin dashed back up the mountain. Inside the cave, working feverishly, he managed to rappel himself down the side of the shaft. Once there, he was relieved to find that Tommy was still alive, still breathing.

"Tommy, wake up. You've gotta wake up so we can get out of here." But there was no response. Finally, desperate and not knowing what else to do, Quentin tied the rope around his unconscious brother's chest—fastening it under both his arms so it wouldn't slip off. Then he climbed back up to haul Tommy out.

It had worked, too. With almost superhuman effort and after a half-hour struggle, Quentin finally dragged Tommy's dead weight up out of the shaft. He heaved him out of the hole and rolled him onto the jagged floor of the cave like a landed fish, but by then Tommy Walker wasn't breathing anymore. He was dead.

"Goddamn it!" Quentin had screamed, gazing down at

his brother's still and rapidly cooling form. "How dare you go and die on me! How dare you!"

He had started to go for help even then, but halfway to the car the second time, he changed his mind. What if, in the process of pulling Tommy up and out, Quentin had done something to him—what if he had broken something else, caused some other damage that hadn't happened in the fall? What if it was Quentin's fault that his brother was dead? And maybe it was anyway. After all, Quentin was the one who had driven them there in the first place. It was Quentin's car, Quentin's driver's license, and Quentin's gas.

And finally, because he didn't know what else to do; because he didn't know how to go about beginning to face the enormous consequences of what he had done, he climbed into the car and drove away. He went home. Later that night, when Janie asked where Tommy was, Quentin said he didn't know. He claimed he had no idea.

And a day later, Quentin Walker had reluctantly agreed, right along with everyone else, that for some unknown reason his brother Tommy must have run away.

From that day on, no amount of drinking ever held the awful memories quite at bay. In his sleep, Quentin Walker often dreamed about his brother lying limp and lifeless on the floor of the cave. And now, after all the intervening years, for the first time, Quentin Walker was headed back there.

He didn't know for sure if Tommy's body was still in the cave. It probably was, but by the time Mitch Johnson arrived on the scene, it wouldn't be there anymore. Quentin couldn't afford for Tommy to be found now. Back at the beginning, when it first happened, people might have believed it was an accident. If they found out about it now, who would believe that story, especially if it was coming from Quentin Walker, from somebody who was an ex-con?

Tommy Walker had been missing all these years, and his brother Quentin was determined that he stay that way—missing forever.

8

As the two men led the woman back toward the village, many of the Little People went away, but there was always a swarm of bees or wasps to guard the woman. On the fourth day of the journey, the woman pointed to the sky and began to dig holes in the ground. And the bees were very excited. They sang, "Rain, rain, rain!"

In two more steps of Tash—the Sun—in what the Milgahn would call hours, the clouds appeared, and the rains came. The two men filled their water baskets and were glad. But the happiest of all was Jeweth—the Earth.

When the rain was over, the two men wanted to continue on, but the woman would not go. So the two men left the woman some pinole and went back to their own people. After a time the Indians returned to their own country. When they came to the place where the two men had left the strange woman, they found many houses. This kihhim—this village—had been built by people from the south. They said *they had come to be near the great Medicine Woman of the* Tohono O'othham. Gohhim O'othham—*Old Limping Man*—*was curious and asked where this Medicine Woman lived. The people of the village took him to a house made of sticks of ocotillo and covered with mud. There were two rooms in this house. The inside room was dark with an odd noise in it—a strange kind of buzzing.*

When Kulani O'oks—*Medicine Woman*—*came out, Old Limping Man saw it was the same woman whom the Little People had saved. And so this great Medicine Woman, whose name was* Mualig Siakam—*Forever Spinning*—*told Old Limping Man how she had been among strangers in the south. When she had returned alone to join her own people, the* Tohono O'othham, *she found her home village deserted. All the Desert People were gone. There was no water. The animals had gone too, and so had all the birds.*

And so this woman, who had been left alone in the burning desert, sent up a prayer for help. Pa-nahl—*the Bees*—*were the first to come. The Bees sent for help and brought* Wihpsh—*the Wasps. Then came* Mumuwali—*the Flies,* Komikam—*the Beetles, and* Totoni—*the Ants. They all came to help her, all the Little People who had not yet left the burning desert.*

The woman said the Little People had told her to go to sleep and they would watch over her. That was all she knew.

As the endless questions droned on, Diana was more than slightly bored. Megan, her publicist in New York, had given her such glowing advance notices on Monty Lazarus that Diana had expected him to be someone who would come up with an original take on the standard author interview. Then, just when she was about to decide the whole thing was destined to be a flop, Monty surprised her.

Sitting back in his chair, studying her over his glasses and under steepled fingers, he finally asked one of the questions she had been waiting and wanting to answer.

"Tell me," he said. "After all this time, what made you finally decide to write this book?"

"I wanted answers," she said. "And some closure."

"After almost twenty years?"

"It's twenty-one now. It was seventeen when I started. That's the thing about being a victim of violent crime. I don't think you ever get over it, not completely. If you let your guard down, the memories are always there, just under the surface, waiting to come flooding back and zing you when you least expect them. I thought that by facing Andrew Carlisle down, by once and for all confronting everything he did to me, that I could put it in the past. I thought that maybe I'd be able to finally reach the other side of the nightmare and gain some perspective."

"Did it work?"

"I don't know. The jury's still out. I still dream about him sometimes."

"About the rape itself? We could talk about that if you like."

After all the innocuous questions that had gone before, that one rocked her. It meant that Monty Lazarus had read *Shadow of Death* after all. Diana felt blood warming her cheeks.

"I've talked about the rape all I'm going to—in the book itself. Megan was supposed to tell you that subject was off limits. Not only that, if you've already read the book, why did you ask me all those other questions?" she asked. "You must have known the answers to most of that stuff."

Monty Lazarus smiled. His eyes were very blue—a startlingly intense sky blue that was almost the color of Garrison Ladd's. Almost the color of Davy's.

"When you're writing, how many drafts do you do on a book?" Monty asked.

Diana shrugged. "I don't know for sure. Three—four maybe. I can't tell. Every time I open up a chapter on the computer, I end up changing something. Maybe it's nothing more than shortening a sentence here and there or breaking up a paragraph in a different way so the words look better on the page. Sometimes I find places where I've used the same word twice within two or three lines. At that rate, everything's a different draft."

"And you're polishing as you go."

"Yes, always."

"Do things ever change in all that polishing?"

"Well, probably, but—"

"You see," Monty Lazarus said with a smile, "the reason I like to do in-depth interviews is that I want to hear what the person is saying in his or her own words—without all the polishing. Without all the real feelings and emotions cleaned up and taken out. Those are the things that never show up on the pages of a book.

"For instance, a little while ago we were talking about your marriage to Brandon Walker. When I asked how long you'd been married, you said twenty years. Were you aware, though, that when you told me that, there was a little half-smile playing around the corners of your mouth?"

"No," Diana conceded. "I wasn't aware of that."

"And when I asked you about your children and you started discussing your stepchildren, you looked as though you'd put what you thought was a piece of candy in your mouth and discovered, too late, that it was really dog shit. See what I mean?"

Diana smiled. "Yes," she said. "I suppose I do."

Monty Lazarus smiled in turn and then leaned back in his chair, regarding Diana thoughtfully over the low coffee table between them. "I want you to tell me a little about the process of this book. Did you seek out Andrew Carlisle, or was it the other way around?"

"He asked me," Diana said. "He wrote to me in care of my publisher."

"Let me get this straight. The man who killed your husband, and raped you, wrote you a letter and asked that you write his story? And despite everything that had happened before, despite all that history, you still agreed?"

"*Shadow of Death* tells both stories," Diana corrected. "His and mine."

"I'd have to say that the book is generally pretty un-flinching," Lazarus said. "Blazingly so at times, but there's a gap that I find puzzling."

"Which gap is that?"

"You barely mention the interviews themselves," Monty Lazarus said. "I'm assuming they took place in the state prison up at Florence, since that's where Carlisle was incarcerated. Is that true?"

"Yes," Diana said. "In the visiting room up there to begin with. Then later on, when he was hospitalized for symptoms related to AIDS, they let me interview him in the infirmary."

"But why didn't you talk about that?" Lazarus persisted. "It seems to me that's an important part of the story, for the victim to triumph over the perpetrator, as it were. For you to see your tormentor laid low—blind, crippled, horribly disfigured, and finally dying of AIDS. I'm surprised you didn't share that satisfaction with your readers, that sense of vindication."

"I didn't write about satisfaction or vindication because they weren't there," Diana answered quietly.

"They weren't?" Monty Lazarus asked. Then, after a moment, he added, "I'm sorry. I didn't mean to put words in your mouth. What did you feel then, when you met him again after all those years?"

"Horror," Diana said simply.

"Horror?" Lazarus repeated. "At the way he looked? Because of the burns on his face and chest? Because of his mangled arm?"

Diana shook her head. "No," she replied. "It had nothing at all to do with the way he looked. It was because of what he was—what he stood for."

"Which was?"

"Evil," she said. "Outside catechism classes, I had never actually met the devil before, somebody who could pass for

Satan. I was afraid that if I wrote about him that way, no one would believe me. He seemed to have an almost hypnotic effect on people, certainly on my first husband. If Andrew Carlisle told Garrison Ladd that black was white and vice versa, I think Gary would have gone to his death trying to prove it was true."

"I see," Monty said, writing something down in his notebook, but Diana Ladd Walker wasn't at all sure he understood. In fact, she wasn't entirely sure she did, either.

The morning of Diana's first scheduled interview with Andrew Carlisle had dawned clear and dry and hot. Already dressed for work himself, Brandon Walker lounged in the doorway between their bedroom and the master bath, drinking a cup of coffee and watching as his wife carefully applied her makeup.

"I could always take the day off and come along with you," he offered. "That way I'd be right there in case anything went wrong."

"Nothing's going to go wrong, Brandon," Diana said, trying to sound less anxious than she felt. "It isn't as though I'll be alone with him. There are guards. There'll be other visitors in the room as well. I'll be fine."

For a time after that, Brandon Walker sipped his coffee in silence. "Are you going to try to see Quentin while you're there?"

Diana put down her mascara brush. Her gaze met Brandon's in the neutral territory of the bathroom mirror's steamy reflection. "I could," she said finally. "Do you want me to?"

Brandon's older son had been locked up in the state penitentiary at Florence for months now. On occasion, Brandon and Diana had talked about driving up there to see him, but each time, Brandon had changed his mind and backed out at the last minute.

"I guess," he said hollowly. "I do want to know how Quent's doing. I just can't bring myself to go there to see him. Still, no matter what he's done, he's also my son. Nothing's going to change that. Since we've already lost Tommy, we can't very well just abandon Quentin, can we?"

Brandon looked away, but not before Diana glimpsed the anguished expression on his face. She tried to read that look, tried to fathom what was behind it. Betrayal? Despair? Pain? Anger?

"No," Diana agreed at last. "I don't suppose we can. I can't promise I'll see Quentin today. It depends on whether or not there's enough time left in visiting hours after the interview with Carlisle is over. If they'll let me, though, I will."

"Thanks, Di," Brandon said gruffly. "I appreciate it."

And it turned out that there had been enough time for Diana Ladd Walker to see both prisoners that day. She had been waiting in the Visitation Room, amidst a group of other women who, armed with whatever difficulties were besetting them on the outside, had come either to rail at or to share their woes with their husbands or boyfriends or sons. Diana had brought only a yellow pad and a pencil, along with a pervasive sense of dread.

As one door after another had clanged shut behind her, Diana felt a sudden resurgence of that long-ago fear. In her ignorance, she had thought of the house in Gates Pass as a safe haven, yet Carlisle had found a way inside the house and had attacked her there, despite her careful precautions and numerous locked doors. Maybe, here in the prison, despite the reassuring presence of guards and iron bars, her presumed safety might once again prove illusory.

Andrew Carlisle was here, and so was Diana Walker. She was already locked inside the same complex. Soon the two of them would be within the same four walls. Would she be able to stand it? For the first time, Diana's courage wavered. At that moment it would have taken only the smallest nudge from Brandon to convince her to walk away and forget the whole project.

Quaking, fighting an almost overpowering urge to bolt and run, Diana followed the escorting guards into the grimly functional prison Visitation Room. It was lit by sallow, artificial light that gave everyone in the place a jaundiced, sickly look. The walls were posted with rules and regulations, many of them made illegible by layers of graffiti. The chairs in the room were all bolted to the floor. It was a hard, desperate place where people with no hope waited to see loved ones who had even less.

The guard leading Diana took her directly to the far side of the room, where the wall was made of thick Plexiglas so yellowed and scratched that looking through it seemed more like peering through a veil of smutty L.A. smog than anything else. Directed to a chair, Diana sat and waited.

The last time she had seen Andrew Carlisle had been years earlier at his double murder trial. One of his arms—the one Bone had snapped in two at the wrist—had been encased in a heavy plaster cast, and his face had still been swathed in bandages. The prison warden had told Diana in advance of that first visit that the injured arm had been permanently damaged, leaving him with only limited use of his fingers.

The mangled arm was one thing—more Bone's doing than Diana's. What she dreaded seeing was his unbandaged face, the one into which she had flung a frying pan full of searing-hot bacon grease. That grease had been Diana's last desperate line of defense against Andrew Carlisle's brute force and sharp knife. The grease had worked far better than she could have hoped. He had fallen on the slick floor, clawing at his scorched face and howling in agony.

This day, though, when Carlisle was led into the room, there was no such mummylike mask to lessen the horrible impact of what she had done to him. The guard brought him into the room, seated him on a chair across from Diana, and then placed the intercom receiver, one used to communicate through the Plexiglas barrier, in his good hand. All the while, Diana could only sit and stare. The third-degree burns had molded his once chiseled features into a grotesquely twisted, lumpy grimace. They had also ruined his eyes. Andrew Carlisle was blind.

No amount of anticipation could have prepared Diana for the way he looked. It stunned her to think that she had intentionally inflicted that kind of injury on another human being. Still, faced with the same set of circumstances, she knew she would have made the same decision and fought him again with the same ferocity.

"I'm told I'm quite ugly these days," Andrew Carlisle said into the intercom mouthpiece as Diana picked up hers to listen. "They're supposedly doing remarkable things with skin transplants and plastic surgery these days, but not for convicted killers with AIDS. Nobody exactly jumped to the plate and offered to get me the best possible care back then, or now, either, for that matter. Come to think of it, I wonder? Doesn't denying someone proper medical care constitute cruel and unusual punishment? What do you think? Maybe I could take the Pima County Sheriff's Department to court and sue them for damages."

"I have no idea," Diana said. "That's up to you."

He laughed then. "You sound quite sure of yourself, Ms. Walker. Have you changed much then since I saw you last?"

"Changed how?"

"Anything," he replied. "You haven't turned into one of those born-again Christians, by any chance, have you?"

"No."

"Good." He sounded relieved. "After you agreed to come see me, I started worrying that maybe you had transformed yourself into one of those religious zealots. They are all eager to come pray over me to save my immortal soul. Some of them even want to grant me forgiveness."

Diana took a deep breath and managed to find her conversational sea legs. "No," she said. "You don't have to worry about that, Mr. Carlisle. I've never forgiven you, and I never will."

"Good," Andrew Carlisle replied. "Very good. I'm delighted to hear it. Now, tell me about the way you look."

"What about the way I look?"

"Are you very different from the way you were that night we were together? You're the last person I ever saw or ever will see," he added, as his puckered mouth twisted into an oddly one-sided smile. "As a consequence, Ms. Walker, I remember everything about that night as vividly as if it had happened yesterday or the day before. I remember every detail about you, and I would suppose that you remember me in much the same way. We were both operating in what the experts call a non-drug-induced altered state of consciousness."

"My hair is turning gray," Diana answered, carefully keeping her voice even. "I'm over fifty. I wear glasses. Two pairs of glasses, actually—one for distance and one for reading."

"I'm far more interested in your body," Andrew Carlisle said.

Some blind people seem to gaze off into the far distance when they speak. Andrew Carlisle's opaque, sightless eyes seemed to pry directly into Diana's very being. She could barely breathe. An involuntary shudder ran up and down her spine while a hot flush covered her face. She wanted nothing more than to race to the door. She wanted out. She longed to be away from this monster, to be back outside in the straightforward discomfort of the hot desert air.

This must be what Brandon was trying to warn me about, she thought, fighting back panic.

When Brandon had said she would be putting herself at risk, he must have seen that even though Andrew Carlisle would not be able to harm her physically, he might still be able to invade her mind and infect her soul.

Pulling herself together, Diana sat up straight and

squared her shoulders. When she spoke, she willed her voice not to quaver.

"Let's get one thing straight, Mr. Carlisle," she said. "I'm the one calling the shots here. If you want to do this project, we're going to do it my way. Basic ground rule number one is that we don't talk about that night. Not now, not ever!"

"But that's pretty much the whole point, isn't it?" Carlisle said, smiling his ruined smile. "Everything that happened before led up to it, and everything afterward led away from it."

"That night isn't *my* point," Diana returned. "And I'm the one writing the book. If you don't like it, hire yourself another writer."

"Hire?" Carlisle croaked. "What do you mean, hire? I already told you I can't afford to pay you anything."

"I'm being paid, all right," Diana answered. "My agent has pitched the idea to my editor in New York. The book I'm writing will be written, and I will be paid. The only question is whether or not any of your point of view actually appears in print. That depends on how well you behave, on whether or not you agree to do things my way."

Diana suspected that Andrew Carlisle was a vain man who was prepared to go to any length in order to be immortalized in print. He must have realized that Diana Ladd Walker was his best chance for getting there. In this case, Diana's instincts were good. Her threat of cutting his perspective out of the project immediately delivered the required result.

"All right," he agreed grudgingly. "I won't mention it again. So where do we start?"

"From the beginning," Diana said. "With your family and your childhood. Where you were born and where you grew up. I'd also like to interview any living relatives."

"Like my mother, you mean?" he asked.

Diana remembered being told that Andrew Carlisle's mother had been there in the yard at Gates Pass the night of her son's attack. Myrna Louise Spaulding had ridden down to Tucson from her home in Tempe with a homicide detective named G. T. Farrell. At the time Diana had been too preoccupied with everything else to notice. Later on, during the trial, Myrna Louise had been conspicuous in her absence. Diana had mistakenly assumed the woman was dead.

"You mean your mother's still alive?" Diana asked.

"More or less. She lives in one of those marginal retirement homes in Chandler. From the sound of it, I'd say it's a pretty awful place, but I doubt she can afford any better."

"Does she come here to see you?"

"Not anymore. She used to. The first time I was here. Still, once a year, on my birthday, she sends me a box of chocolates. See's Assorted. I've never bothered to tell her I hate the damn things. She's my mother, after all, so you'd think she'd remember that I never liked chocolate, not even when I was little."

"If you don't like the chocolates she sends you, what do you do with them, then?" Diana asked. "Give them away?"

Carlisle grinned. "Are you kidding? The guy in the cell next to me would kill for one of 'em, so I flush them down the toilet. One at a time. It drives him crazy."

Another shiver of chills flashed through Diana's body.

"Getting back to establishing ground rules," Andrew Carlisle continued. "How do you want to do this? We could probably sit here chatting this way, or else I could let you review some of the material I've already put together. Some of it is taped, some is on disk. I could print it out for you. That way, you could take it with you, go over it at your leisure, and then you could come back later so we could discuss it."

"How did you get it on disk?" Diana asked.

He gestured with his damaged arm. "I've learned to be a one-handed touch typist," he said. "Fortunately, this is one of those full-service prisons. Inmates are allowed to have access to computers in the library so they can prepare their own writs. I do that, by the way. Compose writs for those less fortunate than myself—the poor bastards who mostly can't read or write. Someone else has to do the editing and run the spell-checker. In a pinch, you could probably do that."

"I suppose we can try it that way." Diana did her best to sound reluctant, although in truth she was delighted at the prospect of any option that might spare her spending unlimited periods of time, shut up in this awful room, sitting face-to-face with this equally awful man.

"When can you have the first segment done?" she asked.

"A week or so," he said. "Sorting out the details of my childhood shouldn't take too long. It wasn't particularly happy or memorable. I doubt there'll be very much to reminisce about."

Diana raised her hand and beckoned to the guard. "I think we're through here," she said.

The guard glanced at his watch. "There's still plenty of time," he said. "Would you like to see your stepson, then?"

"Yes, please," Diana said.

Ten minutes after Andrew Carlisle was led from the room, the guard returned with Quentin Walker in tow.

"Oh," he said, his face registering disappointment as soon as he saw her. "It's you. I was hoping it was my mother. What do you want?"

A year and a half in prison had done nothing to diminish Quentin Walker's perpetual swagger.

"I came to see someone else, but I thought I'd stop by and check on you to see if there's anything you need."

"What exactly do you have in mind?" Quentin returned. "An overnight pass would be great. Better yet, how about commuting my sentence to time served? That would be very nice. And you might bring along a girl next time. Since I'm not married, I don't qualify for conjugal visits, but I'll bet my dear old dad could pull a string or two and help me keep my manhood intact."

"I don't think so," Diana replied. "Your father's not involved in this in any way. I was thinking more in terms of books or writing materials."

The superior smile on Quentin Walker's face shifted into a chilly sneer. "Writing and reading materials?" he asked. "Are we suddenly focused on educating poor lost Quent? Trying to make up for the difference between what you guys did for precious little Davy and that baby squaw you dragged home and what you two did for Tommy and me? I don't think it's going to work. Let's say it's too little, too late."

If sibling rivalry was bad, Diana realized, stepsibling rivalry was infinitely worse.

"This has nothing to do with David and Lani," she said evenly. "And I didn't come here to argue." She stood up. "Why don't we just forget I asked."

"Good idea," Quentin returned. "We'll do that. I don't need anything from you, not now and not ever."

"Good," Diana said. "At least that makes our relationship clear."

"So that's how you did it then?" Monty Lazarus asked. For a moment Diana wasn't sure what he was asking. "He gave you access to the material he had written?"

"Yes."

"But there's not really any acknowledgment of that in your book, is there? Shouldn't there have been?"

The question was a sly one, and Monty Lazarus kept his eyes focused on her face as he asked it. Realizing she was about to fall victim to a case of ambush journalism, Diana tried to play dumb.

"I'm not sure I understand what you're saying."

"If you used Andrew Carlisle's written material, shouldn't you have said that instead of passing it off as your own work?"

It took real effort to hold off a reflexive tightening of the muscles across her jaw. "It is my own work," she said coldly. "All of it. I did my own research, conducted my own interviews."

"Sorry," Monty Lazarus said. "I didn't mean any offense."

The hell you didn't, you bastard! Diana thought. She took a careful sip of her iced tea before she trusted herself enough to speak. "Of course not," she said.

Her reaction was so blatant that it was all Mitch Johnson could do to keep from bursting out laughing. And if she was prickly when it came to questions concerning her literary integrity, he wondered what would happen when they veered off into more personal topics.

"What kinds of interviews?" he asked.

"I tracked Andrew Carlisle's mother down at her retirement home up in Chandler. I thought hearing about him from her might help me understand him better. But he was already several moves ahead of me there."

Mitch Johnson knew exactly what Diana Ladd Walker was leading up to—the tapes, of course. He and Andy had discussed Andy's giving them to her in great detail, long before it happened. But he had to ask, had to convince her to tell him.

"What are you talking about?" he asked.

"Andrew Carlisle was a master at mind games, Mr. Lazarus," Diana answered. "At the time we started the project, I still didn't understand that."

"Games?" he repeated. "What kind of games are we talking about?"

"Andrew Carlisle was toying with me, Mr. Lazarus, the same way a cat torments a captive mouse."

So am I, Mitch Johnson thought, concealing the beginnings of an unintentional smile behind his iced-tea glass.

"In the beginning," Diana continued, "I don't think he had any intention of my writing the book."

"Really. That's surprising," Monty returned. "Why, then, did he bother to write to you in the first place?"

"Of all his victims," she said slowly, "I'm the one who got away. Not only that, even before this book, I had achieved a kind of prominence in writing that Andrew Carlisle could never hope for. I think that ate at him for years. After all, I'm somebody he didn't consider worthy of being one of his students."

"That's right," Monty Lazarus said. "I remember now. Your husband was admitted to the writing program Professor Carlisle taught, but you weren't. Your husband—your first husband, that is—was he a writer, too? Did Garrison Ladd ever have anything published?"

"No," she answered. "He never did."

"But he was enrolled in Carlisle's class at the time of his death. Presumably he was working on something, then. What was it?"

Diana shook her head. "I have no idea," she answered. "I'm pretty sure there was a partially completed manuscript, but I never read it. The thing disappeared in all the confusion after Gary's death. I don't know what happened to it."

"Wouldn't it be interesting to know what was in it?"

Mitch asked the speculative question deftly like a *picador* sticking a tormenting pic into the unsuspecting bull's neck. And it did its intended work. It pleased him to see her struggle with her answer. She took a deep breath.

"No," she said finally. "I don't think knowing that would serve any useful purpose at all. Whatever Gary was writing, it had nothing at all to do with Andrew Carlisle's focus on me, which, in my opinion, boils down to nothing more or less than professional jealousy."

Oh, no, Mitch wanted to tell her. *It's far more complex than that.* Instead, Monty Lazarus looked down at his notes and frowned. "Let's go back to something you said just a minute ago, something about Carlisle being a couple of moves ahead of you. Something about him never really intending for you to write the book. If that was the case, what was the point?"

"He was hoping to humiliate me publicly," Diana answered. "I think he thought he could get me to make a public commitment to writing the book and then force me to back out of it. But it didn't work. I wrote the book anyway."

For the first time, Mitch was surprised. Diana's answer was right on the money. Andy had told him that he didn't think she'd have guts enough to go through with it. That was another instance, one of the first ones Mitch had noticed, where Andy Carlisle's assessment of any given situation had turned out to be dead wrong.

"It still doesn't make much sense," Monty said, making a show of dusting crumbs of tortilla chips out of his lap.

Diana knew it did make sense, but only if you had all the other pieces of the puzzle. Monty Lazarus didn't have access to those. No one did, no one other than Diana. Those were the very things she had left out of the book, the ugly parts she had never mentioned to anyone, including Brandon Walker.

She had absolutely no intention of telling the whole story to Monty Lazarus, either. Those things were hers alone—Diana Ladd Walker's dirty little secrets. Instead, she tossed off a too-casual answer, hoping it would throw him off the trail.

"Let's just say it was a grudge match," Diana said. "Andrew Philip Carlisle hated my guts."

Almost a month after that first interview with Carlisle up in Florence, Diana was still waiting for the first written installment, which had taken far longer for him to deliver than he had said it would.

Davy was home from school for a few weeks. Over the Fourth of July weekend, Diana and Brandon had planned to take Lani and Davy up to the White Mountains to visit some friends who owned a two-room cabin just outside Payson. The four-day outing was scheduled to start Thursday afternoon, as soon as Brandon came home from work. Fate in the form of a demanding editor intervened when the Federal Express delivery man came to the door at nine o'clock Thursday morning. The package he delivered contained the galleys for her next book, *The Copper Baron's Wife,* along with an apologetic note from her editor saying the corrections needed to be completed and ready to be returned to New York on Tuesday morning.

"I'd better stay home and work on them," she said to Brandon on the phone that day when she called him at his office. "You know as well as I do that I can't do a good job on galleys when we're camped out with a houseful of people up in Payson. I have to be able to concentrate, but you and the kids are welcome to go. Just because I have to work doesn't mean everybody else has to suffer."

Brandon had protested, but in the end he had taken Lani and Davy and the three of them had gone off without her. Once they were piled in the car and headed for Payson, Diana had locked herself up with the galleys and worked her way through the first hundred pages of the book before she gave up for the night and went to bed. The next morning, when she went out to bring in the newspaper, she found an envelope propped against the front door. Although it was addressed to her, it hadn't been mailed. Someone had left it on the porch overnight.

Curious, she had torn the envelope open and found a cassette tape—that and nothing else. No note, no explanation. She had taken the tape inside to her office and popped it into the cassette player she kept on the bookshelf beside her desk.

When the tape first began playing, there was no sound—none at all. Distracted by a headline at the top of the newspaper, Diana was beginning to assume that the tape was blank when she heard a moan—a long, terrible moan.

"Please," a woman's voice whispered. "Mr. Ladd, please . . ."

Diana had been holding the newspaper in one hand and a cup of coffee in the other. As soon as she heard her former husband's name, she dropped both the paper and the cup. The paper merely fell back to the surface of the desk. The cup, however, crashed to the bare floor, shattering on the Saltillo tile and sending splatters of coffee and shards of cup from one end of the room to the other.

Diana leaned closer to the recorder and turned up the volume. "Mr. Ladd," the girl's voice said again. "Please. Let me go."

"No help there, little lady," a man's voice said. "He's out cold. Can't hear a word you're saying."

The voice was younger, but Diana recognized it after a moment. Andrew Carlisle's. Unmistakably Andrew Carlisle's and . . . the other? Could it be Gina Antone's? No. That wasn't possible! It couldn't be!

But a few agonizing exchanges later, Diana realized it was true. The other voice *did* belong to Gina Antone all right, to someone suffering the torments of the damned.

"Please, mister," the girl pleaded helplessly, her voice barely a whisper. "Please don't hurt me again. Please . . ." The rest of what she might have said dissolved into a shriek followed by a series of despairing sobs.

"But that's what you're here for, isn't it? Don't you remember telling us that you were taking us to a bad place? It turns out you were right. This is a bad place, my dear. A very bad place."

There was a momentary pause followed by another spine-tingling scream that seemed to go on forever. Diana had risen to her feet as if to fend off a physical attack. Now she slumped backward into the chair while the infernal tape continued to play. Gradually the scream subsided until there was nothing left but uncontrollable, gasping sobs.

"My God," Diana whispered aloud. "Did he tape the whole thing?"

Soon it became clear that he had. It was a ninety-minute tape, forty-five minutes per side. Halfway through the tape, the girl began passing out. It happened over and over again. Each time he revived her—brought her back to consciousness with splashes of water and with slaps to her face so he could continue the terrible process. Sick with revulsion, Diana realized he was orchestrating and prolonging her ordeal so the whole thing would be there. On tape. Every bit of it, even the horrifying finale where, after first announcing his intentions for the benefit of his unseen audience, Andrew Carlisle had bitten off Gina Antone's nipple.

Shaken to the core, Diana listened to the whole thing. Not because she wanted to but because she was incapable of doing anything else. She sat in the chair as though mesmerized, as though stricken by some sudden paralysis that rendered her unable to make the slightest movement, unable to reach across to the tape player and switch it off. Unchecked tears streamed down her face and dripped unnoticed into the mess of splattered coffee and broken china.

And when it was finally over, when Gina Antone's awful death was finished at last and the recorder clicked off, Diana leaned over and threw up into the mess of coffee and broken cup.

For a while after that she still couldn't move. Carlisle had made it last that whole time. He had tortured the girl for a carefully calculated ninety minutes. And that was just the part he had taped. From the sound of it there must have been some preliminaries that had occurred even before that. And for inflicting that kind of appalling torture, for premeditating, planning, and savoring every ugly moment of that appalling inhumanity, what had happened to Andrew Carlisle?

A superior court judge had allowed him to plead guilty to a charge of second-degree manslaughter. The torture death of Gina Antone hadn't even merited a charge of murder in the first degree. The State of Arizona had extracted a price of six short years from Andrew Carlisle in exchange for

Gina Antone's suffering. Six years. After that, he had been allowed to go free. Free to kill again.

Stunned, Diana sat for another half-hour, trying to decide what to do. There was no sense in turning the tape over to the authorities. What would they do with it? What *could* they do? Preposterously light or not, Andrew Carlisle had already served a prison term in connection with Gina Antone's death. Double jeopardy would preclude him from being tried again for that same crime.

So should she keep the tape? Comments made by Andrew Carlisle during the tape seemed to make it clear that Diana's former husband, Garrison Ladd, had been present at the crime scene but drunk and passed out during most of that terrible drama. Twenty-two years after the fact, Diana Cooper Ladd Walker finally had some understanding of her former husband's involvement in Gina Antone's death. It would seem that Garrison hadn't been actively involved in what was done to Gina, but that didn't mean he was blameless. Mr. Ladd. Gina had called him by name. No doubt he was the one she knew. That meant Garrison was probably the one who had lured her into the truck in the first place.

When he did that, when he had offered her a ride, had he known what was coming or not? There was no way of unraveling that now, and listening to the tape again or a hundred times, or having someone else listen to it wouldn't have provided an adequate answer to that haunting question.

Getting out of the chair at last, Diana set about cleaning up the mess of vomit, spilled coffee, and broken pottery. Down on her hands and knees, for the first time ever she was grateful that Rita was dead. Had Gina's grandmother still been alive, Diana would have had to face the moral dilemma of whether or not to play the tape for the old woman. With Rita dead, that wasn't an issue.

But what about Davy? What would happen if he heard it? That thought hit her like a lightning bolt. Diana's son—Garrison Ladd's son—was still alive. If he ever came to know what was on that tape, it would tell him far more about his father than he ever needed to know.

Finally, there was Brandon to consider. He had headed the investigation into Gina Antone's death and he had eventually arrested Andrew Carlisle. The plea bargain that had followed the arrest had been negotiated behind Brandon Walker's back. If he had to endure listening to the grim recorded reality of Gina Antone's death, Diana knew Brandon would be devastated. He would blame himself for the unwitting part he had played in allowing Andrew Carlisle to slip off the hook and escape what should have been a charge of aggravated first-degree murder.

Thinking about what exposure to the tape would do to both Brandon and Davy was what finally galvanized Diana Ladd Walker to action. Brandon was already carrying around a big enough load of guilt. His son Quentin was in prison due to a fatality drunk-driving charge. As another source of free-flowing guilt in Brandon Walker's life, that tape was the last thing he needed.

With a fierce jab of her finger, Diana ejected the offending tape. She popped it out of the player and then carried it out to the living room. It was the first weekend in July. At eight o'clock in the morning, the air conditioner was already humming along at full speed when Diana knelt in front of the fireplace and opened the flue. Carefully, she laid a small fire with kindling at the bottom, topped by a layer of several wrist-thick branches of dried ironwood.

Once the kindling was lit, she sat on the raised hearth and waited until the ironwood was fully engulfed before she tossed the tape into the crackling flames. As the heat attacked it, the clear plastic container began to curl and melt. Like a snake shedding its skin, the magnetic tape slithered off its spindle and escaped the confines of the dwindling case. The tape writhed free, wriggled like a tortured creature, burst into flames, and then withered into a glowing chain of ash.

Only when there was nothing left of the tape and container but a charred, amorphous blob of melted plastic did Diana turn her back on the fireplace. Hurrying into the bathroom, she showered and dressed. Then, after raking the remainder of the fire apart, she left the house and drove straight to Florence. That day, Diana Walker Ladd was the first person inside the Visitation Room when the guard opened the door at ten o'clock in the morning.

Andrew Carlisle was led to his side of the Plexiglas divider a few minutes later. "Why, Mrs. Walker," he said, sitting down across from her. "To what do I owe this unexpected honor? I don't remember our setting an appointment for today."

"We didn't, you son of a bitch," she said.

He brightened. The puckered skin around his mouth stretched into a pained imitation of a smile. "I see," he said. "You must have received my little care package."

"Why did you send it to me?"

"Why? Because I wanted you to know what this was all about."

"That's not true. You wanted someone to know the truth about what you did and what you got away with. You wanted to gloat and rub somebody's nose in it."

"That, too," he conceded. "Maybe a little."

"Where was it all this time?"

"The tape? That's for me to know and for you to find out," Andrew Carlisle answered.

"Who brought it to my house? Who dropped it off? And how many more ugly surprises do you have in store for me?"

"One or two," he answered. "Or does that mean you're quitting?"

"No," Diana told him. "It doesn't mean I'm quitting. You think this is some kind of a game, don't you? You think this is a way to get back at me for what I did to you. Well, listen up, buster. I'm not a quitter. I'm going to write this damned book. By the time I finish, you're going to wish you'd never asked me to do it."

"That sounds like a threat."

"It is a threat."

"In other words, you're abolishing the ground rules."

"I'm writing this book regardless."

"That will make the process far more interesting for me. More hands-on, if you'll pardon the expression. Especially when it's time to talk about the time we spent together."

"Go fuck yourself, Mr. Carlisle!" She stood up, turned her back on him, and stalked over to the door. She had to wait in front of the door for several long moments before a guard opened it to let her out. While she was standing there she glanced back. Behind the Plexiglas barrier he was doubled over. And even though she couldn't actually hear him without benefit of the intercom—the sound nonetheless filled her head and echoed down the confines of the prison hallway long after the heavy metal door had slammed shut behind her.

That ghostly sound was one she would never forget. It was Andrew Philip Carlisle. Laughing.

9

While Mualig Siakam *and* Old Limping Man *were talking, some Indians came carrying a child. The child seemed asleep or dead. The people said she had been that way for a long time. They laid the child on the ground in the outer room of Medicine Woman's house.*

Mualig Siakam *took a gourd which had pebbles in it that rattled. She took some small, soft white feathers, and she took a little white powder. Then she sat down at the head of the child and she began to sing.*

The Indians could not understand Medicine Woman's song because she used the old, old language which is the one I'itoi *gave his people in the beginning. All the animals understand this language, but only a very few of the old men and women remember it.*

As Medicine Woman sang, she rattled the gourd which had on it the marks of shuhthagi—*the water—and of* wepgih—*the lightning. For a long time* Mualig Siakam *sang alone, but when the people who were sitting around had learned the song, they sang with her.*

And then Medicine Woman took some of the white feathers and passed them softly over the child's mouth and nose. She passed the feathers back and forth, back and forth. Sometimes she passed the feathers down over the child's chest. Then again she passed them back and forth across the child's face.

And the face of the child changed. Her body moved. Medicine Woman gave a silent command to the child's mother, who brought water. The child drank, and everyone looked very pleased.

The next morning Old Limping Man *went to the house of* Mualig Siakam. *Medicine Woman was feeding the child, who was sitting up. And that day, the child's people took her home.*

Halfway to the highway, walking in scorching midday heat, Manny Chavez took a detour. The wine was gone. He was verging on heatstroke. In the end it was thirst and the hope of finding water that drove him off-track.

Under normal circumstances, no right-thinking member of the Desert People would have gone anywhere near the haunted, moldering ruins of the deserted village known as *Ko'oi Koshwa*—Rattlesnake Skull. An Apache war party, aided by a young *Tohono O'othham* woman, a traitor, had massacred almost the entire village. The only survivors, a boy and a girl, had sought refuge in a cave on the steep flanks of *Ioligam* several miles away.

More recently, in the late sixties, a young Indian girl named Gina Antone had been murdered there. Anthony Listo, now chief of police for the *Tohono O'othham* Nation, had been a lowly patrol officer during that investigation. From time to time, he had been heard to talk about the girl who had been lured from a summer dance to one of the taboo caves on *Ioligam*, where she had been tortured and killed. Her body had been left, floating facedown, in the *charco*—a muddy man-made watering hole—near the deserted village itself.

A whole new series of legends and beliefs had grown up around that murder. The killer, an Anglo named Carlisle, was said to have been *Ohbsgam*—Apachelike. People claimed that the killer had been invaded by the spirits of the dead Apaches who had attacked Rattlesnake Skull Village long ago.

All the caves on *Ioligam* were considered sacred and off-limits. They had been officially declared so in the lease negotiations when the tribe allowed the building of Kitt Peak National Observatory. In the aftermath of Gina Antone's death, however, the caves close to *Ko'oi Koshwa* became taboo as well. People said *Ohbsgam Ho'ok*—Apachelike Monster—lived there, waiting for a chance to steal away another young *Tohono O'othham* girl. Parents sometimes used stories about the bogeyman *S-mo'o O'othham*—Hairy Man—to scare little boys back in line. On girls they used *Ohbsgam Ho'ok*.

Manny Chavez, thirsty but no longer drunk, considered all these things as he headed for the *charco* near what had once been Rattlesnake Skull Village. It was late in the season. Most of the other *charcos* on the reservation were already dry and would remain so until after the first summer rains came in late June or July. But no one ran any cattle near *Ko'oi Koshwa*. Without livestock to reduce the volume of water, Manny reasoned that he might still find water there—at least enough to get him the rest of the way to the highway.

Earlier, as Manny walked, he had heard and seen a four-wheel-drive vehicle making its way both up and down part of the mountain. Suspecting the people inside of being Anglo rock-climbers, Manny had given the tangerine-colored older-model Bronco a wide berth. He'd be better off on the highway, trying to hitch a ride in the back of an Indian-owned livestock truck, than messing around with a carful of *Mil-gahn*.

Now, though, as Manny approached the *charco*, he was surprised to see that same vehicle parked nearby. A man—an Anglo armed with a shovel—was digging industriously in the dirt. Manny may have been *nawmki*—a drunkard—but he was also *Tohono O'othham*, from the top of his sand-encrusted hair to the toes of his worn-out boots. The thought of this *Mil-gahn* blithely digging for artifacts on the reservation offended Manuel Chavez.

"Hey," he shouted. "What are you doing?"

The man with the shovel stopped digging and looked up.

"You can't dig here," Manny said. "This is a sacred place."

For a moment the two men stared at each other, then the Anglo, who was much younger than Manny, climbed out of the hole he was digging in the soft sand. He came at Manny with the shovel raised over his shoulder, wielding it like a baseball bat.

There was no question of Manny standing his ground. He looked around for a possible weapon. Off to his right was a small circle of river rock surrounding a faded wooden cross, but the rocks were too far away and too small to do him any good. Turning away from the *Mil-gahn's* unreasoning fury, Manuel Chavez tried to run. He tripped and fell facedown in the sand.

The first blow, the only one he felt, caught him squarely on the back of the head.

David Ladd lay in the darkened hotel room waiting to fall asleep and grappling with the overwhelming fear that another panic attack would come over him and catch him unawares. The plague of attacks and dreams had left him feeling shaken and vulnerable. He knew now that another attack was inevitable. The only question was, when would it come? What if it happened while he was with Candace? What would she think of him then? He was young, strong, and supposedly healthy. This kind of thing wasn't supposed to happen to people like him, but it *was* happening.

At last, emotionally worn and physically exhausted, David Ladd fell into a deep and dreamless sleep. Sometime later, he was jarred awake by the sound of a key in the lock and then by the opening door banging hard against the inside security chain.

"David," Candace called through the crack in the door. "Are you in there?"

Groggily, he staggered over to the door and unlatched the chain. "It's you," he mumbled.

Dropping several shopping bags to the floor, Candace stood up on tiptoe and kissed him. "Who else did you think it would be?"

"I was just taking a nap," he said. "I'm still half asleep. I'll go take a shower and see if it wakes me up."

"Sure," Candace said. "Go ahead."

He had finished his shower, shut off the water, and was just starting to towel himself dry when Candace knocked softly on the door. "Can I come in?"

"Sure," he said, wrapping the towel around his waist.

Candace burst into the room wearing little more than a glowingly radiant smile on her face.

"Oh, Davy," she said, throwing both arms around his neck and crushing the soft flesh of her warm breasts against his damp chest. "I love it. It's absolutely gorgeous. And it fits perfectly. How did you know what size?"

For a moment or two, David Ladd didn't understand what was going on or grasp what she was talking about. Then, catching a glimpse of Astrid Ladd's ring on Candace Waverly's finger, he realized she had found it just where he had left it—on the nightstand table with his watch.

Crying and kissing him at the same time, Candace seemed totally oblivious to the droplets of water on his still-wet body. "And the answer is yes," she whispered, with her lips grazing his ear. "Yes, yes, yes! Of course, I'll marry you, even if it means living in your one-horse hometown."

Marry! At the sound of the word, David Garrison Ladd's legs almost buckled under him. For the length of several long kisses he was too stunned to reply. And by the time Candace's impassioned kisses subsided, it was pretty much too late. By then she was leading him back across the artificially darkened room to the bed.

Sinking down on the mattress, she pulled David down on top of her naked body, drawing him into her while her eager hips rose up to meet him. That wasn't the time to tell her that this was all a terrible mistake—that he had never planned to give her Astrid Ladd's ring in the first place. He did the only thing that made sense under the circumstances—he kissed her back.

Other than that, he kept his mouth shut. And after their lovemaking, while he was drifting on a pink haze, she snuggled close and kissed his chest. "What a wonderfully romantic surprise," she murmured. "But I have a surprise for you, too."

"What's that?"

Candace reached over on the nightstand and picked up a piece of paper. A check. "What's that?" he asked.

"Look at it," she said. "It's made out to both of us."

When he looked at it more closely, David Ladd's eyes bulged. It was a personal check in the amount of twenty-five thousand dollars, made out to David Ladd and Candace Waverly Ladd and drawn on a joint account belonging to Richard and Elizabeth Waverly.

"What's this?" David asked.

"A bribe," Candace answered with a grin. "For eloping. Daddy says it'll only work as long as Mother knows nothing about our engagement and hasn't had time to plan anything until it's too late. Once she gets wind of it and starts arranging things, the deal is off. He's already married off two daughters, and he doesn't want to do another one. And I don't blame him."

"Eloping," David Ladd echoed. "What are you talking about? Us? When?"

"Today, dummy," she said, snuggling under his chin and nuzzling his neck. "Right now. I thought you'd catch on as soon as you saw all the suitcases. I have it all figured out. We can drive through Vegas on our way to Tucson and get married there. It's not that far out of the way. I already have a dress and everything."

"What about your job?" David Ladd mounted one small but clearly futile objection.

"With Dad's firm? What about it? I got laid off," Candace beamed. "Yesterday afternoon. So not only do I get the time off, I can collect unemployment benefits, too. Isn't that a great deal?"

"It's great, all right," David Ladd muttered while that post-coital pink haze disintegrated into a million pieces around him. He managed to infuse the words with a whole lot more enthusiasm than he felt, although "great" wasn't exactly the word he would have chosen.

"And I love the ring," Candace continued. "It's gorgeous."

"I'm glad you like it" was all David could manage. After all, what else could he say?

After making a quick trip down the Sasabe Road to take a report on a one vehicle/one steer accident in which only the steer had perished, Deputy Brian Fellows stopped off at the Three Points Trading Post to buy himself a much-needed Coke to get him through the rest of his long afternoon shift.

As summer heated up, daytime temperatures on the arid Sonoran Desert made working the night shift suddenly far preferable to working days. One of the local radio stations held an annual contest, offering a prize to the listener who successfully guessed the correct day, time, and hour when the "ice broke on the Santa Cruz." Loosely translated, that meant the day, hour, and minute the thermometer finally broke one hundred for the year. From that time on, from the moment daytime temperatures crossed that critical century mark until well into September, Brian, along with any number of other low-totem-pole deputies, found himself working straight days.

With school out for the summer, the trading post was full of ten or so kids—two Anglo and the rest Indian—milling around between the banks of shelves. Brian smiled down at them. The Anglos grinned back, while the Indians shied away. The deputy liked little kids, and it hurt his feelings that the *Tohono O'othham* children were frightened of him. Because he knew some of the language, he tried speaking to them in *Tohono O'othham* on occasion. That always seemed to spook them that much more. Was it the color of his skin? he wondered. Or was it the uniform? Maybe it was a combination of both.

Back in his county-owned Blazer, he sat looking up and down Highway 86, watching passing vehicles made shimmering and ghostlike by the waves of heat rising off the blacktop. This quiet Saturday afternoon there didn't seem to be much happening in his patrol area, which covered Highway 86 west from Ryan Field to the boundary of the *Tohono O'othham* Reservation, and along Highway 286 from Three Points south to Sasabe on the U.S./Mexican border.

It was boom time once again in the Valley of the Sun. Tucson and surrounding areas in Pima County were experiencing a renewed population growth, but this part of the county—the part included in Brian's patrol area—wasn't yet overly affected. Sometimes he would be called out to an incident on Sandario Road that led north toward Marana. There he could drive for miles without seeing another human or meeting another vehicle. The same held true for Coleman Road at the base of the Baboquivaris.

And the back and forth chatter on the radio seldom had much to do with the area assigned to Deputy Brian Fellows. Those long straight stretches of highway leading to and from the reservation yielded more drunk drivers than other parts of the county. They also had more than a fair share of auto accidents. Those mostly happened at night on weekends.

Brian had been a deputy four full years. Other officers who had come through the academy after him were already starting to move up while Brian was still stuck in what was—in terms of departmental advancement—the equivalent of Outer Mongolia. But Brian was resigned to the fact that it could have been much worse. If Bill Forsythe had wanted to, he could have figured out a way to get rid of Brian Fellows altogether. In fact, considering Brian's close connection to Brandon Walker, it was a little surprising that the ax hadn't fallen in the wake of Brandon's departure.

Still, Brian didn't dwell on the unfairness of it all. He was too busy being grateful. After all, he was doing what he had always wanted to do—being a cop and following in Brandon Walker's footsteps. As for the rest? Nothing much mattered. Brian was single and living at home. Taking care of his disabled mother in his off-hours pretty much kept him out of the dating game, so the low pay scale for young deputies didn't bother him all that much, either.

There were times when Brian was struck by the irony of his position. He was persona non grata with the current administration of the Pima County Sheriff's Department because of his relationship to the previous sheriff, who was, after all, no blood relation but the father of Brian's half-brothers.

Tommy and Quentin had been four and five years older than Brian, and they had been the banes of the younger child's existence. But if it hadn't been for them, Brian never would have met their father, a man who—more than any other—became Brian's father as well.

None of the other boys—Davy Ladd included—had ever seemed to pay that much attention to anything Brandon Walker said or did. In fact, they all seemed to be at odds with him much of the time. Not Brian. For him, the former Pima County sheriff, even in defeat, had always been larger than life—the closest thing to a superhero that ever crossed the path of that little fatherless boy.

"How's it going, Mr. Walker?" Brian Fellows had asked several months earlier, when he had stopped by the house in Gates Pass on his way back from patrol.

Brandon, working outdoors in his shirtsleeves, had looked up to see Brian Fellows, a young man he had known from early childhood on, step out of a Pima County patrol car.

"Okay," Brandon said gruffly, reaching down to pull out another log of mesquite. "How about you?"

"Pretty good," Brian replied, although the answer didn't sound particularly convincing.

"How's your mother?"

Brian's mother, Janie Walker Fellows Hitchcock Noonan, had been Brandon Walker's first wife. Years earlier, when Brian was a sophomore at Tucson High, his mother had been in what should have been a fatality car wreck. She had been paralyzed from the waist down. Janie's boyfriend du jour— a lush who had actually been at the wheel of the car and who had walked away from the accident without a scratch—had skipped town immediately.

In subsequent years, most of the responsibility for his mother's care had fallen on Brian's narrow but capable young shoulders. Some people rise above physical tragedy. Janie Noonan wasn't one of those. She was a difficult patient. For months she had railed at Brian, telling him that if he didn't have guts enough to use a gun to put her out of her misery, the least he could do was bring her one so she could do the job herself.

By now Janie was fairly well resigned to her fate. She appreciated the fact that Brian had stayed on, patiently caring for her when most young men, under similar circumstances, would have moved out. That didn't mean she treated him any better, though. Janie had grown into a helpless tyrant. In the absence of her other two sons, Brian became her sole target, but he was used to that. It seemed to him that his mother had simply taken up the role formerly filled by his older brothers, Quentin and Tommy.

"Nobody likes a Goody Two-shoes," Quentin had told him on more than one occasion. "They think you're nothing but a stupid little wimp."

The difference between Brian Fellows and his best friend, Davy Ladd, was that Davy would usually rise to Quentin's challenge and fight back, regardless of the bloody-nosed consequences. Brian was a survivor who kept his mouth shut and let the taunts wash over him.

By now, though, at age twenty-six, he was tired of being a "good boy." He was beginning to see that there wasn't much percentage in it, although he didn't really know how to be anything else other than what he was.

"Mom's about the same," he said, answering Brandon Walker's question in a matter-of-fact manner that didn't brook sympathy.

Looking at this handsome young man in his deputy sheriff's uniform, Brandon couldn't help remembering a much younger version of the same young man, a little lost boy who had stood forlornly on the front porch of his ex-wife's home each time Brandon had come by to pick up his own two sons, Quentin and Tommy.

Brandon no longer remembered where they had been going that day—maybe to a movie, maybe to the Pima County Fair, or maybe even to a baseball game. What he hadn't forgotten was the solemn, sad-eyed look on Brian's face that had changed instantly to sheer joy the moment Brandon asked him if he wanted to come along.

"You're not taking *him,* are you?" Quentin had demanded, his voice quivering in outrage.

Brandon's older son had a surly streak. Of all the kids, he had always been the sullen one—the spoiled brat with the chip on his shoulder. Janie had seen to that.

"Why shouldn't I?" Brandon asked.

"Because he's a pest," Quentin spat back. "And a baby, too. He'll probably wet his pants or have to go to the bathroom a million times."

Brian had wavered on the porch for a moment, as if afraid that Quentin's argument would carry the day. When Brandon didn't change his mind, the boy had raced into the house to ask Janie for permission to go along. Moments later, he had come charging back outside.

"She said it's all right. I can go!" Brian had crowed triumphantly, racing for the car.

"I get to ride shotgun!" Quentin had snarled, but Brian hadn't cared about that. The backseat was fine with him. At that point he would probably have been grateful to sit in the trunk.

"You'll take turns," Brandon had told Quent, trying to instill in him a sense of sharing and fair play. And that was how it worked from then on—the boys had taken turns. But Brandon Walker's lessons in enforced sharing had been lost on Quentin. Rather than teaching him how to be a better person, Brandon Walker's kindness to Quentin's half-brother fostered an ugly case of burning resentment that spanned the whole of Brian Fellows's childhood.

"How about a cup of coffee or glass of iced tea?" Brandon had asked finally, emerging from a tangled skein of memory. Brian's face had brightened into almost the same look Brandon remembered from that day on the porch.

"Sure, Mr. Walker," he responded. "Coffee would be great."

In all those intervening years, while the other three boys had gone through their various stages of smart-mouthed rebellion, Brian had never called Brandon anything but a respectful "Mr. Walker."

Shaking his head, Brandon led the way into the house. One of his main regrets at losing the election had been missing the chance to watch this promising young man mature into the outstanding police officer he would someday be. That was something else Quentin had cost him—the opportunity of seeing 'little' Brian Fellows grow into Brian Fellows, the man.

"People at the department are asking about you," the young deputy said, as he settled onto a chair at the kitchen table.

"You don't say," Brandon replied gruffly. "Well, go ahead and tell them I'm fine. On second thought, don't tell them anything at all. If you're smart and want to get anywhere in Bill Forsythe's department, you won't even mention my name, much less let on that you know me."

After Brandon poured cups of coffee, the two men were quiet for a few moments. Brandon didn't mean to pry, but in the end he couldn't resist probing.

"How are things going out there?" he asked. "I mean, how are things at the department really going?"

Brian shrugged. "All right, I guess. But there are lots of people who miss you. Sheriff Forsythe's"—Brian paused, as if searching for just the right word—"he's just different, I guess. Different from you, that is," he finished somewhat lamely.

"You bet he is," Brandon replied, not even trying to keep the hollow sound of bitterness out of his voice. "The voters in this county wanted different. As far as I can see, they got it."

Once again the two men fell silent. For a moment Brandon Walker felt vindicated.

A parade of boyfriends and briefly maintained husbands had wandered through Janie's life and, as a consequence,

through the lives of her three sons as well. One of them—
Brian no longer remembered which one—had told him that
children should be seen but not heard. Brian had taken those
words to heart and had turned them into a personal creed.
What had once been a necessary tool for surviving Quentin's
casual and constant brutality had become a way of life. Brian
Fellows answered questions. He hardly ever volunteered information, although Brandon Walker could tell by looking at
him that the young man was clearly troubled about something.

"So what brings you here today?" the older man asked at
last.

Brian ducked his head. "Quentin," he answered.

"What about Quentin?"

"He's out," Brian answered. "On parole."

"Where's he living?"

"Somewhere in Tucson, I suppose. I don't know for sure
where. He hasn't come by here, has he?"

Brandon shook his head. "He wouldn't dare."

Brian sighed. "He has been by the house a couple of
times, wanting money and looking for a place to stay. I had
to make him leave, Mr. Walker, and I thought you should
know what's going on."

"What is going on?" Brandon asked.

Brian swallowed hard. "He came by to hit Mom up for
money, for a loan, he called it. She had already written him
two checks for a hundred bucks each, before I caught on to
what was happening. She can't afford to be giving him that
kind of money. She still has some, but with the nurse and all
the medical expenses, it's not going to last forever. I don't
know what to do."

"Go to court and get a protection order," Brandon Walker
said at once. "Janie has given you power of attorney so you
can handle her affairs, hasn't she?"

Brian nodded. "Yes."

"As her conservator, you have a moral and legal obliga-
tion to protect her assets."

With a pained expression on his face, Brian nodded again. "But Quentin's my brother," he said.

"And he's my son," Brandon replied. "But that doesn't give him a right to steal from his own mother."

"So you don't think I did the wrong thing, by not letting him stay at the house?"

With his heart aching in sympathy, Brandon looked at the troubled young man sitting across from him. "No," he had said kindly. "I don't blame you at all, and neither will anyone else. With people like Quentin loose in the world, you have a responsibility to protect yourself. If you can, that is. And believe me, Brian, since I happen to be Quentin's father, I know that isn't easy advice to follow."

Months after that last courtesy visit to Gates Pass, Brian was sitting in his air-conditioned Blazer next to the trading post at Three Points, sipping his Coke and wondering how soon his friend Davy would be home when the call came in over the radio. An INS officer was requesting assistance. The dispatcher read off the officer's location.

"Highway 86 to Coleman Road. First left after you cross off the reservation. It gets confusing after that. The INS officer says just follow her tracks. You're looking for a *charco*.

"By the way," the dispatcher continued. "Are you four-wheeling it today?"

"That's affirmative," Brian said, putting the Blazer in gear.

"Good," the dispatcher told him. "From the sounds of it, if you weren't, I'd have to send in another unit."

With lights flashing and siren blaring, Brian Fellows sped west on Highway 86. At first he didn't think anything about where he was going. He was simply following directions. It wasn't until he turned off the highway that he recognized the place as somewhere he had been before. He had gone to that same *charco* years earlier, the summer Tommy disappeared. The four of them had gone there together—Quentin and Tommy, Davy Ladd and Brian.

By then, though, he was too busy following the tracks to think about it. Kicking up a huge cloud of dust, he wheeled through the thick undergrowth of green mesquite and blooming palo verde. He jolted his way through first one sandy wash—the one where Quentin had gotten stuck—and then through another, all the while following a set of tracks that could only have been left by one of the green Internationals or GMC Suburbans the Immigration and Naturalization Service sends out on patrol around the desert Southwest, collecting illegal aliens and returning them to the border.

Brian spotted the vehicle eventually, an International parked next to the shrine he remembered, Gina Antone's shrine. The small wooden cross, faded gray now rather than white, sat crookedly in the midst of a scattered circle of river rocks.

Maybe while Davy's home, Brian thought, parking his Blazer, *we can come out here with flowers and candles. We can paint the cross and fix the shrine up the same way we did before.*

It was nothing more than a passing thought, though, because right then, Deputy Brian Fellows was working. When he stepped out of the Blazer, there was no sign of life. "Anybody here?" he called.

"Over here," a woman's answering voice returned from somewhere in the thick undergrowth. "And if you've got any drinking water there with you, bring it along."

Brian grabbed a gallon jug of bottled water out of the back of the Blazer and then started in the direction of the woman's voice. "Watch out for the footprints," she called to him. "You're probably going to need them."

Glancing down, Brian saw what she meant. Something

heavy had been dragged by hand through the sandy dirt, leaving a deep track. A single set of footprints, heading back toward the *charco,* overlaid the track. As instructed, Brian Fellows detoured around both as he made his way into a grove of mesquite. Ten yards into the undergrowth he came to a small clearing where a woman in a gray-green uniform was bending over the figure of a man. He lay flat on his back, with his unprotected face fully exposed to the glaring sun. A cloud of flies buzzed overhead.

"What happened?" Brian asked.

The woman looked up at him, her face grim. "Somebody beat the crap out of this guy," she said.

Brian handed over his jug of water. By then he was close enough to smell the unmistakable stench of evacuated bowels, of urine that reeked of secondhand wine.

"He's still alive then?" Brian asked.

"So far, but only just barely. I've called for a med-evac helicopter, but I don't think he's going to make it. He can't move. Either his back's broken or he's suffering from a concussion, I can't tell which."

The man lying on the ground, dark-haired and heavy-set, appeared to be around sixty years old. The large brass belt buckle imprinted with the traditional *Tohono O'othham* maze identified him as an Indian rather than Hispanic. One whole side of his face, clotted with blood, seemed to have been bashed in. His eyes were open, but the irises had rolled back out of sight. He was breathing, shallowly, but that was about all.

"Thanks for the water," the woman said, opening the jug and pouring some of it onto a handkerchief. First she wrung out some of the water over the man's parched lips and swollen tongue, then she laid the still-soaking cloth on the injured man's forehead. That done, she sprinkled the rest of his body as well, dousing his bloodied clothing.

"I'm trying to lower his body temperature," she explained. "I don't know if it's helping or not, but we've got to try."

It was all Brian could do to kneel beside the injured man and look at him. His mother's condition had taught him the real meaning behind the awful words "broken back." He wasn't at all sure that keeping the man alive would be doing him any favor. What Brian Fellows did feel, however, was both pity and an incredible sense of gratitude. If the man's back was actually broken or if he had suffered permanent injury as a result of heatstroke, someone else—someone who wasn't Brian—would have to care for him for the rest of his life, feeding him, bathing him, and attending to his most basic needs.

"What can I do to help?" he asked.

"Keep the damn flies and ants away," the woman told him. "They're eating him alive."

Brian tried to comply. He waved his Stetson in the air, whacking at the roiling flies, and he attempted to pluck off the marauding ants that peppered the man's broken body. It was a losing battle. As soon as he got rid of one ant, two more appeared in its place.

"Because there's water in the *charco,* a lot of undocumented aliens come this way, especially at this time of year," the woman was saying. The name tag on the breast pocket of her uniform identified her as Agent Kelly.

"I usually try to stop by here at least once a day," she continued. "I saw the tracks in the sand and decided to investigate. When I first saw him, I was sure he was dead, but then I found a slight pulse. When I came back from calling for help, his eyes were open."

Suddenly the man groaned. His eyes blinked. He moved his head from side to side and tried to speak.

"Easy," Agent Kelly said. "Take it easy. Help is on the way."

Brian leaned closer to the injured man. "Can you tell us what happened?" he asked. "Do you know who did this?"

The man trained his bloodshot eyes on Brian's face. ". . . *Mil-gahn,*" he whispered hoarsely.

The sound of the softly spoken word caused the years to

peel away. Brian was once again reliving those carefree days when he and Davy had been little, when they had spent every spare moment out in the little shed behind Davy's house, with Brian learning the language of Davy's old Indian baby-sitter, Rita Antone. When they were together, Davy and Rita had spoken to one another almost exclusively in *Tohono O'othham*—they had called it Papago back then—rather than English. Over time Brian Fellows had picked up some of the language himself. He knew that the word *Mil-gahn* meant Anglo.

"A white man did this?" Brian asked, hunkering even closer to the injured man.

"Yes," the man whispered weakly in *Tohono O'othham*. "A white man."

"He hit you on purpose?" Brian asked.

The man nodded.

"Do you know who it was?" Brain asked. "Do you know the man's name?"

This time the injured man shook his head, then he murmured something else. Brian's grasp of the language was such that he could pick out only one or two words—*hiabog*—digging, and *shohbith*—forbidden.

"What's he saying?" Agent Kelly asked.

"I didn't catch all of it. Something about forbidden digging. I'll bet this guy stumbled on a gang of artifact thieves, or maybe just one. The Indians around here consider this whole area sacred, from here to the mountains."

"That's news to me," Agent Kelly said.

Overhead they heard the pulsing clatter of an arriving helicopter. "They've probably located the vehicles, but they'll have trouble finding us. I'll stay here with him," she directed. "You go guide them in."

The helicopter landed in the clearing near where the cars were parked. After directing the emergency medical technicians on where to go, Brian went back to his Blazer and called in. "I need a detective out here," he said.

"How come?" the dispatcher wanted to know. "What's going on?"

"We've got a severely injured man. He may not make it."

"You're talking about the drunk Indian the Border Patrol found? We've already dispatched the helicopter—"

"The helicopter's here," Brian interrupted. "I'm asking for a detective. The guy says a white man beat him up."

"But he's still alive right now, right?"

"Barely."

"Go ahead and write it up yourself, Deputy Fellows. The detectives are pretty much tied up at the moment. If one of 'em gets freed up later, I'll send him along. In the meantime, this case is your baby." The dispatcher's implication was clear: a deputy capable of investigating dead cattle ought to be able to handle a beat-up Indian now and then.

Brian sighed and headed back toward the *charco*. Brandon Walker was right. With Bill Forsythe's administration, the people of Pima County had gotten something different, all right.

In spades.

From somewhere very far away, Lani heard what sounded like a siren. She opened her eyes. At least, she *thought* she opened her eyes, but she could see nothing. She tried to move her hands and feet. She could move them a little, but not much, and when she tried to raise her head, her face came into contact with something soft.

Where am I? she wondered. *Why am I so hot?*

Her body ached with the pain of spending hours locked in the same position. She seemed to be lying naked on something soft. And she could feel something silky touching her sides and the bare skin of her immovable legs and arms. A cool breeze wafted over her hot skin from somewhere, and there was a pillow propped under her head.

A pillow. "Maybe I'm dead," she said aloud, but the

sound was so dead that it was almost as though she hadn't said a word. "Am I dead?" she asked.

The answer came from inside her rather than from anywhere outside.

If there's cloth all around me, above and below and a pillow, too, she thought, *I must be in a casket, just like Nana* Dahd.

For weeks everyone, with the possible exception of Lani, had known that Rita Antone was living on borrowed time. The whole household knew it wouldn't be long now. For days now, Wanda and Fat Crack Ortiz had stayed at the house in Gates Pass, keeping watch at Rita's bedside night and day. When they slept, they did so taking turns in the spare bedroom.

Over the years there had been plenty of subtle criticism on the reservation about Rita Antone. The Indians had been upset with her for abandoning her people and her own family to go live in Tucson with a family of Whites. There had also been some pointed and mean-spirited criticism aimed at Rita's family for letting her go. The gossips maintained that, although Diana Ladd Walker may have been glad enough to have Rita's help while she was strong and healthy and could manage housekeeping and child-care chores, they expected that the *Mil-gahn* woman would be quick to send Rita back to the reservation once she was no longer useful, when, in the vernacular of the *Tohono O'othham*, she was only good for making baskets and nothing else.

Knowing that Rita must have been involved, ill will toward her had flourished anew among the *Tohono O'oth-ham* in the wake of Brandon and Diana Walker's unconventional adoption of Clemencia Escalante. Not that any of the Indian people on the reservation had been interested in adopting the child themselves. Everyone knew that the strange little girl had been singled out by *I'itoi* and his mes-

sengers, the Little People. Clemencia had been kissed by
the ants in the same way the legendary *Kulani O'oks* had
been kissed by the bees. Although there was some interest
at the prospect of having a new and potentially powerful
Medicine Woman in the tribe, no one—including Clemencia's blood relatives—wanted the job of being parents to
such a child.

By now, though, with Rita Antone bedridden and being
lovingly cared for by both her Indian and Anglo families, the
reservation naysayers and gossips had been silenced for
good and all.

On that last day, a sleep-deprived Fat Crack came into the
kitchen where Diana and Brandon were eating breakfast.
Gabe helped himself to a cup of coffee and then tried to
mash down his unruly hair. It was still standing straight up,
just the way he had slept on it, slumped down in the chair
next to Rita's bed.

"She's asking for Davy," Fat Crack said. "Do you know
where he is?"

Diana glanced at her watch. "Probably in class right now,
but I don't know which one or where."

"Let me make a call to the registrar's office over at the
university," Brandon had told them. "Once they tell us
where he is, I'll go there, pick him up, and bring him back
home."

Fat Crack nodded. "Good," he said. "I don't think there's
much time."

Forty-five minutes later, Brandon Walker was waiting in
the hall outside Davy's Anthropology 101 class. As soon as
Davy saw Brandon, he knew what was going on.

"How bad is it?" he asked.

"Pretty bad," Brandon returned. "Fat Crack says we
should come as soon as we can."

They had hurried out to the car which, due to law-
enforcement privilege, had been parked on the usually vehi-
cle-free pedestrian mall.

"I hate this," Davy said, settling into the seat, slamming his door, and then staring out the window.

"What do you hate?"

"Having old people for friends and having them die on me. First Father John, then Looks At Nothing, and now Rita."

At age ninety-five, Looks At Nothing had avoided the threat of being placed in a hospital by simply walking off into the desert one hot summer's day. They had found his desiccated body weeks later, baking in the hot sand of a desert wash not a thousand yards from his home.

"I'm sorry," Brandon said, and meant it.

At the house, Davy had gone straight into Rita's room. He had stayed there for only ten minutes or so. He had come out carrying Rita's prized but aged medicine basket. His face was pale but he was dry-eyed. "I'm ready to go back now," he said.

He and Brandon had set out in the car. "She gave me her basket," Davy said a few minutes later.

"I know," Brandon said. "I saw you carrying it."

"But it's not mine to keep," Davy added.

Brandon Walker glanced at his stepson. His jaw was set, but now there were tears glimmering on his face. "I get to have Father John's rosary and Rita's son's Purple Heart. Everything else goes to Lani. It isn't fair!"

Brandon was tempted to point out that very little in life is fair, but he didn't. "Why, then, did she give it to you today?" he asked.

"Because Lani's only seven, or at least she will be to-morrow. She can't have the rest of it until she's older."

"When are you supposed to give it to her?"

Davy brushed the tears from his face. "That's what I asked Rita. She said that I'd know when it was time."

Brandon pulled up in front of the dorm, but Davy made no effort to get out. Instead, he opened the basket, picked through it, and removed two separate items, both of which he shoved in his pocket. Then he put the frayed cover back on the basket.

"Dad," he said. "Would you do me a favor?"

"What's that?" Brandon asked.

"I can't take this into the dorm. No one would understand. And somebody might try to steal it or something. You and Mom have a safety deposit box down at the bank, don't you?"

"Yes."

"Would you mind putting this in there and keeping it? I mean, if it isn't really mine, I don't want to lose it. I need to keep it safe—for Lani."

"Sure, Davy," Brandon said. "I'll be glad to. If you want me to, I'll drop it off this morning on my way to the department."

"Thanks," Davy said, handing the basket over. "And tell Fat Crack that I'll come back out to the house as soon as I'm done with my last class. I should be done by three at the latest."

But Rita Antone was gone long before then. She died within half an hour of the time her little *Olhoni* left, taking Understanding Woman's medicine basket with him.

Nine years later, the bank had gone through several different mergers and had ended up as part of Wells Fargo. The bank had changed, but not the medicine basket, at least not noticeably. Maybe it was somewhat more frayed than it had been a decade earlier, but the power *Oks Amichuda* had woven into it years before still remained and still waited to be let out.

The day after Nana *Dahd* died was the worst birthday Lani ever remembered. It seemed to her that a terrible empty place had opened up in her life. The cake had been ordered well in advance, and everyone had tried to go through the motions of a party, just as Rita would have wanted them to. When it came time to blow out the candles, however, Lani had fled the room in tears, leaving the lighted candles still burning.

Brandon was the one who had come to find her, sitting in the playhouse he had built for her in the far corner of the backyard.

"Lani," he called. "Come here. What's the matter?"

She crept outside and fell, weeping, against him.

"Nana *Dahd's* dead, and Davy's mad at me," she sobbed. "I wish I were dead, too."

"No, you don't," he said soothingly. "Rita wouldn't want you to be unhappy. We were lucky to have had her for as long as we did, but now it's time to let her go. She was suffering, Lani. She was in terrible pain. It would be selfish for us to want her to stay any longer."

"I know," Lani said, "but . . ."

"Wait a minute. What's that in your hand?"

"Her *owij*," Lani answered. "Her awl. She gave it to me yesterday. She said I must always keep making baskets."

"Good."

"But why was Davy so mean to me?" Lani asked. "I called him at the dorm and asked him if he was going to come have cake with us. He said he was too busy, but I think he just didn't want to. He sounded mad, but why would he be? What have I done?"

"Nothing, Lani," Brandon said. "He's upset about Rita, the same as you are. He'll get over it. We just have to be patient with each other. Come on, let's go back inside and have some of that cake."

Obligingly Lani had followed him into the house. The candles were already out. She managed to choke down a few bites of cake, but that was all.

Three days later, at the funeral at San Xavier Mission, Lani was shocked to see Rita lying in the casket with her head propped up on a pillow.

"But Nana *Dahd* doesn't like pillows," Lani had insisted, tugging at her father's hand. "She never uses a pillow."

"Shhhh," Brandon Walker had said. "Not now."

On the face of it, that was all there was to it. There was never any further discussion. Brandon's "not now" became "not ever," except for one small thing.

From that day on, Dolores Lanita Walker never again used a pillow.

Not until now.

10

On the Fourth Day I'itoi *made the Sun—Tash. And Elder Brother went with* Tash *to show him the way, just as Sun travels today.*

For a long time Tash *walked close to the earth, and it was very hot.* Juhk O'othham—*Rain Man—refused to follow his brother,* Chewagi O'othham—*Cloud Man—over the land, and* Hewel O'othham—*Wind Man—was angry and only made things hotter and dryer.*

All the desert world needed water. The Desert People were so thirsty and cross that they quarreled. When u'uwhig—*the Birds—came too near each other, they pulled feathers.* Tohbi—*Cottontail Rabbit—and* Ko'owi—*Rattlesnake, and* Jewho—*Gopher—could no longer live together. So* Jewho *became very busy digging new holes.*

When the animals had quarreled until only the strongest were left, a strange people came out of the old deserted gopher holes.

These were the PaDaj O'othham—*Bad People—who were moved by the Spirit of Evil. They came from the big water in the far southwest, and they spread all over the land, killing the people as they came until every man felt that he lived in a black hole.*

The Desert People were so sad that at last they cried out to the Great Spirit for help. And when I'itoi *saw that the* PaDaj O'othham *were in the land, he took some good spirits of the other world and made warriors out of them.*

These good spirit warriors chased the Bad People but could neither capture nor kill them. And because his good soldiers from the spirit world could not destroy the Bad People, who were moved by the Spirit of Evil, I'itoi *was ashamed.*

"That must have been very interesting," Monty Lazarus was saying.

Diana snapped to attention and was embarrassed to realize that she had once again allowed her mind to wander. Talking and thinking about Andrew Carlisle still had the power to do that. She had thought that writing the book about him would have cleared the man out of her system once and for all. Her continuing discomfort during this interview seemed to suggest that wasn't the case.

She wondered if she'd said anything stupid. Whatever she had said, no doubt Mr. Lazarus would quote her verbatim.

"I'm sorry," she said. "I guess I'm getting tired. What was interesting?"

"Interviewing Andrew Carlisle's mother."

Diana didn't remember when the interview had veered into discussing Myrna Louise, but it must have. "Right," she said. "It was."

"She's still alive then?" Monty asked.

"Not now. She died within weeks of the time I saw her. It's a good thing I went to see her when I did. Other than talking to Andrew Carlisle himself, my interview with Myrna Louise was one of the most important ones I did for the book. I was nervous about seeing her after what I'd done to her son—leaving him blind and crippled. I had no idea how she'd respond to me. Just because a court had ruled I had acted in self-defense didn't mean that would carry any weight with the man's mother."

"Didn't you say in the book someplace that he tried to kill her once?"

Diana nodded. "He did, but she got away. What I found strange was that she didn't seem to hold it against him. She told me that there wasn't any point in carrying grudges and that he was her only reason for still hanging on. She said that if she was gone, he wouldn't have anyone at all."

"So when you went to interview her, how did it go?" Monty Lazarus asked.

"It was fine," Diana said. "Myrna Louise Carlisle Spaulding Rivers couldn't have been more gracious."

The first time Diana had met Myrna Louise, it was mid-morning in the somewhat grubby lunchroom of the Vista Retirement Center in Chandler, Arizona. Andrew Carlisle's mother, with a walker strategically stationed nearby, was seated on a stained bench shoved carelessly up to a chipped table in the far corner of the room. She looked up at her visitor from a game of solitaire played with a deck of sticky, dog-eared cards.

"You must be Diana Walker," Myrna Louise said as Diana walked up to the table. "I've seen your picture before. On your books."

"Thank you for agreeing to see me," Diana said.

Myrna Louise smiled. "I didn't have much choice, now, did I? I'm not going anyplace soon. I figured I could just as well."

Her hair, an improbable color of red, was thin and wispy.

Her face may have been made up with a once-practiced hand, but now there were a few slips. A dribble of mascara darkened one cheek, and some of the too-red lipstick had smeared and edged its way up and down into the wrinkled creases above and below her lips. The teeth were false and clicked ominously when she spoke, as though threatening to pop out at any moment.

"Anyway," she added, "I wanted to meet you. I wanted to apologize."

"Apologize? For what?"

"For my son, of course. For Andrew. He was a good boy when he was little. Good and so cute, too. I used to have the curls from his first haircut, but I finally threw them away when I moved here. Carlton made me get rid of them."

"Carlton?"

"Carlton Rivers, my late husband. My latest late husband. Anyway, when I told him about what Andrew had done—or rather, what he had tried to do—he said I should just forget about him. He said I should forget I'd ever even had a son. He said I should leave him in prison and let him rot. Andrew tried to kill me, you see. The same day he tried to kill you, as a matter of fact. I got away, though. When he got out of the car at that storage place, I just drove myself away. You should have seen his face. He couldn't believe it—that I was driving. I almost couldn't believe it myself. I'd never done it before—driven a car, that is. Not before or since."

Diana took a deep breath. "You're not responsible for your son's actions, Mrs. Rivers. There's no need for you to apologize to me."

"A reverend comes by and conducts church services here every Sunday," Myrna Louise continued as though she hadn't heard Diana's response. "I tried to talk to him about Andrew once or twice after I found out about the AIDS business. I suppose you know about that?"

Diana nodded.

"I asked him if he thought that was God's way of punishing Andrew. You know, an eye-for-an-eye sort of thing. Just like he lost his eyesight over what he did to you."

"God didn't throw the bacon grease," Diana said. "I did."

"But God's responsible for the result, isn't he?" Myrna Louise insisted. "If God had wanted it to work that way, he could have just burned him, but he wouldn't have been blind. Don't you see?"

"Not exactly," Diana said.

"Well, anyway, now I hear you're writing a book about him."

"Yes, although it's not just about him. It's about all the people whose lives he touched. Whose lives he changed."

"Or ended," Myrna Louise added sadly. "It serves him right that he doesn't get to write his own book. He asked you to do that, to write it?"

"Yes."

"That's hard for me to believe, but I don't suppose anything about Andrew should surprise me anymore. I would think he would have wanted to write it himself, even if he couldn't get it published. He's still angry with me about the manuscript, you know."

"What manuscript?"

"Of his book. The book he wrote when he was in prison the first time."

"And what happened to it?" Diana asked.

"I burned it," Myrna Louise said thoughtfully. "One page at a time."

"There aren't any copies left?"

"Not that I know of."

"And what did your son call this book?"

Myrna Louise shook her head. "I don't remember the name of it now. After all these years, I guess I've managed to forget what it was exactly, although I remember the title had something to do with Indians. I didn't read the whole thing, just parts of it. It was awful. I couldn't believe anyone could write such terrible stuff. The things his main character did to other characters were just awful. It made me feel filthy just having in my hands. But of course, I know now that he must not have made some of that up."

"What do you mean, he didn't make it up?" Diana asked.

"That he had actually done some of those things himself. And that there were others."

"Other what?" Diana asked.

"Other victims," Myrna Louise answered. "Ones the police knew nothing about."

For several moments after that, Diana didn't trust herself to speak. She was thinking about the ashes of the cassette tape she had swept out of the fireplace and thrown into the garbage can before Brandon and the kids came home from Payson. If there were other victims, did that also mean there were other tapes?

"You told me a little while ago that he tried to kill you the same day he attacked me."

"He didn't exactly try," Myrna Louise corrected. "He was going to. He planned to, but I drove away before he had a chance."

"Did he have a tape recorder or tapes with him that day?"

Myrna Louise pursed her lips. "It's really hard for me to talk about this," she said.

"About what?"

"About the tape recorder."

Diana felt a chill run up and down her spine. "So there was a tape recorder?"

"Yes," Myrna Louise answered. "Yes, there was."

"What happened to it?"

"That's the part I don't want to talk about. When the detectives found it under the car seat in Jake's Valiant—my second husband's Valiant—I told them it was mine and they let me keep it. If you write into your book that it was really Andrew's, I might still get in trouble over it. For concealing evidence."

"What did you do with the tape recorder, Mrs. Rivers?" Diana asked. "It could be very important."

"I pawned it," Myrna Louise answered. "Andrew asked me about it later, about what had happened to it. I told him the detectives took it. So, please, it's better if you don't say anything about it at all. It could raise all kinds of ruckus."

"When you took the recorder, were there any tapes with it?"

"Only some blanks. A whole package of blanks."

"But none that had been used?"

For a long time after that, Myrna Louise Rivers didn't answer. She had gathered up the deck of cards from the table and sat there absently shuffling them. Finally she reached for her walker and stood up.

"Excuse me, Mrs. Rivers," Diana said. "I haven't had a chance to ask you . . ."

"We have to go back to my room now," Myrna Louise said. "They'll be setting up for lunch in a few minutes anyhow, so we'll need to be out of the way. But I want to give you something."

Vista Retirement Center was laid out in a quadrangle. The front wing of the building was the common area with the dining hall, a recreation area, library, and lobby. One of the side wings was the convalescent wing. The two other wings were devoted to patients who were still well enough to come and go on their own. The wings were connected by shaded breezeways, but in the 110-degree heat, the shade didn't make that much difference.

By the time they reached Myrna Louise's room in the far back wing, Diana was worried the woman was going to faint with exertion. She sank down on the side of the bed, breathing hard.

"I'm not much good in all this heat," she gasped at last when she could speak. "Sit down. Let me catch my breath."

A wall-unit air conditioner grumbled under the screened window, but the air flow didn't make a dent in the hot dusty air of that small, spartan room. In addition to a bed, the room contained a single easy chair, a dresser with a small television set on it, and a kitchen table with two chairs. A door led to a tiny bathroom. The place was grim enough that it reminded Diana more of a monk's cell or prison accommodations than it did a retirement home. Diana sank into the chair and waited until a winded Myrna Louise Rivers was finally able to speak.

"There are some shoe boxes on the top shelf of the closet," the woman managed at last. "If you wouldn't mind bringing me the bottom one, I'd appreciate it."

Diana did as she was told. In the closet she found three shoe boxes stacked one on top of the other. From the weight of the first two, it seemed likely that they contained shoes. The third one seemed to hold something as well, but it felt far too light to be a pair of shoes. When Diana shook the box slightly, it gave a muffled rattle, as though whatever was inside had been packed in tissue paper.

Taking the box over to the bed, she handed it to Myrna Louise. The woman's gnarled, liver-spotted hand shook as she reached out to take it. "That's the one," she said.

Holding it on her lap for a few moments, she gazed off into space as though her thoughts were far away from this grim place where she was living out her final years. She sat with one hand resting on the lid as if she were unwilling to open it.

"I send him candy, you know," she murmured thoughtfully. "Every year on his birthday, I see to it that he has a box of chocolates from me. I know he gets them although he never sends thank-you notes. Andrew never was big on thank-you notes, you see. The problem is, it's hard for me to connect the person I'm sending the candy to—the person who is my son—to this."

She gave the shoe box a desultory pat. "It doesn't seem possible that the little boy I used to make birthday cakes for is the same person. Does that make sense?"

Diana nodded and said nothing.

"He came back home the day before all that happened,"

Myrna Louise continued thoughtfully. "He had been gone overnight in Jake's car. I didn't ask him where he had been—I never asked him that, because he would have told me it was none of my business. But when he came home, he was wearing this."

Carefully she removed the lid. Inside the shoe box Diana saw a splash of vivid-pink material. Slowly Myrna Louise lifted the fabric from the box and unrolled it, revealing a bright pink silk pantsuit. Something hard and small was at the very center of the roll of material—something Myrna Louise deftly covered with one hand before Diana could glimpse what it was.

"That's a woman's pantsuit, isn't it?" Diana asked. "Why was your son wearing that?"

"It's beautiful, isn't it," Myrna Louise said, passing the top to Diana so she, too, could finger the delicate material.

"And expensive," Diana added. "But you still haven't told me why was he wearing it."

"At the time he said it was like kids playing dress-up, but I realized later that it was a disguise he wore when he left that hotel in Tucson after he killed that man, that guy who worked in the movies."

Johnny Rivkin's name leaped to the forefront out of the long-buried past. He had been the second victim in Andrew Carlisle's three-day reign of terror after he was released from prison in June of 1975. Rivkin, a noted Hollywood costume designer, had met Andrew Carlisle at a well-known gay watering hole, a pickup joint, in downtown Tucson. After meeting in the bar at the Reardon Hotel, Rivkin had invited Carlisle to join him for a drink in his hotel suite at the Santa Rita a few blocks away. That casual invitation had ended several hours later with Johnny Rivkin's throat slit.

"When Andrew brought this into my house," Myrna Louise was saying, "I was upset. I hated seeing him dress like that because he wasn't queer—at least I didn't used to think so. But it was made of real silk. I had real silk myself once, back when I was married to Howie—Andrew's father. But not since. And I guess I must have been a little envious, too. So when that police officer came to see me that night in Tempe . . ."

"Detective Farrell?" Diana asked, remembering G. T. "Geet" Farrell, the Pinal County detective who had joined forces with Brandon Walker and Fat Crack in trying to track down Gina Antone's newly released killer.

Myrna nodded. "That's right. That's the one. When he came by asking me questions, I knew they were going to take Andrew away and lock him up again. So when I went down the hall to use the bathroom, I took this out of Andrew's closet and put it in mine. I didn't think he'd mind.

"Everything happened that night. For months afterward, I just left it there in my closet without daring to touch it. Then one day I was invited to go to a senior singles dance and I decided to try it on. I thought if I had the sleeves and pants shortened, maybe it would fit. That's when I found this," she said. "It was there in one of the jacket pockets the whole time."

Myrna Louise moved her hand. There, in her lap, lay a single cassette tape.

Without having to listen to it or even touch it, Diana Ladd Walker knew exactly what it was. In that moment, though, she found herself able to be grateful for one small blessing. In 1968, when Gina died, and again in 1975, VCRs and video cameras had been invented, but they weren't available to everyone.

And most especially Diana was grateful that they weren't available to Andrew Philip Carlisle.

Mitch Johnson tried to listen carefully while Diana told him about the interview with Myrna Louise. What interested him most of all was what she left out. Again, there was no mention of Andy's tape. So he had been right about that. She had kept that part of their exchange a secret—not only in writing the book but probably also in what she told those closest to her. That was all right, she wouldn't be able to keep that secret forever. Not after tonight.

The other item of interest was what she said about Myrna Louise's death. She had said a stroke. When word of Myrna Louise's death had come to the prison, Andy had laughed at the incompetent ninnies who ruled it as death by natural causes.

"Why is that so funny?" Mitch had asked.

"Because they're wrong. Because I made arrangements to have someone slip her a little something."

As well as Mitch knew Andy by then, the whole idea was a little startling. "Your own mother?" Mitch asked.

"Why not?" Andy returned. "Once she handed Diana's little care package over to my hired-hand delivery boy, there was no sense in her hanging around. After all, that damned rest home was costing a fortune. And don't pretend to be so shocked, Mitch. After all, it's in your own best interests."

"Mine!"

"You bet. Myrna Louise's rent at that retirement home was coming directly out of my pocket—and yours, too."

"I suppose you're right," Mitch had said. "But you arranged the whole thing from here?"

"Sure," Andy said. "If you've got enough money, hiring decent help is no problem."

Mitch continued going through the motions of seeming to listen intently and of taking notes, but he was losing interest. There comes a time in every bullfight when it's time to end the capework and uncover the sword. His purpose was to leave Diana Ladd Walker with something to think about later on. Something that would, in the aftermath of what was about to happen between Lani and Quentin, leave her questioning all her smug assumptions about the kind of person she was and how she had raised her children.

He waited until she paused. "Listening to you now and remembering the way you describe Andrew Carlisle's mother in the book, you make her sound perfectly ordinary."

"She *was* perfectly ordinary," Diana said. "That's what I wanted to show about her. Myrna Louise Rivers was far less educated than her son and hadn't had the benefit of all the advantages that accrued to him from his father's side of the family. People like to believe that monsters beget monsters, but she wasn't a monster, not by any means. I think it's far too easy for society to believe that killers inherit their evil tendencies from their parents and then pass them along to their own children. As I said in the book, I don't believe that's true."

"Is that the case in your own situation as well?"

Diana frowned. "What do you mean?"

"In the case of your stepson, Quentin. You don't feel that his upbringing had anything to do with what happened to him or to the other son, the one who ran away?"

Mitch was delighted to see the angry flush that flooded Diana Walker's face. "No," she said firmly. "Quentin Walker and Tommy Walker were both responsible for their own actions."

"But isn't it possible that your relationship with their father closed those two boys out somehow and that's why they ended up going so haywire?"

Gleefully, Mitch saw the muscles on Diana's jawline contract. "No," she said. "I don't think that at all. By the time I met them, both those boys were headed in the wrong direction. There was nothing their father and I could do to change that course."

Maybe it didn't seem like much of a seed, but once Brandon and Diana Walker were trying to come to grips with the fact that their son Quentin had murdered his sister Lani, it would give them something more to think about.

Monty Lazarus made a show of glancing at his watch. "My God!" he exclaimed. "Look at the time. I promised

Megan that I'd have you home in plenty of time for your dinner. Based on that, I booked another appointment. I'm supposed to meet some friends, and I'm about to be late. Would you mind if we finished this up and shot the pictures sometime tomorrow?"

If Diana Ladd Walker had posed for a photo right then, the camera probably would have captured exactly what she was thinking—that it would have given her the greatest of pleasure to shove the camera right back down Monty's arrogant goddamned throat.

"That would be fine," she said, trying not to let her relief show at finally escaping this interminable interview. Maybe by tomorrow she could find a way to be reasonably civil to this jackass.

"What time?"

"Say two o'clock."

"All right. And where? Out at the house?"

"No. Not your place. I have some locations in mind. I'll call you in the morning and let you know where to meet me."

"Fine." Diana got up and started away, but before she went too far, she remembered her manners. "Thanks for the refreshments."

"Think nothing of it," Monty Lazarus said with an ingratiating smile. "It was my pleasure."

The EMTs immediately went to work attempting to stabilize their patient. Agent Kelly and Deputy Fellows suddenly found themselves with nothing to do. Sent packing from the scene of all the action, the two officers retreated to the spot where their vehicles were parked.

Agent Kelly was a short, sturdy blonde with closely-cropped hair, gray-green eyes, and an easy smile. Brian had no idea how long she had been out in the baking sun with the injured man, but her face was flushed. The shirt of her green uniform was soaked with sweat.

Opening the door to her van, she put the two empty water jugs—both his and hers—on the floorboard of the front seat, and then she pulled out another. Screwing open the cap, she held the jug over her head and poured, letting the water spill down. Once she was thoroughly soaked, she handed the gallon jug over to Brian. "Live a little," she said.

After a momentary hesitation, Brian followed suit. "My name's Katherine Kelly, by the way," she told him as he gave the jug back to her. "Kath for short. We didn't exactly have time for official introductions before." She held out her hand.

Before, when they had been working together and dealing with a crisis, Brian had been totally at ease. Now his natural reticence reasserted itself, leaving him feeling tongue-tied and dim-witted. "Brian Fellows," he managed awkwardly.

If Kath Kelly suffered any social difficulties, they didn't show. "Did you call for a detective?" she asked.

Brian nodded. "I did, but they're not sending one," he said. "Everybody's busy, so I'm told. They told me to write it up myself, but the way Dispatch said it, you can tell they'd as soon I dropped the whole thing. After all, the guy's just an Indian."

Kath Kelly's gray-green eyes darkened to emerald. "There's a lot of that going around in my department, too," she said. "So are you going to drop it?"

"No, I'm going to take Dispatch at their word and investigate the hell out of this. Crime-scene investigation may not be my long suit, but I've done some."

"I can help for a while, but as soon as the helicopter leaves, I'll have to get back on patrol. Before I forget, you don't look much like an Indian. Where'd you learn to speak *Tohono O'othham?*"

"From one of my friends, in Tucson," he said.

"Really." Kath smiled. "Pretty impressive," she said. "I speak French fluently and Spanish some, but I couldn't understand a word that poor guy was saying. It's a good thing you showed up. Is that why they have you working this sector of the county, because of your language skills?"

Brian shook his head. "Hardly," he answered with a short laugh. "Nobody at the department knows I speak a word of Papago. And don't tell them, either. It's a deep, dark secret."

For the next half-hour, working in a circle from the outside in, they carefully combed the entire area, finding nothing of interest. They were almost up to the edge of the *charco* before they came to a spot where, although someone had gone to a good deal of trouble to try to cover it up, there was clear evidence that the soil had recently been disturbed.

"It looks to me like this is where the bad guy was doing his forbidden digging," Brian observed.

Kath Kelly nodded. "And the Indian showed up and caught him in the act. What do you suppose was down there?"

"It could be a lot of things," Brian said. "There used to be an Indian village right around here called Rattlesnake Skull. My guess is we've stumbled on your basic artifact thief."

"Sounds like," Kathy agreed.

Before Brian could answer, one of the EMTs came looking for them. "Could the two of you give us a hand?" he asked. "We brought a gurney along, but we can't use it—not in this soft dirt. And this guy's way too heavy for two of us to carry him on a stretcher."

It took all four of them to haul the wounded man out of the mesquite grove toward the waiting helicopter. The man was mumbling incoherently as they loaded him aboard. Again, Brian wasn't able to make it all out, but he was able to pick out one or two words, one of which sounded like *pahl*—priest.

"I think he's asking for a priest," Brian told the EMT. "He's probably worried about last rites."

The man shook his head urgently. *"Pahla,"* he said. *"Pi-pahl."*

The EMT looked at Brian. "What's the difference?"

Brian shook his head. "Sorry," he said. "I know some *To-hono O'othham,* but obviously not enough."

"Just in case, we'll call for a priest all the same," the EMT replied, heading for the door.

"Wait a minute," Brian called after him. "You didn't happen to find any ID on the guy, did you?"

"None," the medic told him. "Not a stitch."

"And where are you taking him?"

"John Doe's on his way to TMC." Moments later, the helicopter took off in a huge man-made whirlwind. When the dust finally settled, Agent Kelly reached in her pocket and extracted a business card.

"If they're gone, I'd better be going, too, but here are my numbers in case you need to reach me about any of this."

"Good thinking," Brian said, fumbling for one of his own cards. "I probably will need to get in touch with you. For my report."

Kath Kelly looked up into his face as she took the card. "You're welcome to call me even if it's not for your report," she said with a smile.

Then, tucking his card in her breast pocket, she turned and walked away, leaving an astonished Brian Fellows staring after her.

For eleven long years, Brian Fellows had been his mother's main caretaker. Her overwhelming physical need had attached itself to Brian's own hyper-developed sense of responsibility. His mother's illness had sucked him dry, robbing him of the last of his adolescence and blighting his social life in the process.

At age twenty-six, faced with clear encouragement from a woman he found immensely attractive, he was left blushing as she drove away.

"I'll be damned," he said to himself. "I *will* be damned."

*   *   *

Diana fumed all the way home. How dare Monty Lazarus imply that whatever had happened with Quentin and Tommy was in any way her fault? She was no more responsible for Quentin ending up in prison than Myrna Louise was for Andrew Carlisle's being there.

By the time she drove past the Leaving Tucson City Limits sign two blocks before the turnoff to the house in Gates Pass, she was starting to feel better. The tension in her jaw relaxed. Their home, as well as five others, sat on a small ten-acre parcel which, because of the attractive nuisance of a nearby target-shooting range, had never been annexed by the City of Tucson.

As she turned off Speedway onto the dirt drive leading up to the house, she could tell by the tire tracks left in the dust that several large, unfamiliar vehicles had come in and out that way earlier in the day. That was one thing about living at the end of a dirt road. You learned to read tracks.

She expected to find Brandon still outside, laboring over his wood. Instead, after hanging her car keys up on the pegboard just inside the kitchen doorway, she wandered on into the living room, where she found a showered, shaved, and nattily dressed Brandon Walker sitting on the couch reading a newspaper. Two champagne glasses and an ice bucket with a chilled bottle of Schramsberg sat on the coffee table in front of him.

"What's this?" Diana asked.

"A little surprise," he said. "Could I interest you in a drink?"

Nodding, Diana sank gratefully down on the couch beside him. "How was it?" he asked.

"Awful. It seemed like it went on forever," she replied. "And it's not over yet. We ran out of time to do the pictures. Those are scheduled for two o'clock tomorrow afternoon."

"After spending half of today, you're still not done? What's this guy doing, writing an article or a biography?"

Diana laughed. Just being home and watching Brandon pour the sparkling liquid into one of the glasses made her feel better. "As a matter of fact, it may be a little of both. Monty Lazarus has an unusual approach to doing an interview. Calling it roundabout is giving it the benefit of the doubt.

"So what have you been up to all afternoon, and what's the big occasion? I haven't seen you this dressed up or happy in months."

Brandon handed her a glass and then touched his to hers. "To us," he said.

"To us," she nodded.

Brandon took a sip. "I spent most of the afternoon loading up three livestock trucks full of wood," he answered. "Fat Crack told me yesterday that he thought he knew someone who could use it. Today Baby Ortiz came by with a bunch of other Indians, and we loaded up three truckloads to take to the popover ladies over at San Xavier."

As a toddler, Gabe's older son, Richard, had wandered around with his diapers at half-mast, much the way his father always wore his low-riding Levi's. It hadn't taken long for people to start calling him *A'ali chum Gigh Tahpani*—Baby Fat Crack. Now forty years old and half again as wide as his father, most people simply called him Baby.

"Baby says he thinks the wood chips might help with the mud problem on the playfield down at Topawa."

"And whoever's going to use the wood will come get it?" Diana asked.

"That's right. They'll come load it and haul it away." Brandon laughed. "I'll bet you thought you were going to be stuck with that mountain of wood permanently, didn't you?" he teased.

"It was beginning to look that way," Diana agreed.

"It makes me feel good that someone's going to get some benefit out of all my hard work," Brandon added seriously. "And as for my being dressed to the nines, I thought I'd straighten up and give the Friends of the Library a real treat, show up as author consort in full-dress regalia."

He put one arm around Diana's shoulder and pulled her close. "It's also an apology of sorts. I've been a real self-centered jerk of late, haven't I?"

"Not as bad as all that," she answered with a laugh.

They sat for several minutes, enjoying their champagne and the comfort of a companionable silence. "What time do we have to be at the dinner?"

Diana looked at her watch. "Megan said six, but we don't really have to be there until seven."

"You mean we have two whole hours all to ourselves?"

She smiled at him over her glass. "Wait a minute," she said coyly. "Are you suggesting what I think you're suggesting?"

Brandon shrugged. "You saw Lani's note. She said she was going directly to the concert . . ."

One of the first and most ongoing casualties of the loss of the election had been to their sex life. Diana had managed to put it out of her mind, but now that Brandon was actually suggesting making love, she wasn't about to turn him down.

Diana stood up and started for the bedroom. "Here goes my hairdo and makeup," she said.

"I didn't think about that," Brandon said. "If you don't want to . . ."

Stopping in the bedroom doorway, she turned and smiled. "Nobody said anything about not wanting to," she said. "It just means that I'll go to dinner with the natural look. It's a lot more like me than this is. Now come in and close the door," she added. "And go ahead and lock it. Lani said she wouldn't be home before the concert, but let's not take any chances."

As Mitch Johnson drove back toward the RV, he was almost wild with anticipation. He had come through the interview with flying colors, done his capework admirably, but the next segment of the adventure would contain the two parts of the plan Andy had lobbied for so adamantly. The rest of the program he had been content to leave entirely in Mitch's hands, to let the person with the ultimate responsibility for putting the plan into action noodle out the details. But for Andy, this was the sine qua non.

"If you can manage to lay hands on the girl," Andy had said, "whatever else you do to her, be sure her mother knows that it's coming from me. Understand?"

Understand? Of course, Mitch had understood. How could he have spent seven and a half years living with Andy Carlisle and listening to the man obsess about women's breasts without understanding? The trick was doing what Andy wanted without being caught.

Women's breasts and what Andy had done to them had been his undoing, at least part of it. Somebody had lost the toothmarks from Gina Antone's mutilated body, but the detectives had matched the ones on the dead woman at Picacho Peak and the ones on Diana Ladd and had used them as part of the evidence that sent Andrew Carlisle to prison for the second time. Andy had talked about that constantly, about how once a woman's breast was exposed to him, he was physically incapable of not biting it.

"So what's the problem here?" Mitch had asked one day, when he was feeling particularly brave and when he felt as though Andy had beaten the subject to death. "Didn't your mother ever nurse you?" he had asked. "How come, when you talk about tits, it's only in terms of mangling them or biting them off instead of using them the way God intended?"

"What my mother did or didn't do is none of your damned business." Andy said the words in a way that made Mitch's blood run cold. He knew at once that he had stepped over some invisible line, and he sincerely wished he hadn't.

"Sorry," he said quickly. "I didn't mean to insult your mother. It's just that sucking on a woman whose boobs are overflowing with milk can be a beautiful thing. I thought maybe you might have tried it."

"No," Andy had responded. "I never have."

"Damn," Lori muttered.

Half-asleep, Mitch rolled over on his side to face her. "What's wrong?"

"Mikey didn't eat," she said. "He already fell back to sleep. He barely touched the one side, and I'm soaking wet on the other."

Mitch reached out and cupped Lori's swollen breast in one hand. She was right. The leaking milk had soaked her nightgown from armpit to waist.

"If you'd let me, maybe I could take some of the pressure off."

"Never mind," she said. "I'll go get the breast pump."

"No, don't," he said. "Let me do it. Please. It won't hurt anything. Mikey won't know."

Lori didn't answer right away, but she didn't move his hand, either. Finally she sighed. "All right," she said. "I guess it would be all right, just this once."

There was no need to unbutton the gown because she slept with it open. Mitch did have some trouble unfastening the nursing bra. He had seen her do it, of course, but watching it done from the inside out wasn't the same as doing it from the outside in and in the dark as well. At last, though, he ran his hand over her damp naked breast. The distended nipple lay erect and inviting beneath his grazing fingertips.

"If you're going to do it," Lori said, "don't take all night."

Whenever he'd had the chance to watch Lori nurse, he'd observed the strange mixture of anticipation and dread with which she greeted Mikey's clamping his hungry lips over her nipple. Sometimes she'd make a sound that was almost like the sigh of satisfaction Mitch's grandmother used to make after taking a sip of too hot coffee.

Raising up on his elbows, Mitch leaned over and clamped on. As his lips closed around her nipple, he felt her body tense and instantly afterward go limp as the sweet, hot milk shot into his mouth. It gushed out at him, shooting all the way to the back of his mouth, teasing his tonsils, almost triggering his gag reflex, but he fought that down and concentrated on sucking, on draining her without ever gripping her with his teeth.

There was more milk inside her than he expected, but at last that one was empty. He sat up to find that in the dark she had deftly unfastened the other side, and now, giggling, she pulled him down onto that one, too, holding him by the back of the neck, pressing him against her, groaning with pleasure as his now aching jaws relieved the pressure on that sore breast as well.

Ever since they had brought Mikey home from the hospital three weeks earlier, Mitch had been intensely curious about the process. For weeks he had begged Lori to let him taste her, but what had never crossed his mind was that the process might pleasure her as well. The fact that she was enjoying it almost as much as he did unleashed months of pent-up sexual deprivation. When he let go of her nipple, she was still laughing so hard that at first she didn't seem to notice that he was prying her legs apart. But she did notice.

"No, Mitch," she said. "It's still too soon. The doctor . . ."

By then Mitch Johnson wasn't interested in what the doctor had said or in what Lori wanted, either. He desperately craved the solace her body had to offer. He craved it and he took it. He had barely shoved himself home when his aching need exploded inside her like a burst of Fourth of July fireworks.

Afterward as he drifted in a mellow haze, he realized she was crying. "What's wrong now?" he asked.

"You raped me." She didn't say it loud, but he knew she meant it.

"No, I didn't," he said. "You wanted it as much as I did. You were *asking* for it."

"You raped me," she repeated dully. "I told you no and you did it anyway."

"I did not rape you," he declared. "How could I? You're my wife."

As far as Mitch Johnson was concerned, the subject was closed. In Tucson, Arizona, in 1975, Lori Kiser Johnson didn't try pressing charges because she knew they wouldn't stick. What she did do, however, was far more effective. From then on, she never said yes to Mitch again, not when it came to sex. Oh, he did get a piece of tail now and then, but only when he took it. And there was never any response. She lay beneath him whenever he did it, dry and unmoving, letting him inside her because she didn't seem to have any choice in the matter, but making sure neither one of them enjoyed it.

Considering that turn of events, it was hardly surprising that a few months later Mitch was out in the desert shooting hell out of a bunch of wetbacks. As frustrated as he was, who wouldn't?

As Mitch turned left on Coleman Road, he saw a huge cloud of dust come roiling up out of the desert about a half mile away. A moment later a helicopter emerged from the cloud and set off toward town. That struck him as odd—worried him a little—but clearly it had nothing to do with him. Two miles down the road, behind a locked gate, the Bounder sat in undisturbed, solitary splendor exactly as he'd left it.

When he stopped the car, he got out and stood for a moment listening. The only sound was the steady thrum of the air conditioner. He had created an extra duct that ran through the storage unit. It was hot, and it wouldn't have done to have Lani Walker baked to a crisp or suffocated before he had his chance at her.

He stood there observing the Bounder and the vast tract

of empty desert around it. He was almost sorry to leave this place. It had been good to him, had allowed the creative juices to flow. But it was time. He had other places to go, other fish to fry, including the stupid-ass second lieutenant from Asheville, North Carolina, who had led his platoon into a Vietcong trap and permanently fucked up Mitch's knee.

Like it or not, it was almost time to abandon the desert. Mitch had already called his landlord to say he was moving and had notified the power company, telling them to shut off the juice as of Wednesday. His would be a planned exit. There would be no question about him deciding to leave after all the shit hit the fan.

If anyone had seen him standing there, they might have thought he was simply admiring the landscape. What he was really doing was seeing how long he could keep from opening the door. Would she be awake or not? Her reaction to the drug had been so pronounced that he worried now that she might still be groggy. That would be too bad. The moment she saw his face, he wanted her to know. Anything less than that wouldn't be enough.

It had been fun toying with Diana without her having the foggiest idea of what was really going on. But with Lani it was different. Diana had said she was a smart girl, and Mitch Johnson desperately wanted that to be so. He wanted her to be smart enough to realize what was happening. To Mitch's way of thinking, knowing in advance, foreseeing the possibilities and dreading them, were the only things that would place Lani Walker any higher on the evolutionary ladder than the dumb little bird he had crushed in his fist years earlier.

Finally, taking a deep breath, he walked up to the door and put his key in the Bounder's custom-made dead bolt. Then he opened the door and stepped inside.

"Honey, I'm home," he called as he pulled the door shut behind him.

*　　*　　*

While Candace was in the bathroom getting ready to go to dinner, Davy paced the room. It wasn't just the ring. It was everything. There was a hole in the pit of his stomach. His palms were wet. Sweat was already soaking through his clean shirt. And the only thing he could think of was that something was wrong—terribly wrong—at home.

Finally, feeling numb, he picked up the phone and dialed. His mother answered, sounding annoyed or sleepy, he couldn't tell which.

"Is Lani there?" he asked.

"She's not home from work yet," Diana said. "And she's supposed to go straight from work to a concert with Jessica Carpenter. Why, is something wrong?"

"No," Davy mumbled. "I just wanted to talk to her."

"What about?" Diana asked. "You sound worried."

David Ladd's mind raced, trying to find a plausible reason for calling that had nothing to do with what he was feeling. "It's a secret," he said, as inspiration struck. "It's about your anniversary present. But that's all right. I can talk to her tomorrow."

"Give me your number," Diana said. "I'll leave her a note in case she does come home before the concert."

Blushing to the roots of his light-blond hair, David Garrison Ladd looked down at the phone on the nightstand and read his mother the number of the Ritz Carlton in Chicago, Illinois. He put down the phone praying fervently that Lani *wouldn't* stop by the house before the concert.

"Who was that?" Candace asked when she came out of the bathroom. "I thought I heard you talking to someone on the phone."

"I just called home to give the folks a progress report," he lied. "My mother worries about me, and I wanted her to know that everything is fine."

Deputy Fellows was used to working on his own. After Kath Kelly left, it took some time for him to get his mind back on the job, but eventually he did. He made plaster casts of what footprints he found. He combed the area again, looking for clues. And three separate times he retraced the path of the dirt track from the place where the attack had taken place to the spot where Kath Kelly had found the injured man lying in the dirt.

It was a long way. Almost a hundred yards. The question was why the killer would drag his victim anywhere at all? Eventually the answer became clear. The attack had been a reaction to being discovered rather than a premeditated crime. As such, the attacker didn't view himself as a killer. Rather than finish his victim off, he had simply dragged the injured man away, and hopefully out of view, expecting nature to take its course.

That meant that the real crime and also the key to the attacker's real intentions and identity had something to do with the digging back on the edge of the *charco*. At four o'-clock in the afternoon, Brian went back to his truck, took a long drink from the last of his water, and collected his shovel. At four-ten, he started to dig.

Digging is a solitary occupation done with an implement that has changed little from ancient times to modern. The act of shoving a sharp spade into the dirt and then extracting a heaping shovel leaves plenty of time for reflection.

With the scattered remains of Gina Antone's shrine mere feet away from him, pieces of Brian Fellows's own life intruded into his thoughts about the case he was working on. Most people would have said that Brian came from a "troubled background." He had found respite from his half-brothers' constant taunting only at school and during those precious hours when he had managed to escape Janie's chaotic household to spend time at the Walker place in Gates Pass.

As Davy Ladd's faithful shadow, Brian had been welcome in places where he never would have been able to venture otherwise. He had walked, wide-eyed, into the dimly lit adobe hut where a blind medicine man named Looks At Nothing had lain confined to a narrow cot. The blind man had been sick, dying of a lingering cough, but he had nonetheless continued to smoke his strange-smelling cigarettes, lighting them one after another, with a cigarette lighter that somehow never once burned his fingers.

Those *Tohono O'othham* people—Rita, Looks At Nothing, Fat Crack, all of them—had been unfailingly kind to little Brian Fellows in a way his own family—mother, stepbrothers, and successive "daddies"—never had.

And now, as he worked in the hot sun with his shovel, he felt as though he was protected somehow from the restless spirits that Davy Ladd had once told him inhabited this place. He had barely come to that conclusion when his shovel bit into something hard. Not wanting to break it, he tossed his shovel aside and then got down on his knees to dig in the sand by hand.

Almost immediately, his hand closed around something long and smooth and straight. When he pulled whatever it was free of the dirt, he saw at once that it was a bone. A leg bone of some kind, he thought. Maybe from a weakened cow that had once become trapped in the muddy *charco* and drowned. He dug some more and was rewarded with another long bone and what looked like a rib of some kind. Up until he found the rib, he kept thinking the bones belonged to an animal. The rib, however, had a very human look to it. Then his hands closed around something round and smooth and hard. The hair rose on the back of his neck. Letting go of the skull, he didn't even bother to finish pulling it free of its earthen prison.

Instead, he climbed out of the hole, walked back to his Blazer, and called in. Fortunately, the dispatcher on duty earlier had gone home for the day. "Where've you been, Fellows? I was about to send someone out looking for you."

"Great," Brian said. "If you're sending somebody, how about a homicide detective? Have him come equipped with shovels and some water—especially the water. I'm about to die of thirst."

"A homicide detective. Why? What have you got? The last I heard you were working on an assault. Did the guy die?"

"Not as far as I know," Brian Fellows said. "That guy was still alive when they loaded him into the helicopter. But somebody else out here is dead as a doornail."

"Dead?" the dispatcher returned. "Who is it?"

"How should I know?" Brian answered. "That's why I need a homicide detective."

"I'll get right on it," the dispatcher said. This time Deputy Fellows was relatively sure the man meant what he said.

It was about time.

11

So I'itoi *gave orders to chase the evil ones to the ocean. When they reached the shore of what is now the Gulf of California, Great Spirit sang a song. As* I'itoi *sang, the waters were divided and the Bad People rushed in to go to the other side. Then Elder Brother called the waters together again, and many of the* PaDaj O'othham—*the Bad People—were drowned, but some reached the other side.*

Great Spirit again tried to have his good warriors kill those evil ones that had escaped the waters, but the warriors would not. And I'itoi—*Spirit of Goodness—felt so ashamed that he made himself small and came back from the other side through the ground, under the water.*

Many of his people returned with I'itoi, *but some could not, and these were very unhappy, for the* PaDaj O'othham *who had not been destroyed were increasing.*

Then I'itoi's *daughter said she would save these good Indians who were not happy. She took all the children to the seashore, where they sat down and sang together. This is the song that* I'itoi's *daughter and* A'ali—*the Children—sang:*

> *O white birds who cross the water,*
> *O white birds who cross the water,*
> *Help us now to cross the water.*
> *We want to go with you across the water.*

Kohkod—*the Seagulls—heard the song. They came down and studied* I'itoi's *daughter and the children. Then* Kohkod *flew up and circled around, singing:*

> *Take these feathers that we give you*
> *Take these white feathers that we give you—*
> *Take the feathers floating round you*
> *And do not fear to cross the water.*

So the Indians took the white feathers that the seagulls gave them. They bound the feathers round their heads and crossed the water safely. That is why, nawoj, *my friend, the* Tohono O'othham *keep those white feathers—the* stoha a'an—*very carefully, even to this day.*

Candace and David had a beautiful dinner together in the hotel dining room. The champagne Candace ordered was Dom Perignon. "It's okay," she said, sending a radiant smile in Davy's direction over the top of the wine list. "Daddy said we could have whatever we want. It's on him."

"Exactly how much did Bridget and Larry's wedding set your folks back?" David asked once the sommelier left the table. Bridget was Candace's next older sister. Her wedding had taken place two months before Davy and Candace met.

Candace shivered. "You don't even want to know," she said. "It was a complete circus. She had nine attendants."

David gulped. "Nine?"

"The reception was a sit-down dinner for three hundred at the club. It was awful. 'Ghastly' is the word Daddy used. He was a little drunk before it was all over that night. I remember him taking me aside and telling me that night that no matter what, he wasn't going to go through that again."

The waiter returned carrying a champagne bucket. Candace winked at Davy. "All Daddy's doing is making good on that promise."

The wine was served with all due ceremony. "I finished reading your mother's book last night," Candace Waverly said over the top of her glass a few moments later. "You hardly ever talk about that, you know. I remember your saying once that your mother was a writer, but until she won that big prize last month, and until Mom saw her on 'The Today Show,' I didn't know she was an *important* writer. My dad only reads boring stuff like *The Wall Street Journal* and *Barron's*, but still he's dying to meet her. So's Mother."

"She'll probably be in Chicago on tour sometime," David said without enthusiasm. "Maybe she can meet your folks then."

"What do you think of it?"

"What do I think of what?" David Ladd asked. "Of her going on tour? Of her meeting your parents?"

Candace glared at him in mock exasperation. "No, silly. Of her book."

In fact, like his stepfather, David Ladd had avoided reading *Shadow of Death* like the plague, and for many of the same reasons. For the first seven years of his life, Davy had been an only child, the son of a woman obsessed by her dream of becoming a writer. In the beginning, maybe Davy hadn't had to contend with sibling rivalry as such, but there had always been competition for Diana Ladd Walker's attention. All his life David had felt as though he was forever relegated to second place, first behind Diana's typewriter, and then behind Brandon Walker and Lani and a succession of ever smaller computers.

With that foundation, it wasn't at all surprising that Davy regarded his mother's increasing success in the world of writing with a certain ambivalence. When it came to *Shadow of Death,* however, ambivalence turned to active abhorrence. He resented the idea that his mother would have anything at all to do with Andrew Carlisle—with the monster who had single-handedly brought so much destruction on the Ladd family. Andrew Carlisle was the single individual who bore ultimate responsibility for the death and subsequent disgrace of David Ladd's father, Garrison. Once released from prison, Carlisle had come back to Tucson. In a binge of vengeance, he had brutalized and raped David's mother while Davy himself remained imprisoned and helpless behind a locked root-cellar door.

Whatever innocuous words Diana Ladd Walker may have used to tell her side of that story, the one thing they couldn't absolve Davy of was the fact that he hadn't helped her. After all, what kind of a son *wouldn't* save his mother? Whenever David Ladd thought of those long-ago events, it was always with an abiding sense of shame and failure. He had let his mother down, had somehow forsaken her, leaving her defenseless in her hour of need. What could be more shameful than that?

For years Davy had fantasized about that day. In those imagined scenarios, he always emerged from the cellar and did battle with the evil *Ohb.* In those daydreams, Davy Ladd always fought Andrew Carlisle and won.

In writing *Shadow of Death,* Davy doubted his mother had taken his feelings on the subject into account. By reporting what happened in a factual manner—and Diana was always factual—she had no doubt held up Davy's glaring inadequacy for all the world to see. Everyone who read the book—even Candace—would know about David Garrison Ladd's terrible failure in the face of that awful crisis.

"I haven't read it," he said after a long interval.

Candace looked shocked. "You haven't? Why not?"

David Ladd thought about that for a minute more before he answered, fearing that just talking about it might be enough to bring on another panic attack and send his heart racing out of control.

"I guess you had to be there," he said finally. "Maybe my mother doesn't mind reliving that day, but I do. I don't ever want to be that scared or that powerless again."

"But you were just a child when it happened, weren't you?" Candace objected.

David nodded. "Six, going on seven," he said.

"See there?" Candace continued. "You're lucky. Most kids never have a chance to see their parents doing something heroic."

"Heroic!" David echoed. "Are you serious? Stupid, maybe, but not heroic. She could have had help if she'd wanted to. Brandon Walker wasn't my stepfather then, but I'm sure he offered to help her, and I'm equally sure she turned him down. The other thing she could have done was pack up and go someplace else until the cops had the guy back under lock and key."

"Still," Candace returned, "she did fight him, and she won. He didn't get away with it; he went to prison. So don't call your mother stupid, at least not to me. I think she was very brave, not only back then—when it happened—but also now, for talking about it after all these years and bringing it all out in the open."

David didn't want to quarrel with Candace, not in this elegant dining room populated by fashionably dressed guests and dignified waiters. "I guess we're all entitled to our opinions," he waffled. "You can call her brave if you want to. I still say she was stubborn."

Candace grinned. "So you could say that you come by that honestly."

David nodded. "I guess," he said.

They lingered over dinner for the better part of two hours, savoring every morsel. Then they went back up to their room and made love. Afterward, Candace fell asleep while Davy lay awake, waiting to see if the dream would come again, and worrying about what he would do if that happened.

How the hell could he be engaged and about to elope, for God's sake? He liked Candace well enough, but not that much. No way was he in love, and yet her suitcases were all packed and waiting by the door. And her father's bribe—her father's astonishingly generous twenty-five-thousand-dollar bribe!—was safely stashed in the side pocket of Candace Waverly's purse.

Davy rolled over on his side. Candace stirred beside him, sighed contentedly in her sleep, and cuddled even closer. The soft curls on her head tickled his nose and made him sneeze.

All his life David Ladd had pondered the mystery of his parents' relationship. He had never met his father. Everything he had heard about Garrison Ladd from his mother had been steeped in the dregs of Diana's disillusion and hurt. As a teenager, David had often asked himself if it was possible that his parents had ever loved one another. If not, if they had never been in love, why had they gotten married in the first place? What had caused them to disregard their basic differences in favor of holy matrimony?

Now, lying next to Candace, he was blessed with an inkling of understanding. Perhaps Garrison and Diana had been swept along on a tide of misunderstanding and confusion neither one of them had nerve enough to stop. Perhaps they had woken up married one day without really intending to. David had read a book once called *The Accidental Tourist*. And now here he was about to become an accidental bridegroom.

And it would happen, too. Candace would see to it. Unless Davy himself had brains and guts enough to do something to stop it.

David Ladd had been brought up by Rita Antone, by a woman raised in a non-confrontational culture. Among the *Tohono O'othham,* yes is always better than no.

He wondered, as he drifted off to sleep, if someone had told Candace Waverly that little secret about him, or if she was simply operating on instinct. Probably instinct was the correct answer, he thought.

As far as he could tell, women were like that.

Mitch hadn't thought that the girl would still be so far out of it, but she was. She lay quietly, making hardly any protest when he donned a pair of latex gloves and scrubbed her whole body with a rough, sun-baked towel—parts he had touched and some parts he hadn't—making sure that no traces of his own fingerprints lingered anywhere on her skin.

It took time to make the tape, asking her leading questions in a way that elicited mumbled but predictable answers. By the end of that, though, Mitch was concerned that it would soon be time to leave for town to keep the date with Quentin. Still Lani Walker dozed on and off. That frustrated Mitch no end. What he required from her—what he wanted more than anything—was awareness and fear. Without those, what he was doing just wasn't good enough. He knew he would have to treat her with scopolamine once more before they left for town—a much lighter dose this time—but in the meantime . . .

Taking out a pair of rubber-handled kitchen tongs he had purchased new for that sole purpose, he laid the metal teeth on the burner of the stove, turned on the fire, and set them to heat. He didn't take them off the flame until the rubber handles were starting to smolder.

When Mitch returned to the bed, he found Lani Walker sleeping peacefully once again. He stood for a moment looking down at her and feeling godlike, observing the smooth skin of her body, flawless still, except for those few white marks. He had the power to leave that body flawless or to mar it forever. There was never any real question of whether or not he would do it. There was only one decision left to make—choosing which one he would take.

"Lani!" he called out sharply. "Lani, wake up."

The long lashes fluttered open, but the dark eyes that looked questioningly up at him were vague and confused. There was no still comprehension in them, still no fear.

"Watch this," he said.

For ease of use, Mitch had left the tape recorder sitting on the floor beside the bed with the controls set on pause. With his gloved left hand, he reached down and punched the "record" button, then he slammed his good knee into her abdomen. The force of the blow sent the wind rushing out of her. Holding her pinioned to the bed with the full weight of his body, he clamped the scorching teeth of the tongs into the fullness of her right breast, an inch and a half on either side of the tender brown nipple.

Even tied hand and foot, Lani bucked so hard beneath him that she almost pitched him off her. He had to grab hold of her waist with his free hand to keep from being thrown onto the floor. Even that far away, the fierce heat from the searing tongs warmed the skin of Mitch's own face. The shockingly sweet smell of singeing flesh filled his nostrils.

It was a magic moment for Mitch. Feeling that naked body writhe in agony beneath his was as good as any sex he ever remembered. But the best part about it was the scream. That was far more than he could have hoped; better than anything he had ever imagined. Hearing Lani Walker's shriek of torment, it was all Mitch could do to hold back an answering moan of his own, one of exquisite pleasure rather than pain.

At last she lay still beneath him. As soon as she did so, he unclasped the tongs. He had to force the metal free from the charred skin. Around the wounded flesh, a wave of shocked goose bumps slid across her body. Mitch was surprised to see them. *Who knows?* he thought. *Maybe it did as much for her as it did for me.*

Reaching down, he quickly switched off the tape before she had a chance to say something that might somehow lessen the impact of that beautifully unearthly scream. Her sudden stillness was so complete that for a moment Mitch was afraid she might have fainted, thus depriving him and putting a temporary end to his fun. But no, when he looked down, her watery, tear-filled eyes were wide open, staring up at him in outraged, accusing silence.

Mitch Johnson wanted her to speak to him then, but she did not. If nothing else, he would have liked her to beg and plead with him not to hurt her again, but she didn't do that, either. After that one shrill, involuntary cry, no further sound escaped Lani Walker's lips, not even a whimper.

As the girl studied him, Mitch thought about Eve in the Garden of Eden. Like Eve growing beyond her mindless goodness, Lani had emerged from the cocoon of her drug-induced slumber. Willingly or not, she had now tasted the forbidden fruit. The dark, burning eyes she focused on him had been forever robbed of their trusting innocence.

"Welcome to the real world, babe," Mitch Johnson said, then he turned and walked away.

He held the tongs under running water from the faucet long enough to cool them down, until the fierce heat sizzled away, first into steam and then into nothing. Once they were cool enough, he put them back in the shopping bag they'd come in originally. Then he rewound the tape to the beginning, returned it to the plastic carrying case, and put that in the bag as well.

This one's for you, Andy, he thought. *It's a promise I made and one I kept. Somehow I doubt Diana Ladd Walker will like it as much as you would. In fact, she won't like it at all, but it's something she and Brandon Walker will never forget, not as long as they live.*

The pain was so blindingly intense that for a time Lani wasn't aware of anything else. The whole universe seemed centered in the seared flesh of her wounded breast. It overwhelmed her whole being. There were no words that encompassed that awful hurt, no thoughts that made such inhuman cruelty understandable.

At last, though, through her unseeing anguish, Lani became aware of the man standing over her, aware of his eyes pressing in on her and of her nakedness under that invasive gaze. She squirmed, as if hoping to escape that look, but the scarves binding her hands and legs held her fast. The only way to combat that look was to stare back at him, holding his gaze with her own.

Studying him, she was suddenly aware that he wanted something more from her, as if what he had already taken wasn't enough; as if he longed for something else in order to achieve real satisfaction.

Trying to imagine what that could be somehow took her mind away from the searing pain arcing through her body like the burning blue flash of her father's welding torch. And then, as clearly as if she had read his thoughts, she knew. Standing there, clothed in his presumed superiority, he was waiting for her to speak, to say something. It was almost as though he needed her to acknowledge his brutality and then bow before it.

Her only weapon was to deny him that satisfaction. She kept quiet, biting her lips to hold them together. After a long moment, he melted out of her line of vision, leaving her to ride out the terrible pain alone and in utter silence.

But somehow she wasn't alone. The vision came surging at her out of the past the moment she closed her eyes.

Lani was five years old again, standing naked in front of the mirror in her parents' bathroom. She had pawed through her mother's makeup and found the tube of concealer, the white lipstick-looking stuff Diana sometimes put under her eyes before she applied her other makeup.

Carefully, looking down at her body rather than watching her reflection in the mirror, Lani drew a perfect pair of half-moons on her flat chest, encircling the little brown knob of flesh that would someday grow into a nipple.

Then, pulling on her nightgown, she went racing through the house. She wanted to show someone her handiwork, but her parents were out. Instead, she went searching for Rita Antone. She found Nana *Dahd* in her room at the back of the house, working on a basket.

"Look," Lani crowed, pulling up her nightgown. "Look at what I did. Now I can be just like Mommy."

Rita's face had gone strangely pale and rigid the moment she saw the circle Lani had drawn on her body.

"Go wash," she ordered, in a terrible voice Lani Walker had never heard before. "Go wash that off. Do not do it again! Ever!"

"But why can't I be like Mommy?" she had said later, after she had showered for a second time. Once again dressed for bed, she had come back to Nana *Dahd's* room to say good night and hoping to make some sense of what had happened.

"Shhhh," Nana *Dahd* had told her. "Your mother looks like that because the evil *Ohb* did something to her. Because he hurt her. You shouldn't say such things. Someone might hear you and make it happen."

Now someone had.

Lani's eyes came open. The pain wasn't any less. If anything, it was worse. She looked down at the angry welt of seared flesh. It was red now and blistered, but someday it, too, would be a pale white scar, almost the same as the one that encircled the nipple on her mother's right breast.

And that was the moment when, without being able to say how, Lani knew this was the same thing. Lani had learned from reading her mother's book that Andrew Carlisle had been blinded and terribly disfigured by the bacon grease Diana Ladd had thrown at him. And she remembered a few weeks earlier, when her mother had told her father at dinner that it had said in the paper that Andrew Carlisle was dead.

Mr. Vega had worn his hair long and in a ponytail when

he had been out on the mountain, painting. This man's hair was very short. He was neither blind nor disfigured, but he was somehow connected to the evil *Ohb*.

Knowing that, Lani had a blueprint of what to do.

"I'm going to untie you now."

Once again the man was standing over her. "Actually, 'untie' isn't the word. Do you see this knife?"

In one hand he held a long narrow knife. The blade was very long and it looked sharp. "I'm going to cut you loose," he continued. "If you don't behave, I'll use it on you. Do you understand?"

Lani nodded again.

"All right then."

One at a time, he cut through the strands of silk that had held her captive. As soon as he set her limbs free, the pins and needles in her arms and legs—the cramps in her shoulders and hips—were bad enough that the new pain took some of Lani's attention away from the pulsing throb in her breast.

"Get up now," he ordered.

She tried to stand and then fell back on the low bed with a jarring thud. "I can't," she said. "My legs are asleep."

"Well, sit there, then." He turned away for a moment and came back holding out a cup. "Drink some of this," he said, sounding almost solicitous. "That must hurt, and maybe this will help deaden the pain."

Lani had figured out by then that he must have drugged her, that he must have put something in the orange juice she had drunk that morning or whenever it was when she was supposedly posing for him. And if he had drugged her once, no doubt he was going to do it again.

She reached up as if to take the cup. Instead of taking it, though, she slapped it out of his hand, gasping with pain at the shock of the cold water slicing across her burned flesh, searing it anew.

"Why, you goddamned bitch!" he muttered. "There's still

some fight left in you, isn't there. But believe me, there's plenty more where that came from."

He walked as far as the kitchen. She saw him pouring something into a fresh cup of water, then he came back. This time, before he gave her the cup, he knotted his other hand into the hair at the back of her neck, yanking her head backward.

"This time you'll drink it like a good girl, or I'll hold you down and pour the stuff down your goddamned throat. Got it?"

She nodded.

He placed the cup in her hand, and this time she drank it down. When she gave it back to him, he checked to make sure it was empty.

"That's better," he said. "You swallowed every drop. Here are your clothes now. Get dressed."

Concerned about fingerprints, he had rinsed out her clothing earlier that morning, but hadn't bothered to dry them. How could he? He didn't have a dryer, and if he had hung them on the clothesline, someone might have noticed. They were still a sodden lump when he tossed them into her lap.

"I can't wear these," she said. "They're wet."

"So? This isn't a fucking Chinese laundry," he told her. "Go naked if you want to. It sure as hell doesn't matter to me."

After a struggle, she finally managed to pull on the jeans. The shirt hurt desperately whenever it touched the burned spot on her breast, but at least the man couldn't look at her anymore. Without further protest she pulled on the wet socks and forced on the boots.

"Come on now," he said impatiently. "Off we go."

With her legs shaking beneath her, she staggered across the room. A few feet away, she stopped beside the easel. There in front of her was a picture—a picture that was undeniably of her.

Mr. Vega saw her stop beside the picture and look. "Well," he said. "What do you think? Is this the kind of thing you had in mind for your parents' anniversary present?"

"Tohntomthadag!" she said.

"You were talking Indian, weren't you," he observed. "What do those words mean?"

Lani Walker shook her head. She never had told Danny Jenkins that *s-koshwa* means "stupid." Not caring what he might do to her, she didn't tell Mr. Vega that in *Tohono O'othham*, the single word she had spoken, *tohntomthadag*, means "pervert."

In the forty minutes between the time Brian Fellows called Dispatch for assistance and the arrival of the detective, Brian stayed in the Blazer. Working on a metal clipboard, he started constructing the necessary paper trail of the incident. He began with the call summoning him to assist Kath Kelly and had worked his way up to unearthing the bones when he realized how stupid he was. Rattlesnake Skull, the ancient village that had once been near the *charco,* had been deserted for a long time, but it had probably been inhabited for hundreds of years before that. It made sense, then, that there would be nothing so very surprising about finding a set of human remains in that general area. In fact, it was possible there were dozens more right around there.

Brian Fellows was still considered a novice as far as the Pima County Sheriff's Department was concerned. He cringed at how that kind of mistake might be viewed by some of the department's more hard-boiled homicide dicks, none of whom would be thrilled at the idea of being dragged away from a Saturday-afternoon poolside barbecue to investigate a corpse that turned out to be two or three hundred years old.

Brian was putting together his backpedal routine when a dusty gray departmental Ford Taurus pulled up beside him. When the burly shape of a cigar-chomping detective climbed out of the driver's seat, Brian breathed a sigh of relief. Dan Leggett. Of all the detectives Brian might have drawn, Dan Leggett would have been his first choice. Dan was one of the old-timers, someone who had been around for a long time. Dan had grown up in law enforcement under Brandon Walker's leadership. He had a reputation for doing a thorough, professional job.

Tossing his clipboard to one side, Brian clambered out of the Blazer and hurried forward to meet the man.

"So what have you got here, Deputy Fellows?" Leggett asked. He handed Brian a plastic water jug and then paused to light a half-smoked cigar while Brian gulped a long drink. "Dispatch tells me they sent you out here to investigate a dead steer," he continued once the cigar was lit. "They claim you turned that steer into first a beating and now a homicide."

"I never said it was a homicide," Brian corrected, hoping to salvage a smidgeon of pride. "And it isn't even a whole body. I dug up some human bones is all. If it turns out to be some Indian who's been dead a few hundred years, you'll probably think I'm a complete idiot."

"Suppose you show me where these bones are and let me take a look for myself. Afterward, depending on the results, we can take a vote on Deputy Brian Fellows's powers of observation and general reliability."

"This way," Brian said. He led Detective Leggett over to his small collection of previously unearthed skeletal remains. "There's a skull down there too," the young deputy said. "Down there, toward the far end of the hole. As soon as I realized what it was, I left it there for fear of destroying evidence."

Leggett blew out a cloud of smoke, held the cigar so he was upwind of both the cigar and the smoke and downwind of the bones. He stood there for a moment, sniffing the air. Finally, he stuffed the cigar back in his mouth.

"Thank God whoever it is has been dead long enough that he or she doesn't stink," he said. Reaching into his pocket, he pulled out a second cigar and offered it to Brian. "Care for a smoke?" he asked.

Brian shook his head. "No, thanks," he said.

Leggett shrugged and stuffed the cigar back in his pocket. "Just wait," he said. "If you're in the dead-body business long enough, you'll figure out that there are times when nothing beats a good cigar. At least, that's what I keep telling my wife."

Clearly amused by his own joke, Leggett was still chuckling as he pulled on a pair of disposable latex gloves and then dropped to his hands and knees in the dirt. Chomping down on the lit cigar, he held it firmly in place while he used both hands to paw away loose sand. Brian kept his mouth shut and watched from the sidelines.

It wasn't long before Dan Leggett picked up a small piece of bone and tossed it casually onto the pile with the others. "Looks like a finger to me," he mumbled.

Still saying nothing, Brian waited anxiously for Leggett to locate the skull. Eventually he did, pulling it out of the dirt and then holding it upside down while sand and pebbles drained out through the gaping holes that had once been eyes and nose. When the skull was finally empty, Dan Leggett examined it for some time without saying a word. Finally, with surprising delicacy, he set it down on the ground beside the hole, then he stood for another long moment, staring at it thoughtfully while he took several leisurely puffs on his cigar.

Brian Fellows found the long silence difficult to bear, but he didn't say a word. Lowly deputies—especially ones who intend to survive in the law enforcement game—learn early on the importance of keeping their mouths shut in the presence of tough-guy homicide detectives. Finally, Leggett looked up at Brian and gave him a yellow-toothed grin.

"Well, Deputy Fellows," Leggett said, "it looks to me like you're in the clear on this one." He knocked a chunk of ash off the end of the cigar, but Brian noticed he was careful none of it landed in the hole or on any of the recently disturbed dirt around it.

Brian had been holding his breath. Slowly he let it out. "Why do you say that?" he asked.

"Because, if this guy had been dead for a couple hundred years, I doubt his head would have five or six silver fillings. I doubt the Indians who lived around here back then were much into modern dentistry."

"No," Brian agreed. "I suppose not. Can you tell what killed him?"

Leggett shook his head. "Much too soon to tell," he said. "Looks like there was quite a blow to his head, but it doesn't mean that's what killed him."

Stuffing the cigar back in his mouth, the detective climbed out of the hole. Brian was surprised to think the detective would give up the search so soon.

"So what do we do now?" Brian asked.

"We dig," Leggett returned. "Or rather, you dig and I watch. I've got a bad back. I trust you were wearing gloves when you handled those first few bones?" Brian nodded.

"Good boy. Chances are there won't be any fingerprints, but then again, you never can tell."

As the sun went down behind the Baboquivari Mountains in the west, Detective Leggett sat to one side of the hole, smoking, while Brian Fellows dug. He pawed in the soft dirt with renewed vigor. Slowly, one bone at a time, the grisly collection beside the hole grew in size. After several minutes of finding nothing, Brian was about to give up when his gloved fingers closed around something thin and pliable.

"What's this?" he asked. "Hey, look. A wallet."

Leggett was at his side instantly, hand outstretched to retrieve the prize. "This hasn't been down there long," he said, holding it up to examine it in the fading light. Leaving the wallet to Detective Leggett, Brian returned to searching the hole for any remaining evidence.

"That's funny," Leggett reported a few moments later.

"What's funny?"

"There's a current driver's license here," Leggett reported. "One that still has a year to run. I would have thought the corpse was far too old for that."

"What's the name?" Brian asked, climbing out of the hole.

"Chavez," Leggett answered. "Manny Chavez. Indian, most likely. There's a Sells address but no phone number. Want to have a look?"

Leggett handed the wallet over to Brian, leaving the plastic folder opened to the driver's license page. Brian glanced at it, started to give it back, then changed his mind to take a second look.

"Wait a minute," he said, pointing to the picture. "That's the guy from this afternoon. I'm sure of it."

"What guy?"

"The one we air-lifted into TMC just before I called for a detective. The one who'd had the crap beaten out of him before Kath Kelly found him."

"You're sure it's the same guy?"

"Hell, yes, I'm sure."

"In that case," Leggett said, "I guess I'd better go talk to him. You stay here and keep the crime scene secure. I'll call for a deputy with a generator and lights to come out and relieve you."

"What are you going to do?" Brian asked.

"I already told you. Go to the hospital and talk to the guy."

"How?"

"What are we doing, playing Twenty Questions?"

"How are you going to talk to him?" Brandon insisted.

"You're some kind of comedian, Deputy Fellows," the detective said. "To quote a former President, read my lips. I'm going to talk to Mr. Chavez with my mouth."

"Do you speak *Tohono O'othham?*" Brian asked.

"No, do you?"

Brian nodded. "As a matter of fact, I do."

"No shit?"

"No shit!"

For a moment Leggett stood looking at him. Finally he shrugged. "In that case," he said, "I guess we'll get somebody else to secure the damn crime scene, because you're coming with me."

Mitch Johnson had a large, trunk-sized box that he sometimes used to haul canvases around. Both the top and floor of the custom-made wooden box had matching grooves in them that allowed him to stack in up to twenty wet canvases without any of them touching each other. In advance of heading into town with Lani, he had emptied the box and loaded it into the back of the Subaru. Then, after blindfolding Lani with one of the cut pieces of scarf, he led her out of the Bounder.

Already the new dose of scopolamine was having the desired effect. Clumsy on her feet, she stumbled and fell against him as she stepped down out of the RV. It gratified him to hear the involuntary moan that escaped her lips when the injured breast, encased now in a still-sodden cowboy shirt, brushed up against his body.

"Smarts, does it, little girl?" he asked.

The Bounder was air-conditioned; the Subaru had been sitting in the afternoon sun. The interior of the box was stifling as he heaved her inside, sending her body sprawling along the rough, splintery bottom. There were ventilation holes in the sides—that was, after all, the point of the thing. He put canvases inside it to dry. That meant that once he turned on the air-conditioning in the car, the temperature inside the box would reduce some, too. Enough to keep her from croaking, most likely. Not enough for her to be comfortable.

Mitch had slammed the tailgate shut and was headed for the driver's seat in the Subaru when he saw a set of blue flashing lights snaking across the desert floor from Tucson. His heart went to his throat. *A damned cop car! Surely they hadn't already discovered the girl was missing. How could they?*

Close to panic, he almost had a heart attack when the car slowed at the turn-off to Coleman Road and then again as the pair of headlights came speeding toward him. By then he could hear the siren wailing through the still desert air.

What the hell do I do now? he wondered. Really, there wasn't any choice. He would have to gut it out. Bluff like hell and hope for the best, but in the meantime, he started the engine on the Subaru and then turned on both the radio and the air conditioner at full blast. That way, if the girl was still aware enough to make any noise, chances were the cop wouldn't hear her.

Moments later, with his heart pounding in his throat, he saw the headlights take a sharp turn to the left a mile or so north of where the Bounder was parked. He could still see the blue lights flashing, but behind them there was only the pale red glow of taillights.

"Whew!" Mitch said aloud. "I don't know what the hell that was all about, but it was too damn close for comfort."

Wanda and Fat Crack were getting ready to go to the dance at Little Tucson. They had always enjoyed going to summertime dances, although Wanda liked it less now than she had before her husband's elevation to tribal chairman. Before when they went to dances, they danced. Now, often as not, she was left to dance with one of her sons or grandsons while Gabe went about the never-ending business of politicking.

"Did you tell her yet?" Wanda asked, as she watched Gabe fasten the snaps on his cowboy shirt.

They hadn't been talking about Delia Cachora, but Fat Crack knew at once who and what Wanda was asking about. Wanda had disapproved of his bringing Delia back to the reservation, after thirty years away, to take on the assignment of tribal attorney.

"We need somebody who knows how to go head-to-head

with all those Washington BIA bureaucrats," Gabe had told his wife back then while the tribal council was wrangling over the decision. "If she can handle those guys, she can take on Pima County and the State of Arizona."

As Gabe expected, Delia Chavez Cachora did fine when it came to dealing with *Mil-gahn* paper-pushers. Where she fell short of the mark was in relating to the people back home, the ones who had never left the reservation. And that was part of the reason Fat Crack had hired David Ladd to serve as her intern. Schooled by Gabe's Aunt Rita and old Looks At Nothing, Davy had forgotten more about being a *Tohono O'othham* than Delia Cachora could ever hope to know.

When Gabe didn't answer, Wanda knew she was right. "You'd better tell her pretty soon," she warned. "Davy's supposed to be here next week, isn't he? She may be real mad when she finds out."

Looking in the mirror, Gabe slipped a turquoise-laden bola tie on over his head. He sighed as he pulled it tight under his double chin. "You're right," he said. "She'll be mad as hell. Maybe I'll tell her tonight, if I have a chance. If she's there. That way she'll have time to get used to the idea before Monday when I have to see her at work."

The shrug Wanda sent in her husband's direction as well as the derisive look said as clearly as if she had spoken that Wanda Ortiz didn't think Delia Cachora would be over the issue of Davy Ladd anytime soon.

"She'll be at the dance, all right," Wanda told her husband. "If her Aunt Julia has anything to say about it, Delia will be working in the feast house."

The painful shock of scraping along the rough wooden floor shattered Lani's druggy haze and brought her back to agonizing awareness. *But it's better to hurt,* she thought. *At least that way I know what's going on.*

The blindfold had caught on a splinter of wood and had been pulled loose as she slid across the floor. When she realized the scarf was gone and opened her eyes, she knew it was daylight from the light leaking in through the ventilation holes. The interior of the box felt like a heated oven. Moments later, a car engine started and she could feel a tiny breath of cool air blowing across her damp clothing. The car started, but for some time it didn't move.

There in the dark and alone, without the man watching her and gloating, there was no need to hold back the tears. Lying flat on her back, she gave in to both the pain and to her growing despair, letting the tears flow. She couldn't understand why this calamity had befallen her, or what she could do about it.

Somehow, in her aching grief, Lani raised one hand to her throat. There, beneath her fingers, she felt the smooth, woven surface of the basket, the *o'othham wopo hashda* she had made from her own hair and from Jessie's.

What if her hair charm, her *kushpo ho'oma*, fell into the hands of this new evil *Ohb*? Lani had woven the maze, the ancient sacred symbol of her people, into the face of the medallion. It was bad enough that Mr. Vega had copied the basket onto that awful picture of his, the one he had drawn of her while she slept, but Lani was suddenly determined that, no matter what, he would not have the basket itself.

Struggling in the dark, she worked desperately to unfasten the safety pin that kept the woven brooch on the slender gold chain. Even as her fingers struggled with the pin, Lani could feel the drug cloud begin to wrap itself around her, dulling her senses at the same time it soothed the terrible throbbing of her wounded breast.

She fought the drug with all the resources she could muster. And even though she couldn't hold it off forever, she did manage to keep it at bay long enough to slip the precious woven disk into the safety of her jeans pocket.

Only then did she give in and let the enveloping sleep overtake her. Whatever the drug was, Lani hated it because it had made her helpless and turned her into a victim. At the same time, she loved it, too, because while she slept, the searing band of pain that was now her right breast no longer hurt her. The drug put her mind to sleep and the pain as well.

Her last waking thought was that Mr. Vega was right. The drug was awful, but it did help.

David Ladd fought his way up out of the nightmare with the awful scream still ringing in his ears. Throwing off the covers, he sat up in bed, shaking all over and gasping for breath.

"David!" Startled out of a sound sleep, Candace sat up in bed beside him. "For God's sake, what's the matter?"

"It was a dream," he managed, through chattering teeth, but already the punishing heartbeat was pounding in his head and chest. Another attack was coming. Helplessly, he fell back on the pillows.

Scrambling out of bed, Candace reached for the phone. "I'll call a doctor."

"No, please. Don't do that," Davy begged.

"But David . . ."

"Please. Just wait! It'll go away in a few minutes. Please."

He held out one trembling hand. Reluctantly, Candace put down the phone and grasped his hand. With a worried frown on her face, she settled back down on the bed beside him. For the next several minutes she leaned over him, murmuring words he could barely hear or understand but ones that somehow comforted him nonetheless. Eventually the terrified beating of his heart began to slow. When his breathing finally steadied, he was able to speak.

"I'm sorry, Candace. I didn't mean for you to . . ."

Realizing that the immediate crisis was past, her solicitous concern turned to a sudden blast of anger. "So what are you on, David Garrison Ladd?" she demanded. "Crack? Speed? LSD? All this time you've had me fooled. I never would have guessed that you did drugs."

"But I don't," David protested. "I swear to God!"

"Don't give me that," she snapped back at him. "I've been around enough druggies in my life to know one when I see one."

"Candace, please. It's nothing like that. You've got to believe me. This has been happening to me for weeks now, every time I go to sleep. First there's an awful dream and then—" He broke off, ashamed.

"And then what?" she demanded.

"You saw what happens. My heart beats like it's going to jump out of my body. I can't breathe. I come out of it soaked with sweat. The first time it happened I thought I was having a heart attack. I thought I was going to die."

"You should see a doctor," Candace said.

"I did. He told me I was having panic attacks. He said they were brought on by stress and that eventually I'd get over them."

"I've heard about panic attacks before," Candace said. "One of the girls in the dorm used to have them. Isn't there something you can take?"

"Nothing that wouldn't be dangerous on a cross-country drive," David told her. "All of the recommended medications turn out to be tranquilizers of some kind."

"Oh," Candace said. "And how long has this been going on?"

"For a couple of weeks now, I guess," David admitted sheepishly.

"And why didn't you tell me before this?"

David shrugged his shoulders. "I was embarrassed. I didn't know what you'd think about me if I told you."

"And it's always the same thing? First the dream and then the panic attack?"

"Yes," David said, "pretty much, but . . ." The rest of the sentence disappeared as he gazed off into space.

"But what?"

David swallowed. His voice dropped. Candace had to strain to hear him. "I used to dream about the day Andrew Carlisle came to the house and attacked Mother. But now the dreams are different."

"Different how?"

"Different because Lani is in them. At the time all that happened, Lani wasn't even born. This one was different, and it was the worst one yet."

Getting up off the bed, David walked over to the window and stared outside at Chicago's nighttime skyline. He stood there in isolation, his shoulders hunched, looking defeated.

"You said this dream was worse than the others," Candace said. "Tell me about it."

David shook his head and didn't speak.

"Please tell me," Candace urged, her voice gentler than it had been. "Please."

David shuddered before he answered. "I was certain the first attack was over," he said at last. "Mother was in the kitchen because I could already smell the bacon cooking. Burning, really. Then the door to the cellar fell open, just the way it always does in the dream, except this time, the room was empty except for Bone, my dog. He was there in the kitchen, licking up the bacon grease, but the house itself was quiet and empty, as though everybody had left."

"Where did they go?"

Davy swallowed. "I'm coming to that. I called Bone to come, and the two of us went from room to room, trying to figure out where everybody had gone. I checked every room but there was nobody to be found, until the last one, Lani's. They were in there, Lani and the evil *Ohb*. He had her on the bed and he was—"

Davy broke off and didn't continue.

"He was raping her?" Candace supplied.

Davy shook his head. "I don't know. I couldn't see. All I know is he was hurting her, and she was screaming." He put his hands over his ears as though Lani's scream were still assailing them. "It was awful."

"It was a dream," Candace said firmly. "Forget it. Come back to bed."

"But Rita, our baby-sitter, always said that dreams mean something. When I was a freshman in high school, I went out for JV football. One day Lani was taking a nap and she woke up crying, saying that I was hurt. Mom was trying to tell her it was nothing but a dream when the school nurse called to say that she thought my ankle was broken and that Mom needed to come pick me up."

"You're saying you think Lani might be hurt?"

Davy shook his head. "I don't know what I'm saying. All I know is, that scream was the worst thing I've ever heard."

"She never called us back tonight, did she?" Candace said thoughtfully.

Davy shook his head. "No," he said. "She didn't."

"So let's try again." Ever practical, Candace sat up in bed, plucked the telephone receiver out of its cradle and handed it over to Davy. "It's only a little after nine there," she said matter-of-factly. "Maybe somebody will be home by now. What's the number?" she said.

Grateful beyond measure that Candace hadn't simply dismissed him as crazy, David Ladd held the phone to his ear while she dialed, then he waited while it rang. "The damned machine again," he said finally, handing the receiver back to her. "Go ahead and hang up."

"Leave another message," Candace ordered. "Tell Lani or your parents, either one, to call you back as soon as they get home."

Eventually the beep sounded in his ear. "Hi, Mom and Dad," he said. "I'm still trying to get hold of Lani, but I guess nobody's home. Give me a call. You already have the number. Bye."

He put down the phone. Candace was looking up at him. "Better?" she said.

David nodded.

"Lie back down, then."

He did as he was told. Moments later Candace snuggled close, her naked leg against his, her fingers brushing delicately across the hair of his chest.

"Whatever happened to Bone?" she asked. "I've read your mother's book, but I don't remember her saying what happened to the dog."

"Poor old *Oh'o*," Davy said. "I haven't thought of him for years. When we first moved to Gates Pass he was my only friend and playmate. Nana *Dahd* always used to say that the first word I spoke was *goks*—dog—the day she brought him home as a gangly puppy."

"What kind of dog was he?"

"A mutt, I'm sure. He looked a lot like an Irish wolfhound—he was that big, long-haired, and scraggly—but he could jump like a deer."

"What was it you called him again?"

"*Oh'o*. In Papago . . . in *Tohono O'othham* . . . that means bone. And that's what he was when Rita first brought him home, skin and bones. But he was a great dog."

"What did he die of?"

"Old age, I guess. The year I turned thirteen. His kidneys gave out on him. My friend Brian Fellows and I carried him up the mountain behind the house and buried him among the rocks where the three of us all used to play hide-and-seek. Bone always loved being It."

"I guess he really messed up the guy's arm. His wrist, anyway."

"Andrew Carlisle's wrist?"

Candace nodded. "From what your mother said in the book, when you let him into the kitchen, he went after the guy tooth and nail."

"He did?"

"Yup. He wrecked it. She talked about that in one of the scenes that takes place in the prison, about how when she saw him again after all those years, his face was all scarred up from the bacon grease. She talked about his arm then, too, about how he had to wear it in a sling."

"Well, I'll be damned," David Ladd said. "I never knew that before, or if I did, I've forgotten."

Slowly, almost unthinkingly, Candace's fingers began to stroke the inside of Davy's thigh. "Stick with me, pal," she said. "I'll teach you everything I know."

She seduced him then, because she thought he needed it. Because it was the middle of the night and because they were both awake and young and had the stamina to do it more than once a night. Afterward, as David Garrison Ladd drifted off into the first really restful sleep he'd had in weeks, he felt as though, for the first time in his life, he had made love.

12

You will remember, nawoj, *that when* I'itoi *divided the water and saved his people, the* Tohono O'othham, *from the Bad People, some of the* PaDaj O'othham *escaped.*

Now these Bad People lived in the south, and they were very lazy. They were too lazy to plant their own fields, so they came into the Land of the Desert People and tried to steal their crops—their wheat, corn, and beans, their pumpkins and melons.

The Tohono O'othham *fought these Bad People and drove them away, but after a time, the beans and corn which the Bad People had stolen were all gone. The* PaDaj O'othham *were hungry again. They knew the Desert People were guarding their fields, so they decided to try a new way to steal the crops.*

Near the village Gurli Put Vo—*Dead Man's Pond—which we now call San Miguel, the corn in the fields was ready to harvest. One morning* Hawani—*Crow—who was sitting in a tree, saw the Bad People coming up out of the ground and begin cutting the grain.*

Crow was so astonished that he called out, "Caw, caw, caw!" This made the people who were living on the edge of the field look up. When they saw their crop disappearing into the ground, they cried out for help.

U'uwhig—the Birds—carried the call for help because the Desert People were always good to the Da'a O'othham—the Flying People—and never let them go hungry or thirsty. And very soon the Indians gathered and drove the Bad People back into the ground. But the bean fields were trampled, and the corn was badly damaged.

It was almost dark before the relief deputy showed up. Detective Leggett parked him in the middle of the road about twenty yards from the *charco*. "You stay right here," he said. "I don't want anyone coming up and down this road until we can get a crime scene team in here tomorrow morning. You got that?"

"Got it," the deputy said.

By the time Dan Leggett and Brian Fellows grabbed a bite of dinner and then turned up at TMC, Manuel Chavez had already been wheeled off to surgery. The clerk on the surgery wing was happy to glean that one bit of information, that John Doe now had a name. She called the information back down to Admitting.

"That John Doe who just went into surgery is from Sells," she told someone over the phone. "That means he's Indian instead of Hispanic, so you might want to update your records." The clerk covered the mouthpiece with her hand and turned a questioning look on Dan Leggett.

"Has anyone notified the family?"

Dan shook his head. "Not yet."

"Are you going to?"

"We're trying," Detective Leggett told her, then he looked

at Brian. "I'm going outside to have a smoke," he said. "Since you're the guy who told me you speak *Tohono O'oth-ham,* you can do the honors."

Obligingly Brian Fellows stood up and went in search of the nearest pay phone. He placed a call to the *Tohono O'oth-ham* tribal police and spoke to an officer named Larry Garcia who spoke English just fine.

"Sure, we know Manny Chavez," Larry told Brian Fellows. "What's he done now?"

"Somebody beat him up pretty badly," Brian replied. "He's in surgery at TMC right now. Can you guys handle next-of-kin notification?"

"We'll try," Larry said. "He's got both a daughter and a son. We should be able to find one of them. What's your name again?"

"Brian Fellows. I'm a deputy with Pima County. I'll be here at the hospital for a while longer. Let me know if you locate someone, would you?"

"Sure thing," Larry said. "No problem. Give me your number."

Brian gave him the surgical clerk's extension, then went outside and found Detective Leggett stationed beside an overflowing breezeway ashtray, smoking one of his smelly cigars.

"What's the scoop?" he asked. "Any luck?"

"The tribal police are working on it," Brian replied. "They'll let us know."

"I've been standing out here thinking," Dan Leggett said. "When you first contacted me, we thought the guy was digging up some kind of artifact. Maybe poor Manny Chavez made the same mistake. For the time being, let's assume, instead, that the first guy was burying something, specifically that pile of bones. Why would somebody go to all the trouble of doing that?"

"Because he had something to hide," Brian offered.

"And what might that be? Maybe our grave digger had

something to do with the first guy's crushed skull. Think about it. We're talking the same MO as with Manny Chavez. Whack 'em upside the head until they fall over dead."

Brian nodded. "That makes sense," he said.

"So we've for sure got assault with intent on this grave-digging guy and maybe even an unknown and consequently unsolved homicide thrown in for good measure. That being the case, I'm not going to let this thing sit until morning. I'm going to go back out to the department and raise a little hell. I asked for a crime scene investigation team for tonight, but all I got was a deputy to secure the scene and the old 'too much overtime' song and dance. I want faster action than that. If I play my cards right, I'll be able to get it. In the meantime, you hang around here and wait for the next of kin. Once they show up, get whatever information you can, but if the doc says we can talk to Manny himself, you call me on the double."

"Will do," Brian replied.

He went back into the waiting room and settled down on one of the molded-plastic chairs. While he sat there and waited for one or the other of Manny Chavez's kids to show up, Brian finished filling out his paper. As he worked his way down the various forms, Brian was once again grateful that Dan Leggett had taken the call. The deputy was glad not only for his own sake, but also for the sake of Manny Chavez's unnotified relatives, whoever they might be. There were plenty of detectives in Bill Forsythe's sheriff's department who wouldn't have given a damn about somebody going around beating up Indians—plenty who wouldn't have lifted a finger about it.

Fortunately for all concerned, Dan Leggett wasn't one of those. He was treating the assault on Manny Chavez as the serious crime it was—a Class 1 felony. Not only that, Brian thought with a smile, the investigation Dan was bent on doing would no doubt necessitate interviewing everyone involved. Including a good-looking Border Patrol agent named Kath Kelly.

Time passed. Brian lost track of how long. He was sitting there almost dozing when the clerk woke him up, saying there was a phone call for him.

"Deputy Fellows?" Larry Garcia asked.

"That's right."

"I just had a call from one of my officers. He's on his way to Little Tucson. There's a dance out there tonight. We're pretty sure Delia Cachora, Manny's daughter, will be there. Once they find her, it'll take an hour or more for them to get her into town. Will you still be there, at the hospital?"

Detective Leggett had given Deputy Fellows his marching orders. "Most likely," Brian told him. "Have her ask for me."

Quentin Walker was more than half lit and still in the bar at seven o'clock when Mitch Johnson finally showed up at El Gato Loco. Among the low-brow workingmen that constituted El Gato's clientele, the well-dressed stranger sporting a pair of dark sunglasses stuck out like a sore thumb.

"You're late," Quentin said accusingly, swinging around on the barstool as Mitch sidled up beside him.

"Sorry," Mitch returned. "I was unavoidably detained. I thought you said you'd be waiting out front."

"I was for a while, but it was too hot and I got too thirsty waiting outside. Want a drink?"

"Sure."

"Well, order one for me, too. I've gotta go take a leak."

The beer was there waiting on the counter when Quentin returned from the bathroom. Coming back down the bar, Quentin tried to walk straight and control his boozy stagger. He didn't want Mitch to realize how much he'd already been drinking, to say nothing of why. Quentin still couldn't quite believe he had killed that damned nosy Indian, but he had, all because he had walked up and caught Quentin red-handed with Tommy's bones right there in front of God and everybody.

Now, Quentin was looking at two potential murder charges instead of one. Jesus! How had that happened to him? How could he have screwed up that badly? The one thing he didn't want to lose sight of, though, was how much the money from those damned pots would mean to him now.

Nobody knew Quentin Walker owned a car. It would take days, weeks, maybe, for all the paperwork to make its way through official channels. With a proper vehicle and a grub-stake of running money, Quentin might even be able to make it into the interior of Mexico. He could leave via that gate on the reservation, the one he had heard so much about from Davy and Brian. It was supposed to be an unofficial border crossing where Indians whose lands had been cut in half by the Gadsden Purchase could go back and forth without the formality of border guards of any kind.

When Mitch Johnson had first shown up with his offer to buy the pots, Quentin had been intrigued more than inter-ested. Now, though, that very same offer of money was of vital importance. The last thing Quentin wanted to do was to spook Mitch into calling the whole thing off. If Mitch walked away, taking with him those five bills with Grover Cleveland's mug shot on them, then Quentin Walker could be left high and dry, without the proverbial pot to piss in. He would have no money and nowhere to run, and he'd be stuck with two possible murder raps staring him in the face. No-body was ever going to believe that Tommy's death had been an accident.

"How about something to eat?" Quentin suggested, thinking that food might help sober him up. "The hamburg-ers here aren't bad."

"Sure," Mitch Johnson said easily. "I'll have one. Why the hell not? We're not in any hurry, are we?"

Shaking his head, Quentin leaned his arms against the edge of the bar to steady himself. "Not that I know of," he said. "I do have some good news, though."

"What's that?" Mitch asked.

"I used some of the money you gave me to buy myself some wheels. I picked up a honkin' big orange Bronco XLT. It's a couple years old, but it runs like a top. If you want, we could drive out to where the pots are in that. I don't know what kind of vehicle you're driving, but the terrain where we're going is pretty rough, and the Bronco is four-wheel-drive."

Mitch Johnson had to fight to keep from showing his disappointment. He had been planning all along that he'd be getting back almost a full refund of that initial five thousand bucks he had given Quentin. And he had less than no intention of giving the little creep his second installment. After all, once Quentin Walker was dead, he wouldn't have any need of money—or of a car, either, for that matter.

Instead of bitching Quentin out—instead of mocking him for his stupidity—Mitch was careful to mask his disappointment. "So, you bought yourself a car?" he asked smoothly. "What kind did you say?"

"A Bronco." To Mitch, Quentin's answer seemed unduly proud. "It's the first time I've had wheels of my own in years. It feels real good."

"I'll bet it does," Mitch Johnson agreed.

After that exchange, Mitch sat for a long time and considered this changed state of affairs. His plan had called for the next part of the operation to be carried out in the Subaru. That way he would have the canvas-drying crate to use to confine either Lani and/or Quentin, should the drugs somehow prove unreliable. The idea of changing vehicles added a complication, but the whole point of being competitive— of being able to capitalize on situations where other people faltered—was being flexible enough to go with the flow. The idea was to take the unexpected and turn it from a liability into an advantage.

"Hang on here a minute," Mitch said to Quentin. "And if

my food comes before I get back, you leave my hamburger alone."

"Sure thing," Quentin said.

Mitch walked out to the far corner of the parking lot where he had left the Subaru. There, he unlocked the tailgate, opened the wooden crate, and checked on Lani, who appeared to be sleeping peacefully. Putting on his rubber gloves, he removed Lani's bike from the crate. Hurriedly he wheeled it over to the orange Bronco parked nearby, an orange Bronco with a temporary paper license hanging in the window next to a prominently displayed AS IS/NO WARRANTY notice. Predictably, the Bronco wasn't locked. Mitch hefted the mountain bike into the spacious cargo compartment and then went over to secure the Subaru.

"Sweet dreams, little one," he said to a sleeping Lani as he once again closed up the crate. "See you after your brother and I finish up at the house."

When Mitch went back inside, the food had been served. Mitch ate his lousy hamburger and watched Quentin wolf his. There was something about the man that wasn't quite right. There was a nervous tension in him that Mitch didn't remember from the night before, but he put his worries aside. Whatever was bothering Quentin Walker, that little dose of scopolamine Mitch had dropped into Quentin's first beer would soon take the edge off. In fact, Mitch's only real concern was that Quentin was far more smashed than he should have been. With Quentin drunk, Mitch worried that even a little bit of Burundianga Cocktail might prove to be too much.

The overheated afternoon had cooled into a warm summer's evening when Quentin and Mitch Johnson finally left the bar. Quentin blundered first in one direction and then in the other as he attempted to cross the parking lot. He finally came to a stop and leaned up against the Bronco to steady himself.

"Geez!" he muttered. "That last beer was a killer. Hey, Mitch," he said. "You wouldn't mind driving, would you?

The food didn't do me a bit of good. I'm having a tough time here. I can give you directions, no problem, but with my record, I can't afford to be picked up DWI."

"No problem," Mitch said. "Where are the keys?"

It took time for Quentin to extract the keys from his pocket and hand them over.

"You don't mind, do you?" Quentin whined.

Mitch shook his head. "Not at all," he said. "After all, friends don't let friends drive drunk."

Detective Dan Leggett was pissed as hell. "What do you mean, you've recalled him?" he demanded.

"Just that," Reg Atkins, the night-watch commander, returned mildly. "We can't send a team of crime techs out there until Monday morning. You know as well as I do that Sheriff Forsythe won't authorize any overtime right now, at least not until the start of the new fiscal year. Overtime is to be scheduled only in cases of dire emergency. One busted Indian and a pile of bones don't qualify, at least not in my book. And in case you're wondering, the same thing goes for deputies. Brian Fellows is off the clock as of fifteen minutes ago and the guy you sent out to Coleman Road just got called to a car fire out by Ryan Field."

Less than six months from retirement, Dan Leggett was a member of the old guard. As someone who still owed a good deal of loyalty to the previous administration, he was a pain in Sheriff Bill Forsythe's neck. Anybody else in his position might have shut up and let things pass. Not Dan Leggett. He was an unrepentant smoker, a loner, and a rocker of boats.

"You called them off?"

"Damned straight. If you think we're going to have a deputy camped out by a *charco* all weekend long, you're crazy as a bedbug."

"But I want those bones examined."

"Well, go get them and bring them back to the lab your-self, if you're so all-fired excited about them. There are plenty of people to work on them if you ever get them here."

Without another word, Dan Leggett stormed out of Reg Atkins's office. Ever since Brandon Walker had been voted out of office, this kind of shit had been happening—espe-cially to older guys, the ones who had been around long enough to know the real score. He had been a rookie deputy toward the end of Sheriff DuShane's term in office. There had been lots of crap like this back then. It looked as though things had come full circle.

But if Sheriff Bill Forsythe thought he was going to run Dan Leggett off a day before his scheduled retirement day, he was full of it. And he wasn't going to be bamboozled out of properly investigating these two possibly related cases.

At the *charco* even though the deputy was long gone, noth-ing seemed to be disturbed. Since Deputy Fellows had already made plaster casts, Dan Leggett simply drove as close as he could to the pile of bones without getting stuck in the sand. After extracting a trouble light from the trunk, he examined the grisly pile by the trouble light's eerie orange glow.

There was nothing but partial skeletal remains here now, but Detective Leggett realized this had once been a living, breathing human being. A person. Somebody's loved one. As such, whoever it was deserved some respect, certainly more than being tossed haphazardly in the trunk of an un-marked patrol car.

"Sorry about this," Dan said aloud, addressing the skull whose empty eyes seemed to stare up at him. "But this is the only way I can think of to find out who you are and what happened to you."

After that murmured apology, he put on his disposable gloves and loaded the bones into three separate cardboard evidence boxes. It was the best Dan Leggett could do.

He took the boxes back to the department and then lugged the surprisingly lightweight stack into the crime lab.

"What's this?" the lab tech asked, opening the top box and peering inside.

"It's what's left of a body," he told her. "When you take them out of the box, I want every single one of them dusted for prints."

"Come on, Detective Leggett. Fingerprints?"

"I'm an old man who's about to retire," Dan Leggett told the thirty-something technician. "Humor me, just this once. And while you're at it, fax a dental photo over to that Bio-Metrics professor at the U. Who knows, we might just get a hit on his Missing Persons database."

As tribal chairman, Gabe Ortiz could easily have gone straight to the head of the line at the feast house in Little Tucson. But that wasn't Fat Crack's style. Instead, an hour or so before the Chicken Scratch Band was scheduled to play, he and Wanda were standing in line waiting to be admitted to the feast house along with their bass-guitar-playing son, Leo, and everyone else who was waiting to eat.

Gabe could remember a time, seemingly not that long ago, when all the guys in the band had been old men. Times had changed. The problem was, the members of the band had always stayed pretty much the same—middle-aged. That was still true. What was different was that Gabe Ortiz was well into his sixties and one of the band members was his unmarried, thirty-eight-year-old son.

They filed into the feast house and took seats at the tables. Moments later, Delia Cachora herself showed up carrying plates. She set two plates down in front of Gabe and Wanda and then went back for more.

Leo caught his father's eye. "When are you going to put in a good word for me with that new tribal attorney?" he asked.

"What do you want me to tell her?" Gabe asked. "That you're a good mechanic? You've never worked on a Saab in your life."

Leo laughed. "I could learn," he said.

Delia Chavez Cachora had returned to the reservation driving a shiny black Saab 9000. In the reservation world where Ford and Chevy pickups ruled supreme, Delia's car had created quite a stir—especially when word leaked out that the Saab's leather seats were actually heated. In the Arizona desert, heated seats were considered to be a laughably unnecessary option. After months of driving in gritty dust, its once shiny onyx exterior had acquired a perpetually matte-brown overlay.

"Why don't you talk to her yourself?" Wanda asked impatiently. "She won't bite."

"I knew her in first grade," Leo said. "But I don't think that counts."

Delia returned to the table with two more plates, one of which she put in front of Leo Ortiz.

"Delia," Gabe said, "this is my son, Leo. He says you were in first grade together. He wants you to know that he's a pretty good mechanic."

Leo Ortiz shrugged. "You never can tell when you might need a good mechanic," he said with a laugh. "Or a bass guitar player, either."

Delia Cachora studied Leo Ortiz's broad face as if searching for a resemblance between this graying, portly man and some child she had known in school thirty years earlier. "I'll bear that in mind," she said. Then she headed back to the serving line to collect more plates.

Wanda looked at her husband. "Are you going to talk to her?" Wanda asked.

Fat Crack nodded. "After," he said.

Wanda sighed, then she turned her attention on her son. "I don't know why you're so interested in her," she sniffed disapprovingly. "Julia Joaquin, her auntie, tells me Delia can't even make tortillas."

Leo caught his father's eye and winked. "Plenty of women can cook," Leo said, "but I'll bet Delia Cachora can do lots of other things."

Gabe Ortiz laughed at his son's gentle teasing, but it surprised him somewhat that Delia Cachora would turn out to be the kind of woman who would interest either one of his two sons, who, at thirty-eight and forty, respectively, were both thought to be aging, perpetual bachelors. If Leo did in fact find Delia attractive, by the time Gabe finished telling her about Davy Ladd's upcoming arrival, Leo's chances would be greatly reduced from what they were right then. Gabe had put the unpleasant task off for far too long already. It was time.

He waited until that group of feast-goers had finished eating. Then, on his way out, Gabe stopped by the dishwashing station where the tribal attorney stood over a steaming washtub of water with soapy dishwater all the way up to her elbows.

"Delia," Gabe said quietly. "I need to talk to you."

"Right now?"

"Whenever you have time," Gabe answered. "I'll wait outside."

Wanda walked over to the dance floor with Leo while Fat Crack lingered outside the door to the feast house. Several minutes later, Delia Cachora joined him.

"Is something wrong?" Delia asked anxiously. "You look worried."

Gabe was worried. The business with Andrew Carlisle had kept him awake for most of two successive nights now. His only regret was that his state of mind showed so clearly to outside observers.

Fat Crack shook his head. "There's nothing wrong with you," he said. "But there is something I need to talk to you about." He led her away from the feast house, through the lines of parked cars, through groups of people gathered informally around the backs of pickups, laughing and talking. When they reached the Crown Victoria, Fat Crack opened the door and motioned her inside.

"Whatever it is, it must be serious," Delia said.

"Not that serious. I wanted to talk to you about a friend of mine. A sort of cousin, actually. My aunt's godson. His name's David Ladd."

In the world of the *Tohono O'othham*—where even the most direct conversational route is never a straight line—this was a straightforward way of beginning.

"What about him?" Delia asked.

"I've offered him a job."

The car was silent for a moment. "David Ladd," Delia repeated at last. "That doesn't sound like a *Tohono O'oth-ham* name."

"It isn't," Fat Crack admitted. "Davy is *Mil-gahn*. He was my aunt Rita's godson—a foster son, more or less."

"Why are you telling me about this?" Delia asked. "Is there some legal problem?"

Gabe Ortiz took a deep breath. "I've offered him an intern-ship," he said. "In your office. He just graduated from law school at Northwestern. He'll be home sometime next week and able to start work the week after that. I've hired him as your special assistant while he's studying for the bar exam. As an in-tern, we won't have to pay him all that much, and I thought that while you're preoccupied by negotiations with the county, he'll be able to help out with some of the day-to-day stuff."

Delia's reaction was every bit as bad as Gabe Ortiz had expected. "Wait just a damn minute here!" she exclaimed, turning on Gabe with both eyes blazing. "Are you saying you've hired an Anglo to come work in my office without telling me and without even asking my opinion?"

"Pretty much."

"My understanding was that the tribal attorney always hires his or her own assistants," Delia said.

"The tribal attorney works for me," Gabe reminded her impassively. The fact that he was using his tribal council voice on her infuriated Delia Chavez Cachora even more.

"But you already told me, he's *Mil-gahn*," she objected. "An Anglo."

Gabe Ortiz remained unimpressed. "So? Are you prejudiced against Anglos, or what?"

At thirty-eight, having fought her way through years of prejudice in Eastern Seaboard parochial schools, Delia Cachora knew about racial prejudice firsthand. From the wrong end.

"What if I am?" she asked. "I'm sure there are plenty of Indian law school graduates we could hire while they're waiting to pass the bar exam. Besides, I can't hire anyone anyway. We talked about that a couple of months ago. I'm already over budget."

"I'm hiring Davy Ladd out of a special discretionary fund," Gabe said. "One that comes straight from my office. The money to pay him won't be coming out of your budget, it'll be coming out of mine."

"In other words, he's coming, like it or lump it."

Gabe Ortiz nodded. "I suppose that's about it," he said. "But wait until you meet him. He's an unusual young man. I think you'll like him."

"I wouldn't count on it," Delia muttered. She opened the car door. "In fact, I wouldn't count on that at all."

Delia started out of the car and would have walked away, but just then a tow truck, red lights flashing, followed by a Law and Order patrol car, pulled up and stopped directly in front of the Crown Victoria. Gabe's other son, Richard, climbed down from the truck.

"Here they are," he was saying to the officer piling out of the patrol car.

As Gabe climbed out of the Crown Victoria, he immediately recognized Ira Segundo, a young patrol officer for the *Tohono O'othham* tribal police. "What's the matter, Ira?" Gabe asked.

"I'm looking for Mrs. Cachora," Ira said. "Baby told me she might be here with you."

"I'm Delia Cachora," she said, stepping forward. "What's wrong?"

"It's about your dad," Ira Segundo said. "There was a problem over off Coleman Road. He's been hurt."

A curtain of wariness more than concern settled over Delia's face. Since she had returned to the reservation, her father and her younger brother, Eddie, had only come to see her to ask for money. "What about him?"

"It happened at a *charco* over by where Rattlesnake Skull used to be—"

"By Rattlesnake Skull?" Gabe Ortiz interrupted.

Ira nodded. "We think maybe there was a fight of some kind. He must be hurt pretty bad. They air-lifted him to TMC."

"You should be telling my brother this instead of me," Delia said. "He's the one who lives with him, but he's probably off drunk somewhere. I'll go get my car."

"No, Delia," Gabe said. "Get in. I'll give you a ride." Gabe Ortiz turned to his son. "Richard, I'm leaving you to take your mother home from the dance when she's ready to go. Ira, I want you to put on your flashers and lead us into town."

"Sure thing, Mr. Ortiz," Ira said.

Still angry, Delia wanted to object, but something about the way Gabe issued the orders stopped her. She did as she was told and climbed back into the Crown Victoria. "I don't know why you're doing this," she said, once Gabe was back inside and had started the engine. "It's my father, and I'm perfectly capable of driving myself."

Already Gabe was threading his way through the army of parked cars. In the reflected glow of the dashboard lights, Delia was surprised by the grim set of his face.

"You've been away from the reservation a long time," he said, sounding suddenly tired. "Have you ever heard of Rattlesnake Skull?"

"Never," she said. "I gather from what he said that it's a deserted village."

They were out of the parking lot now, and the lights on the patrol car were flashing in front of them. "Right," Gabe said. "It is deserted, but a lot has happened there over the

years. Before you go see your father and before you meet
Davy Ladd, you should hear about some of it. I'm probably
the only one who can tell you."

When the banquet was finally over, Brandon and Diana
Walker drove west across town. The evening had been surprisingly fun, and Diana was still giggling.

"You were absolutely great," she told Brandon. "I don't
know why you've ever been spooked at the idea of talking to
little old ladies. You charmed the socks off every one that got
within spitting distance of you."

Brandon grinned. "There's nothing like a little sex in the
afternoon to give a guy's sagging ego a boost. But it turns
out they were a pretty nice bunch of little old ladies . . ."

"And men," Diana added.

"And a few men," Brandon corrected. "The difference between the people we met tonight and most people is that the
ones at the banquet all think I'm lucky to be able to be retired at age fifty-four. Everybody else thinks I'm either
crazy or some kind of laggard."

"They haven't seen your woodpile," Diana said.

Their mood was still light, right up until they drove up to
the house in Gates Pass. "Damn it," Brandon said. "It looks
like Lani left every light in the house burning. One of these
days she'll have to pay her own utility bills. It's going to
come as a real shock."

Brandon hit the automatic door opener and the gate on
the side of the house swung open. "She also left her bike in
the middle of the damn carport. What on earth is she thinking of?"

Diana sighed, dismayed to hear Brandon's mood change
from good to bad in the space of a few yards of driveway.
"Stop the car," she said. "I'll get out and move the bike out
of the way."

She pushed the bike up to the front of the carport, giving

Brandon enough room to park his Nissan next to her Suburban. No doubt the fragile mood of the evening was irretrievably broken. One way or another, children did that to their parents with astounding regularity.

The back door was unlocked, which most likely meant that Lani was home, but that was something else that would annoy her father. When Lani was home alone, she was supposed to keep the front and back doors locked.

Shaking her head, Diana went inside and discovered that Brandon was right. Almost every light in the house was blazing, but the note for Lani that Diana had left on the counter—the Post-it containing Davy's phone number and telling Lani to call him back—was still on the counter, exactly where Diana had left it.

Through years of mothering teenagers, Diana Ladd Walker had discovered that looking in the sink and checking the most recent set of dirty dishes was usually a good way of getting a handle on who all was home, how long they'd been there, and whether or not they had dragged any visitors into the house with them.

The evidence in the sink this time left Diana puzzled. Other than the pair of champagne glasses she and Brandon had left there earlier in the afternoon, there was nothing but a pair of rubber-handled kitchen tongs. Knowing it wasn't hers, Diana picked the utensil up and examined it under the light. The gripper part was somewhat scorched. It looked as though it had been used to cook meat of some kind, but there was nothing in the kitchen—no accompanying greasy mess—that gave Diana any hint of what that might have been.

As Diana automatically moved to the phone to check for messages, she could hear Brandon walking through the rest of the house, calling for Lani and switching off lights as he went. When Diana punched in the code, she found there were a total of five messages waiting for her. That bugged her. It was Saturday night. Couldn't she and Brandon even go out to dinner without having the whole world phone in their absence?

The first message was timed in at three twenty-one. "Lani," a female voice said. "This is Mrs. Allison from the museum. If you aren't able to take your shift, you should always call in as soon as possible to let us know. I know tomorrow is scheduled to be your day off. If for some reason you aren't going to be able to make your next shift on Monday, please call in on Sunday if you can. If I'm not there, leave word on the machine."

Lani hadn't made it to work? That didn't make sense. She had *left* for work. How could it be that she was absent? The next message, at six-eleven, moments after Diana and Brandon had left for the banquet, was from Jessica Carpenter.

"Lani, what are you going to wear? Call me and let me know."

"That figures," Diana muttered as she erased that one.

The one after that was more worrisome. "Lani," Jessica Carpenter said. "I thought you were going to be here by now. Mom has to go someplace after she drops me off, and if we don't leave in a few minutes, she'll be late. She says I should leave your ticket at the box office. I'll put it in an envelope with your name on it."

The next message, at nine-fifteen, was another one from Davy. "Hi, Mom and Dad. I'm still trying to get hold of Lani, but I guess nobody's home. Give me a call. Bye."

The last one was from Jessica once again. "It's intermission and you're not here. Are you mad at me or sick, or what? I'll try calling again when I get home."

Brandon came back into the kitchen just as Diana was putting down the phone. "Still taking messages?" he said.

"Lani didn't go to work," Diana said. "And she didn't go to the concert, either."

"Didn't go to the concert?" Brandon echoed. "Where is she then? I've gone through the whole house looking for her."

"Hang on," Diana told him. "I'll call the Carpenters and see if she ever showed up there."

The phone rang several times and then the answering machine came on. Diana left a message for them to call her as soon as possible. "Nobody's home," she told Brandon. "Maybe they're all still at the concert."

"But Lani's bike is here. Where would she be if her bike's here?"

Brandon looked grim. "Something's wrong. I'll go back through the house and check again. Maybe I missed something. Do you have any idea what she wore when she left the house this morning?"

Diana shook her head. "I heard the gate shut, but I didn't see her leave."

This time they got as far as Brandon's study. Before, Brandon had simply reached into the room and switched off the light without bothering to look into the room itself. Barely a step inside the door, he stopped so abruptly that Diana almost collided with him. "What the hell!"

Sidestepping him, Diana was able to see into the room herself. A fine spray of shattered glass covered most of the floor. In the center of the glass lay several broken picture frames. Looking beyond that, Diana saw that the wall behind Brandon's desk—his Wall of Honor as he had called it—was empty. All his service plaques, his civic honors—including his Tucson Citizen of the Year and the Detective of the Year award—the one he'd received from *Parade Magazine* for cracking a dead illegal alien case years before—were all on the floor, smashed beyond recognition.

"Oh, Brandon!" Diana wailed. "What a mess. I'll go get the broom—"

"Don't touch anything and don't come into the room any farther until we get a handle on exactly what's happened here. It looks to me as though whoever it was broke into my gun case, too."

Diana's stomach sank to her knees. She had to fight off the sudden urge to vomit. "What about Lani . . ."

Brandon turned toward her, the muscles working across his tightened jaw. "Let's don't hit panic buttons," he advised. "The first thing we should do is call the department and have them send somebody out to investigate." Walking back to the kitchen, he picked up the phone. "Did you notice anything else out of place?" he asked as he dialed. After all those years with the department, the number of the direct line into Dispatch was still embedded in his brain as well as his dialing finger.

Diana thought for a minute. "Only that set of tongs over there in the sink. It looks as though somebody used it to cook meat or something, but I can't tell what."

Alicia Duarte was fairly new to Dispatch, but she had been around the department long enough that Brandon Walker's name still carried a good deal of weight. Her initial response was to offer to send out a deputy.

"A deputy will be fine," Brandon told her. "But I think we're going to need a detective too. There's a good chance that our daughter has disappeared as well, and the two incidents are most likely related."

"Sure thing, Sheriff Walker," Alicia said, honoring him with the title even though it was no longer his. "I'll get right on it."

Brandon put down the phone and then walked over to wrap his arms around Diana. "You heard what I said. Someone is on the way, although it'll take time for them to get here."

"What if we've lost her?" Diana asked in a small voice. "What if Lani's gone for good?"

"She isn't," Brandon returned fiercely. It wasn't so much that he believed she wasn't lost. It was just that when it came to his precious Lani, believing anything else was unthinkable.

*   *   *

Brandon's initial reluctance about adopting Clemencia Escalante disappeared within days of the child's noisy entry into the Walker household. He was captivated by her in every way, and the reverse was also true. It wasn't long before his daily return from work was cause for an ecstatic greeting on Clemencia's part. When he was home, she padded around at his heels, following him everywhere, always underfoot no matter where he was or what he was doing.

When it came time to work on turning their temporary appointment as foster parents into permanent adoptive ones, Brandon had forged through the reams of paperwork with cheerful determination. Later, during caseworker interviews, he was charming and enthusiastic. But when the time came to drive out to Sells to appear before the tribal court for a hearing on finalizing the adoption, he was as nervous as he had been on the day he and Diana Ladd married.

"What if they turn us down after all this?" he asked, standing in front of the mirror and reknotting his tie for a third time. "What if we have to give her back? I couldn't stand to lose her now, not after all this."

"Wanda seems to think it'll go through as long as we have Rita in our corner."

The four of them rode out to Sells together. Rita and the baby sat in the backseat—Clemencia sleeping in her car seat and Rita sitting stolidly with her arms folded across her lap. She said very little, but everything about her exuded serene confidence. They found Fat Crack waiting for them in the small gravel parking lot outside the tribal courtroom. While Brandon and Diana unloaded the baby and her gear, Rita turned to her nephew.

"Did you do it?" she asked Fat Crack, speaking to him in the language of the *Tohono O'othham*. "Did you look at her picture through the divining crystals?"

"*Heu'u*—yes," Fat Crack said.

"And what did you see?"

"I saw this child, the one you call Forever Spinning,

wearing a white coat and carrying a feather, a seagull feather."

"See there?" Rita said, her face dissolving into a smile. "I told you, didn't I? She will be both."

"But—"

"No more," Rita said. "It's time to go in."

Molly Juan, the tribal judge, was a pug-faced, no-non-sense woman who spent several long minutes shuffling through the paperwork Wanda Ortiz handed her before raising her eyes to gaze at the people gathered in the courtroom.

"Both parents are willing to give up the child?" she asked at last.

Wanda Ortiz nodded. "Both have signed terminations of parental rights."

"And there are no blood relatives interested in taking her?"

"Not at this time. If the Walkers' petition to adopt her is denied, my office has made arrangements to place Clemencia in a facility in Phoenix."

"Who is this then?" Molly Juan asked, nodding toward Rita.

"This is Mrs. Antone—Rita Antone—a widow and my husband's aunt," Wanda replied.

"And she has some interest in this matter?"

Ponderously, Rita Antone wheeled her chair until she sat facing the judge. "That is true," Rita said. "I am *Hejel Wi i'thag*—Left Alone. My grandmother, my father's mother, was *Oks Amichuda*, Understanding Woman. She was not a medicine woman, although she could have been. But she told me once, years ago, that I would find one, and that when I did, I should give her my medicine basket.

"Do you know the story of *Mualig Siakam*?"

Molly Juan nodded. "Of course, the woman who was saved by the Little People during the great famine."

Brandon Walker leaned over to his wife. "What the hell does all this have to do with the price of tea in China?"

"Shhhh," Diana returned.

"Clemencia has been kissed by the ants in the same way the first *Mualig Siakam* was kissed by the bees," Rita continued. "Clemencia was starving and might have died if the ants had not bitten her and brought her to my attention. Some of her relatives are afraid to take her because they fear Ant Sickness. The Walkers are *Mil-gahn*, so Ant Sickness cannot hurt them. And I am old. I will die long before Ant Sickness can find me.

"The Walkers are asking for her because everyone knows that I am too old to care for her by myself, just as her own great-grandmother was. But I know that this is the child *Oks Amichuda* told me about—the very one."

"And you think, that by keeping her with you, you can help her become a medicine woman?" Molly Juan asked.

Rita looked at Fat Crack. "She already is one," Rita said. "She may not be old enough to understand that yet, and I will not tell her. It's something she must learn for herself. But in the time I have left, I can teach her things that will be useful when the time comes for her to decide."

Rita started to move away, but Judge Juan stopped her. "Supposing you die?" she asked pointedly. "What happens then? If Clemencia is living with a *Mil-gahn* family, who will be there to teach her?"

"The Walkers have a son," Rita answered quietly. "His *Mil-gahn* name is David Ladd. His Indian name—the one Looks At Nothing gave him when he was baptized—is *Edagith Gogk Je'e*—One With Two Mothers."

Molly Juan pushed her wire-framed glasses back up on her nose and peered closely at Rita. "I remember now. This is the Anglo boy who was baptized by an old medicine man years ago."

Rita nodded. "Looks At Nothing and I both taught Davy Ladd things he would need to know, things he can teach Clemencia as she gets older even though the medicine man and I are gone."

"How old is this boy now?"

"Twelve."

"And he speaks *Tohono O'othham*?"

"Yes."

"But what makes you think he would be willing to serve as a teacher and guide to this little girl?"

"I have lived with David Ladd since before he was born," Rita said. "He is a child of my heart if not of my flesh. When he was baptized, his mother—Mrs. Walker here—and I ate the ceremonial gruel together. He is a good boy. If I ask him to do something, he will do it."

That was when Judge Molly Juan finally turned to Diana and Brandon Walker. During the course of the proceedings, in an effort to keep the restless Clemencia quiet, Diana had handed the child over to Brandon. By the time the judge looked at them, Clemencia had grasped the tail of Brandon's new silk tie in one tiny fist and was happily chewing on it and choking him with it at the same time.

"Sheriff Walker," Molly Juan said, "it sounds as though your family is somewhat unusual. What do you think of all this?"

Still holding the child, Brandon got to his feet to address the judge. "Clemencia is just a baby, and she needs a home," he said. "I hate to think about her being sent to an orphanage."

"But what about the rest of it, Sheriff Walker? I know from the paperwork that your wife taught out here on the reservation for a number of years. She probably knows something about the *Tohono O'othham* and their culture and beliefs. What about you?"

Brandon looked down at the baby, who lay in his arms smiling up at him. For a moment he didn't speak at all. Finally he looked back at the judge.

"On the night of my stepson's second baptism," he said slowly, "I stood outside the feast house and smoked the Peace Smoke with Looks At Nothing. That night he asked three of us—Father John from San Xavier Mission; Gabe

Ortiz, Mrs. Antone's nephew; and myself—along with him to serve as Davy's four fathers. It seems to me this is much the same thing.

"If you let us have her, my wife and I will do everything in our power to see that she has the best of both worlds."

Judge Juan nodded. "All right then, supposing I were to grant this petition on a temporary basis, pending final adoption proceedings, have you given any thought as to what you would call her?"

"Dolores Lanita—Lani for short," Brandon answered at once. "Those would be her Anglo names. And her Indian name would be *Mualig Siakam*—Forever Spinning."

"And her home village?" Judge Juan asked.

"*Ban Thak*—Coyote Sitting," he answered. "That is Rita's home village. It would be hers as well."

"Be it so ordered," Judge Juan said, whacking her desk with the gavel. "Next case."

13

hen all the people near the village of Gurli Put Vo—
Dead Man's Pond—were told to come to a council so they
could arrange for the protection of their fields. Everything
that flies and all the animals came with the Indians to the
council. And everybody promised to watch carefully so that
the Bad People of the south should not again surprise them.

When PaDaj O'othham had eaten all the corn which they
had stolen, they were soon hungry again. So they began once
more to think of the nice fields of the Desert People. They began
to wish they could steal the harvest, but they did not know how
to accomplish this because, as you know, the Indians and their
friends, the Flying People and all the animals, were on guard.

Then a wise old bad man told PaDaj O'othham what to do.

Now when the Desert People held that council to arrange
for the protection of their fields, they were so excited that
they called only the people who live aboveground. So this
wise old bad man told PaDaj O'othham to call all the peo-

ple who live under the ground: Ko'owi—the Snakes,
Nanakshel—*the Scorpions,* Hiani—*the Tarantulas,* Jewho—
the Gophers, Chichdag—*the Gila Monsters, and* Chuk—*the
Jackrabbits. The Bad People said they would give all these
people who live under the ground good food and beautiful
clothes if they would go through the ground to the fields of
the Desert People and fight the* Tohono O'othham *while the
Bad People stole the crops.*

Chuk—*Jackrabbit—did not like this plan. The Indians
had always been good to* Chuk, *and he did not want to fight
them. But Jackrabbit did not know what to do.*

Some bumblebees were sitting in a nearby tree.
Hu'udagi—*the Bumblebees—told* Chuk *to run with all his
speed to the Desert People and tell them how* PaDaj O'othham *were planning to steal their harvest. The Bumblebees
said they would tell* U'uwhig—*the Birds.*

*So Jackrabbit ran. He went in such a hurry that he took
longer and longer jumps. As he jumped longer and longer,
his legs grew longer and longer. That is why, my friend, even
to this day, Jackrabbit's legs are so much longer than the
legs of his brother rabbit,* Tohbi—*the Cottontail.*

Lani awakened in the dark. She was hot. Salt, leached from
her sweat-stained shirt, had seeped into the raw wound on
her breast. The smoldering pain from that was what had
wakened her, and it seemed to expand with every breath, filling her eyes with tears. Her whole body was stiff. Her back
ached from lying on what seemed to be uneven grooves in
the floor beneath her.

While she had been asleep, she had been dreaming again,
dreaming about Nana *Dahd*. In the dream Lani had been a
child again. She and Rita had been walking together somewhere, walking and talking, although that was impossible.
By the time Lani first knew Rita Antone, Nana *Dahd* was already confined to a wheelchair.

Lani emerged from Rita's comforting presence in the dream, and she longed to return there, but this time when she wakened, she didn't seem to emerge gradually. There was no lingering fog of confusion the way there had been before. She knew at once that she was a prisoner and that she had been drugged. Perhaps the man named Vega had given her a much smaller dose this time, or perhaps some of the effect had been evacuated out of her system—sweated out of her pores by the perspiration that soaked her clothing.

Lani felt around her, trying to assess the hot, dark cage in which she was imprisoned—a huge wooden crate from the feel of it. Her searching fingers reached out and touched sturdy walls a foot or so on either side of her. They refused to give or even so much as creak when she tried pushing against them. Then she pounded on the wood until her knuckles bled, but if anyone heard, no one came to her aid.

The darkness around her at first seemed absolute, but at last she noticed rays of yellow light penetrating the darkness. The light, as if from street lights, told her that it was still night. She was near a road. She could hear the muffled roar of traffic—the sounds of heavy trucks, anyway. Periodically the box shook with what had to be the earth-shaking rumble of a nearby passing train.

For a while Lani tried yelling for help, but the heavy wooden box swallowed the sound, locking the noise inside with her. Her shouting, like the pounding that had preceded it, brought no help. No one *would* come, she realized at last. Rescue, if it came at all, would have to come from inside, from Lani herself. Otherwise, she would simply lie in this overheated box until the heat got to her or until she died of thirst or starvation.

As she had done countless times in the past, she reached up to her throat to touch her *kushpo ho'oma*—her hair charm—only to discover it was missing. At first, when her fingertips touched only the naked gold chain, she thought she had lost the medallion and she was bereft. Seconds later, though, she remembered taking it off and putting it in her pocket—hiding it there in hopes of keeping it out of the hands of the evil man who had hurt her so badly.

It was still there in her pocket, exactly where she had hidden it. That reassured her. At least Vega hadn't stripped off her clothes again, hadn't discovered where she had hidden the charm, so perhaps, this time, he had left her alone.

She had no idea how long she had been asleep. From that moment early in the morning—some morning—when she sat down on the rock for him to begin sketching her until now could have been one day or several, for all she knew. For one thing, she had been out of it long enough for him to draw that second picture. Just thinking about that— about lying there naked in front of him all that time, for what must have been hours—made her wince with shame. And if Lani didn't remember any of that, there might be other things the man had done to her that she didn't remember, either.

She lay very still and tried to sense the condition of her body. Other than the damaged breast and what felt like a series of splinters in her back, she seemed to be intact. If he had raped her, she would feel it, wouldn't she? There was a sudden feeling of relief that deserted her a moment later. Of course he hadn't raped her. Not yet. That was why she was still here. That was what awaited her once he came back— that and more.

In that moment, Lani saw it all with appalling clarity. Of course Vega would return for her. He had no intention of her staying in the box forever until she died of heat prostration or thirst or starvation. He had locked her in the crate for a reason—so she would be available to him, helpless and waiting, when it was time for whatever came next.

Sooner or later, Vega would come back for her. Closing her eyes in the darkness, she saw him again, with an almost gleeful smile on his face, standing over her with the overheated tongs in his hand. Vega was a man who enjoyed inflicting pain. When he came back, Lani knew full well that he would hurt her again.

Had she been standing upright, that awful realization might have tumbled her to the ground. As a child Lani had heard the stories of *Ohbsgam Ho'ok*—Apachelike Monster—who lived around Rattlesnake Skull and who carried young girls away with him, never to be seen again. Vega was like *Ohbsgam Ho'ok*. They were different only in that Vega was real. He was a bully—strong and mean and powerful. Lani was alone and helpless.

"The best thing to do with a bully is to ignore him," Davy had told Lani once. After yet another run-in with Danny Jenkins at school, she had turned to her older brother for advice.

"Those guys thrive on attention," Davy had continued. "That's usually all they want. If you treat 'em like they don't exist, eventually they melt into the woodwork. The only way to get the best of them is to try to understand them, to figure out what their weaknesses are. Then, the next time they come after you, you'll know what to do."

Following Davy's suggestions, Lani had made a show of ignoring Danny Jenkins all the while she studied him. It didn't take long for her to realize that he was desperately afraid of not being accepted, of not fitting in. Bullying was his sole defense, his weapon against being bullied himself. Once Lani understood all that, she had been able to use that knowledge to turn Danny Jenkins into a friend.

But how could she understand someone like Mr. Vega? And did she want to? How was it possible to comprehend a person who was capable of such cruelty? Trying to find a more comfortable position for her aching back, she settled herself on the rough floor and pulled the cloth of the shirt away from the singed skin of her breast. Then she closed her eyes and tried to think.

Just like Danny Jenkins, Vega thrived on power and on other people's pain. He had hurt her, yes, and he would do so again, but hurting her wasn't the real point, or, at least, not the only one. She sensed that what he had done and would do to her constituted a means to an end rather than an end in itself. His real purpose was to hurt her parents. She didn't understand the why of that, but she knew it to be true. Vega wasn't Andrew Carlisle, but there was some connection, some bond between them. Vega was fueled by the same kind of rage and lust for revenge that had caused the evil *Ohb* to invade the house in Gates Pass long before Lani was born.

So that was most of what she knew. Vega was angry and cruel and hot-tempered. *Bagwwul*—one easily angered. That word, which Rita had taught her, seemed to come to Lani through the coils of the basket pressed tightly in the palm of her hand. She remembered Vega's fierce anger when she had slapped away the cup he was holding out to her; how he had yanked her hair back as he forced her to drink the second one.

Anger was one of Vega's weak spots. He demanded obedience but had to enforce that obedience with either drugs or some other form of restraints. That meant he was also *chu ehbiththam*—a coward. Only cowards attacked their enemies when they were helpless and unable to fight back. His outrageous physical assault on Lani had been staged when she was tied hand and foot, when she could do nothing to defend herself.

Obedience. Lani's thoughts strayed back to that word and stayed there. And once again, out of the past or out of the basket, Lani heard Rita's voice, singing to her:

> *"Listen to what I sing to you,*
> *Little* Olhoni. *Listen to what I sing.*
> *Be careful not to look at me*
> *But do exactly as I say."*

Do exactly as I say.

Lani hadn't even been born on the day of the battle with the evil *Ohb*, but she heard the words to that life-saving war chant as clearly as if she herself had been locked in the long-ago darkness of that root cellar along with Rita and Davy and Father John.

Perhaps the two darknesses—the one in the root cellar and the one here inside Vega's stifling wooden crate—were exactly the same thing.

"That dollhouse looks just like my dad's," Quentin said, taking a confused look around as they pulled up the long curving driveway of the Gates Pass house. "What are we doing here?"

"Dropping off your sister's bicycle," Mitch told him.

Lani Walker's knapsack had yielded a garage-door opener and a door key as well. "Take a look in that paper bag over there," he said. "The gate-opener-door and house key are both inside. Get 'em out, would you?"

Quentin seemed dazed and stupefied. His fumbling movements were maddeningly slow, but he did as he was told. "How'd you get these?" he asked, holding up both the key and the opener once he had finally succeeded in retrieving them.

"I already told you. Lani gave them to me so we could bring the bike back," Mitch answered. "What did you think, that I stole them? And don't just sit there holding the damn thing. Press the button, would you?"

Obligingly, Quentin pressed the button, and the wrought-iron electronic gate swung open. Quentin started to hand the opener over to Mitch. "Keep it," Mitch told him. "We'll need it again on the way out. Now drag the bike out of the back. Where does it go, do you know?"

Quentin shrugged. "Right here in the carport, as far as I know."

By the time Quentin finally managed to unlock the back door, Mitch Johnson was fairly dancing with anticipation—like a little kid who has waited too long to go to the bathroom.

After watching the house for weeks, Mitch Johnson was ready to be inside. He had always planned on invading Brandon's home turf as part of the operation. As the door finally opened, Mitch felt almost giddy. All those years he had been moldering in prison, Brandon Walker had been living here in what he believed to be a safe haven. Well, it wasn't safe anymore.

Carrying the bag with its few remaining goodies, it didn't take long to distribute them. Mitch directed Quentin to leave the tongs in the kitchen sink and the cassette tape under his stepmother's pillow.

Quentin seemed puzzled. He held the tape up to the light and examined it. "What's this for?" he asked.

"It's just a little something Lani wants your dad and stepmom to have. It's their anniversary pretty soon, isn't it?"

"I guess so," Quentin agreed. "So how do you know Lani?"

"We met at her job," Mitch said. "At the museum."

Mitch couldn't help being a little in awe of Quentin's capacity. Based on how much booze he had probably drunk, that little bit of scopolamine should have laid the guy low. As it was, Quentin Walker's mental faculties were noticeably dim, but he was still walking and talking.

"Why are we doing all this?" Quentin asked, leaning up against the doorway to steady himself. "And why's it so hot?"

"I already told you," Mitch said. "It's a favor for your sister."

"Oh," said Quentin.

The last room they entered was Brandon Walker's study. Quentin had told Mitch that was where Brandon Walker kept his guns, and that was what they went looking for—Brandon's gun cabinet. While Quentin pawed through the top desk drawer, searching for the key to the locked cabinet, Mitch Johnson surveyed the room. He was fine until he saw the framed plaque hanging on the wall along with any number of other awards.

The 1976 Detective of the Year award had been presented

to Detective Brandon Walker by *Parade Magazine* as a result of his having solved a homicide case, one in which two
men were murdered and another was severely injured.

The plaque on the wall didn't say that, didn't reveal all
those details. It didn't have to. Mitch knew them by heart.
This was the award—the recognition—that had come to
Brandon Walker for arresting Mitch Johnson himself. For
arresting a man who was engaged in the wholly honorable
pursuit of protecting God and country from the invading
hordes. Those wetbacks had been illegal trespassers on U.S.
soil, intent on taking jobs away from real Americans who
were out of work. Mitch was the one who should have been
given a medal for getting rid of that kind of scum—a medal,
not a jail sentence.

The rage that hit Mitch Johnson on seeing that framed
award went far beyond anything he had ever imagined. Years
of pent-up frustration boiled over when he saw it. That was
the worst part of the whole operation, the moment of his
greatest temptation.

Years ago, in similar circumstances, Andy had simply
fallen victim to Diana's body, losing his focus and purpose
both, in satisfying his biological cravings. By resisting the
pull of Lani's tight little body, by not tearing into her when
it would have been so easy, Mitch Johnson had already
proved to himself that he was a better man than his mentor.
Seeing that plaque sitting smugly on the wall was far worse
for Mitch than merely wanting to be inside some stupid
woman's hot little twat.

What Mitch wanted to do in that moment was take a
gun—any gun would do, but preferably an automatic—and
mow through every picture in the place. It would have been
easy. Even as the thought crossed his mind, Quentin Walker
was in the process of handing Mitch a Colt .357 that would
have blasted the whole room to pieces. And brought cops
raining down on them from miles away.

Taking a deep, calming breath, Mitch caught himself just

in time. He dropped the weapon into his pocket. "What's all this shit?" he said, gesturing.

"What?" Quentin asked. "The stuff on the wall?"

Mitch nodded, not trusting himself to speak.

"Dad used to call it his Wall of Honor."

"Knock it down," Mitch said. "Knock that crap down and break it."

"All of it?" Quentin asked, staring from frame to frame.

"Why not?" Mitch told him. "Your father never did anything for you, did he?"

"No, he didn't," Quentin agreed, reaching for the first piece, a framed diploma from the University of Arizona. "Why the hell shouldn't I?"

Raising the diploma over his head, Quentin smashed it to pieces in a spray of glass in the middle of the floor. While Quentin worked his way down the wall, Mitch took the Detective of the Year Award off the wall. He studied it for a moment with his fingers itching to do the job, but that wouldn't have worked. Quentin's prints wouldn't have been on the frame.

"Do this one next," Mitch said, handing it over. Even as he watched the piece smash to pieces on the tiled floor, he gave himself full credit and gloated over the victory. His was the triumph of rational thought over base emotions.

Had Quentin Walker's mental faculties been a little less impaired, he might have noticed that from the moment they climbed inside his newly purchased Bronco, Mitch Johnson had been wearing latex gloves. Quentin wasn't.

He didn't notice; didn't even question it. To Mitch's way of thinking, that made all the difference.

Do exactly as I say, Lani was thinking.

As the phrase spun through her mind, she suddenly realized that the words to Nana *Dahd*'s war chant, the ones she had sung to Davy so long ago in order to save his life, were also important to Lani—to save her life as well.

She remembered Mr. Vega's instant fury the moment she had disobeyed him. Obviously whatever drug he had given her—both earlier on the mountain and later at his house—was something that produced compliance, that made her do whatever he said. If Lani was going to save herself—and it was unlikely anyone else would—then she had to make sure that he didn't give her any more of it. She would have to watch for a chance to get away. If the opportunity presented itself, she would be able to take advantage of it only so long as she remained clear-headed.

That was the moment when she heard the tailgate of the Subaru swing open. A moment later she heard someone fiddling with the outside of the crate, as though they were opening a padlock hasp. Lani had been lying with the tiny people-hair medallion clutched in her hand, gleaning as much comfort as she could from the tightly woven coils. Now, though, before Vega opened the door on the crate, she stuffed the tiny basket back into the pocket of her jeans. Then she forced herself to lie still, closing her eyes and slowing her breathing. By the time the door swung open, Lani Walker appeared to be sound asleep.

"Come on, sweetheart, rise and shine," Vega said, grabbing her by the ankle and dragging her once again across the rough, splintery floor of the crate. "Wake up. We're going for another little ride."

Yanked upright, Lani found herself standing between the Subaru and an idling sport utility vehicle, an old Bronco. A sleeping man was slumped against the rider's side door. "Come on around to the other side," Vega ordered. "Can you walk on your own, or am I going to have to carry you?"

Lani, planning on acting dazed, didn't have to fake stumbling. Her legs felt rubbery beneath her—rubbery and strangely disconnected from her brain and will. When she staggered and almost fell, Vega grabbed her hair, hard, and held her up with that. The pull was vicious enough that tears came to her eyes, but it also helped clear her head. In a mo-

ment of quiet, she heard a readily identifiable squeak and realized that the fist knotted in her hair was encased in a rubber glove.

Desperate to get away, she looked around. They were
standing in one corner of a large gravel parking lot. There
were no other people visible anywhere. The only other vehicles were parked next to the darkened hulk of a building
half a block away—too far to try running there for help.

After a moment, Vega slammed shut the tailgate of the
Subaru, twisting the key to lock it once more. Lani considered screaming, but just as they started around the back of
the Bronco, with Lani's hair still knotted painfully in Vega's
gloved fist, another train rumbled past on the track that bor-
dered the edge of the lot. With all that noise, there was no
point in attempting to scream for help, not even out in the
open. Over the racket of the train, no one would have heard
her anyway.

Vega wrenched open the driver's door to the Bronco and
shoved her inside. "There you go," he said. "You sit in the
middle. That way I'll be able to keep an eye on you."

The unexpected push sent her piling across the bench seat
and rammed the tender flesh of her already throbbing breast
against the steering wheel of the car. Another intense jolt of
pain shot through her body. She managed to suppress a
shriek. Even so, a yelp of pain escaped her lips. On the far
side of the car, the sleeping man stirred and looked at her.

"Hey, what's this?" he mumbled sleepily. "What's going on?"

Quentin! What was he doing here?

"It's too soon, Quentin," Vega said. "Go back to sleep. I'll
let you know when it's time to wake up."

With his head dropping back to his chin, Quentin did as
he was told.

The odor of beer was thick in the car, and Quentin was
snoring softly. A hundred questions whirled through Lani's
mind, but she asked none of them. Asking questions or
showing too much interest in what was going on around her

was probably an invitation to another drink of whatever Vega had given her earlier. Maybe he had fed some of the same stuff to Quentin.

"I suppose you're a little surprised to see him, aren't you?" Vega said, climbing in behind Lani and shifting the Bronco into gear. "We're just having a little family reunion tonight. Your brother helped me drop off a few presents for your parents. Now the three of us are going for a ride. We have some errands to run."

Vega's earlier ugly mood seemed to have lifted. He was in high spirits, whistling under his breath as he drove out of the lot onto Grant and from there onto eastbound I-10. Whatever had happened during the interval while Lani had been locked in the car seemed to have left him feeling particularly happy.

"Your brother's here," Vega said, instinctively answering Lani's unasked question, "because Quentin's a good friend of mine."

Assuming from the way he made the statement that no reply was necessary, Lani kept quiet. Seconds later, however, an iron grip clamped shut on her leg, just above her left knee. As the muscular fingers dug into her flesh, she squirmed under the punishing grip but resisted the urge to cry out.

"Did you hear me, little lady?" he demanded. "I said Quentin's a good friend of mine."

"Yes," Lani said. "I heard."

"But don't put too much store in it," he added. "Because I'll kill the son of a bitch in a second if you don't behave. Do you understand me? Whether Quentin lives or dies is up to you. If you try to run, or if you make any trouble at all, I'll kill him, no questions asked. Do you understand?"

Lani nodded her head. "Yes," she said quietly. "I understand."

And she did, too. If Vega said he would kill Quentin, then he would, friend or not.

"I don't make idle threats, you see."

"No," Lani said. "I know you don't."

Once again, Nana *Dahd*'s war chant came whirling into Lani Walker's heart out of the darkness of that locked, long-ago root cellar.

> *"Listen to what I sing to you,*
> *Little* Olhoni. *Listen to what I sing.*
> *Be careful not to look at me*
> *But do exactly as I say."*

For a moment it seemed to Lani that Rita herself was riding in the truck with them, telling Lani what she had to do to survive. Lani realized then that she was right. The two sets of darkness and the two evil *Ohbs* were somehow merging into one. And the advice Nana *Dahd* had once given Davy Ladd was the same advice Rita was giving Lani now in the Bronco.

"I'll do it," Lani said quietly. "I'll do exactly what you say."

It might have sounded to Vega as though she were speaking to him, answering him, but in Lani Walker's heart and in her mind's eye, she was actually speaking to Nana *Dahd*.

The words formed clearly enough in her head, but when it came time actually to speak them, they came out fuzzy and disjointed. Like her rubberized legs earlier when she had struggled to walk, the lingering effects of the drug still interfered with Lani's ability to use her tongue. That was evidently exactly what Vega expected.

He loosened his clawlike grip around her leg and gave the top of her thigh a possessive pat. It was all Lani could do not to dodge away under his touch.

"Good girl," Vega said. "Your mother told me you were smart. I'm glad to see some evidence that it's true."

Vega had spoken to Lani's mother, to Diana? When? How? Lani wondered. And what was it he had said earlier about dropping something off at the house? Something about presents? What presents?

Lani cringed then, thinking about the terrible picture she had seen on his easel, the one he had drawn of her, the one with her body naked and with her legs spread open to the world. What if he had taken that one to her parents? Or else, what if he had done something to them? Her heart quailed at the thought.

"Why did you go to my house?" she asked.

Vega reached in his pocket and pulled out a key, one Lani recognized. "Why wouldn't I?" he said. "You gave your brother your key so he could return your bike for you."

By then the Bronco was on I-19 and starting off at the exit to Ajo Way. It seemed to Lani that they were headed for the reservation while off to the right, hidden behind a single barrier of rugged mountain, lay Gates Pass and home. Or whatever was left of home.

"You didn't hurt my parents, did you?" she asked at last.

Vega frowned. "You're awfully full of questions at the moment."

"Did you?" Lani insisted.

He turned his face toward her, his face glowing ghostlike in the reflected headlights of an oncoming vehicle.

"I haven't hurt them yet," he said. "But then, it's probably a little too early. Don't worry, though, they'll be getting your message before long."

"What message?" Lani asked.

"Don't you remember? You made it yourself, a very special tape for both your mother and father."

A tape? Lani could remember nothing about a tape, nothing at all. "I don't remember any tape," she said.

Vega grinned and patted her again. "It's all right if you don't remember," he said. "But what I can tell you is that once they hear it, neither one of your parents is ever going to forget it, not as long as they live."

*   *   *

The patrol car, lights flashing, had barely stopped at the end of the driveway when the Walkers' telephone started to ring. While Brandon went to meet the deputy, Diana raced for the phone, hoping beyond hope that the caller would be Lani. It wasn't.

Jessica Carpenter's mother, Rochelle, was on the phone. "I got your message," she said. "I hope you don't mind my calling this late. We saw the emergency lights as I was bringing Jessie home from the concert. Lani's all right, isn't she?"

"Lani seems to be missing," Diana said, fighting to force the words out around the barrier of a huge lump that threatened to block her throat. "Jessie hasn't seen her then?"

"Not all day," Rochelle Carpenter said. "The last time they talked was last night. Jessie said Lani was all excited about something she was doing for you this morning before work, something about an anniversary present."

Diana caught her breath at the thought that maybe this was a clue, something that might lead them to Lani or at least tell them where to start looking. "Could I talk to Jessie?" Diana asked. "If we could find out what that was, maybe it would help us find her."

Moments later, a subdued Jessica Carpenter came on the phone. "I'm sorry, Mrs. Walker. I hope Lani's going to be okay."

"Just tell me what you know about what Lani was doing earlier this morning."

"What if it ruins a surprise?"

"Please," Diana said. "That's a risk we'll have to take."

"It was something about a picture. Lani said she had met a man who was going to paint a picture of her to give to you and Mr. Walker for your anniversary. When we talked last night, she was all excited and asked me what I thought she should wear."

"Did she tell you what she decided?" Diana Walker asked.

"What she wore in February when she was one of the

rodeo princesses. That pretty flowered shirt, her cowboy hat, her boots. I don't know for sure if that's what she wore, but she said she was going to."

The phone trembled in Diana's hand. She was listening to Jessie Carpenter's voice but she was thinking about Fat Crack's warning about the danger from *Shadow of Death,* the warning Diana had laughed off and dismissed without a thought. Was Lani's mysterious disappearance somehow connected to that?

"Her rodeo clothes?" Diana managed to mumble in return. "Did she say why she chose those?"

"Something about the man, the artist, wanting her to look like an Indian."

The doorbell rang. "I'd better go. Someone's at the door," Diana said hurriedly. "Thank you, Jess. I'll pass this information along to the deputy."

But Jessie Carpenter wasn't quite ready to be off the phone. "You don't think anything bad has happened to Lani, do you, Mrs. Walker?"

Hot tears stung the corners of Diana's eyes. "I hope to God nothing has," she said.

By the time Diana put down the phone in the kitchen and headed for the living room, Brandon was already escorting Detective Ford Myers into the house, leading him to the same couch where Deputy Garrett was already seated with his notebook in hand.

Diana's heart fell as soon as she saw Detective Myers. *Why him?* she wondered.

Ford Myers had gotten himself crosswise of Brandon very early in the course of their professional lives. The two of them had gone head-to-head on more than one occasion over the years, but once elected sheriff, the civil service protections Brandon himself had instituted had made getting rid of Myers tough. As a result, Myers had stayed on, growing more and more disgruntled.

During that critical election campaign, when Brandon

had been running against Bill Forsythe in the aftermath of the Quentin Walker protection-racket allegations, Detective Myers had been one of several members of the department who had been openly critical of Brandon Walker's administration.

"What seems to be the problem?" Myers was saying as Diana walked into the room.

"It's our daughter," Brandon answered. "Her name is Lani. Full name Dolores Lanita Walker. She's sixteen. She left for work on her bike around six o'clock this morning and never arrived. Tonight she was supposed to go to a concert with a friend of hers from up the street. Lani didn't show for that, either."

"That's the last time you saw her?" Myers asked. "This morning?"

"We didn't actually see her then," Brandon answered. "She left us a note. We didn't worry about her all day because we thought she had gone to work at the Arizona Sonora Desert Museum. This evening, though, when we came back from dinner, her supervisor from work had called and left a message. Mrs. Allison said on the phone that when she was going to miss a shift like she did today that she needed to call in."

"You've spoken to this Mrs. Allison?"

Brandon shook his head, but plucked the Post-it note with Lani's handwritten message on it and handed it over to the detective. "Not yet," Brandon said, as the detective perused the note. "As you can see, she had plans to go to a concert this evening."

"What kind?" Myers asked. "One of those rock concerts?"

"I doubt it. She goes in more for country western. You could talk to her friend, Jessica Carpenter. She could tell you what kind of concert it was."

"And you said Lani rides her bike to work?"

"That's right. She could drive one of the cars, but she prefers the bike. When my wife and I came home a little while ago, though, the bike was back home, lying in the middle of the carport. Her bike was here, but Lani wasn't. Every light in the house was on."

The detective glanced at Deputy Garrett. "A break-in then?" Myers asked.

Garrett shook his head. "I haven't been able to find any sign of it so far. Either the doors were left unlocked—"

"They weren't," Brandon interrupted.

"Or whoever it was let themselves in with a key. Other than a gun—a Colt .357—nothing else seems to be missing, although there is some glass breakage in Sheriff Walker's study."

"Where was the Colt?" Myers asked.

"Locked in my gun cabinet," Brandon answered.

"And was that broken into?"

Garrett shook his head. "Again, whoever it was must have used a key," the deputy said.

"The key was in my desk drawer," Brandon said.

Ford Myers raised his eyebrow. "So whoever it was knew where to look. You said something about breakage, Deputy Garrett? What's that all about?"

"Plaques, diplomas, and framed certificates," Garrett answered. "That kind of thing."

"Anything else missing besides the gun?" Myers continued. "Money? Jewelry?"

Brandon shook his head. "We haven't really checked that yet," he said. "We called for a deputy before we went snooping around."

Myers nodded. "I see," he said. "Now, tell me," he continued, "have you two been having any trouble with your daughter recently?"

"Trouble?" Diana asked, interjecting herself into the conversation for the first time. "What do you mean, trouble?"

"Boy trouble, for instance," Myers said with a casual shrug of the shoulders. "Hanging out with the wrong crowd. Problems with drugs or alcohol."

Diana was shaking her head long before he finished.

"No," she declared. "Absolutely not! Nothing like that. Lani's a fine kid. An honors student. She's never given us a bit of trouble."

Myers stuffed his notebook into his pocket and then glanced at Deputy Garrett. "How about if I have the deputy here show me the damage in your office."

Brandon's face was tight with suppressed anger. "Sure," he said. "That'll be fine."

As the two officers started out of the room, Diana made as if to follow them, but Brandon stopped her. "We'll wait here," he said.

As soon as Garrett and Myers were out of earshot, a furious Diana Walker turned on her husband. "What the hell does he mean, hanging out with the wrong crowd?"

"Hush. Don't let him hear you," Brandon said. "You know where the SOB is going with all that, don't you? I do. I'll bet he's going to call this a family disturbance. He'll say Lani's a runaway. He's not going to lift a finger until he has to. He'll go by the book on this one, one hundred percent. Guaranteed."

Diana was outraged. "Not lift a finger? What do you mean?"

"Hide and watch," Brandon told her. "I've seen it before. Nobody plays the official rules game better than Ford Myers. I think maybe he invented it."

They were sitting waiting in grim silence a few minutes later when Myers sauntered back into the room. "If you have any jewelry or cash in the house, you might want to check it," he suggested.

"We don't keep cash around," Brandon said. "And not that much jewelry. But I'm sure Diana will be glad to check."

Wordlessly, Diana got up and walked into the bedroom. Nothing appeared to be out of place. Her jewelry box was where it belonged and nothing seemed to be missing. Fighting back tears, she walked on down the hall and checked

Lani's bedroom. Jessica was right. The flowered cowboy shirt, Lani's Stetson, and Tony Lama boots were all gone from the closet. Diana returned to the living room just as Myers was getting ready to leave.

"I checked," she said. "Everything is here, except for the outfit Jessica said Lani was planning to wear. That one is gone."

"Good enough, Mrs. Walker," Myers said. "Deputy Garrett and I will be shoving off for the time being. If you still haven't heard anything from Lani by tomorrow morning, call in after six and we'll go ahead with the Missing Persons report at that time."

"I can tell you what clothes Lani was wearing when she left the house," Diana said. "In case you're interested, that is."

"That information should go into the Missing Persons report when you make it." Myers smiled. "Chances are, though, it won't even be necessary. Most of the time, these kids turn up long before the twenty-four-hour deadline. I'm sure your husband can tell you how it works, Mrs. Walker. By allowing that day's worth of grace time, we can cut down on unnecessary paperwork. Right, Mr. Walker?"

"Right," Brandon said.

"And as far as the gun theft and the vandalism is concerned, on a low-priority residential robbery like this, I won't be able to schedule someone to come out and lift prints until regular work hours next week. And besides, that may not prove necessary, either."

"What do you mean?" Diana asked. "Why wouldn't it be necessary?"

Myers shrugged. "What if the whole thing turns out to be a family prank of some kind? If your daughter took the gun herself on a lark, just to do a little unauthorized target practice, it might be better not to have those prints on file, don't you think?"

"But Lani wouldn't—" Diana began.

"Sure," Brandon said, urging Detective Myers and the

deputy out the door. "I see what you mean. Thanks for all your help."

Diana was fuming when Brandon turned to face her. "Why did you let him off the hook like that?" she demanded. "Lani doesn't even *like* guns. She would never—"

"I let Detective Myers off the hook because he has no intention of doing anything, and I do." With that, Brandon Walker stalked toward the kitchen, with Diana right on his heels.

"What?" she asked. "What are you going to do?"

"I could lift prints myself, but that might screw up some prosecutor's chain of evidence," Brandon said, picking up the phone. "So instead, I'm going to make a few calls. There are some people in this world who owe me. It's time to call in a few of my markers."

Fingerprints were Alvin Miller's life. From the time an ink pad showed up as a birthday present for his sixth birthday party, he had found fingerprints endlessly fascinating. He had left a trail of indelible red marks across the face of his mother's new Harvest Gold refrigerator and dishwasher. His mother had confiscated the damn thing after that and thrown it in the garbage.

By the time Alvin was sixteen, he had turned an Eagle Scout project into a volunteer position as an aide in the latent fingerprint lab for the Pima County Sheriff's Department. Upon high school graduation, he had transformed his volunteer work into a paying job. Now, at age thirty-four and without benefit of more than a few college credits, he was the youngest and least formally educated person in the country to be placed in charge of a fully automated fingerprint identification system.

The civil service protections former sheriff Brandon Walker had instituted over the years kept his successor from doing politically based wholesale firings, but Bill Forsythe wasn't above finding other ways of unloading what he considered deadwood. One of the people he wanted out most was Alvin Miller. To have some of the best, most up-to-date equipment in the Southwest in the hands of an "uneducated kid" was more than Forsythe could stand. He wanted somebody in that position with the proper credentials—somebody people around the country could look up to, somebody about whom they would say, "Now there's a guy who knows what he's doing."

Since his election, Sheriff Forsythe had hit Alvin Miller where it hurt the worst—in the budget department, chopping both money and staff. The "automated" part of AFIS sounds good, but the part that precedes the automation—enhancing the prints so the computer can actually scan and analyze them—is a labor-intensive, manual process. Forsythe had cut so far back on staffing the fingerprint lab that it should have been impossible for it to function—would have been impossible—had the lab been left in any hands less capable or dedicated than those of Alvin Miller.

He worked night and day. He put in his eight hours on the clock and another eight or so besides almost every day, Saturdays and Sundays included. Only forty hours a week went on the clock; a whole lot more than forty were freebies.

Because Alvin had so much hands-on practice, he was incredibly quick at manually enhancing those prints. He could read volumes into what looked like—to everyone else's untrained eyes—indecipherable circles and smudges. When it came to fingerprints, Alvin found each was as unique as he'd always heard snowflakes were supposed to be. And once he had dealt with a print, he remembered much of what he saw. Twice now, he had managed to make a hit—fingering a current resident in the Pima County Jail for another unrelated crime *before* feeding the information into the computer.

When Carley Fielding, Pima County's weekend lab tech, called earlier that evening to see what she should do with the three boxes of bones Detective Leggett wanted printed, Alvin Miller happened to be in and working. Lifting finger- prints off human bones was nothing Alvin had ever done be- fore. The prospect was interesting enough to take him away from whatever he had been working on before.

It turned out that bones were easy to process. It didn't take long for Alvin to figure out that more than one person had handled the bones. Some had done so with gloves on, but only one had handled them bare-handed. Alvin sorted through one set of dusted prints after another until he was convinced that he had found the best possible one.

That was where he was when his phone rang. "Al?" a fa- miliar voice asked. "What the hell are you still doing there working at this time of night?"

"Sheriff Walker!" Alvin Miller exclaimed. A pleased smile spread over his face as he recognized his former boss's voice. "How's it going?"

"Not all that good. I need some help."

"Hey, if there's something I can do," Al Miller told him, "you've got it."

"I know," Brandon Walker said. "And as it turns out, there is something you can do, Al, because I just happen to have a houseful of fingerprints that need to be lifted."

"What house?" Alvin Miller asked.

"Mine."

"The same one you lived in before? The one out in Gates Pass?"

"That's it. But I don't want to get you in trouble with your new boss by taking you away from something im- portant."

"Don't worry about it," Alvin Miller said with a grin. "My new boss isn't going to say a word. As far as Bill Forsythe and his damned time clock are concerned, I'm not even working tonight. That being the case, I can come and go as I damned well please. See you in twenty minutes or so, give or take."

*　　*　　*

Once Brandon was off the phone with Alvin Miller, Diana took her turn and tried dialing the number Davy had left on his message. She was surprised when a faraway desk clerk told her that she had dialed the Ritz-Carlton. She was even more surprised when the voice of a sleep-dulled young woman answered the phone. Moments later Davy's voice came through the receiver as well.

"Hi, Mom," he said. "How's it going?"

Just hearing her son speak brought Diana close to tears. She had to swallow the lump in her throat before she could answer. "Not all that well at the moment," she said. "Lani's missing."

"What?" Davy asked.

"Lani's gone," Diana said bleakly.

"What do you mean, gone?"

"I mean she's not here. She never showed for that concert with Jessica, and she didn't show up for work today, either."

"Maybe she went to visit somebody else. Have you checked with her other friends?"

"We're checking," Diana said, "but I thought you'd want to know what was going on."

"You don't think she's been kidnapped, or something, do you?" Davy demanded. "Shouldn't somebody contact the FBI?"

"Brandon is handling it."

"What can I do to help?" Davy asked urgently.

"Nothing much, for right now," Diana answered. "I just wanted you to know, that's all."

"Thanks," he said. "Are you and Dad going to be all right?"

Diana felt herself choking on the phone. "We'll be okay," she said. "But hurry home. Hurry as fast as you can. And call every night so we can keep you posted."

"I will," Davy said. "I promise."

A stricken David Ladd handed the phone over to Candace. "I was right," he said. "Something awful *has* happened. Lani's gone."

Candace was the one who put the phone back in its cradle and switched on the light. "Gone where?" she asked.

Davy shrugged. "Nobody knows."

"Your parents think she's been kidnapped?"

"Maybe, but they're not sure. Candace, I've never heard my mother this upset. She never even asked who you were." While he spoke, Davy had crawled out of bed and was starting toward the bathroom.

"What are you doing?" Candace asked.

"I'm going to shower and get dressed."

"But why?"

"So I can leave. You heard me. I told Mom I'd be there as soon as I can. If I go right now, I can be halfway to Bloomington before morning rush hour starts."

"*We,*" Candace said pointedly. "If *we* leave right now. Besides, it's Sunday; there isn't going to be a rush hour."

David nodded. "I meant we," he said.

"Doesn't that seem like a stupid thing to do?" Candace asked.

"Stupid? Didn't you hear what I said? This is a crisis, Candace. My family needs me."

"I didn't say going was stupid. Driving is. Why not fly?" Candace asked. "We can put the tickets on my AmEx. If we take a plane, we can be in Tucson by noon. Driving, that's about as long as it would take us to make it to the Iowa state line."

"What about the car? What about all my stuff?"

"I'll call Bridget," Candace said decisively. "She works only a few blocks from here. If we leave the parking claim ticket at the desk, she can come over on Monday after work, pick up the car, and take it home with her. She and Larry can keep it with them until we can make arrangements to come back and get it later. In the meantime, we can take a cab to the airport. That's a lot less trouble than fighting the park-ing-garage wars."

Candace wrestled a city phone book out of the nightstand drawer and started looking through it.

"What are you doing?" David asked.

"Calling the airlines to find the earliest plane and get us a reservation."

David looked at her wonderingly. "You'd do this for me? Go to all this trouble?"

She looked at him in mock exasperation as the "all lines are busy" message played out in her ear. "David," Candace said, "we're a team. I've been telling you for months now that I love you. If there's a crisis in your life, then there's a crisis in mine, too."

Just then a live person somewhere in the airline industry must have come on the phone. "What's your earliest flight from Chicago to Tucson?" she asked. There was a long pause. "Six A.M.?" she said a moment later.

Looking at the clock on the nightstand, Candace groaned. "Not much time for sleep, is there? But that's the one we need. Two seats, together, if you have them." There was a pause. "The return flight?" She glanced questioningly in David's direction. "I don't know about that. I guess we'd better just leave the return trip open for now."

After making arrangements to pay for the tickets at the counter, Candace put down the phone. "Don't you think we ought to try to sleep for another hour or so? We don't want to get there and be so shot from lack of sleep that we can't help out."

Obligingly, Davy lay back down on the bed, but he didn't crawl back under the sheets because he didn't expect to fall asleep again. He did, though. The next thing he knew, the alarm in the clock radio next to his head was going off. It was four-thirty.

From the light leaking out of the bathroom and from the sound of running water, he could tell that Candace was already up and in the shower. Moments later, David Ladd was, too.

He was standing under the steaming spray of water when he remembered his dream from the day before—the dream and Lani's horrifying scream.

Rocked by a terrible sense of foreboding, Davy braced himself against the shower wall to keep from falling. He knew now that the scream could mean only one thing.

Dolores Lanita Walker was already dead.

14

When the Indians heard the bad news—that PaDaj O'othham *were coming again to steal their crops*—they held *another council. Everybody came.* U'uwhig—*the Birds*—*told their friends the Indians about a mountain which was not far from their village and quite near their fields. The people went to this mountain, and on the side of it they built three big walls of rock.*

Those walls of rock are there, even to this day.

Then all the women and children went up on top of the mountain, behind the walls of rock. But the men stayed down to protect the fields.

Soon the Bad People of the South came once again.

The Wasps, the Scorpions, and Snakes were leading them. But Nuhwi—*the Buzzards—and* Chuk U'uwhig—*the Blackbirds—and all the larger birds were on guard.* Nuhwi—*Buzzard—would catch* Ko'owi—*Snake—and break his back.* Tatdai—*Roadrunner—watched for the*

Scorpions, and Pa-nahl—*the Bees—fought* Wihpsh—*the Wasps.*

So at last the Bad People were driven away. The Desert People returned to their village and their fields. They built houses and were very happy. A great many of the Bad People had been killed in this fight, so it was a long time before they felt strong enough to fight again. But after a while they were very hungry. And Wihpsh—*the Wasps—carried word to them that the Indian women were once again filling their ollas and grain baskets with corn and beans and honey.*

This time PaDaj O'othham *waited until it was very dry and hot. Then they started north.*

This time Shoh'o—*Grasshopper—had listened to the plans of the Bad People.* Shoh'o *started to jump to reach his friends, the Desert People, and warn them. The harder and faster Grasshopper jumped, the longer grew his hind legs. Still he could not go fast enough. So he took two leaves and fastened them on and flew. Before he arrived, he wore out one pair of leaves and put on another pair. To this day* Shoh'o—*Grasshopper—still carries one large thin pair of wings, and another thin small green pair.*

One minute Deputy Fellows was wide awake, staring at the doors to the ICU waiting room. The next minute, Gabe Ortiz was shaking him awake.

"Brian?"

Brian's eyes flicked open. It took a moment for the face in front of his to register. "Fat Crack!" he exclaimed. "How the hell are you, and what are you doing here?"

"Delia Cachora, Manny Chavez's daughter, works with me out on the reservation. When we heard about her father, I offered to drive her into town."

Brian glanced around the waiting room. No one else was there. "Where is she?" he asked.

"A nurse took Delia in to see him," Fat Crack said. "How does it look?"

Brian shook his head. "Not good," he said. "It's his back. Broken."

"How did it happen?" Gabe Ortiz asked. "I heard it had something to do with Rattlesnake Skull."

Brian nodded. "At the *charco*. It sounds as though he came across someone—an Anglo—digging up bones there by the water hole. We think Mr. Chavez thought the guy was digging up ancient artifacts and tried to stop him. The guy attacked Mr. Chavez with a shovel."

Fat Crack was shaking his head when an Indian woman in her mid- to late thirties emerged from behind the doors to the ICU. "He's still unconscious," she said, addressing Gabe Ortiz. "No one knows when he'll come out from under the anesthetic. His condition is serious enough that somebody had a priest come around and deliver last rites. The nurse said he was really bent out of shape about that. My father stopped being a Catholic a long time ago."

Blushing, Brian stood up. "You must be Delia Cachora. I'm Deputy Fellows," he said. "I'm sorry. I'm afraid the priest business is all my fault. When we found your father, he was saying something over and over in *Tohono O'oth-ham*. I thought he was calling for a priest—*pahl*. It turns out he was saying *pahla*."

"Shovel," Fat Crack supplied.

Brian Fellows nodded. "That's right. Shovel. I'm sorry if the priest upset him."

Delia Chavez Cachora gave him a puzzled glance. "Where did you learn to speak *Tohono O'othham*?" she asked.

"From a friend of mine," he answered. "Davy Ladd."

Delia's reaction was instantaneous. Without a word, she turned away from both men and stalked from the waiting room. Brian turned to Gabe.

"I'm really sorry about all the confusion. I guess she's

upset. The problem is, I'm supposed to try to talk to her. The detective left me the job of asking her some questions, but it doesn't look like that's going to work. Was it the priest stuff?" Brian asked. "Or do you think it was something I said?"

Gabe Ortiz smiled and eased himself into the chair next to the one where Brian had been sitting earlier. He folded his arms across his broad chest and closed his eyes.

"No, Brian," Gabe replied. "I believe it was something *I* said. Sit down and take a load off. Delia's upset at the moment, but if we just sit here and wait, eventually she'll come around."

Quentin had told Mitch to wake him up as soon as they got to the turnoff to Coleman Road. It bothered Mitch a little that where they were going was so damned close to where the Bounder was parked. He had chosen that particular spot because there, on the edge of the reservation, was about as far from town as he could get. But it was natural that the edge of the reservation, rather than the middle of it, was where Quentin would have discovered his treasure trove of Native American pots.

Still, as long as Mitch played his cards right, it didn't matter that much. He glanced toward Lani. Obviously he had measured out a better dosage this time. The amount of drug Mitch had used, combined with his threat to kill Quentin, was working well enough. Lani Walker was docile without being comatose. That might prove beneficial. If the terrain was as rough as Quentin claimed it would be, Mitch would probably need Lani to be able to climb on her own power rather than being carried or dragged.

Quentin himself was Mitch's biggest concern as they drove west toward the reservation. Would he be able to rouse Quentin enough when the time came to get him to do what was needed? If not, he might have to do an on-the-fly revision of his plan and let the pots go. They had been gravy all along—an extra added attraction. What was not optional was how he left Quentin and Lani once Mitch was ready to walk away. He would arrange the bodies artfully.

Lani would be found right alongside the remains of her killer. The scenario would be plain for all to see. After murdering and mutilating his sister, the record would show that Quentin Walker had taken his own life.

How do you suppose you'll like them apples, Mr. Brandon Walker? Mitch Johnson grinned to himself. *It should give you something to think about for the rest of your goddamned natural life.*

The turnoff was coming up. "Okay now," Mitch said to Lani. "Nap time's over. Wake him up so he can give me directions."

Lani turned to Quentin. "Wake up," she said. He didn't stir.

"Come on, girl," Mitch said, once again grasping her lower thigh. "I know you can do better than that!" He didn't bother to tighten his grip. He didn't have to. Obviously, Lani Walker had learned how to take orders.

"Come on, Quentin," she said, shaking her brother's shoulder. "You have to wake up now."

Quentin tried to dodge the commanding voice. He didn't want to wake up. He was enjoying his sleep. There was no reason for him not to. And who the hell was this woman who was so damned determined to wake him up?

He opened his eyes and tried to focus on the face hovering in front of his. When the world spun on its axis, Quentin shut his eyes immediately. He tried to shut his ears as well.

"Quentin!" Another voice this time. A male voice. "Wake the hell up and get busy!"

Mitch. Mitch Johnson, and he sounded pissed. Quentin struggled to open his eyes. "Where are we, Mitch?" Quentin mumbled, not quite able to make his tongue and mouth work in any kind of harmony. "Whazza problem?"

"The problem is we're almost to Coleman Road, and I don't know what the hell to do next."

"Doan worry 'bout a thing," Quentin murmured, closing his eyes once more. "Just lemme sleep a little longer."

"Wake him up!" Mitch demanded. "Slap him around if you have to, but get his eyes open."

Quentin felt a small hand on his shoulder, shaking him. He opened his eyes once more.

A woman's face—a girl's, really—hovered anxiously over him. It took a matter of seconds for the dark hair and eyes to arrange themselves into a recognizable creature. As soon as that happened, Quentin could barely believe it. Lani! The shock of recognition stunned him and brought him out of his stupor, although as soon as he tried to sit up, a fierce attack of vertigo once again sent the interior of the Bronco whirling around him.

"What the hell is she doing here?" Quentin demanded. "I said I'd take you to the cave. Bringing someone else along wasn't part of the bargain, especially not her."

Quentin didn't like being around his sister. Lani was almost as weird as that old Indian hag named Rita who used to take care of her when she was little. Lani had funny ways about her, ways of knowing things that she maybe shouldn't have, just like Rita. If Quentin had been able to, he would have climbed in the backseat right then, just to put some distance between them.

"She's your sister, isn't she?" Mitch returned mildly. "I didn't think you'd mind if I brought her along for the ride."

"Mitch," Quentin said, speaking slowly, trying to make his lips and brain work in conjunction, trying to make it sound as though his objection were more general and less personal. "Don't you understand anything? She may be my stepsister, but she's also an Indian. Once the tribe hears about my pots, they'll raise all kinds of hell."

"Lani's not going to say anything to anybody, are you, Lani?"

Once again, Vega's warning fingers caressed the top of her leg. Dreading his viselike grip, Lani flinched under the pressure of his hand and shook her head.

"No," she said at once. "I won't tell anybody. I promise."

The turnoff to Coleman Road was coming up fast. Mitch Johnson switched on his signal. "Now what?"

"Go about half a mile up. There's a road off to the left. A few yards beyond that, there's a wash off to the right. Turn there."

"Up the wash?"

"Right," Quentin said, grateful that his tongue and lips seemed to be working better now, although he felt like hell. This was one of the worst hangovers he'd ever encountered.

"Before we turn off, though," he continued, "you'll need to stop and let me drive. The trail isn't marked. You won't know where to go."

Mitch glanced dubiously across the seat. "You're sure you can drive?"

"What do you think I am, drunk or something?" Quentin asked irritably.

"Definitely or something," Mitch Johnson whispered under his breath.

Lani sat quietly between the two men—between her brother and the man Quentin had just called Mitch. At least she now knew what the *M* stood for in Vega's signature. Mitch.

As the Bronco's heavy-duty tires whined down the pavement, Lani looked up at the shadow of mountain looming above them. *Ioligam*'s stately dark flanks were silhouetted against a starry sky.

They were going after pots. If they had been found here on the reservation, they were actually *Tohono O'othham* pots that might have been hidden inside the mountain for hundreds of years. Perhaps they had remained hidden from view in one of the sacred caves on *I'itoi's* second favorite mountain.

She remembered once listening to Davy and Brian Fellows talking about the day Tommy and Quentin Walker had found a big limestone cave out on the reservation.

"They didn't go inside, did they?" Lani had asked.

Davy shrugged. "Of course they did."

"But that's against the rules," Lani had objected indignantly. "Nobody's supposed to go inside those caves. They're sacred. You should have stopped them."

Davy and Brian had both laughed at her. "What's so funny?" she had demanded. "Why are you two laughing?"

"Fortunately, you're much too young to remember growing up with Quentin and Tommy. When we were all kids, those two were a pair of holy terrors. As far as they were concerned, rules were made to be broken."

"So what happened?"

"As far as I know, they went there just that once," Brian said. "It wasn't long after that when Tommy ran away. If Quentin went back out to the reservation to go exploring the cave by himself, he never mentioned it."

"If they went inside the cave, maybe that's what happened to Tommy."

"What?" Brian asked.

"Maybe *I'itoi* got him," Lani said.

Brian shook his head. When he spoke, the laughter had gone out of his voice. "Don't ever say anything about this to your dad," he said seriously, "but from the rumors I heard, I'd say drug-dealing is what got Tommy. What I've never been able to understand is why it didn't get Quentin, too."

As they turned up Coleman Road, Lani felt a growing certainty that the place where they were going was the same cave Brian and Davy had talked about. Off to the left was the dirt track that led off to Rattlesnake Skull *charco,* the place they used to go every year to redecorate the shrine dedicated to Nana *Dahd*'s murdered granddaughter.

"We shouldn't go there," Lani said softly, unable to keep herself from issuing the warning. Even someone as cruel as Mitch Vega deserved to be warned away from danger.

"See there?" Quentin yelped angrily, glaring at her. "I knew you shouldn't have brought her."

"Shut up, Lani," Mitch said.

Lani closed her eyes and tried to hear Rita's words. *Listen to me and do exactly as I say.*

Alvin Miller was a talented guy who was able to do his work in a seemingly focused fashion, all the while carrying on a reasonably intelligent conversation with whoever happened to be within earshot.

In this case, as he carried his gear into Brandon and Diana Walker's house in Gates Pass, Brandon was giving Alvin an earful. He had responded to former Sheriff Walker's call for help without asking for any specific details on the situation. Now, though, Brandon was venting his frustration over the way Detective Ford Myers was—or rather *was not*—handling the disappearance of Brandon's sixteen-year-old daughter, Lani.

Other than having been one once, Alvin wasn't especially wise to the ways of teenagers. Nonetheless, he did see some merit to Detective Ford's inclination to go slow and not push panic buttons. Although Alvin sympathized with his former boss, he could see that the whole thing might very well turn out to be nothing but a headstrong teenager pulling a stunt on her too-trusting parents. After all, armed or not, most missing kids did turn up back home eventually.

So Alvin listened and nodded. Betweentimes, he went to work. "What all would you like me to check for prints?" he asked.

"Lani's bicycle," Brandon answered. "That's outside in

the carport. There's a pair of rubber-handled tongs in the kitchen sink. And back in my study, somebody went to the trouble of breaking up a couple thousand bucks' worth of custom-framing."

For comparison purposes, Alvin took prints from both Brandon and Diana Walker as well as prints from places in the daughter's room that would most likely prove to belong to Lani herself. He packed up the tongs, the bicycle, and the better part of the picture-frame display. Alvin knew he'd be better off dusting those in the privacy of his lab. What he couldn't take back to the department with him was the house itself and furniture that was too big to move.

"Where did you say you kept the key to the gun cabinet?"

"In the desk." Brandon had been following Alvin from room to room, watching the process with intent interest. As Alvin settled down to dust the desktop, Brandon left the room. The print—one with a distinctive diagonal slash across the face of it—leaped out at Alvin the moment he delicately brushed the graphite across the smooth oak surface.

Alvin Miller could barely believe his eyes. He knew he had seen that same print, or else one very much like it, on the wallet Dan Leggett had brought in earlier and on several of the bones in the detective's boxed collection. For a moment, Alvin was too flustered to know what to do.

He was here in Brandon Walker's home collecting prints as an unofficial favor to an old friend. The problem was, if he was right, if this print and the other one were identical, then Alvin Miller had stumbled across something that would link the newly discovered bones with the break-in here at the Gates Pass house. Not only that, connecting those two sets of dots could put him in the middle of a potentially career-killing cross fire between two dueling detectives—Dan Leggett and Ford Myers.

In addition, if Lani Walker was somehow involved in an assault and a possible homicide, the chances of her disappearance being nothing but ordinary teenaged rebellion went way down. Whatever was going on with her was most likely a whole lot more serious than that. The same went for Brandon Walker's missing .357.

Feeling as though he'd just blundered into a hive of killer bees, Alvin considered his next move. For the time being, saying anything to Brandon Walker was out, certainly until Alvin actually had a chance to compare those two distinctive prints. In the meantime, he took several more reasonably good prints off the desktop and drawer.

"Getting any good ones?" Brandon Walker asked, reappearing in the door to his study.

"Some," Alvin Miller allowed, "but my pager just went off." That was an outright lie, but it was the best he could do under the circumstances. "I'll stop here for now. I'll come back tomorrow sometime. Just don't touch anything until I do. The stuff I've already picked up I'll work on in the lab."

"Sure thing, Al," Brandon Walker said. "I appreciate it."

Alvin Miller drove straight back to the department. There, after simply eyeballing the two dusted prints, he picked up the phone and dialed Dan Leggett's home phone number. "Who's calling?" Leggett's wife asked in a tone that indicated she wasn't pleased with this work-related, late Saturday-evening phone call.

"It's Alvin Miller. Tell him I'm calling about the prints."

"So there were some?" Leggett asked, coming on the phone. "Did you get a hit?"

"Not yet. I haven't had a chance to run them yet, but there's a problem."

"What kind of problem?" Dan Leggett asked.

"How well do you get along with Detective Myers?"

"He's a jerk, why?"

"Because I've got a match between one of your prints and prints on a case he's working. Actually, a case he hasn't quite gotten around to working on yet."

"This is beginning to sound complicated."

"It is. The matching print came from the top of the desk

in Brandon Walker's study in his home office. Somebody broke into the place, smashed up some of his stuff, and stole a gun. But the real kicker is that Lani Walker, Sheriff Walker's sixteen-year-old daughter, is among the missing and has been since early this morning. Myers refused to take the MP report because of the twenty-four-hour wait. Claimed it was probably just kid bullshit. But with the matching print . . ."

"You think her disappearance may be linked to our assault case from this afternoon?"

"Don't you?" Alvin asked. "It's sure as hell linked to your bones and wallet."

Detective Leggett considered for a moment. "So how did you get dragged into all this? Into the Walker thing, I mean?"

"Myers told Brandon Walker that the soonest anybody could come check for prints was Monday, and Walker called to see if I could do it any earlier. I couldn't very well turn the man down, now could I?"

"Ford Myers is going to be ripped when he finds out," Leggett said. "He'll be gunning for you."

Alvin Miller laughed. "That's nothing new. He already is."

"So what are you going to do with the prints you have?"

"Get them ready, scan them into the computer, and run them."

"Tonight? How long will it take you?"

"An hour or so to get them ready. After that, it's just a matter of waiting for the computer to do its thing. Do you want me to give you a call later on if I get a hit?"

"You'd better," Dan Leggett said. "But do me one favor."

"What's that?"

"Don't tell Ford Myers until I give you the word."

"Don't worry," Alvin Miller said. "Why should I? After all, he isn't expecting fingerprint results before Monday morning. Do you want me to call you there and let you know what I find?"

"Don't bother. I'm heading back out."

"Where are you going?"

"Back over to the hospital to see if Brian Fellows has had a chance to talk to Mr. Chavez."

A few yards beyond the turnoff to the Rattlesnake Skull *charco,* Mitch swung the wheel sharply to the right. Pulling over to the side, he stopped. "Time to switch into four-wheel drive," he said.

Quentin reached for the door handle. "How'd you know this was it?" he asked.

"I can see your tracks heading off across the wash, dummy," Mitch Johnson replied. "And if I can see them, so can the rest of the world."

Lani was dismayed to see that once on his feet, Quentin could barely stand upright. She stayed in the car while Quentin struggled with the hubs. Finally Mitch ordered Quentin back into the truck, the backseat this time.

"You come with me," he said to Lani. Once she was on her feet, he handed her a branch he had broken off a nearby mesquite. "I want you to follow behind the truck," he said. "Brush out the tire tracks, and yours, too. Do you understand?"

Lani nodded.

"And if you do anything off the wall, if you try to run, not only will I shoot your brother with his father's own gun, I'll come get you, too. Is that clear?"

"Yes."

Lani watched Mitch climb back into the truck, knowing that he was wrong about that. Quentin Walker was Brandon Walker's son, her father's son, but as far as Lani was concerned, Davy Ladd was her only brother. Still, she couldn't stand the thought that some action of hers, even an action that might save her own life, could cost Quentin his. She didn't like him much and she owed him nothing. And had she turned and fled into the desert right then, she might very well have managed to hide well enough and long enough to get away.

But how would she feel when she heard the report of gunfire, a shot that would come from her father's own gun, one that would snuff out Quentin's life? It didn't matter if he was drugged or just drunk. Either way, he was almost as incapable of defending himself against Mitch as Lani had been earlier.

While Mitch backed up and turned the Bronco to head off across the wash, that was Lani's dilemma—to run and try to save herself or to stay and try to save Quentin's life as well as her own. There was a part of her that already knew Mitch's real intention was to kill them both. He had no reason not to.

The Bronco bounced across the wash and then paused on the far side. "Come on," Mitch yelled out the window. "Hurry it up."

The moment Lani Walker heard his voice, shouting at her over the idling rumble of the Bronco, she made up her mind. Brother or not, she would try to be Quentin's keeper. If they both lived, she might once again be able to tell her parents in person that she loved them. If not, if she and Quentin were both doomed and if seeing her parents again was impossible, then she was determined to leave some word for them, some farewell message. Slipping one hand into the pocket of her jeans, Lani pulled out her precious *O'othham* basket. Resisting the temptation to press its reassuring presence into her palm once more, she dropped it, allowing it to fall atop the small hump of rocky gravel that formed the shoulder of the road.

If someone happened to find the basket and was good enough to give it to Lani's parents, then perhaps Diana and Brandon Walker would understand that it was a last loving message sent from Lani to them. If not—even if the carefully woven hair charm came to no other end than to grace *Wosho koson*'s—Pack Rat's—burrow—Lani could be assured the sacred symbol of the *Tohono O'othham*, the maze, would not be defiled by Mitch's evil *Ohb* touch. He might manage to claim other trophies, including some ancient Indian pots, but Lani's basket would never be his.

Fighting back tears, Lani bent herself to her assigned task, wielding the makeshift broom. As she scraped the tire tracks out of the sand, Lani realized that with every stroke she was also erasing any hope that some rescuer might find them in time.

That meant she and Quentin would most likely die. If it came down to a fight between her and Mitch, there could be little doubt of the outcome. He would win. Lani and Quentin would die, but the terrible pain in her breast told her that in the hands of someone like Mitch Vega, there might be far worse things than death.

That awful knowledge came over Lani in a mind-clearing rush, calming her fears rather than adding to them. Perhaps she would not be able to save either Quentin's life or her own from this new evil *Ohb,* but by leaving the basket behind, she had at least saved that.

As long as those few strands of black and yellow hair stayed woven together, then some remnant of Lani's own life would remain as well, for she had woven her own spirit into that basket—her own spirit and Jessica's and Nana *Dahd*'s as well.

No matter what he did, Mitch would never be able to touch that.

For some time after Alvin Miller left, Brandon and Diana simply sat in the living room together, sharing many of the same thoughts, but for minutes at a time, neither of them spoke.

"Should we call Fat Crack?" Diana asked at last.

"I don't see what good that would do," Brandon said.

"But what if . . ."

"If what?"

Diana paused for a moment before she answered. "What if he's right and this is what he meant yesterday when he was talking about the evil coming from my book?"

"How could it be?" Brandon returned. "I don't see how Lani's disappearance now can have anything to do with Andrew Carlisle showing up here twenty-one years ago."

"I don't either," Diana said. "Forget I even mentioned it."

Again they were quiet. "What if we've lost her forever, Brandon? What if we never see her again?"

Swallowing hard, Brandon Walker leaned back and rested his head on the chair. He had already lived through this agony once when they lost Tommy. It had never occurred to him that he might lose a second child.

"Don't say that," he said. "We'll find her. I *know* we'll find her."

But even as he said the words, Brandon's own heart was drowning in despair. He had heard those same platitudes spoken by other grieving parents about other missing children, some of whom had never been heard from again.

"At six o'clock sharp, I'm going to be on the phone to the department, raising hell. Ford Myers may not be the one who comes out here to take the Missing Persons report, but someone sure as hell will be, or I'll know the reason why!"

Diana glanced at her watch. It was ten of one. "Maybe we should go to bed. Even if we can't sleep, it would probably do our bodies some good if we lay down for a while."

Brandon looked at Diana. Other than having kicked off her shoes, she was still wearing the dress she had worn to the banquet, but she looked bedraggled. Her hair had come adrift. Brandon was startled by the dark shadows under her eyes and by the bone-weary strain showing around the corners of her mouth.

"You're right," he said quickly, standing up and helping her to rise as well. "If there's a phone call, we can take it in the bedroom just as easily as we can take it here."

They walked into the bedroom together. Brandon stripped to his shorts while Diana undressed and hung up her dress. The bed was still in disarray as a result of their afternoon lovemaking. As Brandon set about straightening the covers, a plastic cassette tape slid out from under Diana's pillow.

"What's this?" he asked, picking it up. Other than the manufacturer's label, there was no marking on it of any kind. "Did you leave this tape here, Di?" he asked.

Diana, dressed in a nightgown, came out of her walk-in closet. "What tape?" she asked.

"This one," Brandon said, holding it up so she could see it. "I found it under your pillow."

Diana Ladd Walker swayed on her feet and groped for the door-jamb to keep from falling. Her face turned deathly pale. "Where did that come from?" she whispered.

"I told you. I found it under your pillow. Maybe it's a message from Lani."

"No," Diana said. Shivering, she looked at the tape and shook her head. "No, it isn't."

But Brandon's mind was made up. "She probably decided to leave us a tape instead of a note," he said.

Tape in hand, Brandon was already on his way to the living room, headed for the stereo deck with the built-in cassette player. Diana came after him. "It's not from Lani, Brandon. Don't play it."

The brittle note of warning in her voice was enough to cause him to turn and look at her in alarm. "Why not?" he asked.

"Don't play it," she said again. "Please don't."

Brandon looked at his wife impatiently. "What's gotten into you?" he asked.

"The tape isn't from Lani," Diana said. "It's from Andrew Carlisle. I know it is."

Disgusted and impatient, Brandon turned to the stereo. As he inserted the tape into the player, he glanced back at his wife. "You and Fat Crack," he said. "Dead men don't do tapes. How could he?"

Hunching her shoulders and doubling over as if in pain, Diana Walker sank down on the couch. "Brandon, listen to me. It is from Carlisle. You don't want to play it."

"Diana, if there's a chance this is going to help us locate Lani, of course we're going to play it," he said.

As the sound filled the room, they both recognized Lani's voice almost at once, but it was muffled and difficult to understand, as if it had been recorded from a great distance. Pressing the remote volume control, Brandon turned it up several notches.

"What was that?" he said, frowning with concentration. "Didn't it sound as though she said something about Quentin?"

Still bent over and staring at the floor, Diana shook her head and said nothing. Brandon hit the "stop" button, rewound the tape a few rotations, and then hit "play" once more.

And he was right. It was Lani's voice, louder now, but still fuzzy and indistinct, saying her brother's name over and over. "Quentin," she was saying. "Quentin, Quentin, Quentin."

"What the hell does Quentin have to do with all this?" Brandon asked.

Almost like a sleepwalker, Diana got up off the couch and walked over to where Brandon was kneeling in front of the stereo. "Shut it off," she begged, leaning against him, putting both hands on his shoulders. "Please, Brandon. Don't listen to any more of it. You don't understand. I can't stand to listen to any more."

"Diana," Brandon said curtly. "This is bound to help us find Lani. We've got to listen to all of it—every single word. Be quiet now for a minute so I can hear what they're saying."

Trying to decipher the tape over Diana's continuing objections, Brandon punched the volume control one more time. And that was where it was when the unearthly scream came tearing through the speakers.

The sound ripped into Diana's whole being, robbing her legs of the strength needed to stand upright. Her beseeching hands went limp on Brandon's shoulders and slid down his back. While Brandon stared uncomprehendingly at the now silent speaker, Diana dropped to her knees, leaning against him.

"Oh, my God," she sobbed. "He's killed her. I know Andrew Carlisle's killed her."

Slowly, an ashen Brandon Walker turned around to face her. Grasping his wife by the shoulders, he shook her. "You knew what was coming, didn't you? That's why you didn't want me to play the tape. How did you know?"

It was a question, but the way he said the words turned it into an accusation. At first Diana didn't answer. "How?" he demanded again.

"We've got to call Fat Crack," she murmured. "He's the only one who can help us now."

She reached out then as if to cling to him, but he moved away from her. The sudden fury rising in Brandon Walker's soul was so overwhelming that he no longer dared allow himself to touch her.

"It's got nothing to do with Andrew Carlisle!" he snarled back at her. "You heard what she said. Quentin was the one who was with her. Whatever happened just then, Quentin is the one who did it, the little son of a bitch. And once I lay hands on him . . ."

The rest of the uncompleted threat hung in the air as Brandon got to his feet and headed for the kitchen. Diana was still sitting there when he returned. Without another word, he ejected the tape from the player and then put both it and the carrying case into a paper bag.

When he headed for the kitchen once again, Diana got up and followed him. "Where are you going?" she asked, when he took his car keys down from the Peg-Board.

"I'm going to take these to the department so Alvin Miller can check them for prints. Then I'm going to ask him to run Quentin's prints as a comparison."

"Lani's dead, isn't she?" Diana said.

Brandon Walker bit his lip and nodded. The agony in that scream left him little else to hope for.

"Yes," he said at last. "I suppose so."

For a moment husband and wife stood looking at each other. The fury Brandon had felt earlier was gone. "You knew what was coming, didn't you?" Diana nodded wordlessly. "How?"

"There were others."

"Others?"

Diana looked away then, refusing to meet his eyes. "Other tapes," she answered.

"Of other murders?"

"Yes."

"But you never mentioned anything about it."

Diana shook her head, still refusing to meet her husband's probing gaze. "They were so awful, I never told anyone about them, not even you. I didn't want anybody else to know or to have to listen."

"You mean like snuff films, only on audio?" Brandon's voice trembled as he asked the question. He felt suddenly slack-jawed. "You mean you've heard them?"

"Yes." Diana took a deep breath. "Two of them. There was one of Gina Antone's death. The other was about that costume designer that he killed in downtown Tucson. This one makes three."

"But that's Andrew Carlisle. Lani was talking to Quentin. To my son."

"Quentin and Carlisle were in prison together," Diana suggested quietly, in a voice still choked with emotion. "Carlisle had an almost hypnotic effect on Gary Ladd. He was there with Gina when she died, and I'm sure that's why he killed himself. Maybe Carlisle did the same thing to Quentin."

The anger that had been holding Brandon upright collapsed inside him and sent him lurching drunkenly into Diana's arms. Still holding the paper bag in one hand, he used his other arm to pull Diana against his chest while he buried his head in her hair.

"We're going to need help," he murmured. "Go get dressed now, Diana," he said, pushing her away. "I'll start the car and we'll go do whatever it is we have to do. We'll take this thing to the department. We'll take it to the FBI Missing and Exploited Children unit. If it's the last thing I ever do, I'm going to find Quentin and put him away."

"I'm sorry," Diana said. "I'm so sorry."

"Not nearly as sorry as I am," he murmured back, wiping the tears from his eyes. "Not nearly."

The ICU waiting room Dan Leggett returned to was far more crowded than when he had left it several hours earlier. Off to one side of the room sat a group of Indians that included an attractive woman in her mid- to late thirties, a solidly built man in his mid- to late forties, and an elderly woman. The three of them were talking together in low voices.

In the middle of the room, Deputy Brian Fellows snoozed in a chair next to another Indian, a portly man somewhere in his sixties, who was also dozing.

Leggett stopped in front of Brian Fellows's chair. "What's happening?"

Brian's chin bounced off his chest. Blinking, he straightened in his chair. "Sorry about that, Detective Leggett. I must have fallen asleep."

"So I noticed. What's going on?"

"That's Delia Cachora over there," he said. "The younger woman. The older one is Delia's aunt, Julia Joaquin. And that's Julia's son, Wally Joaquin. And this," Brian added, motioning toward the man seated next to him, "is a friend of mine named Gabe Ortiz."

Dan Leggett nodded politely and held out his hand. "Any relation to the *Tohono O'othham* tribal chairman?"

Fat Crack straightened himself in the chair. "I am the tribal chairman," he said. "Mr. Chavez's daughter, Delia, works for me," he added as if to explain his presence. "I gave her a ride into town."

"Has anyone been able to talk to him yet?"

Brian shook his head. "Not as far as I know, although you might try talking to Ms. Cachora."

"Let's do it then," Dan Leggett said. "Come over and introduce me. There's no time to lose."

"Why? What's wrong?"

Dan Leggett shook his head. "You're not going to believe it," he said. "Lani Walker's turned up missing, and she may be involved in all this."

As soon as he made that last statement, Dan noticed that Gabe Ortiz came to attention, but the detective was too focused on Delia Cachora to wonder at the connection. "I'm Detective Dan Leggett from the Pima County Sheriff's Department," he said, stopping in front of the trio of Indians and not waiting for Brian to make introductions. "I'm in charge of investigating the assault against your father. It's important that we ask him some questions as soon as possible. When's the last time you tried to speak to him?"

"It was almost an hour ago now. Why? What's so important?" Delia asked.

"We're working on what may be a related case. I need to know if there's anything he can tell us about the attack. We're wondering if his assailant acted alone or if there was someone else involved."

"Lani Walker isn't involved," Gabe Ortiz declared forcefully. "She couldn't be. I've known her since she was a baby. She would never do anything like this."

Accustomed to Gabe Ortiz's usually soft-spoken ways, Delia looked at the tribal chairman in some surprise. "You think a woman is involved in the attack on my father?"

"It's possible," Dan said.

Delia stood up and leveled another questioning look in Gabe Ortiz's direction. "I'll go check," she said. "The problem is, even if he's awake, they probably won't allow anyone in other than family. Do you want me to ask whether or not a woman was there?"

Dan shook his head. "Don't put words in his mouth. Just ask if he remembers anything about it, especially whether or not his attacker was operating alone."

Delia left. The waiting room was silent for a long moment after the doors swung shut behind her. "Lani didn't do it," Gabe said again.

Brian Fellows nodded. "I know her, too, Dan. The Lani I know wouldn't harm a fly."

Dan Leggett turned to face Gabe. "Mr. Ortiz," he said, "we have a fingerprint from the bones that matches one found in the Walkers' house. I said she may have been involved. What I didn't say is that her involvement may have happened under duress."

"Duress? What does that mean?"

"It means Lani Walker may have been kidnapped," Dan Leggett said. "No one has seen her since she left to go to work sometime around six yesterday morning. She didn't show up for her shift or for a concert date with a friend yesterday evening."

"Kidnapped?" Brian Fellows echoed.

Delia came to the door and motioned to her elderly aunt. "He's talking, but in *Tohono O'othham*. I don't remember enough of that to be able to understand."

Again the people left in the waiting room drifted into silence. Gabe Ortiz walked across the room and sat down in a chair, burying his face in his hands. "Mr. Ortiz seems very upset about all this," Dan Leggett observed. "Is he related to Lani Walker somehow?"

Brian Fellows nodded. "He and his wife are Lani's godparents."

"Oh," Dan Leggett said. "That explains it then."

A few minutes later, Julia Joaquin emerged from the ICU. Walking stiffly, she passed directly in front of the

waiting detective and deputy, going instead to where Gabe
Ortiz was sitting. Dan Leggett and Brian Fellows trailed
after her.

"Manny only remembers seeing a man, not a woman,"
the old woman said, speaking to the tribal chairman, addressing him softly in *Tohono O'othham* rather than English. "The man was tall and skinny—a *Mil-gahn*. And he
was driving an orange truck of some kind."

"The girl wasn't there?" Gabe asked.

Julia Joaquin shook her head. Gabe Ortiz sighed in obvious relief.

"What are they saying?" Dan Leggett asked, and Brian
translated as well as he could.

"Manny Chavez's back is broken and he may be paralyzed," Julia Joaquin continued, still addressing Gabe Ortiz,
rather than any of the others. "Do you know of a medicine
man who is good with Turtle Sickness?"

"I do not," Gabe answered. "But I will find out."

"Thank you," Julia said. She turned to the detective just
as Brian finished translating once more.

"Turtle Sickness?" Dan Leggett repeated.

Julia Joaquin nodded.

"How can you call it a sickness? Somebody hit him in the
back with a shovel!"

"Turtle Sickness—paralysis—comes from being rude,"
she explained firmly. "My brother-in-law has always been a
very rude man."

Just then Delia Cachora returned to the waiting room.
"Aunt Julia told you what you needed to know?" she asked.

Dan Leggett nodded. "She certainly did," he said.

Gabe stood up and took Julia Joaquin's hand in his. "I'm
glad the ant-bit child wasn't there."

Julia nodded. "I am, too," she said.

"Ant-bit child?" Delia Cachora asked. "What are we talking about now?" She seemed almost as puzzled about that as
Dan Leggett was about Turtle Sickness.

Julia Joaquin turned to her niece. "There was an old blind medicine man, years ago, who was always telling people that an ant-bit child would someday show up on the reservation and that she would grow up to be a powerful medicine woman."

Delia glanced warily at Detective Leggett. "Aunt Julia," she cautioned, but Julia Joaquin disregarded the warning.

"*Kulani O'oks,*" she continued. "She was the woman who was kissed by the bees. Looks At Nothing said the ant-bit child would be just like her, that she would save people, not harm them, not even someone like Manny."

"Thank you," Gabe Ortiz said to Julia. "I'm sure you're right."

The tribal chairman left then. Dan Leggett handed Delia Cachora a business card. "I'd appreciate it if you'd keep us posted on your father's condition," he said. "In the meantime, Deputy Fellows and I will head back out to the department to see if there's anything else we can do."

The two officers left the waiting room together. Once outside, Dan Leggett stopped long enough to light a cigar. "So Lani Walker's supposed to be a medicine woman when she grows up," he said. "That one takes the cake. Have you ever heard anything like it in your life?"

As the cloud of smoke ballooned around Detective Leggett's head, Brian Fellows realized there was a certain olfactory resemblance between that and *wiw*—the wild tobacco Looks At Nothing had always used in his evil-smelling, hand-rolled cigarettes. The smell brought back a string of memories, including Rita Antone saying much the same thing Julia Joaquin had just said, that Davy's new baby sister would one day grow up to be a medicine woman. It came as no surprise to him that Looks At Nothing would have been the original source of that story, and it hardly mattered that the old medicine man had been dead for years before Lani Walker came to live in the house in Gates Pass.

"Actually, I have," Brian Fellows said. "I've heard it before from any number of people."

"The medicine-woman part?"

Brian nodded.

With the cigar now lit, Dan Leggett waved the flaming match in the air until the fire went out. "And you believe it?" Dan asked.

"As a matter of fact I do," Brian Fellows said.

With a quizzical frown on his face, Detective Leggett stared hard at the young deputy. "I think you're all nuts," he said at last. "From the tribal chairman right on down."

After laboring up the steep mountainside for what seemed forever, Mitch finally parked the Bronco in a grove of mesquite. By the time Lani reached the truck, Quentin and Mitch were both outside, with Quentin directing Mitch as they placed several pieces of camouflaged canvas from the back of the Bronco over the top of the vehicle.

Quentin was still none too steady on his feet, but he was clearly proud of his ability to plan ahead. "This way, nobody will be able to spot it," he said. "Not from down below, and not from up above, either."

"Great," Mitch said. "Which way now?"

"Up here," Quentin said. He staggered off across the brush-covered slope, somehow managing to stay upright. "The entrance is hard enough to spot during the daylight, but don't worry. We'll find it."

"You go next," Mitch ordered, shoving Lani forward behind Quentin. "I'll bring up the rear."

For what seemed like a very long time, the three of them clambered single-file on a diagonal up and across the flank of mountain. Mitch and Quentin both carried flashlights, but they opted to leave them off, for fear lights on the mountain might attract unwanted attention. Instead, the trio accomplished the nighttime hike with only the moon to light the path. After half an hour or so, Quentin suddenly disappeared. One moment he was there in front of Lani, the next he was gone. Looking down the side of the mountain, she expected to see him falling to his death. Instead, his unseen hand reached out and grabbed hers.

"In here," Quentin said, dragging her into what looked like an exceptionally deep shadow. "It's this way."

Only when she was right there in front of it was Lani able to see Quentin crouching just inside a three-foot-wide hole in the mountain. "Watch yourself," he added. "For the next fifteen yards or so we have to do this on hands and knees."

Plunged into total darkness, Lani crawled forward into the damp heart of the mountain. At first she could feel walls on either side of her, but eventually the space opened up and the rocks underneath gave way to slimy mud. A light flickered behind her and was followed by the scraping of someone else coming through the tunnel. Moments later Mitch emerged, flashlight in hand. Standing up, he shone the light around them. When he did so, Lani was dumbfounded.

They were standing in the middle of a huge, rough-walled limestone cavern with spectacular bubbles of rock surging up from the floor and with curtains of rock flowing down from above. The place was utterly still. Other than their labored breathing, the only sound inside the cavern was the steady drip of water.

Dolores Lanita Walker had grown up hearing stories of Elder Brother and how he spent his summers in the sacred caves on *Ioligam*. Rita had taught her that the Desert People, sometimes called the People With Two Houses, were called that because they had two homes—a winter one on the flat and a cooler summer one high up in the mountains. It made sense then that *I'itoi*, the *Tohono O'othham*'s beloved Elder Brother, would do much the same thing. In the winter he was said to live on Baboquivari—Grandfather Place Mountain. But in the summertime he was said to come to *Ioligam*— Manzanita Mountain.

Lani had spent all her life being told that caves like this were both dangerous and sacred; that they were places to be avoided. Now, though, looking around at the towering, ghostly walls, lit by the feeble probing of Mitch's flashlight, Lani Walker felt no fear.

She felt not the slightest doubt that this was a sacred, holy place. And since it was summer, no doubt *I'itoi* was somewhere nearby. That made this a perfectly good place to die.

By the time David Ladd emerged from the bathroom shaved, showered, and dressed, Candace's suitcases were zipped shut and stacked beside the door. Candace herself was on the phone with her sister, Bridget.

"Thanks, Bridge," Candace was saying. "You know I wouldn't ask you if it weren't an emergency. And yes, we'll let you know what's going on as soon as we know exactly what it is . . . Sure, that'll work. We'll leave the parking receipt in an envelope for you at the front desk," she said. "Just drive the Jeep home. We'll make arrangements to come get it later."

While Davy finished throwing the few things he had brought to the room into his small bag, Candace gave him a quick thumbs-up, all the while staying tuned to the telephone conversation.

"Sure I know Mom will kill me," Candace replied. "But another wedding like yours would kill Dad, so there you are . . . No, we don't need a ride to O'Hare. I've already called for a cab. It'll be here in a few minutes, so I'd better go. Tell Larry thanks for being so understanding about me waking you up at this ungodly hour."

"You'd better decide what you're going to leave and what

you're going to take," David suggested when Candace put down the phone.

"Oh," she said. "I'll take them all. Two checked and two carry-ons. What about you?"

David looked down at his single bag. What he'd brought upstairs for one night wasn't enough to see him through more than a couple of days. "I'd better go down to the garage and see about repacking," he said.

"Sure, go ahead," Candace told him. "I'll call for a bell-man and meet you down in the lobby."

In the parking garage, Davy hauled out one other suitcase to take, along with the shirt and shaving gear he had taken upstairs. *That'll do,* he thought. *At least until I can get back here to pick up the rest of my stuff.*

He closed and locked the door and started to walk away, then he stopped and went back. Unlocking the cargo door, he rummaged through the boxes until he found the one he was looking for. It was a small wooden chest Astrid Ladd had given him, one that Davy's father had made in wood shop while he was still in high school and had given to Astrid as a gift. "Happy Mother's Day, 1954" had been burned into the bottom piece of wood.

Astrid had given Davy the box only three days earlier, and it contained only two items—Rita Antone's son's purple heart and Father John's *losalo*—his rosary. David Ladd stuffed the purple heart in the outside pocket of his suitcase, then stood for a moment staring down at the olive wood cru-cifix and the string of black beads. He had been only five years old, but he still remembered the day Father John had taught him to pray.

His mother had opened the front door and discovered Bone staggering around drunkenly outside. She had no idea what was wrong with the animal but Father John, who had come to the house to give Davy his first-ever catechism class, did.

"That dog's been poisoned," Father John had told them. "We've got to get him to a vet."

Before they could even lead Bone to the car, the hundred-pound dog collapsed in helpless convulsions. It took both Davy's mother and the priest to lift him, carry him to the priest's car, and load him inside. Davy had wanted to go along, but Diana had turned him back, ordering him to stay with Rita.

Worried about the poor dog, Davy was in tears as Father John started the car. Before driving out of the yard, however, the priest stopped the car beside the devastated child.

"Remember how we were talking about prayer a while ago?" the priest asked, rolling down the window. "Would you like me to pray for Bone?"

"Yes," Davy had whispered. "Please."

"Heavenly Father," the priest had said, bowing his head. "We pray that you will grant the blessing of healing to your servant, Bone, that he may return safely to his home. We ask this in the name of the Father, of the Son, and of the Holy Ghost. Amen."

David Ladd had learned a good deal more about prayer since that fateful day long ago, when God had spared not only his dog but the rest of the family as well. He had learned, too, what Father John meant when he said that the answer to prayer could be either yes or no.

Davy had never forgotten the priest's powerful lesson, and it came rushing back to him now, out of the distant past. Closing his fist around the smooth crucifix, David Ladd closed his eyes, envisioning as he did so both his parents and his little sister, Lani.

"Heavenly Father," he whispered. "We pray now for the blessing of healing for your servants Brandon, Diana, and Lani Walker and for Davy Ladd and Candace Waverly. See us all safely through this time of trouble in the name of the Father, of the Son, and of the Holy Ghost. Amen."

Then, putting the rosary in his shirt pocket so he could feel the beads through the thin material of his shirt, David Ladd locked the Jeep Cherokee, picked up his suitcase, and headed home.

15

The people went to the mountain, where they had fought before, but this time Tho'ag—*the Mountain*—*was covered with snakes and scorpions and Bad People.*

U'uwhig—*the Birds*—*had all gone away to a distant water hole, so they were not there to help their friends, the Desert People. Many of the* Tohono O'othham *were killed, among them many women and children.*

Tho'ag—*the Mountain*—*felt so bad when so many of his friends were being killed that he opened holes in the rocks so the Desert People could see through. That is why he is called* Wuhi Tho'ag—*which means Eye Mountain. And you can see the eyes in this mountain today, just as you can see the walls of rock.*

At last Wuhi Tho'ag *called to his brother mountain,* Baboquivari, *for help.* Baboquivari, *who watches over everything, answered. Wind Man, whose home is on Babo-quivari, called his brother Cloud Man to help. Cloud Man*

*came down low over the fighting and made cradles for the
Indian children, and Wind Man carried the children in the
cloud cradles to* Baboquivari, *where they were safe.*

The fighting grew worse, and I'itoi *was ashamed of his
people.*

*So Great Spirit spoke. Heavy dark clouds came down
over the mountain where they were fighting, so that no one
could see.*

In these big black clouds Hewel—*the Wind—carried
many of the Desert People safely to the valley of* Baboquivari.

The Tohono O'othham *were so bloody from fighting that
they stained the clouds and the mountains all red.*

*That is why, even to this day, about the top of the great
mountain peak,* Baboquivari, *nearly always there are a few
clouds. And these clouds are not white, but are colored a little with blood. This,* nawoj, *you may see for yourself.*

Scrabbling across the steep flank of the mountain with only
the moon to light the path, Mitch Johnson had twisted his bad
knee and almost tumbled down the mountainside himself.
Now, crawling through the entryway with his flashlight in
hand, a stabbing pain in Mitch's leg caused beads of sweat to
pop out on his forehead. Hurting himself wasn't something he
had counted on, but he wasn't about to let it stop him, either,
not after all the years of planning and waiting.

Mitch had expected a hole in the mountainside, but once
he made it into the cavern itself and sent the thin beam of his
flashlight probing the distant ceiling and walls, he was
awestruck. The cave was huge.

"It's something, isn't it?" Quentin said as he joined them.
"Whatever you do, watch where you step. It's slicker 'an
snot in here, and there's a hole over here just to the right
that's a killer. It'll break your neck if you fall into it. And
there's snakes, too."

There wasn't much in life that scared Mitch Johnson, but snakes did. "Rattlers?" he asked.

"That's right. I killed a diamondback just outside the entrance earlier this afternoon," Quentin was saying. "It was a big mother, and I threw the body down the side of the mountain. The problem is, where there's one snake, there's usually another."

While Mitch carefully scoured the surrounding area for snakes, Quentin once again took his position at the head of the line, picking his way through the forest of stalagmites that thrust themselves up out of the limestone floor.

"This way," Quentin said. "There's sort of a path here."

If there was a path, Lani couldn't see it. The rocks were so slippery that she was having some difficulty walking.

"I thought you said somebody lived in here," Mitch complained as he gingerly negotiated the rough and treacherously slick floor of the cavern. "How could they?"

"Not here," Quentin said. "In the other room."

Paying close attention to every twist and turn in the path, Lani listened to everything—not just to the words Quentin and Mitch were exchanging, but to what the mountain was saying as well. There seemed to be other voices there too, and Lani strained to hear them. Maybe this was where the Bad People lived, the *PaDaj O'othham* who had come time and again to steal the crops from the Desert People and to do battle with *I'itoi*.

She had thought Mitch Vega to be a messenger of Davy's Evil *Ohb,* but maybe the *Ohb* were really part of the Bad People. Maybe that's why they had come to this underground place. Maybe the people who said *I'itoi* lived in *Ioligam's* sacred caves were wrong and had been all along.

The thought of being in the presence of the Bad People plunged Lani back into despair. Behind her Mitch heard her sharp intake of breath.

His clawlike fingers clamped shut across the top of her

shoulder. "What is it?" he demanded. "What did you see? A snake, maybe? Where?"

He shone the flashlight directly into Lani's eyes, temporarily blinding her and then turning away as he scanned the ground around him. But something had happened in that moment as his face pressed so close to hers that Lani could feel his hot breath on her skin. She had heard something in his voice that hadn't been there before and her heart beat fast when she realized what it was—fear. Not a lot of it. No, just the tiniest trace. But still, it was fear, and knowing Mitch Vega was afraid gave Lani something else that hadn't been there before—hope, and the possibility that maybe somehow, someway, she would survive.

She looked again at Quentin. The walk up the mountain seemed to have sobered him some. At least his movements were steadier. If Mitch had given him some of the drug, perhaps that was wearing off as well. Maybe, between the two of them . . .

The thought that Quentin's dose of scopolamine might be wearing off too soon was worrisome to Mitch Johnson. He needed the right combination of mobility and control. It was important to have Quentin able to get around under his own steam, but it was also important for his thinking capabilities to be somewhat impaired.

Following Quentin and Lani through the cavern, Mitch was shocked when Quentin suddenly seemed to melt into a solid rock wall, taking Lani with him. Mitch, limping hurriedly after them, had to pause and examine the wall with the beam from his flashlight before discovering a jagged fissure in the rock. After squeezing through the narrow aperture, he found himself in a long narrow shaft that seemed to lead off into the interior of the mountain, away from the much larger cavern behind them. Yards ahead, Mitch could see Lani Walker disappearing around a curve.

As soon as Mitch stepped into the passage, the ground underfoot was different—smoother, but slicker as well. Here, the rocky floor had been painstakingly covered with a layer of dirt that constant moisture kept in a state of goopy muck. It was possible there had once been stalactites and stalagmites, just as there were in the other room. If so, they had been cut down and carted away, making the narrow shaft passable.

Hurrying after the others, Mitch rounded the curve and was suddenly conscious of a slight lifting in the total darkness that had surrounded him before. Now his flashlight probed ahead toward a hazy gray glow. At first Mitch thought that maybe Quentin had lit a lantern of some kind. Instead, as Mitch entered a second, much smaller, chamber, he realized this one was lit—almost brilliantly so—by a shaft of silvery moonlight slanting into the cave from outside, from a narrow crack at the top of a huge pile of debris.

Mitch had thought that the passageway was leading them deeper into the mountain. Instead, they had evidently angled off to the side, to a place where the shell of mountain was very thin.

"There used to be another entrance here," Quentin was saying, pointing the beam of his light up toward the narrow hole at the top of the debris. "At one time this was probably the main entrance. I figure it used to be larger than the one we came in, but it looks like a landslide pretty well covered it up. All that's left of it is that little opening way up there."

Not only was there more light here but, because of the presence of some outside air, the second chamber was also slightly warmer and dryer. Here the texture of the dirt underfoot changed from mud to the caliche-like crust that forms in desert washes after a summertime flood.

"You said you came out here earlier today?" Mitch asked. Quentin nodded.

"Why? What were you doing?"

"Just checking things out," Quentin said. "Making sure

nothing had happened to any of this stuff since the last time I was here. It turns out nothing did. The pots are all still here. Come take a look." As Quentin spoke, he aimed the beam from his flashlight at something in the far corner of the room. "What do you think?" he added.

Mitch Johnson thrust Lani aside and hurried past her. There on the floor, half-buried in the dirt, lay the shiny white bones of a human skeleton. And around those bleached bones, spilled onto their sides as though having been investigated by some marauding, hungry beast, lay a whole collection of pots—medium-sized ones for holding corn and piñon nuts, grain and *pinole,* and larger ones as well—the kind used for carrying water and for cooking meat and beans.

"It doesn't look like all that much to me," Mitch said, "but the guy I told you about wants them, so we'd better pack 'em up and get 'em out of here."

"You can't," Lani Walker said. Those were the first words she had spoken since Mitch had dragged her out of the Bronco down by the wash. She hadn't intended to say anything at all, but the words came choking out of her in spite of her best effort to hold them back.

Mitch swung around and looked at her. "We can't what?"

"Take the pots," she answered. "It's wrong. The spirit of the woman who made them is always trapped inside the pots she makes. That's why a woman's pottery is always broken when she dies, so her spirit won't be trapped. So she can go free."

"Trapped in her pots? Right!" Mitch scoffed. "If you asked me, it looks more like she was trapped in the mountain, not in her damn pots. Now sit down and shut the hell up," he added. "I don't remember anybody asking for your opinion."

Without a word, Lani sank down and sat cross-legged on the caliche-covered floor. When Mitch looked back at Quentin, he was staring at the girl while a puzzled frown knotted his forehead.

"What's she doing here anyway?" he asked. "I don't understand."

"She just came along for the ride, Quentin," Mitch said jokingly. "For the fun of it. Once we get all these pots out of here, the three of us are going to have a little party." Mitch paused and patted his shirt pocket. "I brought along a few mood-altering substances, Quentin. When the work's all done, the three of us can have a blast."

"You mean Little Miss Perfect here takes drugs, too?" Quentin's frown dissolved into a grin. "I never would have guessed it. Neither would Dad, I'll bet. He'll have a cow if he ever finds out."

Lani started to reply, but before she could answer, a swift and vicious kick from the toe of Mitch's hiking boot smashed into her thigh. She said nothing.

"Tripping out is for dessert," Mitch said quickly. "First let's worry about the pots."

"How are we going to carry them out?" Quentin asked.

"In your backpack."

"But we only have one."

"You should have thought of that before. I guess you'll have to do it by yourself then, won't you?"

"By myself?"

"Sure," Mitch responded. "You're the one getting paid for it, aren't you?"

"But if everybody does their share . . ." Quentin began.

"I said for you to do it," Mitch said, his voice hardening as he spoke. "If the damned pots don't get down the mountain to that car of yours, you don't get your five thousand bucks, understand?"

Obligingly, Quentin slipped off his backpack, went over to the corner, and loaded three of the larger pots into it. "That's all that'll fit for right now," he said.

"That's all right," Mitch said. "Make as many trips as you need to. We have all the time in the world."

As Quentin turned to leave, Mitch breathed a sigh of relief. The drug was still working well enough. With Mitch's knee acting up, he needed Quentin's physical strength to haul the pots down the mountain to the car. After that, all bets were off.

As Quentin took flashlight in hand and started back through the passage, Lani sat on the floor of the cave, staring at the bones glowing with an eerie phosphorescence in the indirect haze of moonlight.

Looking at the skeleton, Lani knew immediately that the bones belonged to a woman of some wealth. The pots alone were an indication of that. Most likely there had been baskets once as well, but those, like the woman's flesh, had long since decayed and melted back into the earth—leaving behind only the harder stuff—the clay pottery and the bones. And one day, Lani's bones would be found here as well. Unknown and unrelated to one another in life, she and this other woman would be sisters in death. Lani took some small comfort in knowing that she would not be left there alone.

Across from her, Mitch sat down on something hard, something that supported his weight—a rock of some kind. In the moments before he switched off his flashlight, Lani realized he was rubbing his knee, massaging it, as though he had twisted it perhaps. It was a small thing, but nevertheless something to remember.

Sitting cross-legged on the hard ground, Lani reached out one arm, expecting to rest some of her weight on that one hand. Instead of encountering the dirt floor, her hand blundered into one of the remaining pots—one of the smaller ones. As Lani's exploring fingers strayed silently around the smooth edge of the neck of the pot, a powerful realization shot through her, something that was as much *chehchki*—dream—as it was understanding.

This pot had once belonged to *Oks Gagda*—to Betraying

Woman. Lani knew the story. She had heard the legend from Nana *Dahd* and from Davy as well. The legend—the *ha'icha ahgidathag*—of Betraying Woman—was a cautionary tale that told how a young girl whose birth name had long since disappeared into oblivion had once fallen in love with an Apache—an *Ohb*. When an enemy war party had attacked her village, the girl had betrayed her people to their dreaded enemy. Much later, the bad girl was brought back home and punished. According to the legend, *I'itoi* locked her in a cave and then called the mountain down around her, leaving her to die alone and in the dark.

Lani had lived all her life with those beloved *I'itoi* stories and traditions, but there was a part of her that discounted them. Over the years she had stopped believing in them in much the same way she eventually had stopped believing in Santa Claus. Although legends of Saint Nicholas and the *I'itoi* stories as well may both have had some distant basis in fact, by age sixteen Lani no longer regarded them as true. The stories and the lessons to be learned from them were part of her culture but not necessarily part of her life.

She had been eight years old when Davy broke the bad news to her, that Santa Claus didn't exist. Nana *Dahd* was gone by then, so Lani hadn't been able to go to her for consolation. For the first time, without Rita there to comfort her, Lani had turned to her mother—to Diana Ladd Walker. And it was in her mother's arms that she had learned that the wonder and magic of Christmas hadn't gone out of her life forever.

Feeling the cool, smooth clay under her fingertips, Lani felt the return of another kind of magic. *Oks Gagda*—Betraying Woman—did exist. She had been locked in a cave by the falling mountain just the way Nana *Dahd* had said. But now Lani knew something about that story that she had never known before. Betraying Woman had been locked in a cave with two entrances. If she had known about the other entrance, she might have simply walked away, rather than staying to endure her punishment. In a way she would never be able to explain to anyone else, Lani Walker grasped the significance of what had happened. *Oks Gagda* had willingly chosen to remain where she was, choosing the honor of *jehka'ich*—of suffering the consequences of her wickedness—rather than taking the coward's path and running away.

A wave of gooseflesh raced across Lani's body. She had left her people-hair basket behind, but *I'itoi* had sent her another talisman to take the basket's place. Carefully, making as little noise as possible, she lifted the small sturdy pot from where it had sat undisturbed for all those years and placed it, out of sight, in the triangular space formed by her crossed legs.

"What are you doing over there?" Mitch demanded, shining a blinding beam from his flashlight directly in her eyes.

"Nothing," Lani said. "Just trying to get comfortable."

"You stay right where you are," Mitch warned. "No funny business."

Lani said nothing more. Covering the perfectly round opening of the pot with the palm of her hand, Lani closed her eyes. With the cool rim of clay touching her skin, Lani let the words of Nana *Dahd*'s long-ago song flow silently through her whole being.

Do not look at me, Little Olhoni
Do not look at me when I sing to you
So this man will not know we are speaking
So this evil man will think he is winning.

Do not look at me when I sing, Little Olhoni,
But listen to what I say. This man is evil.
This man is the enemy. This man is Ohb.
Do not let this frighten you.
Whatever happens, we must not let him win.
I am singing a war song, Little Olhoni.
A hunter's song, a killer's song.

I am singing a song to I'itoi, *asking him to help us.*
Asking him to guide us in the battle
So the evil Ohb *does not win.*

Do not look at me, Little Olhoni,
Do not look at me when I sing to you.
I must sing this song four times,
For all of nature goes in fours,
But when the trouble starts
You must listen very carefully
And do exactly what I say.
If I tell you to run, you must run,
Run fast, and do not look back.
Whatever happens, Little Olhoni.
You must run and not look back.

Remember in the story how I'itoi *made himself a fly*
And hid in the smallest crack when Eagleman
Came searching for him. Be like I'itoi,
Little Olhoni. *Be like* I'itoi *and hide yourself*
In the smallest crack. Hide yourself somewhere
And do not come out again until the battle is over.
Listen to what I sing to you, Little Olhoni.
Do not look at me but do exactly as I say.

Lani paused sometimes between verses to listen. Outside
the cave's entrance, cool nighttime air rustled through the
manzanita, making a sighing sound like people whispering—or like *a'ali chum*—little children—gossiping and
sharing secrets. Maybe it was that sound that brought Betraying Woman back to Lani's attention. Not only had she
been left to die in the cave, her spirit was still there, trapped
forever in the prison of her unbroken pots.

"Pots are made to be broken," Nana *Dahd* had told her
time and again. "Always the pots must be broken."

And that was why, in Rita's medicine basket, there had

once been a single shard of pottery with the figure of a turtle etched into it. The piece of reddish-brown clay had come from a pot Rita's grandmother, *Oks Amichuda*—Understanding Woman—had made when she was a young woman. After Understanding Woman's death, Rita herself had smashed the pot to pieces, releasing her grandmother's spirit. The only thing Rita had saved was that one jagged-edged piece.

For just a moment, in that dim gray light, Lani thought she saw the pale figure of a woman glide behind the man who called himself Mitch Vega. Lani saw the figure pause and then move on.

The shadowy shape was there for such a brief moment that at first Lani thought, perhaps, she had made her up. But then, as Lani kept on singing, a strange peace enveloped her. She felt perfectly calm—as though she were being swept along in the untroubled stillness inside a whirlwind. And since Lani understood by then that, like Betraying Woman, she was going to die anyway, there was no longer any reason for her to remain silent.

"Why do you hate them?" she asked.

"Hate who?" Mitch returned.

"My parents," Lani answered. "That's why you've done all this—drugged me, drugged Quentin, brought us here. That's the reason you drew that awful picture of me, as well. To get at my parents, but I still don't understand why."

"It's not your parents," Mitch said agreeably enough. "It's your father."

"My father? What did he do to you?"

"Did your father ever mention the name Mitch Johnson to you?"

"Mitch Johnson? I don't think so. Is that you? I thought your name was Vega."

"Mitch Whatever. It doesn't really matter, does it?" He laughed then. The brittle laughter rattled hollowly off the walls of the cave. "That's a pisser, isn't it! Brandon Walker cost me my family, my future, and twenty years out of my life, but I'm not important enough for even the smallest mention to Brandon Walker's nearest and dearest."

"What did my father do to you?" Lani persisted.

"I'll tell you what he did. He locked me up, and for no good reason. Those goddamned wetbacks are sucking the lifeblood out of this country. They were wrecking things back then, and it's worse now. All I was trying to do was stop it."

The word "wetbacks" brought the story back. "You're him," Lani said.

"Him who?"

"The man who shot those poor Mexicans out in the desert."

"So your father did tell you about me after all. What did he say?"

"He wasn't talking about you," Lani answered. "He was talking about the award. I was dusting in his study and I asked him about some of his awards. The *Parade Magazine* Detective of the Year Award was—"

"He was talking about his damned award?"

Lani heard the change in the tenor of his voice, the sudden surge of anger. The lesson she should have learned when she had slapped the drug-laden cup away from her lips seemed so distant now, so far in the past, that it no longer applied. What difference did it make? He was going to kill her anyway.

"That's why they gave it to him," she said quietly. "For sending you to prison. You killed two people and wounded another. I think you got what you deserved."

"Shut up," Mitch Vega-Johnson snarled. "Shut the hell up. You don't know the first goddamned thing about it."

Listen to me, Little Olhoni, *and do exactly as I say.*

Once again Nana *Dahd*'s song came to mind and she

began to sing quietly—*jupij ne'e*. She whispered the strength-giving words, not loud enough for Mitch to hear, but loud enough that they might fall on the ears of Betraying Woman, that they might reach out to that other trapped spirit who had spent so long shut up in the cave.

When Mitch had taken her prisoner and when he had hurt her, he had caught her unawares. Lani had learned enough about him now to realize that he was simply waiting for Quentin to finish loading the pots. When that task was accomplished, Mitch would come after Lani again—after Lani and Quentin both.

Minute by minute, the danger was coming closer, and singing Nana *Dahd*'s song was the only way Lani knew to prepare for it, to achieve *ih'in*. This time, when he came after her, she would be ready. Perhaps she would not escape—escape did not seem possible—but with the help of *I'itoi* and of Betraying Woman, Lani would meet her fate in a way that would make Nana *Dahd* proud. In the face of whatever Mitch Vega-Johnson had to offer, Lani would be *bamustk*—unflinching.

That was the other thing *Siakam* meant—to be a hero, to endure. Nana *Dahd* had given her that word as part of her name. Dolores Lanita Walker was determined that, no matter what, she would somehow live up to the legend of that other *Mualig Siakam*, to the other woman from long ago, the one who had been Kissed by the Bees.

Driving to the department, Brandon and Diana Walker said very little. Brandon had always thought that having a child die a violent death had to be a parent's worst nightmare. But it turned out that wasn't true, because having one child murdered by another was worse by far. There was no way for him to come to grips with the enormity of the tragedy, so he took refuge in action and drove.

Pulling into the familiar parking lot, he was struck by the

difference between then and now, between when he used to park in the slot marked RESERVED FOR SHERIFF. Back then, he would have walked into the building to issue orders and direct the action. Tonight, instead of calling the shots, he was coming in as a family member—as the father of both victim and perpetrator. Instead of being able to tell people what to do, he was going to have to ask, maybe even beg, for someone to help him.

Shaking his head at his own powerlessness, he parked the car in a slot marked VISITOR.

"What are we going to tell them?" Diana asked, as they headed for the public entrance.

Brandon was still carrying the paper bag that held the cassette tape and plastic case. "Before I tell anybody anything, I'm going to try to get these to Alvin. That way he can start lifting prints. Once he's done with the tape, we'll try to get someone to hold still long enough to listen to it."

"Will they believe it?"

"That depends," Brandon told her.

"On what?"

"On the luck of the draw," he answered. "With any kind of luck, Detective Myers will still be home in bed."

Walking into the reception area, the young clerk recognized Brandon Walker immediately. "What can I do for you?" he asked.

"I'm looking for Alvin Miller," Brandon answered.

The clerk frowned. "I doubt he's here. I'm not showing him on the 'in' list."

"Do me a favor," Brandon said. "Try calling the fingerprint lab and see if he answers."

And he did. Within minutes, Alvin Miller had come out to the reception area to escort Brandon and Diana back to the lab. "What's going on?" he asked.

Brandon handed over the bag. "Do me a favor," he said. "We need prints lifted off these."

"All right," Alvin returned.

"Then I'll need something else."

"What's that?"

"You can call up prints by name, can't you?"

"Sure," Alvin answered. "If the prints went into the system with a name, then we can get them out that way, too. Whose name are we looking for?"

"My son's," Brandon Walker said, his voice cracking as he spoke.

"Your son's?"

Brandon nodded. "His name is Quentin—Quentin Addison Walker. He's only been out of Florence for a matter of months, so his prints should be on file."

Without another word, Alvin Miller walked over to a computer keyboard and punched in a series of letters. The whole lab was silent except for the air rushing through the cooling ducts and the hum of fans on various pieces of equipment. For the better part of a minute, that sound didn't change. Then, finally, with a distinctive *thunk*, a printer snapped into action.

Eventually, the print job was complete. Only when the lab was once again filled with that odd humming silence did Alvin reach out to retrieve the printed sheet from the printer. Preparing to hand it to Brandon, he glanced at it once. As soon as he did so, he snatched it away again and held it closer to study it more closely.

"Holy shit!" Alvin exclaimed.

"What is it?" Brandon asked.

"I haven't run the prints yet," he said. "I was just about done enhancing them, but I recognize one of these. Has your son been out to visit you recently?"

"My son and I are currently estranged," Brandon Walker said carefully. "He hasn't been anywhere near Diana's and my house since *before* he was sent to prison. Not as an invited guest," he added.

"But this print—the one right here on the end," Alvin said, handing the sheet over to Brandon at last. "That's the same print I took off the desk in your office and also off one of the pieces of broken frame."

Brandon looked down at the piece of paper in his hand. The last print, the one in the corner, had a diagonal slice across it. Nodding, he handed the set of prints back to Alvin.

"He almost cut his thumb in half with my pocket knife when he was eight," Brandon said quietly. "He took my pocket knife outside and was showing off with his little brother when it happened. You'll probably find the same prints on the tape and tape case as well."

"You think your son Quentin has something to do with your daughter's disappearance?"

Brandon Walker sighed. In the space of a few minutes' time, the former sheriff seemed to have aged ten years.

"With my daughter's murder," he corrected. "It's all on the tape, but before you turn it over to a detective, I want it checked for prints. Diana's and mine are on there along with whatever others there are. You understand, don't you, Alvin?" he asked. "I need to know for sure." He glanced in Diana's direction. "We both need to know."

"Right," Alvin said.

He took the bag and carried it over to his lab area, where he carefully dusted both the tape and the case with graphite, bringing out a whole series of prints. Then, using a magnifying glass, he examined the results for several long minutes.

Finally, putting down the glass, he turned back to Brandon and Diana. "It's here," he said. "On the case, at least."

Brandon Walker's eyes blurred with tears. His legs seemed to splinter beneath him.

"I was afraid it would be," he said. "We'd better go out front and talk to a detective. I'm sure whoever's assigned to this case will need to hear that tape as soon as possible."

"How come?" Alvin Miller asked. "What's on it?"

Brandon Walker took a deep, despairing breath before he answered. "We believe . . ." he said, fighting unsuccessfully to keep his voice steady, ". . . that this is a recording of our daughter's murder."

Together, Diana and Brandon Walker started toward the door. "Ask to talk to Detective Leggett," Alvin Miller called after him. "He doesn't know it yet, but it turns out he's already working this case."

By the time Davy and Candace picked up their tickets at the counter and then went racing through the terminal to the gate, they were both worn out. Once aboard America West Flight 1, bound for Tucson, Candace fell sound asleep. Davy, although fidgety with a combination of nerves and exhaustion, fought hard to stay awake. They were flying in a 737, and Davy was stuck in one of the cramped middle seats, sandwiched between Candace, sleeping on his left, and a bright-eyed little old lady on the right. The woman was tiny. Her skin was tanned nut-brown. The skin of her lips and cheeks was wrinkled in that distinctive pattern that comes from years of smoking. Rattling the pages, she thumbed impatiently through the in-flight magazine.

David sat there, bolt upright and petrified, worried sick that if he did fall asleep, he would instantly be overtaken by yet another panic attack. If, as the emergency room doctor had insisted, the attacks were stress-induced, then Davy figured he was about due for another one. There was, after all, some stress in his life.

His experience with Candace in the hotel earlier meant that he was no longer quite so concerned about what she would think of him when another attack came along. What would other people think, though? The lady next to him, for instance, or the flight attendants hustling up and down the aisle, dispensing orange juice and coffee, what would they do? He could imagine it all too well. "Ladies and gentlemen," one of them would intone into the intercom. "We have a medical emergency here. Is there a doctor on board?"

Stress. Part of that came from finishing school and going home and getting a real job without even taking whatever had happened to Lani into consideration. In the years while Davy was attending law school in Chicago, he had held himself at arm's length from his family back home. Somehow it seemed to him that there wasn't room enough in his heart for all of them at once—for the Arizona contingent and for the Ladd side of the family in Illinois. To say nothing of Candace.

Looking at her sleeping peacefully beside him, Davy couldn't quite believe she was there. In his scheme of things, Candace had always been part of his Chicago life, and yet here she was on the plane with him, headed for Tucson. Not only that, she was going there with Astrid Ladd's amazingly large diamond engagement ring firmly encircling the ring finger on her slender left hand.

Davy hadn't exactly popped the question. Nevertheless, they were engaged. Candace was planning a quick wedding in Vegas while Davy squirmed with the knowledge that his mother and stepfather had barely heard her name. He hadn't told them any more about her than he had told them about his other passing romantic fancies. It hadn't seemed necessary.

Now, given the circumstances, telling was more than necessary. It was essential and tardy and not at all one-sided. Just as he hadn't talked about Candace to his parents, the reverse was also true. There was a whole lot he hadn't told Candace, either.

The lush lifestyle in which Candace Waverly had grown up in Oak Park, Illinois, was far different from what prevailed in the comparatively simple house in Gates Pass. And if Candace's experience was one step removed from the Tucson house, it was forever away from Rita Antone's one-room adobe house—little more than a shack, really—which had been Nana *Dahd*'s ancestral home in *Ban Thak*.

Coyote Sitting, Davy thought. Just the names of the villages were bad enough. *Hawani Naggiak*—Crow Hanging;

Komkch'eD e Wah'osidk—Turtle Wedged; *Gogs mek*—Burnt Dog. Davy knew them equally well in English and in *Tohono O'othham*, but what would Candace think when he tried to explain them to her?

Conflicting geography was one thing. What about when he started dealing in the crossed wires of personalities? There had been no particular need to tell Candace much about being raised by Rita Antone, who in turn had been raised by her own grandmother, Understanding Woman. Over time Davy had mentioned a few things, of course, but only the simple, straightforward parts, not any of what Richard Waverly, Candace's father, would derisively call the woo-woo stuff.

Davy had never mentioned Looks At Nothing's Peace Smoke, for instance. He hadn't told Candace or any of her family how the blind old medicine man from his childhood would light his foul-smelling wild tobacco with a flame sparked by his faithful Zippo lighter. He hadn't told them about Looks At Nothing's spooky way of knowing things before they happened or of the blind man telling others what he had "seen" in his divining crystals.

How would Candace and her family react to a discussion of medicine men and divining crystals—and medicine baskets, for that matter? Or try scalp bundles on for size. The one from Rita's medicine basket—an *Ohb* scalp bundle, no doubt—was the main reason Rita's medicine basket was still sitting in his parents' safety deposit box eleven years after Rita's death.

Davy was sure now that the scalp bundle had been the primary reason Rita had insisted that it be kept out of Lani's hands until she was old enough to handle it with proper respect. Davy cringed at the idea of sitting down and trying to explain to Richard Waverly how improper handling of a scalp-bundle could bring on a bout of Enemy Sickness, the best cure for which was a medicine man singing scalp-bundle songs at night.

Old Man Waverly will just love that one, Davy thought.

And yet, those things—which he could imagine Candace and her family not quite understanding—were far too much a part of Davy's life and experience for him to dismiss them. The stories about *I'itoi* and Earth Medicine Man were as deeply woven into Davy's background as *Aesop's Fables* and the Brothers Grimm were into Candace's. How would somebody raised on watered-down versions of *Little Red Riding Hood* and *Cinderella* respond to having her son or daughter hear about how *I'itoi* chopped the head off the monster Eagleman's baby?

Almost without realizing what he was doing, Davy reached into his pocket and pulled out Father John's rosary. At age twenty-seven, David Ladd closed his eyes and saw in his mind's eye those three aged adults who had played such important roles in his childhood—Rita, Looks At Nothing, and Father John. They were all so very different and yet, despite those differences, they had drawn a healing circle of love around him—a little half-orphaned Anglo boy—and held him safe inside it.

How had they done that? And if, from the vantage point of being that well-loved child, Davy himself couldn't answer that question, how in God's name would he ever be able to explain it to anyone else, including Candace Waverly?

By then the beads were laid out across his palm. He began slowly, one bead at a time, silently moving his lips as he recited the words. "Holy Mary, Mother of God, pray for us sinners now and at the hour of our death. Amen."

Halfway through the process, probably somewhere over Colorado, someone tapped on his right arm. Startled, he looked up. The lady next to him was smiling a benignly cheery smile.

"I know just how you feel," she said. "I used to be afraid of flying, too, young man. But they have classes for that kind of thing these days. I took one at Pima Community

College a few years back. You might look into taking one yourself. Those classes don't cost very much, and they help. They really do."

Blushing furiously, Davy dropped Father John's *losalo* back into his pocket. "Thank you," he said. "I'll try to look into it as soon as I have a chance."

Leaving the hospital, Fat Crack Ortiz stopped by the Walker house in Gates Pass long enough to see that no one was home. After that he headed the Crown Victoria toward Sells. No doubt the dance was still going strong, but he didn't even pause at the Little Tucson turnoff. Instead, he drove on home.

When he had warned Brandon Walker of danger the day before, it hadn't occurred to him that the danger in question, the evil emanating from Diana's book, might fall on Lani. He had expected Diana herself to be the target, never Lani.

Once he reached the house, he was grateful to discover that Wanda still wasn't home. Although she tolerated his medicine-man status, she certainly wasn't thrilled by it. Gabe went straight to the wooden desk and retrieved Looks At Nothing's medicine pouch. Then he went outside. Using a stick of mesquite, he stood in the middle of the dirt-floored patio and used the stick to draw a circle around himself. Then he eased himself down on the hard ground in exactly the way the old blind medicine man would have prescribed.

With the porch light providing the only light, he opened the pouch and took out a rolled cigarette made from *wiw*—wild tobacco—that Fat Crack had carefully gathered and rolled into the ceremonial cigarettes. Digging further, he located Looks At Nothing's old Zippo lighter, which had become almost as much a part of the *duajida*—the nighttime divination ceremony—as the billowing smoke itself. Then, opening a second, smaller bag made of some soft, chamois-like material, Fat Crack peered inside at the crystals he knew were there.

In all the years Fat Crack Ortiz had been in possession of the medicine pouch, he had seldom touched the crystals or taken them out of their protective bag. But if any occasion called for the use of Looks At Nothing's most powerful medicine, this was it. Lani Walker was in danger. The old medicine man had been dead long before Rita Antone's ant-kissed child had been born. Nonetheless, his influence, even from the grave, had directed almost every aspect of Lani's young life, from her unusual adoption to the things she had been taught by the people who had been placed in charge of caring for her.

The responsibility of caring for the child had been left to a number of people, but Looks At Nothing's medicine pouch had been entrusted to Fat Crack alone. The treasured pouch had come to him with the understanding that the Medicine Man with the Tow Truck would save it for Looks At Nothing's real successor. For a time, while the children were young, Fat Crack had fooled himself into believing that the mantle would fall to one or the other of his own two sons—to either Richard or Leo. And then, when Rita had insisted on taking Clemencia Escalante to raise, she had told her nephew that perhaps the ant-marked baby was the one Looks At Nothing had told them about. Over the years, Fat Crack had come to believe that was true.

Carefully, patiently, Fat Crack unknotted the drawstring that held the chamois bag closed. Holding out an upturned hand, he dumped the collection of crystals into his palm. There were four of them in all. As soon as Fat Crack saw the four of them winking back the reflected glow of the porch light, he had to smile. Four crystals made sense. After all, as everyone knows, all things in nature go in fours.

Arranging them side by side, Fat Crack laid the crystals and the cigarette and lighter out on the spread leather surface of the pouch, then he reached into his hip pocket and pulled out his wallet. Carefully he thumbed through the school pictures of his own children and grandchildren until he found the one Lani had given him the year before at Christmas.

He lit the cigarette and let the smoke swirl around him in the late-night breeze. There was no one sitting in the circle with him, but Fat Crack raised the cigarette and blew a puff of smoke in each of the four directions, just as Looks At Nothing had taught him, saying *"Nawoj"* as he did so.

While the cigarette still glowed in his fingertips, Fat Crack lifted up the first crystal and held it over Lani's picture. Nothing happened. It was the same with the second crystal and with the third as well.

The sky was gradually lightening in the east and Fat Crack was already thinking how foolish he must look sitting there on the ground when he picked up the fourth crystal and held it over the picture. What happened then was something he could never explain. It simply was. The picture on the paper changed ever so slightly until something else superimposed itself over Lani's smiling face.

At first Fat Crack thought he was seeing the head of a rattlesnake, its jaws open wide to swallow something, its fangs fully exposed. This was not a snake's head. It was, in fact, a snake's skull—*ko'oi koshwa*. Then, as Fat Crack leaned down to examine the picture more closely, he realized the picture underneath the skull seemed changed as well. In the slowly eddying smoke, he saw that Lani's eyes were missing. Instead of eyes smiling back at him, there were only empty sockets.

The message from the divining crystals was clear. If Lani Walker wasn't already dead, she soon would be.

Fat Crack's hands shook as he carefully returned the crystals and lighter to the medicine pouch. He was just closing it and trying to decide what to do with this newfound, awful knowledge when the headlights from Richard Ortiz's tow truck flashed across the yard. With an agility that surprised Fat Crack even as he did it, he heaved his hefty frame up off the ground and hurried toward the truck. He reached the rider's door just as Wanda climbed out and turned to tell Richard good-bye.

"*Oi g hihm*," Fat Crack said to his son, hoisting himself up into the seat Wanda had just vacated. Literally translated, *oi g hihm* means "Let's walk." In the everyday language of the reservation, however, it means "Let's get in the pickup and go."

"Where are you going?" Wanda demanded, catching the door before Gabe had a chance to close it.

"To Rattlesnake Skull Charco," he said. "Call Brandon Walker and tell him to meet me there. Tell him that's where we'll find Lani. Tell him to hurry before it's too late."

"What's wrong with Lani?" Wanda Ortiz asked in alarm. "Is she hurt, sick? What's going on?"

"She's been kidnapped," Fat Crack answered without hesitation. "I believe she's been taken by someone connected to the evil *Ohb*. If we don't find her soon, that person is going to kill her, if he hasn't already."

Wanda nodded and stepped back from the truck. "I'll call the Walkers right away," she said.

Richard Ortiz shifted the tow truck into reverse. "We're not talking more of that old medicine-man nonsense, are we?" he asked dubiously.

This was no time for a philosophical discussion. "Shut up and drive, Baby," Fat Crack told his son. "And while you're at it, put the flashers on."

"You think it's that serious?"

"You bet," Fat Crack told him. "It's a matter of life and death."

Quentin had come back to the cavern, picked up the second load of pottery, and had gone to carry it back down the mountain. Soon he would be back for the third and last load. Lani knew that was when Mitch Johnson would make his move. That was when he would kill them.

But even with death looming closer, Lani no longer felt frightened. The whispered words of Nana *Dahd*'s war chant were helping Lani to remain calm in the face of whatever was to come. And the pot was helping her as well. Still undetected by either Quentin or Mitch, it lay nestled between her legs. Stroking the cool, hard clay seemed to offer as much comfort as Nana *Dahd*'s song. The presence of the pot seemed to take up where the people-hair basket had left off.

Across the darkened cave, Mitch Johnson was talking, his voice droning on and on, as much to himself as to Lani. When she finally started paying attention, he was talking about Quentin's reaction to the drug. "Scopolamine's interesting stuff, isn't it? Sort of like a combination of drug and hypnosis. I guess those guys down in Colombia aren't so stupid after all."

"That's what you used on us?" Lani asked.

"Andy claimed that scopolamine poisoning makes 'em hot as hell, red as a beet, mad as a hatter, and blind as a bat."

In that throwaway remark Lani almost missed the crucial name—Andy. Her heart lurched inside her chest. All night long she had been forging spiritual links between this man and the evil *Ohb*. Now, though, for the first time, there was some outside confirmation that connections between Andrew Carlisle of old and this new evil *Ohb* did exist. Lani had to know for sure.

"Who's Andy?" she asked, swallowing an entirely new lump of fear that rose dangerously in her throat.

"Did you say 'Who's Andy?' " Mitch Johnson asked in mock disbelief. "You mean here you are, smart enough to go to University High School, but you're not smart enough to figure all this out for yourself?"

"Who's Andy?" Lani repeated.

"A friend of mine," Mitch Johnson told her. "It turns out he was a friend of your mother's as well. If you've read your mother's book, then you know a whole lot about him. His name was Carlisle. Andrew Philip Carlisle. Ever heard of him?"

Sitting there in the dark, Lani's body was covered by another wave of gooseflesh. She felt sick to her stomach. It was true, then. She was shut up in the darkened cave with a man named Mitch Johnson, but she was there with Andrew Carlisle as well, with the vengeful spirit of the evil *Ohb* who had raped and tortured her mother.

"That's why you burned me, isn't it?" she said. Her voice seemed very small. In the emptiness of the darkened cave, it was hardly more than a whisper. "You did it for him."

"So maybe you aren't so dumb after all. This way your mother is bound to make the connection, but there won't be any tooth impressions for someone to take to court the way there were with Andy."

Andy. It was hard for her to comprehend that word. How could a person who was "Andy" to Mitch Johnson also be Andrew Carlisle, the monster who had frequented the stories of Lani Walker's childhood? She had spent long winter evenings, snuggled in Rita's lap, hearing the story again and again. Lani had loved hearing how two women, the priest, the boy, and the dog had overcome the wicked *Mil-gahn* man. Again and again Nana *Dahd* had told the powerful tale of how *I'itoi* had helped them defeat the enemy who was, at the same time, both Apachelike and not-Apache.

"I don't suppose you ever met him," Mitch continued. "You're much too young. He was already in prison for the second time long before you were born, but if you had met him, I think you would have been impressed. To put it in terms you might understand—the Indian vernacular, as it were—I'd say he was a very powerful medicine man."

Lani knew something about medicine men—especially about Looks At Nothing, who had been a friend of Rita's. And Fat Crack Ortiz was a medicine man as well. Whatever powers they had weren't used for evil or for hurting people. Mitch Johnson's sarcastic remark burned through Lani's fear and changed it to anger, like a powerful magnifying glass focusing the rays of the sun to ignite a piece of paper.

"You can call him a medicine man if you like," she said softly. "I call him *ho'ok*."

"Ho'ok," Mitch Johnson repeated. "What does that mean?"

"Monster," Lani replied.

For a moment after she said it, there was no sound in the dark stillness of the cave, then there was a short hiccup followed by a hoot of raucous laughter.

Except it didn't sound like laughter to Lani Walker. In the dark it reminded her of something else—of the rasping, unearthly, bone rattling sound a cornered javelina makes when it gnashes its teeth.

16

Now this is all that is known of Mualig Siakam. *She was one of the greatest of all the medicine women in all the Land of the Desert People. She lived to be very, very old. And she taught some of her songs to a few men.*

Some women tried to learn the songs, but the buzzing of the bees joined with the song in the heads of the women and made them afraid. Because they were afraid, the women would not let sleep come. Sleep was necessary in order to know all the powers which one does not see, and which are used in healing.

The Indians would take a new baby many miles to see Great Medicine Woman, and Mualig Siakam *would sing over the baby. She would sing over it with the white feathers of goodness which would help guard its spirit from meanness. And she would feed the baby a little of the very fine white meal which would make its body strong.*

But sometimes Great Medicine Woman would refuse to

sing. Then the people knew there was no hope for the child.

If the people grew angry and tried to make Mualig Siakam *sing over such a child, Great Medicine Woman would scold. She would ask them what right they had over* Tash—*the Sun*—*and* Jeweth—*the Earth*—*and all of* I'itoi's *gifts. Then she would go into the dark inner room of her house, and the* Pa-nahl—*the bees*—*would begin to roar with anger.*

When that happened, all the people—*even Old Limping Man*—*would go away.*

Alvin Miller wasn't used to doing his work in front of a live audience, but that night the lab was jammed with onlookers. The Walkers were there along with Deputy Fellows and both detectives on the case, Leggett and Myers. At the last moment Sheriff Forsythe even showed up, probably summoned by Detective Myers.

"All right," Forsythe said, looking around the room. "What exactly's going on here?"

Brandon Walker looked at the man who had replaced him. "My daughter's missing," he said. "We're afraid she may have been kidnapped."

Forsythe glowered at Detective Myers. "Kidnapped. I thought you said this was a Missing Persons case. And what's all this about bones?"

Miller came across the room and handed the papers over to the sheriff. "This set of prints matches individual prints we took off the collection of bones Deputy Fellows discovered out near the reservation yesterday afternoon as well as items from the break-in at the Walker residence last night that Detective Myers was called to investigate."

Slipping on a pair of reading glasses, Bill Forsythe studied the report. "Quentin Walker," he read aloud. Then he looked up at Brandon. "Your son?"

Brandon nodded. "I want you to call in the FBI," he said.

"The FBI!" Forsythe exclaimed. "For a little domestic thing like this? Not on your life. Chances are your son and daughter were drinking or something, just the way Detective Myers said . . ."

Brandon turned to Alvin. "Do you still have that tape recorder here?"

Miller nodded. "Yes."

"I want you to play the tape," Brandon said.

"But I haven't finished lifting—"

"Play it," Brandon ordered. "That's the only way they're going to believe what we're up against."

A few seconds later, Lani Walker's voice was playing to all the people crowded into the lab. "Quentin," she was saying. "Quentin, Quentin, Quentin."

"Your daughter?" Forsythe asked.

Brandon Walker nodded. By the time the scream tore through the room, Diana Walker was sobbing quietly into her hands.

"You're right," Sheriff Forsythe said, when Alvin Miller finally switched off the tape player. "It's time to pull out the stops."

Breathing a sigh of relief, Brandon Walker reached out and squeezed Diana's hand.

Quentin Walker had deposited his second load of pottery in the back of the Bronco and was on his way back to the cave for the third and last one when he saw the flashing red lights turn off Highway 86 onto Coleman Road.

Climbing up and down was hard physical labor. His head was far clearer now than it had been when he started out. Even though there was no chance of the people in the police car seeing him, he froze where he was and waited for it to go past. But it didn't. Instead, it slowed and turned left, heading for the *charco*.

Blind panic descended on Quentin Walker. *Someone's*

found Tommy, he thought. *And now the cops are coming for me.*

For the space of thirty seconds, he stood paralyzed by fear and indecision. And then, without a thought for the other people in the cave—without even recalling their existence, to say nothing of the third batch of pottery—he turned and ran back down to the Bronco. There was a single car key in his pocket. Sweeping the camouflage cover off the top, Quentin clambered into the vehicle and shoved the key home in the ignition.

Switching on the engine, he gunned it, testing the power, trying to remember exactly how he had come to be here on the mountain. Dimly he remembered driving up here, but it had seemed lighter then. In the dark, he was hard-pressed to remember how to reverse course and get back down.

He began trying to turn the Bronco around. There was little room for maneuvering inside that little clump of mesquite trees, especially when he didn't dare turn on the headlights. Those would certainly attract the attention of the cops with their flashing red lights. Even now, the cop car was headed straight for the *charco.*

Realizing that's where the cops were heading drove Quentin into a frenzy. The next time he backed up, he high-centered on a boulder he hadn't been able to see in the rearview mirror. Even with four-wheel drive, the Bronco didn't come loose the first two times he tried to go forward. The third time, he really goosed it, slamming the accelerator all the way to the floor, giving the Bronco every bit of power he had.

And it worked. Too well.

With a roar and a spray of pebble-sized rocks, the Bronco shot forward—through the grove of mesquite and right over the edge of a limestone cliff that had lain, shrouded in darkness, just beyond the sheltering trees.

Quentin mashed desperately on the brakes, trying to stop, but by then it was too late. The Bronco was already airborne.

It came to earth the first time twenty yards from where it had taken off. It landed nose-first and then bounced end for end. With the screech of tortured metal and to the accompaniment of breaking glass, it turned over and over. The battered remains finally came to rest, roof down, in the soft sand of the wash that skirted the bottom of the mountain. There was no fire, no explosion, only a cloud of dust that rose up into the nighttime sky and then silently dispersed.

Not having fastened his seat belt, Quentin Walker was thrown clear the first time the Bronco rebounded off the unforgiving mountainside. He flew through the air like a rag doll and then landed with a bone-jarring thump into a sturdy thicket of low-lying manzanita.

Quentin never saw Mitch Johnson come scrambling up over the landslide debris and out the crack of that second entrance, never heard him yelling into the gradually graying nighttime sky.

"Come back here, you rotten son of a bitch!"

Lani heard the engine turn over and stutter to life. The sound was faint but distinct. Other than the Bronco, there was no vehicle within hearing distance.

Mitch Johnson roared out his dismay. "Goddamn it! What the hell does he think he's doing?" Moments later, Johnson hurtled himself toward the pile of debris that blocked the second entrance. As he scrambled up it toward the crack at the top, loose rocks and pebbles rained down. A few of them smashed into Lani's legs and arms. Grabbing the pot, she scrambled to safety, stopping only when her body was pressed against the far side of the cave.

She could hear Mitch Johnson shouting at Quentin. For a moment, until the rocks quit falling, Lani stayed where she was. She might have remained there longer, but something outside herself urged her to action.

Now's your chance. Run!

Responding to that silent command, Lani stood and tried to walk. Her feet had fallen asleep. When she tried to stand on them, they were unfeeling boards beneath her. Seconds later they were alive with a thousand needles and pins.

Halfway across the floor of the cavern, she realized what she was doing and stopped cold. She had been trapped there in the cave with Mitch Johnson as surely as the spirit of Betraying Woman had been caught in her unbroken pottery. Now Lani had a chance to escape, but if the pots remained, so would *Oks Gagda*, imprisoned in her pottery long after the debt for betraying her people had been repaid.

Turning back toward the half-buried skeleton and her cache of pots, Lani was determined that the spirit of Betraying Woman would at last be set free.

Lani fell to her knees and felt around the dirt surface until she located the last half dozen pots—the ones Quentin hadn't been able to fit into either his first or second trips to the Bronco. Setting the one little pot aside, reserving it in case she needed to use it as a weapon, Lani set about breaking the other pots. One at a time, she heaved them against the rock wall, hearing them splinter to pieces.

At last only the little one remained. Lani reached down and picked it up. She started to take it with her, but reconsidered. If even one pot remained, Betraying Woman would still be trapped. Hating to do it, but knowing she had to, Lani raised her arm high overhead and smashed that pot as well.

There were tears in her eyes as Lani turned back toward the interior of the cave. She was truly alone now. Her first instinct was to follow Mitch Johnson up over the pile of debris, but what if he was still out there? What if she came out on the other side only to run straight into him. No, her only chance was to find the passage that led into the outer cavern.

In a sudden panic, she realized she had lost track of the exact location of the opening of the passage.

The moon had long crossed the peak of the mountain,

leaving the cave in total darkness. There was no light—at least there shouldn't have been. But as Lani searched the darkness for which way to go, a light did appear. Not a ray of light, and not a beam either. It looked more like a shadow glowing in the dark. It seemed to hover there on the far side of the cave before disappearing into nothing.

Some people have claimed that what Lani saw was little more than a cloud of dust set loose by Mitch's scrambling feet. But for Lani, for someone steeped in the ancient legends of *I'itoi* and in the traditions of the *Tohono O'othham,* there was no doubt about what she had seen.

The phosphorescent cloud came from the pots, all right, but not from dust. Freed now from her clay prison, *Oks Gagda* herself had come to show Lani the way.

Setting off across the dirt floor of the cave once again with more confidence than the darkness warranted, Lani walked to the place where it seemed to her the cloud had disappeared. She held one arm in front of her to keep from running into the rock wall, but that wasn't necessary. At the very spot where the cloud had disappeared, the passageway into the outer cavern opened up before her.

She paused there for a moment, wondering. If Betraying Woman had deceived her own people, could her guidance now be trusted? But there were no other options. One step at a time, Lani set off down the passage. Any moment, Mitch Johnson might return to the cave to find her, bringing the spirit of his friend, Andrew Carlisle, with him, but Lani Walker was no longer alone. Elder Brother himself was with her and so was Betraying Woman.

Lani had reached the point in the passage where she felt rather than saw the walls open out around her. She was just congratulating herself on getting that far when she heard cursing and scraping coming from the front entrance of the cave. Mitch Johnson was coming back. For one heart-stopping moment, she froze. There was nothing more she could do. Mitch had her trapped in the cave. Now he would surely kill her. Or worse. Either way, she had come to the end of her endurance.

Out of the depths of Lani's despair, Nana *Dahd*'s comforting words returned to the girl once more:

> "Remember in the story how I'itoi *made himself a fly*
> *And hid in the smallest crack when Eagleman*
> *Came searching for him. Be like* I'itoi,
> *Little* Olhoni. *Be like* I'itoi *and hide yourself*
> *In the smallest crack. Hide yourself somewhere*
> *And do not come out again until the battle is over.*
> *Listen to what I sing to you, Little* Olhoni.
> *Do not look at me but do exactly as I say."*

Lani Walker was already *inside* a crack in the mountain; already in a cave very much like Eagleman's cave, with a pile of bones moldering in the far corner just the way the bones of the people Eagleman had eaten had moldered in the corner of his cave. And there were cracks inside this crack. The curtains of falling stalactites and the growing mounds of stalagmites that she had glimpsed with Quentin's flashlight earlier all offered places where *I'itoi* could possibly have hidden and where Lani might hide herself as well.

Lani Walker had grown up in two worlds, understanding much of each. She knew instinctively that the *Mil-gahn*, Mitch, might look at the pile of debris and immediately assume that she had followed him out, climbing up and out. It might not occur to him that she would stay inside the mountain; that without benefit of a light she would have nerve enough to trust herself to *I'itoi*'s power and move into the enveloping darkness rather than away from it.

With him scrabbling through the one passage and with Lani trapped in the other, there wasn't a moment to lose. Halfway down the passage, the man-made earthen covering yielded once more to bare, jagged rocks. She could feel the sharp edges under the soles of her boots. She remembered that just before Quentin had ducked into the passage, she had glimpsed the walls of the huge cavern receding far into the mountain.

Clinging to the dank, wet wall and using it as a guide, she turned left from the mouth of the passage and fled along the side of the cavern, into the heart of the mountain.

Into the heart of I'itoi's *sacred mountain,* she told herself. *That is where I am going. Either I will be safe there, or that is where I will die.*

Hardly daring to breathe, she scraped along, still clinging to the wall, testing each tentative stepping place before she put her weight down. She came to the first break in the wall. Feeling around it with both arms, she realized it was a stalagmite, one three feet wide and about that tall, rising up from the floor of the cave. It wasn't large, but perhaps it was large enough to hide her. She ducked behind it just as the first jagged beams from Mitch's flashlight flickered into the cave and then slid across the otherworldly surface of the far wall.

Lani pressed herself against the sheltering stalagmite and held her breath. She didn't dare peek out for fear the beam from the light might reveal her face glowing white in the darkness. She marked his progress by watching the bouncing ray of his flashlight as he came across the room and by the curses and moans that accompanied his every step. She couldn't make out exactly what he was saying, but every once in a while the word "knee" surfaced and there was something about "cops."

Perhaps, in clambering up and over the debris, he had reinjured the knee that had been bothering him earlier. That would explain the knee part. As for the cops, Lani couldn't imagine what he meant. It didn't seem possible that there would be police officers outside looking for her. How could there be? How would anyone know where to look?

After what seemed an eternity, Mitch disappeared into the second passageway. Lani was tempted to stay where she was, but since this was the first hiding place she had found and the one nearest the opening to the second cavern, it was also most likely the first place Mitch Johnson would look when he came searching for her again. She would have to do better than that.

Hoping the noise of his own movements would mask hers, she crept on, trying to suppress the ragged breaths that threatened to catch in her throat and ignoring the sweat that trickled down the back of her neck. Two steps farther, her foot slipped off a sharp edge into a pool of icy water. The splash sounded like an explosion in her pounding ears, but when she stopped still and waited, there was no answering sound from the other room. Perhaps he hadn't heard it.

Barely able to breathe, she moved on. A dozen more steps into the mountain, she found a gap between two sta- lagmites and burrowed her way into that, stopping only when she came up against solid rock.

Closing her eyes against the darkness, she let Nana *Dahd*'s comforting words spill over her soul:

Be like I'itoi, *Little* Olhoni.
Be like I'itoi *and hide yourself*
In the smallest crack. Hide yourself somewhere
And do not come out again until the battle is over.
Listen to what I sing to you, Little Olhoni.
Do not look at me but do exactly as I say.

Trying to obey Nana *Dahd*'s instructions, Lani pressed herself even deeper into the crack in the wall. She had just eased her way down into a reasonably comfortable sitting position on another low-slung stalagmite when she heard the roar of rage in the other room. She cringed. Now it's com- ing, she thought.

Now the evil *Ohb* knows I'm gone.

* * *

Summoned by Sheriff Bill Forsythe, a loose coalition of officers from several jurisdictions converged on the Walker home in Gates Pass. They were just starting to work when the doorbell rang and Brandon went to answer it. Standing there was FBI Agent in Charge, Brock Kendall. After years of working together, Kendall and Brandon Walker had gone from being colleagues to becoming friends.

Kendall held out his hand. "I heard you were having some trouble," he said. "How does that old saying go? I'm from Washington and I'm here to help."

Brandon Walker's face cracked into a pained grin. "Thanks, Brock," he said. "Come on in."

"How bad is it?"

Walker shook his head. "The worst," he said. "About as bad as it can get."

"And the perpetrator may be Quentin, your own son?"

As a father, Brandon could barely stand to answer that question. "Yes," he said. "That's the way it looks."

Even with Brian Fellows and Dan Leggett doing the briefings, it still took precious time to bring all the players up to speed. Brandon Walker tolerated the seemingly interminable interviews as best he could because he knew they were necessary. And he understood that a meticulous crime scene investigation conducted by FBI-trained personnel was equally essential. Even so, it was hard not to fall prey to the thought that nothing much was happening.

At six o'clock in the morning he went into the bedroom. Diana, fully dressed, lay on the bed, staring dry-eyed up at the ceiling. "What's happening?" she asked.

"Brock Kendall is here, on an unofficial basis, of course, unless it starts looking like someone crossed state lines or until he can clear the way under missing and exploited children. Detective Leggett just sent out for a search warrant for Quentin's apartment over on Grant. Dan's a thorough kind of guy. He isn't going to make a move until he has all his ducks in a row."

"If Lani's already dead, what difference will being thorough make?" Diana asked despairingly.

"Don't say that," Brandon returned. "Don't even think it."

"You heard the tape," Diana said. "What else is there to think? And why would Quentin do such a thing? What did Lani ever do to him? Is it jealousy? Is that what this is all about? We would have done exactly the same things for Tommy and Quentin that we did for Davy and Lani if they had ever shown the slightest interest. And every time we tried to do something, Janie was right there saying it wasn't good enough for them. No matter what we did, it wasn't enough."

"Shhhh," Brandon said, laying a finger on Diana's lips. They were as parched and dry as if she had been running a fever. "It isn't Janie's fault that Quentin's gone off his rocker," Brandon said. "Don't waste your time blaming her, and don't blame us either."

"That's what you're saying then? Quentin's gone crazy and what's happened has no connection to the book? Nothing tonight has anything to do with the danger Fat Crack warned us about?"

Brandon slumped wearily against the headboard on his side of the bed. "I can't see what the connection would be," he said. "Insanity is the only thing that makes sense."

Just then there was a tap on the door. A young deputy poked his head inside the room. "Brock Kendall was trying to use your phone a few minutes ago. He said there's evidently a message on your answering machine. He said you should probably listen to it just in case it happens to be a ransom demand. We're in the process of setting a trap on your line. This call must have come in before that."

Brandon played back the message. Using the speaker phone, they both listened to Wanda Ortiz's voice.

"Gabe and Baby just left for Rattlesnake Skull Charco," Wanda said. "He wants you to meet him there. He says that's where you'll find Lani."

By the time the message ended, Brandon had already slipped his shoes back on and was bent over tying them. "What are you going to do?" Diana asked.

"You heard Wanda. Fat Crack wants me to meet him at Rattlesnake Skull Charco, and that's where I'm going."

Diana started to slide off the bed. "If that's where she is, I'm going too."

"No, you're not."

"Why not?" Diana demanded, slipping on her own shoes. "Why the hell shouldn't I? Lani's my daughter, too."

Brandon didn't want to say the real reason, that he was afraid of what they would find at Rattlesnake Skull Charco—afraid of what they would see. He couldn't seem to do much, but at least he could spare Diana that.

"One of us needs to be here to answer the phone," he said. "What if a ransom call does come in?"

Diana's voice rose, verging on hysteria. "There's not going to be any ransom call. You know that. You just—"

"Please, Diana," Brandon said huskily. He reached out and touched her, letting his fingers graze gently down the curving line of her cheek. "Please stay here. I can't order you to stay, but do it because I need you to, Di. Because I'm asking."

Diana sank back down on the bed. "All right," she said. "I'll stay."

"Thank you," Brandon said. He started toward the door.

"You'll take the cell phone?"

"It's already in my pocket."

"Call the moment you hear anything," Diana added. "The moment you find her. Promise me you'll call, no matter how bad it is."

Brandon stopped at the door and looked back at his wife. "I promise," he said. "No matter how bad."

Leaving Diana alone, he hurried out into the living room. "What's up?" Brock Kendall asked.

"Hitch up the wagons. We need to go out to the place

where they found those bones yesterday afternoon. According to Gabe Ortiz, that's where we'll find Lani—at Rattlesnake Skull Charco."

Brian Fellows leaped to his feet. "I can take you there," he offered. "It's not easy to find but—"

"I've been there before," Brandon Walker said. "It's the same place where we found Gina Antone all those years ago. Besides, Brian, I want you to stay here."

Disappointment washed over the young deputy's face. He started to argue. "But I—"

"Most of the other officers here are strangers, Brian," Brandon Walker said. "You're family. I'd like you to be here to be with Diana just in case. To give her some emotional backup. I only pray she won't need it."

"All right, Mr. Walker," Brian said. "If that's what you want me to do, I'll be glad to stay."

Brandon had left the Suburban parked out in front of the house. "Gabe Ortiz," Brock Kendall was saying as they climbed in. "That name sounds familiar. Who is he again?"

"A friend of the family," Brandon answered. "He's also the *Tohono O'othham* tribal chairman."

"But what does he have to do with all this, and how would he know that's where Lani might be?"

"He's a medicine man," Brandon answered, heading for the door. "He knows stuff. Don't ask me how, but he does."

Sitting in the mouth of the cave, watching the flashing red lights in the desert below, Mitch Johnson fought his way through an initial attack of panic. He was convinced that the lights had nothing to do with him. What he couldn't understand was why the hell they didn't finish up whatever it was they were doing and go away. The little Indian slut was still missing, but he was beginning to think that maybe she hadn't made it out of the cave after all.

He couldn't believe he had screwed up that badly, but

there was no one to blame but himself. He had counted too heavily on the drugs to control Quentin. He had kept the Bronco's ignition key in his pocket, but Quentin must have had a spare. He had raced out of the cave in a rage when he heard the Bronco start up without taking the precaution of securing the girl first. When he first discovered that Lani was missing, he had figured she had simply followed his own path up and over the landslide debris in the smaller cavern and out to the steep surface of the mountain.

Now, though, he wondered if that was true. Had she gone that way, she, too, would have seen the lights. If she had gone straight there, hoping to be rescued, wouldn't her appearance have provoked an almost instantaneous reaction? By now the mountainside would have been crawling with cops ready to use Mitch Johnson for some high-tech nighttime target practice. No doubt a bunch of eager-beaver searchers would have combed every inch of the surrounding terrain. One of them was bound to have stumbled across the crumpled hulk of Quentin Walker's Bronco.

No, as the still night slid into early morning, as the sky brightened in the east, and as the flashing red lights stayed right where they were, Mitch grew more and more convinced that Lani Walker was still somewhere inside the cave and probably freezing her cute little tush off as well.

He had already decided on a backup plan of action. All he had to do was make it to the Bounder. Even with his knee acting up again, he could walk that far. Then, if he drove into town, hooked on to the Subaru, he could drive off into the sunset and no one would be the wiser. He understood, however, that a plan like that would work only so long as Lani Walker wasn't alive to point an accusing finger in his direction.

Which meant that, inside the cave or out of it, Mitch Johnson had to find her first.

Had time not been an issue, he could simply have settled into the passage and waited. Eventually Lani would be faced with two simple courses of action: she would either have to come out or starve to death.

Mitch's real difficulty lay in the fact that time *was* an issue. By now the Walkers knew something was up and had probably called for reinforcements. And so, after checking the flashing lights one last time, Mitch Johnson turned back into the first passageway. He did so with only one purpose in mind—to find Lani Walker and kill her.

Somewhere over southeastern Colorado, Davy Ladd finally did fall asleep. The next panic attack hit while the Boeing 737 was cruising over central New Mexico. An observant flight attendant realized something was wrong and quickly moved the little old lady out of the way to an empty seat several rows forward.

As the dream started, it was similar to the others. The evil *Ohb* was there once again, armed with a knife, and chasing Lani and Davy through miles of mazelike tunnels. Once again he was awakened, gasping and sweating, by Lani's chilling scream.

"Something's happening," David said when he could finally speak again as he sat mopping rivulets of sweat off his face with a fistful of napkins the flight attendant had provided.

"What do you mean?" Candace asked.

"Something's happening, and it's happening now," Davy declared.

"How do you know that?"

"I don't know how I know, I just do."

Candace reached in her purse, pulled out a credit card, and removed the air-to-ground phone from its holder in the seat ahead of them. "Call," she said, running the magnetic strip through the slot to activate the phone. "Call and find out."

"Hello?" Diana answered. Her voice wasn't as strong or

as clear as it usually was on the phone. Whether that stemmed from nerves or weariness, Davy couldn't tell. "Mom? It's Davy."

"Where are you?" she asked. "Still in the hotel?"

"No," he answered. "We're on a plane somewhere over New Mexico. Maybe even Arizona by now. What's happening?"

"All hell has broken loose. There are investigators all over the house tearing the place apart. They've been here for hours and—" Diana stopped. "You're flying?" she asked as what Davy had said finally penetrated.

"Yes."

"And you'll be here soon?"

"Yes. The plane should be on the ground in about half an hour. We'll rent a car and—"

"Oh, Davy!" Diana whispered into the phone. "Thank you. I can't believe it. This is an answer to a prayer. But don't rent a car. Brian's here with me right now. I'll have him come to the airport and meet you at the gate. What flight?"

"America West, flight number one, from Chicago. And, Mom?" he added. "I'm not alone."

"You're not?"

"No. My fiancée is with me," David Ladd said, reaching out and taking Candace's hand. "Her name is Candace, Mom. You're going to love her."

The unrelenting cold of the larger cavern had crept into Lani's body, bringing with it a strange lethargy that robbed her of purpose—of the will to fight as well as of the will to live. The first time Mitch had gone cursing through to the outside in search of her, she had tried leaving one hiding place in favor of a better one.

She had barely ventured beyond the sheltering cover of the stalagmite when she lost her footing and fell. She came to a stop with one leg hanging out over a void. Unable to tell how deep the hole was, she broke off a small splinter of icicle-shaped rock and dropped it over the edge. It fell for a long, long time before finally coming to rest.

Shaken, Lani had crawled back into her original hiding place and there she stayed. At first she tried to maintain her connection to Nana *Dahd*'s song, but gradually the cold robbed her of that as well. The words slipped away from her. She could no longer remember them. She had almost drifted off to sleep when Mitch Johnson returned to the cave once more.

"Come out, come out, wherever you are," he called. "You can't hide from me forever."

The sound of Mitch Johnson's voice jarred Lani to alert consciousness. She had hoped to convince him that she had left the cavern. Now, however, as the beam from his flashlight began flickering here and there across the far wall of the cavern, probing one shadowy hollow after another, she realized that wasn't true. With the light moving ever closer, Mitch was searching for her—searching systematically. Fortunately for Lani, he had started on the far side of the cave, but gradually he was working his way closer. It was only a matter of time before the revealing light found its way into Lani's shallow hiding place.

In this unequal contest where one opponent had light and the other did not, Lani knew there was no hope. And it wasn't just the light either. He had other advantages as well—a gun for sure and probably even a knife. Once Mitch found her, it would all be over. There would be no further possibility of escape. If only there were some way . . .

No longer able to summon Nana *Dahd*'s war song, Lani shrank back against the wall, trying to make herself as small a target as possible. As she did so, she felt something brush against the back of her neck. A bat! It was all she could do to keep from screaming as the invisible wings ruffled her hair and fluttered across the skin of her cheek.

Possibly the bat was as startled by Lani's presence as she was by the wings fluttering past her. Soaring on across the chamber, the disoriented creature must have swooped past the man as well.

"What the hell!" Mitch Johnson exclaimed while, at the same time, the flashlight fell to the rocky floor, rolled, flickered briefly, and then went out.

"Damn it anyway!" Mitch bellowed. "Where the hell did it go?"

Lani Walker closed her eyes in prayer, although the darkness both inside and outside her head remained the same.

"Thank you, little *Nanakumal*," she said silently to the bat, wishing that she, like the *Mualig Siakam* of old, could speak *I'itoi's* language well enough so the animal could understand her. "Thank you for stealing the evil *Ohb's* light."

With her heart pounding gratefully in her chest, she waited to see if Mitch Johnson was carrying a spare flashlight. She could hear him scuttling around in the dark. And then, just when she was beginning to think she was safe, she heard a distinctive scraping. Suddenly a match flared.

Mitch's fall had taken him several yards from where he had been before. The flame of the match flickered in a part of the cave where Lani hadn't expected to see it. Not only that, in her eagerness to return to her hiding place, she had gone too far. Instead of being completely sheltered by the stalagmite, she had moved a few critical inches to the other side.

"Why, there you are, little darling," he said. "Come to Daddy."

And then the match went out.

Brian was waiting at the gate when Candace and Davy finally stepped off the plane. He grinned when he saw Davy. "You guys must have been at the very back of the bus."

"Close," Davy said. "Candace, this is Brian Fellows, my best friend. Brian, this is Candace Waverly. We're engaged."

Suppressing a blink of surprise, Brian nodded again, taking charge of one of Candace's bags while she carried the other. "Your mother mentioned something to that effect, but things are so chaotic right now, I'm not sure the information's really penetrated."

"What's going on?"

"It's a very long story," Brian said. "And if you don't mind, I think I'll wait until we're in the car before I tell it to you."

"It's that bad?" Davy asked.

"It ain't good," Brian replied.

On the way down the concourse and while they waited for the luggage, Candace chattered on and on about how brown everything was and about how small the airport was compared to O'Hare. She seemed oblivious to the seriousness of the situation, but Davy had seen the bleak look in Brian's eyes.

Brian had gone home and traded the Blazer for his personal car, a low-slung Camaro. The mountain of luggage didn't come close to fitting in the trunk. Candace finally clambered into a backseat already piled with two leftover suitcases.

"All right," Davy said to Brian as soon as they were all in the car. "Tell me."

As Brian related the story, Davy became more and more somber. Tommy and Quentin had been the banes of Davy's childhood just as they had of Brian's. In fact, it was the older boys' casual meanness that had, in the beginning, united the younger two. Mean or not, though, Brandon Walker's sons were still part of both families. To have to accept one of the two as Lani's killer was appalling.

"You're sure he did it?" Davy asked.

"I heard the tape," Brian replied. "Believe me, it was pretty damned convincing."

"How's Mom taking it?"

"About how you'd expect," Brian said. "Not very well."

"And Brandon?"

"He's better off than your mother is. At least he's able to do something about it. The last I saw of him, he was on his way out to Rattlesnake Skull Charco with Brock Kendall, an FBI agent."

"Rattlesnake Skull? Why there?"

"To meet Fat Crack. Wanda Ortiz called and said that according to Gabe, that's where we'll find Lani."

"Is that where we're going?" Davy asked.

"No. We're supposed to go to the house."

"If the *charco* is where the action is, that's where I want to be," Davy said. "Let's go there."

Brian cast a dubious look across the front seat toward his friend. "All right," he said. "But first let's drop Candace off at the house."

"No way," Candace Waverly said from the backseat. "Where did you say you're going?"

"To a *charco* to see if there's anything we can do to help."

"What's a *charco*?" Candace asked.

"A stock tank," Brian answered.

"A retention pond," Davy said at the same time.

Candace sat back in Brian's cramped rear seat and crossed her arms. "If you're going to the *charco,* I'm going too," she announced.

Davy looked at Brian. "I guess that's settled then," he said.

"I guess it is," Brian agreed.

"How can it be so empty?" Candace asked, as Brian's fully loaded Camaro swept west along Highway 86.

"Empty," Brian repeated. "You should have seen it years ago when Davy and I were kids. That's when it was really empty. There are lots more people living out here now than there used to be."

Candace looked out across the seemingly barren and endless desert and didn't believe a word of it.

Davy, meantime, seemed preoccupied with something

else. "You told me about finding bones at the *charco,* and about Quentin's fingerprints showing up on some of them. What I don't understand is why Quentin would have taken Lani there. It doesn't make sense."

"Nobody says it has to make sense," Brian told him. "All I know is Fat Crack said that's where your dad should look and that's where he's looking."

"Who said that?" Candace asked.

"A friend of ours," Davy answered quickly. "His name's Gabe Ortiz. He's actually the tribal chairman."

"He's an Indian, then?"

"Yes."

"But it sounded like Brian called him by some other name."

"Yes." Davy rolled his eyes. "*Gihg Tahpani,*" he said. "Fat Crack."

"So is Fat his first name and Crack's his last?"

Candace asked the question so seriously that Brian burst out laughing while Davy was reduced to shaking his head. Obviously he had failed miserably in preparing Candace for the culture she was stepping into.

"Fat Crack is a first name," Brian explained good-naturedly. "But it's also sort of a friendly name—a name used between friends. So when you meet him, and until you know him better, you probably ought to call him plain Mr. Ortiz."

They turned off onto Coleman Road. "What kind of shoes do you have on?" Brian asked, looking at Candace's face in the mirror.

"Heels. Why?"

"I was just over this road in a Blazer yesterday. If the Camaro doesn't high-center on the first wash, I know it will on the second."

"On the what?"

"Wash. It's a dry riverbed. A sandy riverbed. We're going to have to walk from here, so the car doesn't get stuck."

"That's all right," Candace said. "I have some tennis shoes in my roll-aboard."

Brian pulled over on the side of the road. The suitcase in question was one of the ones that had wound up in the back-seat with Candace. While she dug through it to find her tennis shoes, Davy and Brian stood outside the car, waiting and looking off up the road toward the *charco*. Finding her shoes, Candace kicked off her heels and then moved to the front seat. She was sitting there tying her shoes when she saw something strange on the shoulder of the road a few feet away.

As soon as she had her shoes tied, she walked over and picked up a small medallion with a strange black-and-white design woven into it. "Hey, you guys," she called to Brian and Davy, who were waiting for her on the other side of the road. "Come see what I found."

Davy sauntered over. As soon as he saw what was in her hand, though, his jaw dropped. "Where did you get that?" he demanded.

"It was right here. Along the side of the road . . ."

"Brian, come here, quick. Fat Crack's right. Lani's been here. Look!"

Sprinting across the road, Brian Fellows stopped in his tracks the moment he caught sight of the basket. "You're right," he said. "She has to be here somewhere . . ."

The three of them were standing there in stunned silence, staring up the mountain, when they heard a cry. "Help."

The voice was so faint that at first they all thought they had imagined it. Then it came again. "Help. Please."

Brian Fellows was the first to start off up the mountain. Davy followed directly on his heels, with Candace bringing up the rear.

Tackling the mountain straight on, with no zigzagging to ease the ascent, made the going slow and difficult. From time to time they had to pause for breath, but each time they did, the voice was a little stronger. "I'm here. In the bushes."

"It sounds like Quentin, doesn't it?" Davy asked.

Nodding grimly, Brian Fellows drew his weapon. He was wearing a bulletproof vest. Neither Candace nor Davy were. "You'd better drop back and let me go on by myself."

"Like hell," Davy said. "Come on."

Frozen in terror, Lani crouched against the wall. The stalagmite that had once provided shelter was now a trap. If she moved away from behind it, he would see her and shoot her. She could hear him out there, crawling ever closer to her hiding place. She could hear him breathing in the dark. Now that he had located her, he came forward without bothering to squander any more of his precious matches, trusting that she would stay exactly where he had seen her last.

And the truth was, she didn't have any choice. She was so cold and had sat in one position for so long that her legs ached with cramps. The pressure was so great that she was tempted to come flying out of her hiding place and make straight for what had to be the passage to the outside. But she didn't do it.

Even as the thought crossed her mind, she realized that the darkness in *I'itoi*'s sacred cave was far stronger than Mitch's matches. If he'd had plenty of them, he would have been using them by now instead of scrabbling along in the dark. And without light, the power of darkness and the power of bats was far greater than the evil *Ohb*'s.

Deep in the cave, Lani had met *Nanakumal*. By touching her, Bat had taken away Lani's fear of the darkness and had infused her with his power. From now on Dolores Lanita Walker would still be Forever Spinning to some, but in her own heart she knew that she was changed. As soon as the bat's wings grazed her skin she was also someone else. From that time on, Lani would call herself *Nanakumal Namkam*—Bat Meeter, knowing that Bat Strength and Ant Strength would both be part of her strength.

Suddenly Lani's spirit was alive again, like one awaking from a deep sleep or else from death itself. Something Nana *Dahd* had told her was called *e chegitog*. The cold no longer mattered. She had come into her own just the way Nana *Dahd* had told her she would someday. No matter what Mitch Johnson did to her, he couldn't take that away.

The song spilled into her mind without her even being aware she was thinking about it.

> *O little* Nanakumal *who lives forever in darkness,*
> *O little* Nanakumal *who lives forever in* I'itoi's *sacred*
>   *cave*
> *Give me your strength so I will not be frightened,*
> *So I will stay in this safe place where the evil* Ohb *cannot come.*
> *For years Betraying Woman has been here with you.*
> *For years your strength has kept her safe*
> *Waiting until I could come and set her free*
> *By smashing her pottery prison against the rocky wall.*
>
> *Keep me safe now too, little* Nanakumal
> *Keep me safe from this new evil* Ohb.
> *Teach me* juhagi—*to be resilient—in the coming battle,*
> *So that this* jiawul—*this devil—does not win.*
> *O little* Nanakumal *who lives forever in darkness,*
> *Whose passing wings changed me into a warrior,*
> *Be with me now as I face this danger.*
> *Protect me in the coming battle and keep me safe.*

Brian was the one who found Quentin Walker, found him trapped faceup and helpless in a bed of manzanita. Knowing at once that his half-brother was too badly hurt to pose any danger, Brian holstered his weapon.

"What happened?" he asked.

"I didn't do it," Quentin sobbed. "Tell Dad I didn't do it."

"Didn't do what?" Brian asked.

"I didn't kill Tommy. He fell. He fell in the cave. I tried to help him. I swear. But he died anyway."

Davy, who had stopped to help Candace up a ledge, arrived just in time to hear the last sentence.

"Lani's dead?" he demanded.

When Quentin looked up at Davy, his eyes wavered as though they wouldn't quite focus. "Lani's not dead," he said. "Tommy's the one who's dead. He's been dead a long, long time."

"But where's Lani?"

"Lani? How should I know where Lani is?"

Davy reached down and grabbed the neck of Quentin's shirt. He would have shook him, too, if Candace hadn't stopped him. "Leave him alone, David," she gasped, fighting to regain her breath. "Can't you see he's hurt?"

Letting go of the shirt, Davy turned and looked up the mountain. "She has to be in the cave," he said. "I'll go. You two stay here with Quentin."

"Lani! It's Davy. Where are you?"

Davy! For a moment, Lani thought she must be dreaming. It was impossible. Davy was in Chicago. He couldn't be here.

"Lani!" he called again. "Can you hear me? Are you in here?"

She heard him then, heard the sound of movement in the passageway. It was true. Davy was here. He had come to find her, to save her. Instead, he was crawling directly into the arms of Mitch Johnson. Somehow she had to stop him.

"Davy," she screamed. "Go back! Don't come in here. He'll kill you. Go back."

The cavern reverberated with a hundred echoes and then fell silent. There was no further sound of movement from the passageway.

"Thank God you're alive," Davy called back. "But it's

okay, Lani. We found Quentin down the mountain. He can't hurt you anymore."

Once again there was movement in the passageway. "The killer's still in here, Davy. It's not Quentin!" Lani howled. "Go back, Davy, before he kills us both."

"Davy!" Mitch Johnson called out. "Did you say Davy? Not little Davy Ladd. Come on in, Davy. I won't hurt you. I won't hurt anybody. You're right. It was all Quentin."

Now there was movement again, but not in the passageway. Now it was in the cave itself. "Keep talking, little girl," Mitch Johnson whispered hoarsely. "Just keep talking. I'll find you, you little bitch, if it's the last goddamned thing I do."

Another match flickered to life.

"Lani," Davy demanded. "What's going on in there? Who's in there with you?"

For a moment Lani was quiet. Mitch Johnson was an implacable enemy—more determined to find and destroy her than he was concerned about his own capture.

Nana *Dahd* had told Lani more than once that the *Tohono O'othham* only kill to eat or to save their own lives. In relating the story of the evil *Ohb,* Rita had always said how proud she was that, in the moment when Diana Ladd might have killed Andrew Carlisle, she had chosen instead to spare him, trusting his punishment to the *Mil-gahn* system of criminal justice.

In a moment of understanding that went far beyond her years, and far beyond anything Mitch Johnson had told her, Lani understood that somehow, still alive and in prison, Andrew Carlisle had taken that piece of *Tohono O'othham* honor and turned it into something evil. He had used it *cheawogid*—to infect—someone else with the same evil that had fueled and driven him.

Nana *Dahd* had died too soon to know how wrong she was. But Lani knew. The telltale *cheposid*—the brand— Mitch Johnson had burned into her breast was proof enough that, as long as he lived, so did Andrew Carlisle.

Those thoughts streaked through Lani Walker's mind as she sat bat-still in the cave, watching the momentary light of the match flickering in the darkness and listening as Mitch came stumbling toward her. Had she screamed again, the echoes might have thrown him off and sent him in the wrong direction, but suddenly she knew that was the wrong thing to do. Instead of hiding from the evil *Ohb,* Bat Meeter wanted him to find her.

"I'm here," she said quietly, pulling herself to her feet. "I'm waiting." A storm of needles and pins shot down her numbed legs. She had to cling to the stalagmite to keep from falling, but she held her ground.

"Lani!" Davy shouted. "Please. What's going on?"

"He has a gun, Davy," she said, speaking slowly in *Tohono O'othham.* "His name is Mitch—Mitch Johnson. The evil *Ohb* sent him here. He wants to kill us both."

"Speak English, you little bitch," Mitch Johnson swore. "You're a goddamned American, speak English."

He was only a matter of yards away from her now, creeping along the wall on the same path Lani had followed, as that match, too, flickered and burned itself out. Pulling herself around the rock, she stood directly in his path.

"You'll have to come get me, Mitch," she taunted. "I'm right here. I'm waiting."

Grunting with effort, she tugged off one of her boots. "Here," she said. She tossed the boot a few feet in front of her. The explosion that followed reverberated back and forth inside the cavern. Clinging to the cold stalagmite, grateful for its solid presence, Lani thought there had been a dozen shots instead of only one.

She had ducked her head and closed her eyes, so the flash of light hadn't affected her. But her ears were roaring. From far away she could hear Davy calling to her. "Lani! Lani! Are you all right?"

"I'm still here, Mitch," Lani said again, not raising her voice, barely speaking above a whisper. "I'm here and I'm waiting."

Carefully judging the distance, she pulled off the second boot as well, tossing it slightly behind her and to the left. She heard him rush forward, close enough that she felt him brushing past her as she ducked back behind the stalagmite once more. There was another explosion of gunfire, another ear-shattering roar. And then nothing.

For a second or two Lani thought she really had gone deaf. She was afraid that the silence that suddenly surrounded her would always be there, that it would never lift. But then, from very far away, she heard Davy calling again, pleading this time.

"Lani, please. Answer me. Are you all right?"

There was a groan—little more than a moan, really. It came from beyond Lani's hiding place. From beyond and below it. From the bottom of the hole into which Lani herself had almost fallen.

She heard the sound and was chilled. It meant that down there somewhere, far beneath the surface of the cave, the evil *Ohb* was still alive. He had taken her bait. The boot had done its work, but the fall hadn't killed him. Even now she could hear movement as he struggled to rise from where he had fallen. Lani knew with a certainty that she had never known before that as long as Mitch Johnson lived, every member of Diana and Brandon Walker's family would be in mortal danger.

Coming out from behind the stalagmite, Lani felt around her in the dark. She remembered being told once that limestone caves are fragile—that the formations break off easily and that they need to be protected from human destruction.

"I'm okay, Davy," she called. "But don't come in right now. I think he's hurt, but he may still be able to shoot. We need help. Go get someone with guns and lights and bullet-proof vests."

"You're sure you'll be all right?"

"I'm fine," she answered. "Go now. Please go!"

She heard Davy shuffling back down the passageway just

as Mitch Johnson groaned again. Feeling her way around the floor of the cavern, she located another stalagmite, one that was much smaller than the hulking giant behind which she had hidden. This one was about a foot in circumference and three to four feet high.

"Ants are very strong," Nana *Dahd* had told her. "When they have to, they can carry more than their own weight."

Positioning her back against the large stalagmite, she pushed against the smaller one with both her feet and all her might. She pushed as hard as she could, straining until stars of effort blazed inside her head. At first it seemed as though the rock would never come loose. But then she remembered who she was—*Mualig Siakam*—a powerful medicine woman, someone who, with the power of her singing, could determine who would live and who would die.

Had Mitch Johnson been a little baby, surely the Woman Who Was Kissed by the Bees, *Kulani O'oks,* would have refused to sing.

Pushing again, Lani Walker felt the stalagmite give way slightly, rocking gently and trying to come loose from its moorings like a giant baby tooth in need of pulling. She pushed again and the rock was looser.

All things in nature go in fours. It was the fourth push that broke the huge rock free. She felt it tottering toward her and she had to push it yet again to send it tumbling in the other direction. She heard it scrape across the lip of the hole. Then, for a space of several seconds, there was no sound at all, then there was a muffled bump as the limestone boulder hit something soft and came to rest.

Holding her breath, Lani listened. In the whole of the cave, except for the steady drip of water, there was no other sound, no other being. Mitch Johnson was dead. In the emptiness of his passing, Lani realized that the spirits of Betraying Woman and Andrew Philip Carlisle had disappeared as well. The three of them had joined *huhugam*—those who are gone.

This time, they would not come back.

"Lani, I'm here," Davy shouted. "Brian is with me. Are you all right?"

"I'm fine," she called back. "It's safe to come in now. The evil *Ohb* is dead."

17

They say it happened long ago that after the Tohono O'othham *defeated* the PaDaj O'othham—*the Bad People*— *the Desert People settled in to live near* Baboquivari— I'itoi's *sacred mountain—which is the center of all things. Much later, when the first* Mil-gahn, *the Spaniards, came, they mistakenly called the* Tohono O'othham *the Bean Eaters after some of the food the Indians ate. And even later, other* Mil-gahn—*the Anglos—came to call them Papagos.*

But the Desert People have always preferred to call *themselves* Tohono O'othham. *They have lived forever on that same land near the base of* Baboquivari. *There they have raised wheat and corn, beans and pumpkins and melons. There they learned to make* chu-i—*flour, and* hahki—*a parched roasted wheat that is also called pinole. There they learned to make baskets in which to store all the food they raised.*

Other people knew that the Indians who lived in the

shadow of Baboquivari *were a good people—that they were always kind to each other. It was that way then, and it is the same today.*

Together, Davy Ladd, Brian Fellows, and Lani Walker made their way on hands and knees down the long passageway to the hidden outside entrance. Only when the two men helped the girl to her feet did they realize that other than a pair of bloodied socks, her feet were bare.

"Where are your shoes?" Brian asked. "You can't be out here on the mountain in bare feet. I'll go back and look for them."

"No," she said. "Don't bother. I'll be fine."

The morning sky was blue overhead. Lani stretched out her bare arms and let *Tash's* warm rays begin to thaw her chilled body. She was standing on her own when a sudden dizzying spell of weakness overtook her, causing her to sink down onto the warm ground itself.

Concerned, Davy knelt down beside her. "Are you all right?"

"A little dizzy is all."

"How long is it since you've had anything to eat or drink?"

"I don't know," Lani said. "I don't remember." For her, time had stopped the moment she sat down to pose for the man she thought was Mr. Vega.

Brian stood up. "I have a Coke down in the car, and a blanket, too. Wait here while I go get them."

"Did he hurt you?" Davy asked quietly after Brian had hurried away.

Lani looked down at her chest. There was a stain on her flowered cowboy shirt where the wound on her breast had seeped into the brightly colored material. The stain barely showed. "Not too badly," she said.

A moment later she glanced up at Davy with a puzzled

frown on her face. "What day is it?" she asked. "How did you get here so fast, and how long have I been gone?"

"It's Sunday," he answered. "Candace and I flew in from Chicago early this morning."

"Sunday?" Lani repeated. "You mean I lost a whole day?"

Davy nodded. "You disappeared yesterday morning on your way to work. You never made it."

She looked at him and frowned. "And who's Candace?"

Davy ducked his head. "My fiancée," he said. "We're engaged. But tell me what happened. Did he run you off the road? What?"

"I went to pose for him," she said. "He was going to let me have a painting to give to Mom and Dad for their anniversary. It was stupid. I see that now. He offered me orange juice and he put something in it, something that knocked me out. He did the same thing to Quentin. What about Quentin? Is he dead?"

Davy shook his head. "Not yet. He's halfway down the mountain, and he's hurt. It looks pretty bad to me. Brian is going for help. Dad and Brock Kendall are over at the *charco*. They'll have to bring in a helicopter. We won't be able to carry him out on a stretcher."

"How did you and Brian know where to look for me?"

Davy looked off down the mountain. Before he answered, he found it necessary to brush something from his eye. "Candace," he croaked. "Wanda Ortiz had called the house and left word for Dad to meet him at Rattlesnake Skull. Brian met Candace and me at the airport and brought us along out here. We were getting ready to walk over to the *charco* to find Dad when Candace sat down to tie her shoes and found this."

Reaching into his shirt pocket, Davy pulled out the tiny people-hair basket and placed it in Lani's hand. As her fingers closed over the precious *kushpo ho'oma*—her hair charm—tears of gratitude filled her eyes.

"But how did you know to look in the cave?" she asked a moment later.

Davy shrugged. "Brian and I saw it years ago on the same day Tommy first found it. Since the cave was right here and since we knew Quentin was involved, it was logical that's where you might be, that maybe he'd take you there." He paused. "According to Quentin, the cave is where Tommy died. He fell into a hole."

The same hole, Lani thought at once. *It has to be the same hole.* "Do you remember the story of Betraying Woman?" she asked.

"Yes."

"This is her cave, Davy," Lani said softly. "That old story Nana *Dahd* used to tell us was true. After the *Tohono O'oth-ham* captured her, they brought her back here and locked her inside the mountain along with all her pots—her unbroken pots. Quentin had found the pots and was planning to sell them, at least he thought he was going to sell them. I broke them. All of them. Or at least as many as I could find.

"Afterward, when I was there in the dark and didn't know which way to go, *kokoi*—a spirit—showed me the way out. I think Betraying Woman's spirit led me to the passageway. Do you believe that? Is that possible?"

"Yes," Davy replied. "I believe it."

Lani laughed. "Probably you, but nobody else," she said. "I was in there for a long time," she continued. "At first I was so scared I could barely think, but then somehow I remembered the words to Nana *Dahd*'s old war chant, the one she sang to you that day in the root cellar. Do you remember? Repeating those words over and over helped me—made me feel brave, and strong.

"Later on, when the song quit working and I was scared again, a bat came to me in the dark. It touched my skin and taught me not to be afraid of the darkness. The bat showed me how the darkness could work against the evil *Ohb*. The next time I sang after that, the song wasn't Nana *Dahd*'s anymore. It was my own song, Davy, but it worked the same way hers did. You believe that, too, don't you?"

"Yes," Davy Ladd said. "I do believe it."

For a time he looked off across the wide expanse of desert. "It's happened, hasn't it, *Kulani O'oks*," he added quietly, with a rueful smile that was, at the same time, both happy and sad. "You've become Medicine Woman, Lani, just like the Woman Who Was Kissed by the Bees, just as Nana *Dahd* said you would. I guess it's time I got her medicine basket out of safekeeping and gave it to you."

"Her medicine basket?" Lani asked.

Davy nodded. "She gave it to me the day she died," he answered. "But only to keep it until you were ready. Until it was time for you to come into your own."

Davy watched Lani's face. He expected her to brighten—to be his little sister again, delighted by some unexpected surprise. Instead, she frowned. He reached out to her, but she drew away from him.

"What's wrong?" he asked.

"I have killed an enemy," she said. "I will need to undergo *e lihmhun* in order to be purified. While I am here alone for sixteen days, I'll have plenty of time to make my own medicine basket. There are only two things from Nana *Dahd*'s basket that I would like to have—the scalp bundle and that single broken piece of Understanding Woman's pottery. The rest of it should go to you, Davy, to Nana *Dahd*'s little *Olhoni*."

Davy Ladd ducked his head to hide his tears. "Thank you," he said.

The first glimpse Brandon Walker had of his future daughter-in-law, Candace Waverly, she was on her hands and knees, huddled close to Quentin Walker's badly injured body. With her face close to his, she was comforting him as best she could while they waited for the med-evac helicopter to show up and fly him off the mountain.

Brandon Walker and Brock Kendall had left the *charco* and were heading for Gates Pass when the call came telling them that Lani had been found. The Pima County dispatcher reported that Lani was all right but that Brandon's son, Quentin, had been severely injured.

When it came time to climb *Ioligam,* the months of woodcutting served Brandon Walker well. He might have been fifty-five years old and considered over the hill by some, but he scampered up the steep mountainside without breaking a sweat, leaving Brock Kendall in the dust.

"Who are you?" Brandon demanded, looking down at the young woman crouched beside Quentin. He immediately assumed that she was somehow connected to the injured man. "And what the hell has this son of a bitch done to his sister?"

"You must be Mr. Walker," Candace said.

Brandon nodded.

"I'm Candace Waverly," she said. "Your son David's fiancée. Quentin wanted me to give you a message. He said to tell you that he didn't kill Tommy. He said it was an accident, that Tommy fell in a hole in the cave. By the time Quentin was finally able to get him out, Tommy was dead. Quentin didn't tell anyone what really happened because he was sure people would think it was all his fault."

"Tommy?" a winded Brock Kendall gasped as he finally reached the limestone outcropping. "I thought we were here about Lani. What's this about Tommy?"

All the way out from Tucson, Brandon Walker had agonized over how he would treat his son, over what he would say. As a father, how could he forgive Quentin for hurting Lani? And now there was responsibility for Tommy as well?

Brandon's legs folded under him. He dropped to the ground and buried his face in his hands. This was too much—way too much. More than he could stand.

"Dear God in heaven, Quentin," Brandon Walker sobbed. "How could you do it? How could you?"

"Take it easy, Mr. Walker," Brian Fellows murmured, appearing out of nowhere and placing a comforting hand on Brandon's heaving shoulder. "Quentin didn't do it. He didn't take Lani, and he didn't hurt her."

Brandon quieted almost instantly. "He didn't? Who did then? Who's responsible for all this?"

"The man's name is Mitch Johnson," Brian answered.

"Mitch Johnson!" Brandon exclaimed. It took only seconds for the name to register. "The guy I put away years ago for shooting up those illegals?"

"That's the one."

"Where is the son of a bitch? I'll kill him myself."

"You don't have to," Brian said softly. "I think Lani already did it for you."

Pima County Detective Dan Leggett was used to calling the shots when it came to conducting interviews. He would have preferred talking to Lani Walker in the air-conditioned splendor of the visiting FBI agent's Lincoln Town Car, but the medicine man—the one Brandon Walker called Fat Crack—refused to let the girl come down off the mountain. *Ioligam* was well inside reservation boundaries. The road where the Town Car was parked was not. Short of escorting Lani down to the car at gunpoint, Leggett wasn't going to get her to leave.

And so the detective took himself up the mountain to her. He found Lani and Fat Crack sitting together off to one side of the entrance to the cave. Lani was still wrapped in a blanket, as though the increasing heat of the day still hadn't penetrated to the chilled marrow of her bones. She sat watching in somber silence while several deputies trudged down the mountainside lugging the stretcher holding the crushed earthly remains of one Mitch Johnson.

Detective Leggett was still mildly irritated with Mr. Tribal Chairman, Gabe Ortiz. After all, it was the medicine man's message, sent via his wife, that had pulled Brandon

Walker, Brock Kendall, and a number of other operatives off on an early-morning wild-goose chase to Rattlesnake Skull Charco. As a police officer, Leggett didn't put much stock in medicine men even if Ortiz's prediction of where they would eventually find Lani Walker had been off target by a mere mile or two.

"If you'd excuse us for a little while," Detective Leggett said to Gabe Ortiz, "I'll need to ask Miss Walker a few questions now."

Lani motioned for Gabe to stay where he was. "I'd like Mr. Ortiz to stay," she said.

"If Mr. Ortiz were your attorney, of course, he'd be welcome to stay, but I'm afraid regulations don't make any provisions for medicine men . . ."

"I'm not an attorney, but I am the tribal chairman and this is tribal land," Gabe Ortiz said with quiet but unmistakable authority. "I am here as Lani's elder and as her spiritual adviser. Since this is my jurisdiction, if she wants me to stay, I stay."

Leggett may not have been much of an advocate of ethnic diversity when it came to medicine men, but the words "tribal chairman" struck a responsive chord.

"Of course," he said agreeably, turning back to Lani. "Since Miss Walker wants you here, you're more than welcome to stay."

The interview, conducted in the full glare of what was now midday sun, took an hour and a half. When it was over, Dan Leggett's shirt and trousers were soaked through with sweat, and he was so parched he could barely talk. Lani still sat swathed in her blanket.

Despite her ordeal, Lani answered his questions with a poise that was surprising to see in someone so young. She responded to simple and complex questions alike with calm clarity. Her harrowing version of Mitch Johnson's physical assault with the kitchen tongs was enough to make Leggett feel half sick, but Lani recounted her ordeal without seeming to be affected by what she was saying. Her steadiness made Leggett wonder if she was really as fine as she claimed or if, perhaps, she might still be suffering from shock.

"That's about it," he said, closing his notebook after the last of his questions. "I think we probably should get you into town and have you checked out by a doctor."

"No," Gabe Ortiz said firmly. "Lani has killed an enemy. She can't go to town. She has to stay out here by herself, away from her village and family, until she finishes undergoing the purification ceremony."

"How long will that take?" Leggett asked, imagining as he did so an evening's worth of cedar drumming.

"Sixteen days," Gabe Ortiz answered.

"Sixteen days? Even though it's most likely self-defense, there'll have to be an inquest or maybe even a preliminary hearing."

"They will have to wait for the sixteen days," Gabe Ortiz told him.

Leggett looked around at the empty desert. "She's going to stay here? In the middle of nowhere?"

Ortiz nodded. "I've already sent my son off to pick up a tent and whatever other supplies she may need. I myself will bring her food and water. Her wounds will be treated in the traditional way."

For the first time in the whole process, Lani Walker's eyes filled with tears. "Thank you," she said.

Diana met Brandon at the door when he came home from the hospital late that evening. "Is Quentin going to make it?"

Brandon paused long enough to hang his keys up on the Peg-Board. "Probably," he said.

"And the bones?"

Brandon sank down beside the table and Diana brought him a glass of iced tea. "I called Dr. Sam," he said. "He ran the dental profile through his computer. The bones they found at Rattlesnake Skull belong to Tommy, all right."

Dr. Sam was short for Swaminathan Narayanamurty, a professor of biometrics at the University of Arizona. Together Dr. Sam and Brandon Walker had come up with the idea of amassing a database of dental records on reported Missing Persons from all over the country. Brandon Walker's effective lobbying before a national meeting of the Law Enforcement and Security Administrators had enabled Dr. Sam to gain some key seed money funding years earlier. That initial grant had grown into a demonstration project.

During the election campaign, Bill Forsythe had brought that project up, implying that Brandon's interest in the project had been based on personal necessity because of his own son's unexplained disappearance rather than on sound law enforcement practices. Personal or not, the connection had been strong enough that on this warm summer Sunday, Dr. Sam had been only too happy to interrupt a week-long stay in a cabin on Mount Lemmon to run the profile of the skull Dan Leggett had retrieved from Rattlesnake Skull Charco.

"Detective Leggett says he thinks Quentin was in the process of moving the bones out of the cave for fear Johnson would see them, when Manny Chavez stumbled into the area. Quentin must have panicked and attacked the man."

"I'm sorry," Diana said. "About Quentin and Tommy."

"Don't be sorry about Tommy," Brandon told her. "At least we know now that it was over quickly for him, that he didn't suffer. It's closure, Di. It's something I've lain awake nights worrying about for years."

The doorbell rang. "Oh, for God's sake," Brandon grumbled irritably. "Who can that be now?"

A moment later, a sunburned Candace Waverly appeared in the kitchen doorway. "It's Detective Leggett," she said. "He was wondering if he could see you two for a few minutes."

Wearily, Brandon rubbed his whisker-stubbled chin. "Sure," he said. "Send him on in."

"Sorry to bother you," the detective said, placing a worn

Hartmann briefcase on the kitchen table. "I know you've both had a terrible two days of it, but I wanted to stop by and show you some of this before I turn it over to the property folks."

Opening the case, he pulled out a pair of latex gloves. While he was putting them on, Diana glanced at the loose piece of paper—a faxed copy of a mug shot—that lay fully exposed in the open briefcase. A sharp intake of breath caused both men to look at her with some concern as all color drained from her face.

"Diana, what's the matter?" Brandon demanded. "What's wrong?"

Diana's hand trembled as she reached out and picked up the paper. "It's him," she moaned. "Dear God in heaven, it is him!"

The paper fluttered out of Diana's hand. Brandon caught it in midair and studied it himself. "That's Mitch Johnson, all right," he said.

"It may be Mitch Johnson, but it's Monty Lazarus, too," Diana whispered. "He looked older and he wore a red wig, but I'd recognize him anywhere."

"Monty Lazarus!" Brandon repeated. "The reporter who interviewed you?"

"Yes."

Confused, Detective Leggett looked from husband to wife. "Who the hell is Monty Lazarus?" he asked.

Brandon put both hands protectively on Diana's shoulders before he answered. "The publicity department at Diana's New York publisher set her up to do an in-depth interview yesterday with someone named Monty Lazarus who was supposedly a stringer with several important magazines. Except it turns out he isn't a stringer at all. He isn't even a writer. He's Mitch Johnson, ex-con, somebody who vowed that he'd get me one day for sending him up."

Leggett shook his head. "It's actually worse than that," he said. "These are documents I've just now removed from Mitch Johnson's motor home out on Coleman Road."

Saying that, he handed Diana Walker a pair of gloves and a pair of manuscript boxes. One was packed to overflowing while the other was less than half-full.

"You might want to take a look at these, Mrs. Walker, but put on gloves before you do it. Fingerprints and all. Meantime, Brandon, there's something I need to show you out in the car."

Brandon Walker followed Leggett out to the driveway where the detective popped the trunk on his Ford Taurus. There, illuminated in the slanting rays of the late afternoon sun, lay Mitch Johnson's awful charcoal nude of Dolores Lanita Walker.

"Where did this god-awful thing come from?" Brandon choked.

"From Mitch Johnson's motor home," Kendall answered. "I smuggled it out. Along with this one, too." He took out a second sketch, one of Quentin Walker. "Neither one of these is on any of the evidence lists. I brought them here so you'd have a chance to get rid of them."

"Thank you, Dan," Brandon Walker said gratefully. "I'll take care of them right away."

With Brandon carrying Lani's picture by the corners, holding it as though it were the rancid carcass of some long-dead thing, and with Dan Leggett lugging the sketch of Quentin, the two men walked into the backyard. There Brandon grabbed an armload of chopped firewood from his never-ending stack and threw several branches into the barbecue grill. Minutes later, the two offending pictures had been reduced to a pile of paper-thin ashes.

"That's that," Brandon said, dusting soot from his hands and onto his pant legs.

"There are two other pictures," Dan Leggett said quietly.

"Of Lani and Quentin?"

"No," Leggett said somberly. "If there are others of them, we haven't found them yet. The two pictures I'm talking about are of someone else. They're titled 'Before' and 'After.'"

"They're both of the same man," Leggett replied. "Before and after a murder. Unless I'm sadly mistaken, the victim will turn out to be Mitch Johnson's ex-wife's second husband. That big-time developer who got carved up down in Nogales a few months back."

"Larry Wraike?" Brandon Walker croaked in surprise. "But I thought a prostitute did that."

"So did everybody else," Leggett replied. "Me included."

The two men went back inside. In the kitchen they found Diana sifting through a stack of papers. Her haunted eyes met Brandon's the moment he stepped into the room.

"Fat Crack was right," she said. "The danger did come from my book."

"What do you mean?" Brandon asked.

"Some of this is Andrew Carlisle's personal diary, Brandon," she told him, holding back the single detail that some of the passages had been addressed directly to her, that even back in 1988, Carlisle had intended that someday Diana Ladd Walker would read what he had written.

"Carlisle and Mitch Johnson were cellmates for years up in Florence," Diana continued. "It's all here in black and white. It started the first day when I went to Florence to interview Carlisle for the book. That's when Carlisle found out Quentin was up there, too. They targeted him that very day, Brandon. They set him up, and that's what this whole thing is about—revenge. Andrew Carlisle was still after me and Mitch Johnson was after you. Lani was the perfect way to get to us both. And that's not all."

"Not all?" Brandon echoed. "How could there be more?"

"This," Diana said. She held up what seemed to be the title page of a manuscript.

"What is it?" Brandon asked.

"Do you remember when Garrison died I told you the manuscript he was working on disappeared?"

Brandon nodded.

"This is it," Diana said. "I recognized the typeface from

his old Smith-Corona the moment I saw it. It's called *A Death Before Dying*. It's supposedly a work of fiction about a college instructor—a handsome man—presumably happily married to a lovely wife. Gary didn't have sense enough to change things very much. The husband taught freshman English; the wife was an elementary school teacher."

"So?" Brandon asked a little impatiently. "I've heard you say yourself that first novels are always autobiographical."

Diana nodded. "They are, and there was an ugly secret running just below the surface of this one. All the while the teacher thinks she's happily married, the husband is carrying on with another professor—a *male* professor. Believe me, it's a very special relationship to which the young wife proves to be an unyielding obstacle."

"You're saying Garrison and Carlisle had something going, something sexual?"

Diana nodded. "I think so," she said.

"That would make sense then," Brandon said. "It would certainly explain some of the hold Carlisle wielded over the man."

"Some of it," Diana agreed. "The kicker is here, though, on the very last page. The last *written* page because the manuscript is clearly incomplete. The last scene is mostly a dialogue between the two men. They're sitting in a bar, talking. Planning exactly how they're going to unload the inconvenient presence of that meddlesome wife."

"You?" Brandon asked.

Diana nodded. Her voice sounded far more self-possessed than she felt. "If I had gone to the dance with them that night," she said, "my guess is I would have been the one who died at Rattlesnake Skull Charco, not Gina Antone."

For sixteen days and nights Lani Walker stayed in the tent Baby and Fat Crack Ortiz had erected for her near the base of *Ioligam*. She spent her days weaving a rectangular medi-

cine basket. When it was finished, the lid fit perfectly. Lani
held it up to the light and studied the final product with no
small satisfaction. It was not as well done as one of Nana
Dahd's own baskets, but it would do.

Each evening, about sunset, Gabe Ortiz would arrive by
himself, bringing with him an evening meal and the next
day's salt-free food. The traditional dictates of the enemy
purification process—*e lihmhun*—specify a period of fast-
ing and of avoiding salted food.

On the final day of her purification exile, with the medicine basket complete, Lani took a flashlight and ventured
into Betraying Woman's cave one last time. There, shoved
up against the stalagmite behind which she had hidden for
hours, Lani found one of her two missing boots. She picked
it up and took it with her when she continued on into *Oks
Gagda*'s burial chamber.

This time when Lani entered the earthen-floored chamber, there was a feeling of utter emptiness about it. The spirits—*kokoi*—that had once inhabited the place were no
longer there. Careful not to touch or disturb the decaying
bones, Lani placed the shoe beside Betraying Woman's
bones as a kind of memorial, then she stepped over to the
wall where all the broken pieces of blasted pottery lay in a
dusty heap. Kneeling down, Lani picked up one shard of
clay after another, examining each in turn, looking for one
that would speak to her, the one that was worthy of inclusion
in Lani Walker's newly woven medicine basket.

The fragment she finally settled on was all black, inside
and out. She chose it because the fine black texture reminded
her of the touch of the bat's wings against her skin. Pocketing
her treasure, Lani was about to stand up and leave when she
caught sight of something else reflected in the glow of the
flashlight, something that would have remained completely
hidden had she not moved several pieces of the pottery.

When Lani saw the tiny bones, she thought at first that
she had discovered the skeleton of a tiny baby. It wasn't,

though. When she picked it up and the bones fell apart, she realized that what she had found was the moldering skeleton of a bat's wing.

Awareness made the hair on the back of her neck stand on end. *I'itoi* had given her a sign. Dolores Lanita Walker was *Mualig Siakam*—Forever Spinning, and *Kulani O'oks*—Medicine Woman as well. But she was also *Nanakumal Namkam*—Bat Meeter. Elder Brother had led her to this place and had shown her it was true.

Why not four names? Lani thought with a laugh. *After all, all things in nature go in fours.*

On that last night, Fat Crack brought along Looks At Nothing's medicine pouch. After Lani and he had eaten, the medicine man drew a circle on the ground, a line that encircled both man and girl. The two of them settled down on the ground inside the circle.

"It's time for your first Peace Smoke," he told her. "Davy and Candace flew out of Tucson for Vegas this afternoon. They're supposed to get married tomorrow, but before he left, Davy brought me these. He said they belong to you."

Opening the medicine pouch, he pulled out two items and handed them to her. She recognized them at once as the treasures from Nana *Dahd*'s old medicine basket—the piece of pottery with the distinctive turtle design etched into the clay and the precious scalp bundle.

"Thank you," Lani said. Opening her basket, she put the two additions inside and closed the lid.

"What else do you have in there?" Fat Crack asked.

"Nothing much," Lani said. "My people-hair charm. A finger from a bat's wing. And a piece of Betraying Woman's pottery."

"Bring it," Fat Crack said. "The piece of pottery, I mean. After we have the Peace Smoke, you and I will study the pottery together."

Using Looks At Nothing's old Zippo lighter, Fat Crack carefully lit the *wiw*. And then, one puff at a time, they smoked the bitter-tasting wild tobacco, passing the lit cigarette back and forth, saying *"Nawoj"* each time it changed hands.

"How is Quentin?" Lani asked.

"Out of the hospital," Fat Crack replied. "But he checked himself into a drug and alcohol rehab program."

"Will he be better?" Lani asked.

Fat Crack shrugged. "Maybe," he said. "He has let go of the secret of his brother's death. Secrets like that can be very bad. They eat at you. Perhaps now, he'll be able to get better."

"Perhaps," Lani agreed.

They were quiet again. Far off to the east, flickers of lightning touched the horizon. The summer rains were coming. They would be here soon—by the end of the week at the latest. In a way, Lani was sorry that when the deluges began she would be living back inside the house in Gates Pass with a regular roof over her head rather than a canvas tent.

Lani Walker wasn't a smoker—not even of regular cigarettes. By the time the last of the wild tobacco smoke had eddied away into the nighttime air, she felt light-headed.

"Have you ever heard of divining crystals?" Fat Crack asked. His voice seemed to come to her from very far away.

"I've heard of them," she said. "But I've never seen any."

Fat Crack reached into the medicine pouch and pulled out the chamois bag. Untying it, he held open Lani's hand and poured the four crystals into it.

"Looks At Nothing said I should keep them until I found a successor worthy of them," he said. "It was through using these that I knew to look for you near Rattlesnake Skull that morning. Now I want you to try it."

"Me?" Lani asked. "But I don't know what to do."

"Take your piece of pottery," Fat Crack directed. "Look at it for a time through each of the different crystals and tell me what you see."

One at a time, holding them up to the firelight, Lani examined the pottery through each of the first three crystals. "I'm not seeing anything," she said, when she put down the third. "It's not going to work."

"Try the last one," Fat Crack urged.

This time, instead of putting the crystal down, Lani continued staring at it for a long time. First a minute passed, and then another. Finally she looked up at him.

"The Apache warrior—*Ohb-s-chu cheggiadkam*—came back here looking for his lover, didn't he? He came looking for Betraying Woman. Somehow his spirit found its way into Andrew Carlisle."

Fat Crack nodded. "That's right," he said. "And into Mitch Johnson as well."

"And now they're free?"

"Yes," Gabe Ortiz answered. "When you broke Betraying Woman's pots after all this time, you set all of them free."

Gabe reached out. One at a time he picked up each of the four divining crystals and returned them to the bag. When the bag was tied shut, he placed the crystals—chamois bag and all—inside Lani's medicine basket.

"They belong to you now, Bat Meeter," he said with a smile. "They are a gift from Looks At Nothing to you, from one wise old *siwani* to a young one. Use them well."

Acknowledgments

The author gratefully acknowledges the work of Dean and Lucille Saxton and their invaluable book, *Papago/Pima-English Dictionary,* and Harold Bell Wright for his wonderfully vivid retelling of Tohono O'othham legends in *Long Ago Told.* She also expresses her thanks to Special Collections at the University of Arizona Library for making available materials that otherwise would have been impossible to obtain. Without these crucial contributions, this book would not exist.

Now available in paperback
from HarperTorch
The *New York Times* Bestseller

HUNTING BADGER

by

Tony Hillerman

0-06-109786-1/$7.50 US/$9.99 Can

Three armed men raid the Ute tribe's gambling casino, and then disappear in the maze of canyons on the Utah-Arizona border. The FBI takes over the investigation, and agents swarm into the area. Making an explosive situation even hotter, these experts devise a theory of the crime that makes a wounded deputy sheriff a suspect—a development that brings in Tribal Police Sergeant Jim Chee and his longtime colleague, retired Lieutenant Joe Leaphorn to help.